RUNNING

THE COBBLESTONES

C. K. MACDONALD

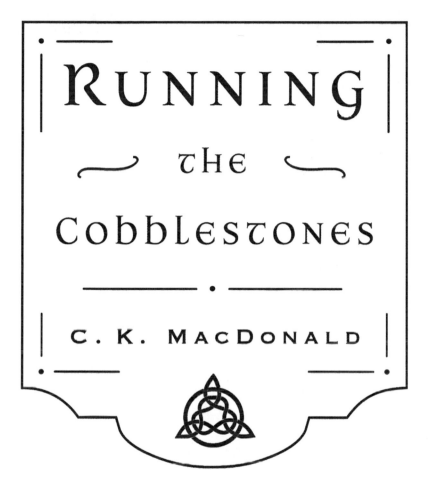

Running the Cobblestones

C. K. MacDonald

This book is a work of fiction. Any references to real people or real places are used fictitiously. Other names, characters and events are products of the authors' imaginations, and any resemblance to actual persons or events is entirely coincidental.

FIRST EDITION
First Printing, 2017

Book design by Donna Burch-Brown
Cover design by Kevin R. Brown
Cover illustration by Shutterstock.com/433564771/©Bildagentur Zoonar GmbH
Interior ornament by iStock/104877373/ericx

MCP
2301 Lucien Way #415
Maitland, FL 32751
407.339.4217

Printed in the United States of America

ISBN: 978-1-63505-609-9

DEDICATION

To the astonishing parents of children with disabilities.

The example you set in your daily lives
sends out more ripples than you will ever know.

CHAPTER 1

Always forgive your enemies—nothing annoys them so much.

~OSCAR WILDE

March 2010, Stillwater, Minnesota

The radiator was no longer whistling so Kate McMahon slammed her toolbox shut with an air of finality. She noticed it was getting easier to swallow the sadness as she prepared to leave this home she had loved and nurtured.

She flipped open the laptop perched on a packing crate. Taking a deep breath, she hit the "purchase now" button. With one tap of the finger she chose a new life.

She told herself she wasn't running away from her problems. Rather, she was taking inspiration from her Irish ancestors, who were forced by the famine to brave a new beginning in a foreign country. Within seconds she got confirmation of her one-way ticket to Ireland. If this venture in the Emerald Isle didn't pan out, her only option would be to move in with her mother in that retirement community in Arizona—and sleep on a futon. She shuddered at the thought.

Everything was all set now ... well, almost everything.

She padded to her bedroom and climbed onto the bed, opening her jewelry box. She fingered the emerald tennis bracelet, the opera-length string of pearls and her Cyma watch. Kate thought she'd feel pain when she picked up the diamond earrings, but no, none. The engagement ring found its way onto her finger one last time. Resetting her shoulders, she placed everything back in the box, her wedding band perched atop it all. She felt strangely detached. In the last three years she'd passed through seasons of denial, anger, despair, embarrassment and now acceptance. It was time to let go of all this and move on.

The estate jewelry stores in town offered a better price than Craigslist, and she needed every penny she could get from these pieces. Their financial value had decreased gradually over the years, and their sentimental value took a sudden plunge a few months after her husband did, when she learned the truth about him. The jeweler assured her the stones were genuine, and the auditors determined Bryan had bought them with legitimate funds.

She grabbed her lumberjack plaid coat to ward off the Minnesota winter chill, stowed the box of jewelry in a big purse, and marched out of the bed and breakfast that had been her home and business for the past nine years. On the brass knocker she hung a sign that read: "Welcome. Check-in is at 4:00 p.m. Please return then." The smell of bacon followed her outside.

She tramped down the porch steps, which she had shoveled before her morning run, and sighed at the "Sold" sign in the front yard. When she and Bryan bought this place, they called it their "forever house." She wished the new owners better luck as she tugged her tam over her ears.

Legally, she would be allowed to keep the equity she had accumulated in the B&B, but that didn't sit well with her. She decided to divide the money among the people on Bryan's sucker list, to try to make amends. Her attorney advised her against it, sounding as if he had never heard of a moral obligation.

A fleeting image of Ireland's green hills crossed her mind, and a smile warmed her numb cheeks. She trudged back through the deep snow, and pressed some into a snowball. She tossed it at the realtor's sign, yelling, "Wipe out!"

On the sidewalk, Mrs. Lulu Benton, her mom's childhood friend, rounded the corner and pretended not to notice her. Kate was getting used to the cold shoulder. Bryan got the blame, but she was left with the shame. And shame wasn't a gentle grey cloud hanging over her—it was a thundering punch to the gut.

"Whoa!" Mrs. Benton yelped, her arms flailing as her feet flew out from under her. Her bony butt landed with a *thunk*, and she rocked back into the snowbank. Kate ran to her aid and helped her to her feet, making sure nothing was broken.

Mrs. Benton brushed the snow from her down jacket and cocked an eyebrow. "It's your fault I'm out here, missy! I was retired, but because of your husband I had to take a job as a hostess at the Dock Café."

"I'm so sorry. I had nothing to do with his business …"

"I don't want to hear your excuses. When you sleep with dogs, you get up with fleas!" She jerked her arm out of Kate's protective grasp and scuttled away.

Kate retrieved her purse and continued on her mission, laughing behind her muffler as her mind replayed the slapstick footage of Mrs. Benton's tumble. It felt good to laugh.

She passed St. Michael's Church and paused at the cemetery next to it, where two of the gravesites stood out for her. Wrapping her arms around herself, she whispered, "I miss you, Dad." She pulled a photo from her purse, and set it into the snow, propping it against his headstone. "This is a picture of my new home. It's in Ireland. Can you believe it? Remember, you used to say that I never quite got Dublin out of my heart? Well, you made the down payment possible."

As she walked away, she bent over, pressed together another snowball and hurled it in the direction of her husband's grave. "Goodbye, Bryan." If her aim had been better, it might have covered the "beloved husband" part of his epitaph, which was etched too soon—before she knew the ugly truth.

She glided gingerly down the plowed and sanded Chilkoot Hill to Main Street, stopped at Stillwater Treasures and stomped the snow off her boots.

Thirty minutes later, she had a fat check in her purse and her boots felt lighter. Kate was certain her Irish ancestors had a lot less in their pockets when they took the giant leap.

The frosty air caught in her throat as she looked around the town she was leaving. Trying to rein in her lingering bitterness, she recalled a reflection she had read that morning and tossed aside: "Forgiveness is the great tool of healing and repair."

So, in order to really move on and heal, I need to master forgiveness? What an impossible concept. It didn't fit into her toolbox. Unthinkable! It would require taking a leap larger than the leap across the Atlantic.

Glancing at the frozen gazebo on the banks of the icy St. Croix River, she had an urge to stop in at No Neck Tony's Bar and see if the one friend she had left in town could join her for an Irish Coffee. She pulled out her phone and dialed Rose.

Soon she'd be leaving behind all the cold shoulders and frigid former friends. Soon she'd be in Dublin, surrounded by warm pubs, faithful old friends and untold new possibilities.

CHAPTER 2

There are no strangers here; only friends we haven't yet met.

~WILLIAM BUTLER YEATS

Two weeks later, Glasnevin, Ireland

Kate stepped out of the cab and paused on the cobblestone street, standing in the shadow of the McFadden Guesthouse—her new home and livelihood. Anxiety shot up her spine. She glanced at the "Sold" sign swinging on a post in front of the red brick beauty and pictured a "No Vacancy" sign hanging there permanently. The March wind ruffled her hair as she exhaled a slow steadying breath and inhaled bold determination.

"Jaysus, is that you, Kate? What're you doin' just standin' there in the road? The neighbors will think you're off your nut," said a familiar voice. Deirdre Kennedy's head was poking out of the large house next door, her mop of copper curls bouncing like Slinkies.

Kate ran to her friend. "Oh, Deirdre, it's so good to see you. God, I can't believe I'm really here."

"Ah, it's grand havin' you here," Deirdre said as they embraced. "I have the keys the estate agent left with us in my pocket."

"You and Mark will rue the day you told me about the McFadden Guesthouse being for sale."

"Ah, go on—We'll love having you close so we can keep an eye on yeh."

"Where are the kids?" Kate asked as she followed Deirdre's steps.

"The big kids are at school and the twins are at my mam's."

Deirdre led the way, stepping over puddles and clutching a bottle of champagne—a housewarming gift from her mother. The sun poked out from the curtain of clouds and spotlighted Kate's new home.

"T'ank God it's a soft day for yeh. It's been pelting rain lately." Deirdre readied the keys. "Now, let's go inside, pour us some bubbly, and give a toast, shall we?"

Kate glanced to the right toward Terry and Myrna Riley's house. "The Rileys' home hasn't lost any of its charm. I can't wait to see them," she said.

"Oh, I bet my granny's black pudding Myrna will be running over here straightaway, when she's done minding the grandkids."

"It's hard to picture them as grandparents. Their kids were so young when I lived with them for that semester—Geez, that was 15 years ago!" Kate said, as the door squeaked open.

Joy settled into her, warm and comforting, as she crossed the threshold into her new home. She expected dim corners and a musty smell, but every lamp was glowing in welcome and a fresh breeze fluttered the lace curtains.

"Oh, Deirdre! You're so thoughtful. I can tell you were here making the place cozy for me. How ever did you have the time?"

Deirdre threw her a smile. "Truth be told, I had the little snappers help. Isn't it a grand thing altogether when folks are neighborly? It was the least we could do and indeed a lovely lesson for the little ones."

Kate tried to remember the last time someone made her feel welcome around the town she left behind. Nothing came to mind. There's an old Gaelic saying, *Céad míle fáilte,* "A hundred thousand welcomes." The Irish take their welcoming to heart. That was one of the reasons she loved this place. She resolved to give her future guests a proper Irish welcome so they'd feel the warmth she felt now.

Deirdre led Kate into the kitchen and they rummaged through the glassware in search of proper flutes. Deirdre popped the cork and said, "The celebratin' starts now and Terry and Myrna will be wantin' to buy you a welcoming drink this evening."

"Are we meeting at O'Gara's tonight? I'd love that. That pub holds a lot of memories for me. More good than bad."

Deirdre held up her glass. "Let's toast to kicking those bad memories in the bollocks!"

Each woman took a sip and then Deirdre played tour guide. "Catriona Ryan has done a marvelous job managing the place. She holds the key to your success. This old building has many quirks and Catriona knows how to keep it humming." Deirdre bit her lip and turned her gaze away from Kate. "Ah, just be sure to get on her good side straightaway."

"What do you mean? Does she think she owns the place?"

"Well, now. Didn't we all think she would buy it when it went on the market? Rumor had it that just then one of her sisters needed a few quid, and being the generous soul that she is—there went the nest egg. So she withdrew her bid. When she heard that an American bought the place, she was worried she'd lose her job. She and her husband had no children and she needs to keep busy."

"Is she hard up for money now?"

"Ah, we don't dig too deeply into her finances, but she has a massive heart and loves to help others."

"How so?"

"Ah, I'm thinkin' you'll be hearin' stories. She's always up to something. But know that she speaks her mind, and doesn't put on a polite front. She's a big, strong, capable woman, and was so loyal to the McFaddens. And she'll be loyal to you, too, once you earn her respect."

Kate smiled. "You're scaring me!"

"Not at all," Deirdre said. "Just don't ruffle her feathers and she'll be as content as a mama puffin sittin' on her eggs. This guesthouse is truly a part of her, and she's grand with the guests."

Sipping their bubbly, they climbed upstairs. Kate took in every detail. "I know it was updated two years ago. So far, I think it looks even nicer than the estate agent's photos." They peeked inside a few guest rooms.

"Catriona told me the mattresses are new," Deirdre said. "Isn't that grand? The crud those things accumulate is disgusting! Even in a proper establishment such as this." She set her champagne on a nightstand, hopped onto the bed and said in a spunky Meg Ryan voice, "Hey Goose, take me to bed or lose me forever!"

Kate pulled her back to her feet. "No wonder you guys have seven kids."

"And need a new mattress."

They headed back downstairs. Deirdre pointed out: "The kitchen's in good form, as you can see, much nicer than my slop-keep. It recently received a facelift as tight as yer woman Joan Rivers." She pulled the skin on her cheeks taut. "And of course, Catriona does a lovely Irish breakfast for the guests."

"If they've gotten on her good side straightaway?"

Deirdre laughed as they moved to the breakfast room. "I love this antique sideboard and cereal dispenser. I could use a set-up like this feeding my troops."

The bay windows with their lace curtains looked out on the quiet street of semi-detached brick homes. The spire of St. Columba's Church cast a blessing on the area. Kate decided she'd take a walk around the neighborhood later, once she unpacked a few boxes.

Her eyes caught the glistening of crystal sconces perched on the moss green walls. They looked like a pair of diamond baubles that might dangle from Liz Taylor's earlobes. As the sun shone on the prisms, bands of color flashed around the room.

Deirdre giggled, "Look at those rainbows. We Irish say they're harbingers of good luck; they promise success, happiness and love. I'd say that's a good sign for you, Kate McMahon."

"Success and happiness sound appealing, but I'm staying away from romance. I could really use that pot of gold, though."

"Ah now, I'll bet your heart will warm up to the idea of love all in good time."

Kate sighed and shook her head. "I don't know. Once bitten, twice shy."

"Right," Deirdre said. "But I'm not givin' up on yeh."

The friends moved on to the adjoining sitting room and then to the office. A check-in stand was nearby. Deirdre pointed to an envelope pinned up on the cork board. "The McFaddens wanted to make sure you read this note." The seal on the envelope was roughed up and the flap was now secured with tape.

"It looks like someone already read my note. Did you do that?"

"Heavens no! Haven't I got better things to do?"

A sketch of the McFadden Guesthouse was featured on the front of the notecard. Kate read the hand-written message while Deirdre peeked over her shoulder:

Dear Ms. McMahon,

We hope you will love this place as much as we do. We have many lovely memories of this home and its gardens. Our hope is that it will bring you much happiness and good fortune. May your guests find the place endearing and return to its warm hearth again and again. We know you will find Catriona Ryan a reliable manager. We hope you will keep her on and work in harmony. She is as much a part of these premises as the brick and mortar. Don't hesitate to call with any questions.

Best of luck,
Connor & Aisling McFadden

P.S. We apologize, but some minerals spilled on the computer's keyboard during our move. We tried to dry it out, but the power light neglects to go on. We've arranged for a repairman from Computer Serve to come to the guesthouse. Please mail us the bill if the repair is not covered under warranty.

"What a nice couple," Kate said, "but not having the computer working is a real bummer. I wish I hadn't sold my laptop last week. It's

9

going to be hard running this business until the darn thing gets repaired."

"Well, now, aren't there cyber cafes and libraries? And I'm t'inkin you could also use our computer."

"Thanks, I might take you up on it. But I need to get familiar with the new reservation and bookkeeping software. I hope the repairman can fix it right away."

She re-pinned the note on the board and studied the name *Catriona Ryan*. "I had no idea the Irish spelled 'Katrina' that way. I'm learning something new every minute."

They moved on to the owner's quarters. Kate hesitated by the queen-sized bed, running her free hand along a linen pillow. She said with a catch in her voice, "Damn these tears! They're right beneath the surface all the time."

"Let them come, luv. Folks around here know you're a young widow and they'll t'ink it's pure grief. Only a few of us know the whole story—at least the story that was in your local newspaper. Mark's Minnesota relations sent it to us. So I know it's not simple grief you're dealing with, but layers of anger and shame, too." She held open her arms and Kate fell into them.

"You went through hell—but you kept on goin' and walked right through the bloody fire." Deirdre rubbed the tears from her own eyes. "You go ahead and cry now. Let it all out and good riddance to it."

They sat on the bed for a time, clinging to each other, careful not to spill a drop from either glass. Then Kate pulled away, honked her nose into some tissue and stiffened her back.

"This bed, like most of the world, is made for a couple. I said I can't be bothered to think about love, but I'm afraid I'll think about it every time I climb into this half-empty bed! My love life, my marriage, all my happy memories were just part of a con game. Bryan wasn't for real, so none of what we had was real. I'll never be able to trust a man—or my judgment—again!"

Deirdre stiffened, too. "I'm sorry I can't change what's happened to you in the past, but I won't let you give up on the future. You best

10

remember that a man *can* be genuine and good, and there are still good ones out there." She glanced at the bed. "Oh, I wish everyone could have what I have with Mark. He understands teamwork. He wears me out and he gives me strength. Now, don't go t'inkin' it's perfect, but he's a good man with integrity—and he puts a smile on my face."

"If only I could believe there's another man like Mark out there…" Kate stopped abruptly and met Deirdre's eyes. She wondered if Deirdre was having the same thought she was. They were just tipsy enough to laugh at the irony, but she hoped Deirdre wouldn't mention Mark's twin brother, Joe. Deirdre and Mark might still be bristling from the old wound Kate had inflicted when she chose Bryan over Joe 15 years ago, but God bless them for not doing a little I-told-you-so dance. Kate wouldn't admit to anyone, including herself, that thoughts of Joe might stir up banked ashes.

Deirdre cleared her throat and raised her glass. "Well, now, here's to you and the new life you're cobblin' together. *Sláinte!*"

Kate jumped to her feet as the glasses clicked, upsetting a few drops of the good stuff. "That's it!"

"What's it?"

"The name—you gave me the name I've been looking for. I'll re-name this place … The Cobblestones!"

"Ah now, that's a lovely idea." Deirdre held up her glass once again. "Here's to The Cobblestones being filled each night. And may you and your guests be cozy and safe."

"Safe? Like … safe from bill collectors? I'll drink to that!" Kate said, taking a long sip. "And here's to getting on Catriona's good side … straightaway." They were still laughing when they began un-packing the boxes shipped from America.

CHAPTER 3

Our prime purpose in this life is to help others.
And if you can't help them, at least don't hurt them.

~DALAI LAMA

Ultan Ferrian was going to hit Fitzsimmons' Sandwich Shop for his lunch, and was so hungry he could eat a farmer's arse through a blackthorn bush. It was two hours later than his usual break. Mr. Doyle ordered him to finish fixing the computer belonging to a professor at DCU. The pompous arsehole needed it straightaway to do his grading. He had looked at Ferrian from across the counter like he was a no-account piece of shite. Schools were plagued by feckers who thought they were better than everyone else. Ever since Ultan dropped out when he was 16, life was much sweeter. He could do what he wanted, when he wanted, unless some eejit entered the picture.

"Bloody hell!" he yelled. "Would it kill that bollocks to just wait a few more days?" Ferrian had things on his own computer he was trying to download on the sly at work, and he had to put that off in order to get Mr. Know-It-All's crap done. Maybe he'd slip out and key the professor's BMW when he came to pick up his computer. That's what happened when people messed with Ultan Ferrian. How's that for customer service?

As he flicked a cigarette butt out the car window, a gust of wind blew one of his sketches out the passenger side. He scowled as the yellow paper swept across the street and fluttered away. "Ah bugger!"

Along the side of Iona Road he spotted a gacky looking teenager sporting cowboy boots and farting around on a bike. He had a half-wit look about himself and a daft smile on his mug as if he didn't have a bloody care in the world.

Fookin' mentaller. Without slowing down, Ferrian jerked his steering wheel to the right—just messing around—heading right toward the bloke. Then just as suddenly, he jerked to the left, correcting his "mistake." The abrupt swerve hurled his *Hustler* magazine off the seat, smashing the cover girl's silicone diddies onto the floor mat.

The kid yelped, swerving his handlebars, and lurched into the curb, catapulting off his bicycle. Ferrian laughed as he looked in his rear-view mirror and watched the fool eejit rub his knee and climb back on his bike, pedaling away like mad with those clunky boots.

"That one's not the full shilling," he snickered to his reflection. He noticed his eyes were still red and puffy. The joints he had smoked the night before were brilliant, but now his supply was nearly gone. He would need cash to buy more, so he couldn't afford to lose his job. His boss, Doyle, had chewed his arse more than once on account he looked and smelled like he'd had a rough night. Ferrian pulled over beneath a beech tree. His hand went to his crotch and scratched his wab before reaching into the front pocket of his trousers. He fished around for a bottle of Red Out and squirted solution into each burning eye. "Shite! That kills!" he hollered, rubbing his lids with clenched fists and wishing he could pluck out his flaming eyeballs.

When he could see again, he spotted the McFadden Guesthouse a stone's throw away. A "Sold" sign swung from a post in the front garden. He wracked his brain, trying to think why the place was familiar. He grabbed the phone from his breast pocket embroidered with the "Computer Serve" logo, and checked his calendar. Sure enough, he was scheduled to make a service call there to fix a desktop.

Ferrian steered his white and dented Ford Ka into the bottleneck traffic on Finglas Road. He needed to make a right-hand turn to the sandwich shop. "Don't any of these gobshites know how to drive?"

Out of frustration, he lit another fag and cranked up the radio while he sat and waited for the light to change.

"I guess nobody wants me to get any fookin' lunch today," he complained to himself. And that's when he saw her—a lovely lady walking on the footpath. She had long, golden hair that hung over a red Minnesota Twins hoodie. He guessed her to be somewhere in her thirties. Probably an American staying at one of the hotels around here. She had the look of a Yank about her. Before the traffic started to move, he snatched the phone from his pocket and snapped a quick photo of her when she wasn't looking.

"Fine bit o' stuff, indeed! Now I'm *really* hungry."

CHAPTER 4

The soul is healed by being with children.

~FYODOR DOSTOYEVSKY

After her walk around Glasnevin, Kate was ready for a cup of tea. She found the kettle in the pantry and placed it on the Aga stove. She inhaled slowly, promising not to let herself be intimidated by the size and complexity of the industrial dinosaur dominating the kitchen. She was familiar with the smaller model that sat in Myrna's kitchen when she was living there, but this one would require a few lessons.

Her thigh scraped something hard protruding from the front of the stove. "Ouch! What the …?"

An old vise grip pliers was attached to a control stem where a knob was missing. She released it and placed it on the counter thinking, "Crap! Am I going to need a new range? That would really throw a wrench into my plans." She'd have to ask Catriona if the thing was on its last leg. Until she could learn more, she'd have to be content with knowing how to boil water.

She headed to the parlor, pulled the lace curtains aside and marveled at the garden. To her delight, a purple camellia posed with perfect posture center stage. She felt an urge to touch its soft petals.

Walking through the flowerbed was like stepping into a Monet painting. She enjoyed gardening, but maintaining this masterpiece was going to be a handful, even with Catriona Ryan's help.

She caressed the beautiful purple blossom, and a deep sense of peace enveloped her body and soul. She closed her eyes and felt the sunshine spill across her face.

A kind male voice spoke from next door in Deirdre's garden, "Are you M-M-Miss Kate?"

She opened her eyes and turned. The thick teen before her had an angelic smile. As he sat cross-legged on a limestone slab, he rocked back and forth. Black cowboy boots covered his feet and one knee was wrapped in gauze.

His beautiful face had the blueprint of Down syndrome.

"Why ... Yes, I'm Kate."

"I'm M-M-Michael Farley and I'm a sheriff around here. Right now I'm protecting the ants. See how they march in a straight line? From their ant hill to that squished banana?"

Kate glanced around the neighborhood. "Umm, where do you live?"

"Over there b-by the church. And I have a job! I help Father Criagáin and Father Hurley at the church. I get the bulletins ready, and sweep, and put flowers in vases, and welcome people on Sundays. I'm swimmin' in the Special Olympics and ... and ... I like John Wayne."

"Well it's nice to meet you. The Special Olympics? Wonderful! And I like John Wayne, too." Kate walked over to him and extended her hand. He met her handshake with another smile as big as the great cowboy himself.

"You talk like John Wayne ... but like a cowgirl. Father Criagáin told me to call on you ... to welcome you and ... and to see if it'd be grand to pick the pretty flowers in your garden for M-M-Mary. But not *all* the flowers. The McF-F-Faddens used to let me come every day." Kate noticed that when Michael stuttered he took his right hand and gently stroked the underside of his left arm. She surmised it was a calming technique used to help slow down his words.

"Oh, you mean you pick the flowers for Mary's altar in St. Columba's?"

He struggled to his feet and led her back into her own garden.

"Yeh. I bring my own tools and a basket my m-mammy gave me. So … would it be fine with you? Do you swim really, really fast, too? Like a torpedo?" He fiddled with the bandage on his knee and then pushed his Ben Franklin glasses up the bridge of his nose.

"No, I don't swim fast like a torpedo, but I can swim okay. There are lots of lakes where I come from. And of course it would be just fine if you picked some of my flowers. There's enough here for all of Glasnevin. In fact, Michael, look at this beautiful purple camellia. I bet Mary would love this one."

Michael retrieved his basket from the limestone slab, cut the blossom, kissed it and laid it in the basket. "I've had m-my eye on that one. T'anks a m-million!" He gave Kate a high-five, wiggled his butt and twirled her around and around in some sort of dance move. Before she could catch her breath, he rushed toward a bike that was resting against the fence.

"Good bye, M-M-Miss Kate! When I ride m-my bike I pretend it's a horse because John Wayne rides a horse."

Michael strapped his basket onto the handlebars and flicked the kickstand up with a booted heel. He said to his bicycle, "Giddy-up, Duke! W-Watch out for white cars!"

Kate smiled and watched her new acquaintance ride into the sunset. She pulled off her sweatshirt, yanking it over her head, thinking about all the neighbors she had yet to meet. *Will I fit in? Did I do the right thing by moving to Ireland?*

She caught another glimpse of Michael in the distance and wondered how in the world he pedaled so well in those cowboy boots. He pulled to the curb, planted his feet and twisted around so he could yell to her. "John Wayne says, 'Life's tough, Pilgrim. It's even tougher if you're s-stupid.'"

Her head jerked and then a chuckle tumbled from her mouth. She was spurred back into Positive Mode. *Buck up, Kate McMahon. Think of the great cast of characters that will play in this homesteading adventure.*

"Hey, M-Miss Kate!" Michael called from a little farther down the street. "Welcome home!"

Yep, this cowgirl was home. Her kettle was whistling and she was glad to be removed from the Wild, Wild West of her old life.

CHAPTER 5

Dogs never bite me, just humans.
~MARILYN MONROE

Myrna Riley had just returned from minding her grandkids, when through her open windows, she heard Michael Farley yell something. She peered through the lace curtains to check on him and realized he was waving toward the McFadden Guesthouse at none other than Kate McMahon. "Ah look, Kate arrived safe and sound. Isn't that lovely! We must run over and welcome her." She said this with an air kiss to her Dalmatian, Pooka.

She and Terry bought the dog when their nest emptied. Their youngest, Helen, had moved to Australia a few years ago to prove her independence. There was no point in trying to dissuade her. You can't put an old head on young shoulders. But working three jobs to support herself made it difficult for the lass to return home for visits. Their sons were living in their own homes now, and t'anks be to God, the grandbabies came to visit often. Otherwise, Myrna believed she'd go daft from missing her chisellers so much. At least they had the dog to keep them company.

Pooka was one lucky pooch. No canine creature ate better or got more attention than this one. Terry stroked her fur while they watched soccer matches on the telly, and he often brought her to the seashore for runs along the strand. Since Pooka was so well behaved, she roamed Glasnevin freely, and had become the local dog.

Rushing to the kitchen, Myrna sliced two pieces of homemade brown bread. "Egg sandwiches were Kate's favorite when she lived with us during that semester long ago. What do you say we take this over to her, Pooka? She must be famished."

Pooka wagged her tail with a *woof*.

"Has it really been 15 years since young Kate slept under this roof? My, oh my … how the years speed by like a Yank in a rented car on the country roads!" Myrna placed the sandwich on a plate garnished with kiwi and strawberries. Finalizing the presentation, she added a few salt-and-vinegar crisps—"potato chips" to the Americans.

She had one last thing she needed to do. She rummaged through the refrigerator and removed her Humira. Every two weeks, Myrna had to give herself a shot to help reduce the symptoms of the rheumatoid arthritis that plagued her joints. She hoisted up her skirt and plunged the medicine into her thigh. "Ah bugger, that hurt, so it did. Must have hit a vein." Clenching her teeth, she extracted the large needle and carefully disposed of the syringe.

"Come along, girl." She called to her pet, pushing the door open with her aching hand.

As they approached the McFadden Guesthouse, Myrna caught sight of her "American daughter."

"Ah Kate, it's grand havin' you here in Ireland for good. It's like havin' one of my own return from across the sea, so it is."

"Oh, Myrna! Thanks. I owe you Rileys so much. If you hadn't been such a great host family, I wouldn't have fallen so deeply in love with Ireland."

"I brought you an egg sandwich. I thought you might be needin' a bit of a snack after all the travelin' you've been doin'. Let's take a look at you now … Aren't you lovely with your hair all long? And I can see you've been keeping up with the runnin'. You're still fit and trim, so you are."

"Thanks, Myrna, you look great yourself, like the Rose of Tralee, actually. I love your bobbed hair," Kate said. "Is Terry home?"

"No, he's still over at Stephen's minding the grandbabies, but he'll be meetin' up with us tonight at O'Gara's. Rose of Tralee? Hee, hee, hee... aren't you a dear. Now, why don't you eat this egg sandwich before it starts smellin'."

As they walked into the kitchen, Myrna said, "I saw Michael Farley waving to you. He's a grand young man, so he is. His ma and da both work at the church, which is lovely because they can keep an eye on him. We all like to look out for him."

Kate fished for another tea bag from the caddy. "I'll look forward to seeing him each day. His comments crack me up."

When the tea was properly steeped they added just the right amount of milk. Myrna remembered teaching young Kate to take tea this way. "How are you doin'?" Myrna asked. "I know it's been a tough t'ree years, all right."

They headed toward the front sitting room as Kate nibbled the egg sandwich flavored with Chef's sauce. "The past three years have been pure hell. My pride was hurt as much as my bank account."

"You poor t'ing. You're not to blame." Myrna wondered again if the drowning was really an accident or Bryan's way of escaping the shame of being discovered.

Kate took another bite of sandwich and then swallowed it with a gulp. "Thanks again, Myrna, for being there when I really needed that second set of parents."

"Ah, your poor mam. Will she be comin' to visit soon?"

"After I get settled."

The gentle atmosphere changed as quickly as the Irish weather when the two matching Kennedy twins tumbled through the front door and rushed at Kate and Myrna. Deirdre was close behind them and a bit out of breath. "Now, now, me boyos, mind your manners."

"Oh, let them be, Deirdre." Kate squatted down and opened her arms to the toddlers. "Hi boys! Aren't you handsome?"

Myrna watched as the boys smacked Kate's cheeks with shy kisses.

"This is just what I needed. It's the perfect tonic for me," said Kate.

Myrna and Deirdre gave each other smiles tinged with sadness. Myrna had three children by the time she was Kate's age. And Deirdre's cup was overflowing.

Through the window, Myrna saw Deirdre's three middle kids running across the street toward the guesthouse. Their burgundy plaid uniform skirts looked like little kilts as the girls leapt through the front door.

"Auntie Kate! Auntie Kate!"

Myrna was delighted to hear the lasses use the term "Auntie" even though Kate was not related to the Kennedys. Kate and Mark were college classmates, and weren't Kate and Deirdre like sisters?

The girls rushed past Myrna—messenger bags, backpacks and all. They were a mass of ginger hair and freckles—traits inherited from both parents. Kate pointed to each girl in turn: "Let's see, you're Mary Margaret, you're Mary Kathryn and you're Mary Cecelia. You've all grown several inches, er, centimeters since I've seen you."

The girls nodded, and Kate added, "I brought you some Regina's Chocolates from St. Paul, and they're sitting on my bed. If you can find them, they're yours to share."

The girls took off down the hall and the twins clambered behind. Myrna noted, "The boys may not talk much yet, but they're no eejits. They know the word 'chocolate,' so they do."

They prattled on about children until Mary Margaret rushed back into the room. "Mammy, Mammy...the twins got themselves into Kate's boxes of clothes and they took her knickers!" As if on cue, the chocolate-covered duo emerged. Sure enough, in the clutches of one twin was a pair of Kate's hot pink Calvin Kleins, resplendent with chocolate smudges.

"Pooh, pooh...Biiiiig pooh!" exclaimed one. Myrna knew it was Gavin because of his gapped teeth.

"Meeeeow!" said his twin, Murphy, lifting his curled claws and licking chocolatey paws.

"Well," Myrna heard Kate whisper, attempting an Irish brogue, "'Tis been a bloody long time since someone's had his paws on me knickers!"

CHAPTER 6

Vodka is tasteless going down, but it's memorable coming up.
~GARRISON KEILLOR

The next morning, Kate was out of breath and feeling way too sluggish as she hit the road on her early morning run. Her stomach was rumbling. She wanted to blame jetlag, but truthfully, it was the drinks she consumed last night at O'Gara's Pub. She hoped a jog would help her recover.

As she found her rhythm, a line from a song popped into her head: *Whiskey yer the devil, yer leadin' me astray.* Old Man Poppy Flynn, a regular at O'Gara's, sang it with gusto last night at the pub. She recalled the octogenarian's comment after she approached his barstool to compliment his voice: "When I'm dead and gone, lovely lady, don't be forgettin' me name. It's *Poppy Flynn*... now put your lips up to mine and repeat it five times!"

Smiling split her head. *Geez, how many Jameson lemonades did I have? Oh, well... it took a lot to keep the memories of Bryan at bay.*

She glanced at her watch. She needed to be back in a half-hour to get a shower in before Catriona Ryan, the manager, came over to meet her.

This route through Glasnevin was one of the three-mile loops she used to traverse when she was a student. Back then she was the only runner about. She'd see a lot of people walking, or riding their bikes, not for exercise, but for transportation.

She recalled the day she first arrived at the Rileys' home. Eight-year-old Helen was helping her unpack.

"What is this?" Helen inquired of Kate's running shorts and tank top.

"My running clothes."

"You must be jokin'!" Helen said, "You can't go out in public with those on!"

That comment sent Kate scouring all over Dublin, until she found a proper sweatsuit. She blew her first month's beer money on ugly, but modest, athletic gear.

The local runners she saw out on the streets this morning were sporting authentic running attire—proof that the Irish were finally bitten by the jogging bug. Now she was certain that her Nike shorts and tops would be acceptable.

She exited Griffith Park, chugging along the Tolka River, until she reached the Botanic Gardens. A plaque stating, "Founded in 1795" graced the wall. Passing through the elaborate gate, she jogged on the path leading to Palm House—a wrought iron glasshouse exhibiting tropical plants. It rose 65 feet high and resembled a multi-faceted diamond.

There was something romantic about this Victorian complex, something enchanting. It served as the perfect backdrop for wedding photos, rendezvous of clandestine lovers, or even for lonely hearts meeting by chance encounters.

Out of the corner of her eye, Kate spotted a male runner on the grounds. His navy Spandex T-shirt couldn't pretend to conceal his muscles. She took a better look at the eye candy, noticing that he was headed toward a double drinking fountain built of fine stone masonry. He removed his 49ers baseball cap and bent over to take a sip. *Is that my heart jumping? Or am I about to retch?*

She sped toward the fountain and bent down to the spigot next to him, their shoulders nearly touching. His body heat was making her hotter. It was the first time since Bryan died that she felt such magnetic attraction. She gave an involuntary "Ahhh" once the water washed the dryness from her mouth. When she felt his eyes turn toward her, she adjusted her cap and smoothed her ponytail. *Dang, I'm sure I look like the dog's breakfast!* She was pretty sure the fluttering in her stomach was from the whiskey. A cold sweat prickled her forehead as she held in her cuss words.

He stood up and replaced his hat.

Is the ground swaying, or is that just me? She closed her eyes.

"Ah, are you … um … okay?" he said.

She could feel him moving closer. She opened her eyes and saw the concern on his face.

Damn, he's drop-dead gorgeous and I'm gonna puke all over his running shoes!

She clutched her stomach. "I'm fine. Just … thirsty."

When it seemed he was going to reach for her, she mumbled, "Gotta run!" and headed toward a wooded path. She turned around for one more glance at the guy. He was retrieving a sweatshirt from the bench and looked mighty fine bending over. She picked up the pace, telling herself to never mind. *I need a man like I need a hole in my head!*

She made it to Wellington Duck Pond before she heaved behind a giant sequoia. She hoped the acid didn't damage the monumental tree. Wiping her mouth on a sleeve, she scanned the area, relieved nobody saw her spewing.

Feeling better now, she commenced jogging. As she curved around the wedding gazebo, she swooped down to grab a leaf that had fallen from a rhododendron, and clutched it in a moist hand. Quickly heading south, she peered at her watch again. She didn't want to smell like a sweaty pool hall when meeting her manager for the first time.

Waiting to cross Botanic Road, Kate glanced back once again, hoping to get another glimpse of Spandex Man. The only people behind her were kids on their way to school.

The steeple of St. Columba's Church loomed in the distance. It was hard to believe that this whole suburb of Dublin was once a monastery where St. Columba himself studied. The monastery was destroyed by the Vikings, and then the area became farmland.

She had to tread carefully because she was running on cobblestones. Glasnevin was a mere village in the 1600s, and by the 1700s many distinctive families lived here on large estates. And the Carroll estate opened up for development in the early 1900s, when these cobblestone roads were laid. Kate's mother's maiden name was Carroll, so she felt like this was her "auld sod."

Jumping onto the sidewalk, she sped up until she rounded the corner into her front garden. Glancing at her watch, she saw it was 7:30 on the dot. She had a half hour before Catriona arrived. The thought of it formed a new lump in the pit of her empty stomach.

Letting go of the rhododendron leaf, she made a vow to drink in moderation from this day forward.

CHAPTER 7

*In 1953 there were two ways for an
Irish Catholic boy to impress his parents:
Become a priest or attend Notre Dame.*

~PHIL DONAHUE

Running up the 16 steps, two at a time, Luke O'Brien identified with Rocky. But in all reality, these days he was more like a down-and-out street brawler. At 38, he was starting to feel as if his joints and muscles had suffered too many body punches. Sometimes he longed for the days when he could run a six-minute mile and was a middle-weight champion for Notre Dame's Bengal Bouts. He gave up boxing when his college days were over, but he was determined to keep running until he went down for the final count—and he hoped it would be a while before that bell rang.

He fished for his key in the hidden pocket of his Spandex shorts and let himself into his townhouse. Usually, if it wasn't raining after his morning workout, Luke would wolf down a big glass of orange juice, toast and hard-boiled eggs while sitting on his second-story balcony, and that is precisely what he did on this fine March morn. After living in Ireland for eight years, he knew to make the most of the fair-weathered days.

As he sat in the breeze, he let his body cool a bit while he munched on his post-run breakfast, glancing around the neighborhood, searching for something, but not finding it. Nonetheless, it was still a beautiful view. From this vantage point he could see

O'Gara's Pub—where he often had a beer and a bite to eat. He could take in the beauty of the brick homes, a big, stately guesthouse, and canopy of treetops. On clear days he actually could see the Botanic Gardens, the Queen Mother of parks, off in the distance.

As the Ireland correspondent for *Associated Press*, Luke had a lot of research to do each day. Beginning at breakfast time, he'd peruse several Irish newspapers. To make his job easier, if these publications had an online version, he could scan them quickly on his laptop. But he still preferred the smell and texture of the crinkly papers.

He kept in touch with news in The States by reading, electronically, *The Wall Street Journal, USA Today, The Washington Post* and the paper of his hometown, *The San Francisco Chronicle*. Since Irish news was a little slow this morning, he clicked onto Notre Dame's website and downloaded *The Observer* to see if it had any good articles, and it did. There was a story about Raghib Ramadian Ismail, also known as "The Rocket," who was a wide receiver for the Fighting Irish's 1988 national championship team and went on to star in the NFL. The story said that in Ismail's retirement he did some bull riding, coached in the extreme sports league and was an inspirational speaker.

"Damn, that guy's got a few years on me and he's still going a lot stronger than I am." Luke walked toward the master bedroom, removed his 49ers ball cap and studied gray flecks in his black hair. "Makes me feel like a slug," he said out loud to no one as he sniffed his armpits, hoping that gal at the drinking fountain didn't get a whiff of his B.O. Then he pulled his navy spandex shirt over his head and threw it basketball-style into the laundry hamper. He missed an easy basket.

"For shit's sake!"

Luke took off his shorts and boxers, balled them up together and tried for a basket once again. This time he made it. "Hot dog!" he whooped.

He sat on his unmade bed. Reaching over to the nightstand, he picked up a framed photo of Christy and himself taken at the football stadium when they were in college, three years before they married. It was his favorite picture.

If all had gone as planned, Luke wouldn't be living in Ireland. They would still be in Dallas, Christy would be a full-time mom and Luke would be bringing home a ton of bacon.

His dream was violently stripped away the moment he received that God-awful visit from Officer Geiger who had found Christy's ID in a zippered pouch stowed under her bicycle seat. She had been sideswiped by a UPS truck on a slick county road. Luke became a widower at 28. Unfortunately, they didn't have any kids in the short three years they were married. They were "waiting." He couldn't remember why.

He reached for his phone and saw that he had three texts from Nora.

The first one: "Where are you?"

The second: "Are you running? Can you pick me up earlier tonight? Xoxo."

The third message made him groan: "I signed you up as emcee. Wear your tux."

He met Nora Connelly six months ago and she'd been coming at him full throttle ever since.

A knock on the door startled him. He hoped it was Buck Hubbell, his photographer sidekick—and not Nora. Luke wrapped a towel around himself and opened the door. He looked at Buck's unshaven face and glanced at his running watch. "Wow … Let's see, you're only 25 minutes early today. Don't you have a life, Buck?"

"Well, while you were out running this morning, O'Brien, I was working my ass off. I had a 5:00 a.m. photo shoot of the shrimpers at Howth Harbour for a freelance story. Now, get your sorry self into the shower so you'll smell pretty for our meeting."

"All right, I'm going, I'm going. Help yourself to the coffee."

"Already on it. And I'm going to sit on your balcony and ogle the hot babes walking to the bus stop."

"Sounds good," Luke said. "If you see a runner in a red shirt with a long, blond ponytail, let me know."

"Whaaat?" Buck just about dropped his cup of Joe. "Did you finally break it off with Nora? And you're noticing other women now? Maybe you should go back to being a neuter."

"Oh, shut up, you little punk. Do you want me to drop my towel and put you to shame? This thing with Nora isn't working out."

"Well, did she whack you over the head with her Prada purse when you told her?"

Luke's shoulders collapsed. "No, I haven't told her yet … Maybe tonight after the fundraiser."

"Fundraiser? You hate fundraisers."

"I know. But she signed me up to emcee. And it's for a good cause—the animal shelter—so I don't want to back out."

"Did you say you're emceeing? You hate public speaking."

"Well, I know that, and she knows that. And I have to wear a damn tux. Can I borrow your bow tie with the great danes all over it?"

"Nora hates that tie, remember? When I wore it to Dan's wedding she told me that I was a 'brazen strap of a woofter for wearing something so desperate altogether.' "

"Precisely. That's why I want to borrow it."

"Okay, Mr. Passive-Aggressive. Watch out for flying evening bags."

Luke laughed and tightened his towel. "I'll be glad tomorrow, when I'm free of Nora and her baggage."

"So, tell me about the runner. The blond in the red shirt?"

"Oh, yeah. On my run this morning I saw a good-looking gal." *Who wasn't looking too good* he almost added.

"Good looking from the front … or the back?"

"Both!" Luke said over his shoulder on his way to the bathroom.

"Which way did she go?"

"I don't know. She was too fast for me."

"We like 'em fast … or have you forgotten?"

"I've forgotten a lot, but this runner jogged my memory." Luke turned on the shower, leaving the bathroom door open, in case Buck spotted the the mystery woman and sounded the alarm. He lathered up and belted out:

Cheer, cheer for Old Notre Dame,
Wake up the echoes cheering her name …

He didn't see Buck lean over the balcony, and he didn't hear him yell to an elderly gent passing by, "Pardon the racket, sir. Have you seen any fast women out there on the street?"

"Not for the past 60 years, so I haven't."

"That's too bad. My buddy's desperate altogether."

CHλPTER 8

Your battles inspired me—not the obvious material battles—
But those that were fought and won behind your forehead.

~JAMES JOYCE

When her manager first arrived, Kate could tell that Catriona was a take-charge kind of gal. After shaking hands, Catriona led her boss around, instructing her about the ins and outs of the place. Kate struggled to pay attention and hoped the older woman wouldn't notice that her pupil was suffering from a hangover. In the hallway, Catriona gave a couple of sniffs. Could she smell the essence of whiskey escaping from her pores or lingering on her breath?

As they passed through the dining room, Kate stumbled, upsetting a basket of fruit on the sideboard. She started to retrieve an orange that was rolling under a chair, but as she bent over, her head felt like it was being pulverized in a juicer. Catriona stepped in to complete the task and harrumphed. "Are you too incapacitated to finish the tour?"

Busted! "Oh, no! I want to finish the tour. But do you mind if we sit down first and have a cup of tea?"

"Not at all. I'll prepare a tray."

Rising from the kitchen was a cacophony of clanging, clinking and more harrumphing. Catriona emerged with her hands on her unwieldy hips. "Jaysus! Why did you remove the spanner from the cooker?"

"Ah ... What did I do?"

"The cooker's knob is banjaxed and I use the spanner to set it to right."

"You mean the wrench? I put it on the counter." Kate's stomach felt like it was being pressed in a vise.

"Don't be tearin' down a fence before findin' out why it was put up."

"Um…What?" She rubbed the bump that had formed on her thigh. "Does the wrench have to hang there all the time?"

"It does indeed. A repairman is too dear, but my husband is happy to serve as the guesthouse's handyman. And didn't he jimmy the cooker well? Now, don't be removin' that spanner again. I can't be replacin' the bloody thing every time I cook eggs and porridge." As she scuttled back to the kitchen she added, "The McFaddens understood how much scurrying I do around here in the mornings."

Kate had a flashback to her very first encounter with Shame, when she was in seventh grade. At a detention during recess, Principal "Mean Monster" Miller stood over her while she scraped globs of gum off the sidewalks.

She took comfort in the hot tea when it arrived. But she could feel the housekeeper's eyes on her as she stirred honey into her cup with shaky hands.

"Is it a sore head you have?" asked Catriona, peering closely at her. "Are you circling over Shannon, then?"

"What? Am I circling over Shannon?" Kate was resting her head on her hand.

With a smirk the older woman said, "Ah, now. I forget that you Yanks don't know all of our jargon. Let me explain: A few years back, Mr. Boris Yeltsin was makin' an official visit to Ireland. He was too polluted to disembark, so the plane circled over Shannon Airport six times, until he sobered up."

"No way! Is that story true?" Kate asked, now putting her hand to her stomach.

" 'Tis indeed. Give it a Google."

"Well, to tell the truth, my stomach sounds like it gave a gargle. I have to admit, I had one too many last night."

"I'm not a tippler myself bein' that me father overindulged before he went on the dry. But I'm not above seein' the humor in it. That Englishman, Churchill, used to say: 'One's not enough. Two's too many. T'ree's just right.' And I'm sure Boris Yeltsin, thought the same. God rest both their souls ... and that of me father."

"Well ... I think I had four or five."

Catriona's eyebrows shot up. "Jaysus! Well then, there's no sense boiling your cabbage twice, now is there?"

Kate didn't have the energy to inquire about that one. She wondered if it was too late to get on Catriona's good side "straightaway."

"Seein' that you're of no use anyway, why don't we take this time to talk business? How much do you know about running a guesthouse?"

Kate swallowed and forced a smile. "My um ... late husband and I ran the Lumberjack Inn back in Minnesota for nine years." Kate peered at Catriona over her cup and guessed her housekeeper's age to be about mid-fifties. "The man who built the place was a lumber baron." Kate pulled out her phone and found a picture of it.

"Oh, I see. How many guests could you accommodate?"

"It had ten suites, and this place—The Cobblestones—has thirteen. So it was a little smaller.

"Right. You're changin' the name? The Cobblestones, is it? I wonder what the McFaddens would t'ink of that. You Americans make such a big to-do about our cobblestones."

"And a lot of Americans will be renting these rooms. I think they'll like the new name."

"Are you after makin' any other changes?"

"Um, well I'm on a tight budget, but I was thinking that some new bedding and lamps would be nice. Plus a new coat of paint here and there would freshen it up."

Catriona shrugged. "You're the boss."

Kate blotted the back of her neck with her napkin. "I am. I'm lucky I was able to buy this place. I wouldn't have been able to do so if it weren't for Ireland's property crash. I know you thought about buying it, too. Running it will take teamwork and Deirdre and the McFaddens told me you're a great manager."

Catriona's eyes traveled to the cork board were the McFaddens' letter was pinned. "They were lovely people to work for. Won't I miss them, though?"

They sipped their drinks, silence stretching between them. Eventually, Catriona tapped the tabletop with her pointer finger and announced, "I get a two-hour break at noon, and my husband, Declan, expects me to be finished here at four o'clock. I like to prepare him a proper meal."

"OO ... kay."

"And every Thursday I have a compulsory appointment, so I need to leave precisely at half-three."

"All right. Anything else?" *Apparently this woman isn't too concerned about getting on MY good side straightaway.*

"Ah no. Not at the moment."

Kate leaned across the table and tried to assume her most authoritative expression. "I'll need you to be here promptly at six o'clock each morning to start the guests' breakfast. I begin most days with a morning run and I'll join you when I'm home and showered, around seven o'clock."

Catriona tilted her head. "Me Declan says that watching the Yanks do their exercising always makes him want to reach for the nearest Toblerone."

Kate smiled. "Well, I run so that I can eat chocolates and Mexican food and keep depression at bay."

Catriona tapped the tabletop once again and said, "Folks who are disposed to depression would be well advised to leave the drink alone ..."

Kate couldn't help thinking this woman resembled the actress, Kathy Bates, portraying The Unsinkable Molly Brown in *Titanic* ... or ... maybe that psychotic literary fan in *Misery*.

CHAPTER 9

I'm not a stunning woman.

~KATHY BATES AS ANNIE IN *MISERY*

Myrna knocked on the guesthouse door as she watched Pooka meander over to Kennedys. "Yoo-hoo Kate, are yeh home?" She let herself in and found Kate and Catriona sitting at a table taking tea. Kate had a face on her like a beagle. Myrna was in bits, hoping the two were getting on.

"Ah now, pet ... are yeh sick? Your face is all droopy like, and a bit pale." She put her hand up to Kate's forehead.

"She's circlin' over Shannon," Catriona said, folding her arms across her bulky bosom.

"Is she now?" Myrna understood. "Ah, yeh poor t'ing. It's not yer fault. Mark Kennedy and my Terry kept buying rounds of drinks last night. It was all part of the craic, so it was."

Kate looked up and shook her head. "No, it wasn't only because of the celebrating. It was because ... because I was trying to drown out the memories of Bryan, and now I'm paying the price. And wouldn't you know ... I'm out of antacids."

Myrna turned to Catriona and explained, "Bryan was Kate's husband and they met here in Ireland even though he was also American." She pulled out a chair, plopped down and looked at Kate. "Indeed. O'Gara's would hold a lot of memories for yeh, now, wouldn't it? You students used to gather there often enough."

"Yeah. And then I start thinking about ... you know ... the Triple Whammy." Kate dropped her head onto her folded arms.

Myrna caressed Kate's shoulders. "Right. The damn Triple Whammy."

Catriona gasped. "Myrna, I don't t'ink I've ever heard you swear before. This Triple Whammy must be somethin' horrible."

"Damn right it was," Kate mumbled into the tabletop. "You might as well know ... straightaway ... that my language is saltier than Myrna's."

"What's the Triple Whammy then?" Catriona leaned in.

Kate lifted her head and took a pensive sip from her teacup. Myrna knew she didn't like to talk about it.

"Go ahead and tell her, Myrna, she'll find out sooner or later, and it's better that she hear it from us."

Myrna rubbed Kate's back. "Sure, luv, and yeh don't have to worry about Catriona blathering it to others. She used to mind our children. I know she's trustworthy."

Myrna turned toward Catriona and cleared her throat. "Shortly after Bryan drowned, while Kate was a grieving widow, she discovered that he was a bloody crook. He was after swindling his investors in one of those Ponzi schemes. Knowin' my Kate, she could have been satisfied just livin' on the income from the inn, but her man wanted something grander. I'm t'inkin' he was too greedy, and let his moral compass get off-kilter. Right, Kate?"

Kate sat up straighter. "I blame myself for not paying more attention. When we would go to parties, his clients would rave about the fantastic returns they were getting on the money they invested with him. No other financial advisor was getting those results. They begged him to let their friends in on it, too. He enjoyed the applause, but I could see he was under more and more stress at the end of every quarter. When I tried to talk about it, he withdrew. He died, quite conveniently, just before it would have been exposed."

"How did he die?" Catriona asked, pouring a cup for Myrna.

"Every year he and three friends would take a daring dive off an old bridge during a town festival. That year, he didn't surface, and they found his body downstream the next day. He simply drowned, no head injury or foul play."

"How awful for you. I can't imagine." Catriona said, adjusting her generous frock.

Myrna gave a wee cough and waited for Kate's response.

"Yes, it was a major shock, but when I learned of his criminal activity—which made it a Double Whammy—my grief over losing him quickly shifted to rage and shame. If he hadn't died, I would've killed him. And if it weren't for my brother Lee, I'd have gone crazy."

"I talked to your mam, Kate," Myrna said. "She told me Father Lee is planning to visit soon." She turned toward Catriona to explain. "Kate's brother is a priest, so he is." She knew this would impress.

"Ah now, isn't that marvelous? How grand to have a priest in the family. My mam was always hoping one of my brothers would choose the collar, but none did. I'll wager your brother was an angel to have on hand when those Whammies happened."

"Yes. I was a broken spirit, so Lee handled the funeral details. He also called each morning just to make sure I was out from under the covers and running the B&B properly. He even came over once or twice to help make beds and bake muffins."

"Em…I'm surprised he let you off of your leash in order to move to Ireland. It appears you were very dependent on him." Catriona noted, cocking an eyebrow.

Myrna shifted in her seat, wondering if she'd need to step in as a referee. "Father Lee is a lovely man," she said.

"He is great…and I was never on a leash—as you say. He was my rock," Kate said. "I was in such a state of despair that I couldn't envision climbing out of the abyss and getting a fresh start. You see, Bryan's story was in the papers, and I couldn't escape the shame. My brother helped me break it down into managable pieces. First of all, when the FBI ransacked our house and took our computers…"

Catriona gasped. "Bejappers! They didn't!"

39

"Oh yes. Then Lee found a lawyer to help me deal with the investigators and the auditors, and to prove my innocence."

Myrna clanked her cup against its saucer. "Indeed Lee did more than bake muffins!"

Catriona shook her head. "You'd have surely lost your business if he hadn't taken over. But over-dependency can be a massive problem. Declan is quite dependent on me, but not to that degree."

"Ah now, Catriona!" Myrna said. "Enough about Declan...I mean...enough with you actin' the judge. Let Kate finish the story."

Kate rubbed her stomach. "My brother took over for me when I felt paralyzed, but he did it wisely. He didn't want me to become too dependent, so he kept telling me: 'You're a clever girl, Kate. You can figure this out.' And he knew I had finally turned the corner when I made several decisions on my own: I filed papers to resume my maiden name; I sold the inn, sold my jewelry, held a garage sale; and I repaid the people Bryan defrauded."

"Kate didn't want to keep a penny of the money he made dishonestly," Myrna explained.

Kate nodded. "And I found a buyer for my burial plot..." she gave a nervous laugh. "...because my plot was located right next to Bryan's."

The ladies giggled at that scenario.

"Indeed that Bryan was nothin' but an arsehole with legs!" Catriona said.

Myrna stifled a pleased little laugh. "And yerself t'inks *I'm* the one with the foul mouth!"

Kate's laugh was so forceful that the tea in her mouth flew back into her cup.

Catriona stood and shrugged her shoulders. "A dishonest husband is really and truly nothin' more than an arsehole with legs. T'anks be to God me Declan is the perfect angel."

"Emmm...Catriona, while you're up," Myrna said, "why don't you go see if Deirdre can spare some antacids for Kate's tummy trouble? I can hear it rumbling to almighty heaven."

As soon as Catriona was out the door, Myrna leaned in to Kate. "Speakin' of heaven, I must be tellin' you somethin'...Catriona's Declan is an angel indeed. He's been dead for the past two years, so he has."

"What?"

Myrna held up a hand. "Wait 'til I tell yeh...She's not as daft as you may be thinkin'. Yourself knows what it's like to suffer desperately with overwhelming grief. She had a fierce love for her Declan, and as I understand it, the poor woman has been stuck in what is called 'denial' since his heart attack."

"Denial? She's delusional. Why didn't anyone tell me? She could ruin my business. You all foisted her on me and she's a whack job!"

"Ah now, Kate. Don't be too annoyed. She's only partially off her rocker and she's harmless. The woman has a big heart and she's a fine worker. We weren't holdin' back information from you, we just didn't know *when* to tell you. Weren't we all hopeful you'd come to love her, as we do, once you grew to know her?"

"But Myrna, the woman clearly needs professional help. You can't just ignore it and let her live unsupervised."

"Right. We watch over her like we do young Michael. Don't all her relations live out the country, though? Now, don't go thinkin' it was an easy task, but we neighbors collectively persuaded Catriona to seek psychiatric counsel. And Terry drives her once a week to Dr. Roddy's clinic so we know she's keepin' to the schedule."

"Oh, that must be her Thursday afternoon 'compulsory appointment.'"

"'Tis," Myrna stated, glancing out the window at Deirdre's back door.

"And I thought her biggest problems were that she's judgmental...and doesn't drink."

"Ah, she drank her fair share, but her medication won't permit it now."

"Well, how am I supposed to act around her when she talks about him?"

"We don't want to interfere with Dr. Roddy's progress, so when she blathers on about Declan, we try to turn a deaf ear toward it."

"But … but she told me he's the handyman here. How am I supposed to play along with that? And she's got this … spanner thing …"

They heard the back door swing open and Catriona say, "Here's your tummy tablets and while you're chewing on them, why don't you finish tellin' me about that Third Whammy?"

Myrna could tell Kate was still in shock, so she took it upon herself to begin. "Ah yes, the Third Whammy. 'Twas her father's fatal heart attack. It seems he blamed himself for not seeing what Bryan was up to. The shame of it all took a toll on him."

Catriona nodded. "I suppose when you're deceived by someone you love, the pain eats up your insides, one bite at a time, until you t'ink you're going to die."

"And some do," said Kate. "Dad's death was such a blow, and I still feel responsible because I brought Bryan into the family."

"I happen to know a therapist—a friend of a friend—who's mighty fond of saying, 'You must let go' … and I can see in your case, Kate, he's quite right."

Kate plucked a sugar cube, crumbled it in her fist, and released it into her tea.

"In order to let go," Myrna said, trying not to look at Catriona, "one must accept reality." Turning to Kate, she added, "And learn to forgive. I know it seems an impossible task, but 'tis the only way to peace."

"Oh, Myrna! How would I even start?" Kate moaned, dropping her head onto her folded arms.

"Baby steps," said Myrna.

Kate lifted her head. "What do you mean?"

"If you're not yet ready to forgive, perhaps you can at least *get ready* to get ready to forgive … take baby steps."

Kate inhaled. "That's just the image I need. Baby steps. I promise I'll try to remember it."

Myrna felt warmth rush through her maternal heart, and wanted to heal Kate's broken one. So she said, "I'm after t'inkin' your da would be so proud of all you've overcome so far."

Kate sniffled. "I hope so. If it weren't for him I wouldn't have been able to afford this place and have a fresh start." She straightened her spine, pushed out a sigh and her voice was barely a whisper. "But if this business doesn't succeed," she peered at Catriona, "my only option will be to move into my mom's condo in the middle of the desert, surrounded by retirees riding golf carts and giant tricycles."

Myrna said, "I t'ink the worst is behind you, and the McFadden Guesthouse ... I mean The Cobblestones ... will be a success for yeh, Kate."

Catriona added, "If you can stay on your feet."

"It *has* to be a success." said Kate. "It's all I've got to my name ... thanks to that ... 'arsehole with legs.'"

Myrna leaned over and patted Kate's leg. "Baby steps, now, luv."

CHAPTER 10

Too often we ... enjoy the comfort of opinion
without the discomfort of thought.

~JOHN F. KENNEDY

After Myrna left, Catriona squatted on her hunkers and scrubbed a toilet in places most humans fear to go. She could hear Kate digging around in the medicine chest in her private W.C. She had to admit that the lass had courage of some sort. *I'm definitely no prissy-girl myself, but indeed I'd be shakin' like a chicken if I had to move to a different country. But this much I know: Surely, I wouldn't be startin' off my new life by gettin' into the drink.*

Catriona stood up and poured bleach into the bowl. With a brush, she scoured the underside of the rim until sweat ran down her neck and between her breasts. She thought about the lunacy of people running for exercise—like Kate. But Catriona found this job was a workout in itself. What with all the hooverin', moppin', sweepin' and gardenin' she did in a day's time, she should sport a smashing figure like Marilyn Monroe's. But she didn't, on account she liked to nibble. And truth be told, she could really pack it away. Ah, sure, Ms. Monroe was a bawdy sex symbol, but what did that anatomy bring her anyhow? A load of unhappiness indeed: illness, addictions, a bad reputation—not to mention three divorces and who knows how many sordid affairs.

She asked the toilet bowl, "Who'd want to sleep with President Kennedy, anyhow?" She knew the answer to that query from a documentary she watched on the telly: Quite a few. But no one with a lick of common sense, surely.

Since the thought of infidelity made Catriona scour the toilet with jack-hammer force, the bloody handle broke right off the brush. "Ah look, now it's as useless as a chocolate teapot," she said to herself on the way to the rubbish bin.

Next, she took a squiz around the kitchen, making a mental note of the tasks she needed to accomplish. Mopping was highest on her agenda. Kate joined her and they worked silently until the cream tile shone like the froth on a perfectly poured Guinness.

At last, Catriona asked her boss, "Do you have any questions for me?"

"Tell me about the part-time maid that comes in the afternoons," Kate said, pushing her mop along the floorboards.

"Ah now, Molly Flood is her name. She'll be in tomorrow. She's a nursing student at UCD and a lovely lass, but in a fortnight she'll be workin' in hospital full time and we'll need to replace her—if business is goin' well enough."

"Well, I'm determined to have a positive outlook. My budget is tight, and I need to buy ads on travel websites, but of course we can't skimp on staffing." Kate pulled her hair into a ponytail, and Catriona noticed a pensive look about her as she added, "We'll have to start searching now for a new assistant to take Molly's place."

Through the lace curtains, Catriona caught sight of Terry and Myrna Riley's home, and the seed of an idea was planted. "Leave it to me."

"Okay. But don't forget to keep me in the loop."

In the loop? These Yanks and their silly terms. I suppose she's trying to tell me she's the boss.

Kate's voice softened. "Where did you learn all the tricks of the trade, Catriona?"

"I grew up on a farm in County Kildare. I was the youngest in a brood of 11 chisellers. My da bred horses, and my dear mam had us girls help feed the men folk. That's where I learned how to cook and bake for a crowd. And we girls also helped with the cleanin' and gardenin'."

"Did you live on the farm until you moved here?"

"Aye. I married at 18 and moved to Glasnevin. I met me Declan at a fair and immediately I was crazy altogether for him. We were in line for the ring toss. He was a grand young man. And he couldn't take his eyes off of me, I'll let you know. Called me 'flah.'" She laughed while shaking her head.

"'Flah'? What does that mean?"

Am I goin' to be spendin' all my days interpreting? "It means attractive." Catriona felt her face redden as she wrung out her mop in the bucket. "And truth be told, he still calls me that, and it's been nearly 40 years. Which is better than Marilyn Monroe could say."

Kate took a few steps back and looked up at the ceiling, mumbling something about Marilyn Monroe being long dead.

Catriona put the mop aside and grabbed the belly fat hanging over her apron, "Wait 'til I tell yeh ... With every stone I put on, Declan seems to love me all the more. It's a miracle, really. We've had our bumps and our share of sadness, but we've stayed the course. I don't know what I'd do without the auld bugger."

Catriona caught a stricken look in Kate's eyes.

"Ah, 'tis daft I am! Here I'm goin' on and on about my happy marriage, not t'inking about the sad end to your own married life. Forgive me."

Kate wiped her brow and muttered, "Um ... Of course I'll forgive you ... Myrna says I need the practice."

Catriona tapped her pointer finger on the counter. "If you listen to my advice, maybe you'll find yourself in a happy marriage like mine someday."

CHAPTER 11

What happens in a romance novel
doesn't always have to stay in one.

~RENEE ALEXIS

D eirdre Kennedy fell asleep by 9:00 that night, with the lamp on and her face smack-dab in a book. Not because it was a dull read by any means, but because she was so exhausted from the trials of her long day. She was reading the flagship novel by Mary Higgins Clark called *Mount Vernon Love Story*, a romance about President George Washington and his wife Martha. When it was first published ages ago it hadn't sold well, but Deirdre was enjoying it. Mark had bought it for her as a sort of bribe. He was hoping she would learn more about American history and share his love for it. He wanted their children to know not only their Irish heritage, but that of their father's homeland, too.

She preferred to read romance novels for the escape they provided when she had a rare ten minutes to herself. She had playfully teased her husband that he was trying to lure her toward history and away from passionate prose because he was afraid he couldn't compete with the studs in the stories. She let him know she sure as hell wasn't going to limit her reading to the likes of *Ulysses, War and Peace* or *Moby Dick*. Escaping into those bloody behemoths wouldn't lighten her own day-to-day whale-sized challenges, now would it?

She once argued with Mark about the content of these romantic novels, telling him, "They're quite tame, really. Nothing disgusting in the stories, but the erotic cover art mistakenly gives that impression." In fact, Deirdre explained that she never read these paperbacks in public because of the covers—diddies bursting forth from bodices, the women's raptured poses of surrender, and the might-as-well-be-naked chaps with their unyielding gluteal muscles.

Deirdre kept insisting that there wasn't anything at all in bad taste within the stories she fancied. He called her bluff, saying, "I bet I could open that book you're reading right now, turn to any page, and it will be a sexual passage and in poor taste." She handed over *Savor Me Slowly* with a smug confidence. He opened the novel and started reading—and bloody nuisance; it *was* a sensuous scene in which the "bad boy" was described as having a "fire in his loins."

Since then, whenever Mark was feeling playful, he would approach his wife by saying, "Come on, Hot Mamacita, there's a fire in my loins!" A few times he'd even said it when they were out in the pub with friends, who were aghast at his bawdy comment. He gave an innocent look and explained, "Whaaat? There's nothing in poor taste about that phrase. I found it in the finest of literature."

Deirdre heard a door slam and one of the big boys yelling, "Yeh eejit! You spilled pink nail varnish on the toilet. Clean it up now!"

She wished she could escape this unfolding scene. Well…she was fully awake now. What page was she on before she had those visions of manly musculature? Oh yes, she had been reading about the Washingtons' love life. George was a commanding, tall bloke with a ponytail like the sexy Fabio type. Deirdre decided that his wooden teeth could be overlooked if he had muscles under his frilly shirt and tight riding pants. Indeed if the cover of this book would have featured George in a titillating pose with a sultry Martha, more copies would have been sold.

Deirdre had to admit, she did like learning about history. But she would never tell her husband this. Today she read that Martha and George could not have children together, but George was a loving stepfather to Martha's two children. Before her first husband died,

Martha had buried two babies; such a tragedy. How some people suffer!

She lay on her stomach, slowly pulling at the sheets and flipping through the pages of her paperback. *And I thought I had a bad day! The chisellers may "chisel" at us all day long, but t'anks be to God, they're alive and healthy.*

Deirdre cleared her mind and drifted into a euphoric twilight... until she was back to head-bobbing, this time on page 179. At some point she awoke enough to click off the light before falling asleep again.

A while later, Mark slid into the sheets, naked. "Oh, yes!" he exclaimed lustfully. "I knew you were up here waiting for me!" He reached for her in the darkness. She knew he was hoping to find her wearing his favorite sexy nightie, but instead she had donned her comfy flannel PJ bottoms and baggy terrycloth pullover. She pressed her fuzzy socks against his legs, letting him know his chances of getting lucky were thinner than a potato crisp.

Her green eyes fluttered open and met the anticipation dancing in his.

He murmured, "There's a fire in my loins."

"You must be jokin'! You t'ink I possess the energy for *that* after the day I had? Away with you now!" She delivered her husband a playful smack on the shoulder and then rolled onto her side, facing away from him.

Mark scooted over to the back side of his wife. "I'm glad to see you've got your warm-up suit on. I bet you're hoping to get put in the game."

She loved it when he tickled her funny bone. "Okay coach, I'm game." She flopped over onto her back and let her arms fall into the mattress like two lead weights. "But you'll have to do all the work. I'm knackered. Just cover me up when you're done."

"I'm just joking about messing around," Mark fibbed. "I actually wanted to tell you that Joe is thinking of coming here to visit over

Easter. I just got done Skyping with him and I wanted to check with you to make sure it would be okay."

"That'd be grand. 'Tis hard to keep you twins apart."

"How do you think Kate will take the news?"

Deirdre turned on the lamp and looked toward her husband. "That was a long time ago, and I'm sure they've both put the past to rest. But I'm thinkin' it could work out for them this time."

"Promise me you won't play at matchmaking. We all got burnt last time. Now, about that fire in my loins..." Mark got out of bed to blow his nose, but Deirdre knew he didn't really need a tissue. It was just a ploy so she'd see his nakedness and get romantic-like.

"You sure are determined and full of yourself." Deirdre smiled as she admired his pecs and biceps. "I'm wide awake now," she purred, opening the sheets to invite him in.

And right at that precise moment, little Mary Cecelia walked through the door. The poor child caught brief sight of her father's lily white butt as he dove under the covers.

"Eew!" She ran down the hall, yelling to her brothers and sisters, "I just saw Da's bum!"

Giggling, Deirdre said, "Umm, Luv? Go grab your screwdriver. You might want to fix that lock properly once and for all."

"I've been working on it... and I've identified the problem: The mating drive system was worn out and the screws were stripped. So, the protruding latch bolt was having difficulty inserting itself into the hole."

"I love it when you talk dirty to me," she said, wriggling out of her pullover.

Down the hall a toddler's voice called, "Me want wa-wa!"

Slithering out of bed Mark reached for his boxers saying, "I'll go get him some water. Why don't you keep slipping out of something comfortable?"

CHAPTER 12

Start by doing what is necessary; then do what is possible;
and suddenly you are doing the impossible.

~SAINT FRANCIS OF ASSISI

Kate could run better this morning. It didn't seem like someone was bludgeoning her head with a shillelagh. Her stomach was settled, too.

"Howya? Lovely mornin'," a dapper gent said to her as she jogged in place at the traffic signal on Botanic Road.

" 'Tis," she said trying to sound Irish.

Kavanagh's pub was just ahead. Swinging above its door was a red sign with its nickname: "The Gravediggers." A chalkboard displayed on the sidewalk announced that Dublin Coddle was their specialty. The aroma of pork and onion threatened to lure her into the premises, but she pushed forward.

Sitting cheek-by-jowl to Kavanagh's was the old entrance of Glasnevin Cemetery. Kate dashed under the stone arched gateway and was immediately humbled by the 1.5 million headstones huddled together like the hungry throngs lined up at soup pots during the famine.

She marveled at the faces of the angel statues. Celtic crosses surrounded her. Tradition had it that the shape of these crosses was formed by St. Patrick himself, superimposing the Latin cross over the circle, which was the druids' sign of the moon goddess.

Yews were everywhere, too. Terry Riley told her they are associated with the tree of life and eternity. She still remembered Myrna pointing out the weeping willows, symbolic of forgiveness.

Kate neared a willow and paused under its branches just long enough to find a tiny spent leaf in the grass. She cradled it in her hand and continued jogging.

The weeping willow, with its downcast pose of surrender, reminded Kate of those horrid months following The Triple Whammy. Lee came over at noon one day, found her crying in bed, and insisted they go for a jog. It wasn't until they were into the second mile that Kate realized he was wearing khakis, a button down dress shirt and loafers. But, her brother didn't let his attire hinder his mission.

She recalled the two of them running through a quiet wooded area just beyond the Stillwater Marina, when she had suddenly stopped, flopped her limp body over a stone wall, drooping like the wisps of a willow. The span of the St. Croix River—a designated national scenic waterway—lay below the bluff. The waters of Bryan's final surrender. She looked at its churning current and felt something primeval move inside her. Lee told her later that she had let out the most gut-wrenching wail he had ever heard in all his years of counseling the bereaved.

"That-a-girl…Let it all out," he said, as he cradled her head against his chest. She was clinging to the fabric of his shirt, grabbing the pressed cotton by the fistfuls; pulling and tugging. Her knees buckled from time to time, making it hard for him to hold her up. Eventually he soothed her, and led her back to the wall. He grabbed an oak leaf from the adjacent tree, and handed it to her.

"You need to get out and go for a run every morning for a while now. And when you do, I want you to take something from nature— like this leaf, a sprig of lilac, or a feather…" Kate recalled being puzzled until he explained, "You're going to hold on to this gift for a bit as you run and think about lessons we learn from nature. Consider that 'nothing remains the same for very long; for everything, there is a season.' And then, very deliberately, open your hand and release the gift. Let it go. Trust that there will be more gifts."

Father Lee turned his sister toward the sunshine and looked into her face. "This is what I learned from studying the life of St. Francis of Assisi. Accepting these three gifts will get you through each day: the lessons from nature, your own hard work, and the goodness of others."

Kate was grateful she'd come a long way since that day. She thought about how happy her big brother will be to witness her progress. Last night they had talked and Lee confirmed he was planning a trip to Ireland after Easter, along with their widowed cousin Nick from Pennsylvania.

She rounded the grassy knoll where a large boulder sat, etched simply with "Parnell," below which rested the leader of Home Rule. Her feet took her past two more modest gravesites of freedom fighters, Eamonn De Valera and Michael Collins.

Looking up she saw an imposing structure resembling Rapunzel's tower. A path circled around the monument, and Kate slowed her pace to take in its grandeur. Daniel O'Connell's tomb. Walking down the steps she entered his crypt. An inscription was chiseled into the wall: "My body to Ireland. My heart to Rome. My soul to Heaven." The liberator died in 1847 from a brain condition. He had never healed completely from his time in prison after being charged with conspiracy by the British government.

Kate climbed out of the monument and walked to the fresh cut flowers that were laid at this tomb each day. *I wonder if O'Connell had to take baby steps, too?*

Kate shivered as she exited the cemetery and read a sign proclaiming: "This watchtower was completed by 1842 to prevent bodies being snatched from Glasnevin Cemetery for anatomical use in medical schools."

She ran by the Brian Boru Pub where Bryan had taken her on their first date. She recalled how they sat at a quiet corner table. The sizzle and snap of the fire in the fireplace fueled the ambience. Her heart beat a lusty bodhran rhythm as she looked at his handsome face and reached over to grab a fried potato from his plate. This inched her up from the stool just enough so she could plant a salty kiss on him.

The fiddler and flutist played an ancient piece called *The Brian Boru March*. Kate loved the energy of the tune and had begun clapping to the rise and fall of the rhythm. When she looked the musicians' way, she let out a squeal. "Oh my God…It's Pierce Brosnan sitting over there! I don't believe it!" And just like a foolish girl in a fan club, she rushed over to him, upsetting their table on her way. A pint of Smithwicks landed right on Bryan's lap, soaking his khakis. He stood up and yelped. The music stopped, and the whole bar went dead silent.

Everyone could hear Kate gush all over the actor: "Oh, gosh…Mr. Pierce…I mean, Mr. Brosnan, I just love you in that show *Remington Steele*! I watch reruns every week when I'm in The States."

"Why, that's a grand compliment, indeed. Especially comin' from someone as beautiful as yourself. Thank you, my lady," he answered with a chivalrous kiss to her hand.

Kate went down like a sack of potatoes. She had never swooned before, and it's a memory she would never forget, for on the cover of the *Irish Daily Mirror* the next morning was a huge color photo of herself, flat on her back on the pub floor, looking cross-eyed. Pierce Brosnan was bending over her, more impressive and suave than ever, and in the right-hand corner, Bryan was caught on camera with his beer-soaked clothing and the look of an eejit on his face.

A few days later more gossip magazines ran the story with headlines screaming: "Boyfriend so Jealous of Pierce Brosnan that he Wets Himself!" Brosnan's popularity continued to soar. He moved on to become the celebrated 007. Kate liked to think that her debacle at the Brian Boru contributed to his rising success. You know—free publicity.

Terry and Myrna Riley sent an enlarged copy of the photo, mounted on a display board for guests to enjoy at Kate's wedding reception three years later. *Dang! Pierce was single back then. I should have pursued him instead of Bryan!*

She came to a shop with baby clothes displayed in the window. Once again the familiar ache of childlessness returned. Along with the haunting question: *Were you lying to me about the infertility, too, Bryan? How deep did your betrayal go?* She made a decision to let go of these painful questions and confirmed her resolve by opening her hand and freeing the willow leaf.

Determined to redirect her focus, she began to "fartlek"—a form of interval training devised by the Swedes. Once a week, or so, Kate practiced this "speed play" method, going as fast as she could for bits of time and following that rush with a normal-paced segment. It exhausted her, but made her a faster runner.

She smiled and took a giant leap over a puddle in front of a computer repair shop. She could see that there was someone looking out the window at her, but she didn't care. It was great to feel so alive and lighthearted. And she was blessed to be back here in Ireland, gifted with lessons from nature, plenty of hard work and the goodness of the Irish folks.

Even Catriona has a core of goodness underneath her crazy denial and judgmental attitude. Or so the neighbors say.

There were a few people on the streets, but they were a bit of a blur as Kate sped by. Ahead she spotted a male runner with buns of steel. As she passed him, she sucked in her tummy and tried to look her best. It dawned on her when she overtook the guy that he looked like the runner she had noticed the other morning. His Spandex was light blue today. *I sure hope my butt isn't jiggling right now!*

Fleetingly, she thought about stopping and thanking him for his concern at the Botanic Gardens drinking fountain. But then another thought darted through her brain: *Why the heck do I care, when men should be the farthest thing from my mind?* She started fartleking faster.

CHAPTER 13

Diplomacy is the ability to tell a man to go to hell
so that he will look forward to the trip.

~IRISH SAYING

Luke was pushing through a leg cramp when he saw a green flash speed by him. His testosterone-fed brain made a quick analysis: *Nice ass!* By the time he came to his senses, and realized that it was "The Lady in Red," she was gone—just like that. Fervently he scanned the nearby streets, but there was no sign of her blond mane and kelly shirt.

"Shit! That is one fast lady!" he said breathlessly.

This neighborhood near Griffith Park was a labyrinth of lanes, gates and alleys. He cussed himself for losing sight of her.

He saw a guy in a white Ford Ka craning his neck like he was searching for a certain address. When Luke was alongside him, the jerk swerved, brushing Luke's arm with his side mirror.

The driver slammed on his brakes and yelled, "You fookin' eejit! Watch where you're goin'!"

"Hey pal . . . take it easy!" Luke countered, as the guy pulled away, giving Luke a one-finger salute.

Just then the light turned red and once again the driver slammed on his brakes, yelling, "Bloody hell!"

"That guy would make a great New Yorker," Luke said to an old woman who was standing on the sidewalk and watching the road rage.

The itty-bitty lady answered, "And a good repentant in the confessional. He has a mouth as foul as a snot rag, that one does."

Luke laughed and bid her a good day. He watched the granny hobble on her way, clutching a well-worn cardigan around her torso. She looked like she was in her nineties. The elderly Irish folks never ceased to amaze him. He'd been living here for nearly eight years and had never come across a crab apple. Even though a lot of them had suffered hardship in their time, they all seemed to maintain a wonderful wit.

His journalistic mode clicked "on" and he jogged back over to the woman for a quick chat. He asked her if she had seen a lady in green sprinting by. But she hadn't noticed anyone except Luke and that vulgar driver who was "in need of a good whippin'."

Then, thinking of a story he wanted to write, Luke handed her a sweaty business card from his sock. He lived by the Boy Scout motto, *Be Prepared,* and it often paid off. He explained to the woman, who introduced herself as Rita Middleton, that he was a writer. For a long time now, he had tossed around the idea of doing a freelance piece on the two Bloody Sundays that Ireland suffered.

Mrs. Middleton said she recalled her parents' stories of the first Bloody Sunday in 1920. And she most certainly remembered the second, which happened during The Troubles—the era of Catholic-Protestant conflict, which began in the 1960s and continued throughout the '80s.

"Things still aren't perfect today, lad, but sure haven't they come a long way?"

Luke arranged a meeting with the spunky Mrs. Middleton—and he scheduled it soon, before she could claim her eternal reward.

With his leg cramp eased, and U2's hit song, *Sunday Bloody Sunday* rocking his brain, he continued on his run. His ego had suffered a blow this morning. Not because of the low-life motorist by the park, but because no woman had ever passed him up during a run before. His competitive spirit didn't like second place.

A few minutes later he was on his balcony drinking a glass of orange juice. He tried to tell himself that he wasn't hoping to get a glimpse of that runner, but if she did happen to pass by, he'd love to lean over the balcony and ask her if she was still thirsty.

He waited with bated breath for twenty minutes or so and then gave up. Maybe he'd see her out another day. *Damn! I haven't been this curious about a woman in ages.*

With a mouthful of toast and marmalade, he flipped open his laptop. Since he was on top of his *AP* assignments, he decided his interviews for the Bloody Sundays feature could be scheduled soon. But an email from his editor made him swallow hard and reach for his phone.

"Buck, it's me. Can you be ready in an hour? Maybe you already heard this. George Clooney's coming to Tullahought, in Kilkenny this weekend. The town's going ape shit—and guess who got the assignment? Might as well be writing for tabloids. Celebrity gossip goes above the fold these days, I guess. And you get to play at paparazzi, buddy."

"Well, I wouldn't mind scoring a shot of Clooney. And hey … maybe there'll be lots of lovely ladies hanging around, hoping to get a glimpse of Pretty Boy."

"Hell, maybe if you're lucky some of his spillover will flow your way—someone who digs the Austin Powers type."

"Real funny. Say, did that Lady in Red 'flow your way' when you were jogging today?"

"Umm, more like zoomed past me."

"Seriously? Geez, Mr.Athlete! You sound like the puppy chasing the pickup truck. You wouldn't know what to do if you caught it anyway. By the way, did you unload Nora last night? And her baggage?"

"Uhh, nope. We were sitting with her folks, but her mother loved your Great Dane tie."

Buck laughed. "Well hurry up and call it off with Nora. You need to get your balls back."

"Yeah, yeah. I will. Now shut the hell up, get your camera ready and slap on that toupee. I'll be there in an hour."

When Luke brought his dishes inside, he missed seeing the white Ford Ka cruising around the neighborhood.

CHAPTER 14

He occasionally takes an "alcoholiday."

~OSCAR WILDE

Ultan Ferrian stopped his car near the curb and whacked the steering wheel with the hand that was holding a Pall Mall cigarette. "Shite! I've bloody lost her!" he screamed aloud. Two businessmen getting out of their parked car glanced his way when they heard his explosive outburst.

"Whaya lookin' at, huh? Fookin' eejits!" he yelled to them. And when they just stood there gawking, he added, "Póg mo thóin!" telling them to kiss his arse.

The computer whiz took a deep pull off his cigarette and sped away from the curb, his wheels screeching. He had to head back to work and he wasn't too happy about it. He was vexed that he wasn't able to catch up to that jogger. She was one of the hottest blonds he had seen in a long time. He seethed as he placed the blame. *If it hadn't been for that wanker, I coulda followed her home. I shoulda just run over that jogging ball-bag!*

When he got back to the computer shop, Ferrian was relieved to discover that his boss was still out on a family emergency. Doyle's mother fell getting off the lift at the old folks' home and needed stitches on her noggin. Since business was slow, Ferrian decided to quell his frustration by fueling his favorite addiction: porn.

He really enjoyed himself when his boss was out. A few months ago, when Doyle was gone for a whole week due to knee surgery,

Ferrian was able to steal a laptop from a large shipment sent from a travel business that was closing down. Before Computer Serve had itemized the used goods, Ferrian removed a security device from the laptop, deleted it from the inventory listing and brought it home. He carried it to work with him each day, concealed in a Manchester United duffle bag, just in case he got a little free time. Doyle was not the full shilling, and still didn't know the laptop ever existed.

As he clicked away, Ferrian thought about how the fookin' Yanks were brilliant. They furnished the world with more than 80 percent of the porno sites. He read in one of his IT magazines that the porn industry racked up more bucks than all of the top U.S. tech companies combined: Microsoft, Earthlink, Google, Netflix, Amazon, eBay, Apple and Yahoo!.

Ferrian just wished the fierce-hoor-owners of his poison of choice didn't fill their pockets so deeply. The exclusive porn sites were costing him too damn much. He made extra cash by selling copies of his favorite downloads, enough dosh for food and those little extras a body craved. But, one of these days, if things got real tough like, he might have to bunk off, and sneak away when the rent came due.

Rarely could he afford a pint in the pubs these days. It was cheaper buying the black stuff at the off-license anyway. And the mates he used to knock around with had long forgotten to invite him to the boozers. Once in a while, if he came across an extra fiver, he'd treat himself and sit at the back of a bar, order a pint of Arthur's, and just watch people. He was turning into a loner, but he couldn't care less. He had all he really needed—except for a woman in the flesh, but there were ways around that problem.

When a photo of a naked female looking like that runner popped up on his screen, Ferrian closed his eyes and tried to picture what the blond jogger looked like when he saw her earlier in the day. She was jumping over that puddle right in front of the shop's window. He had been sitting at the counter when he happened to glance up and see her. She was a fine bit of stuff altogether. She looked like Sharon

Stone in a sweat, actually. Her long, golden hair was plastered to her head and neck even though the weather was cool. He noticed that she had a nice pair of diddies under that green sweaty shirt. And as if she could feel his stare, she turned her head and peered into the shop window. Their eyes met for just an instant, but it was long enough to get Ferrian's juices flowing.

After she ran past, he quickly locked the shop doors and grabbed his computer. Thanking his lucky stars that Doyle was gone, Ferrian rushed to his car in hopes of following her home. He spotted her green shirt down the road as he pulled out of the parking lot and that's when he began his pursuit. He was doing right well until that gobdaw appeared out of nowhere and blew his plans.

Ah, bloody hell! Maybe I could draw a charcoal sketch of her using that photo I took the other day when she was out walking. If any customers came in, he'd have to put it away for a bit. After a good session of sketching, he'd lock up. Then when he got back to his flat in Ballymun, he'd download some new images as he watched repeats of *EastEnders* on the telly.

Maybe he'd have a bit of luck and spot her another day soon enough.

CHAPTER 15

Porkchops and bacon, my two favorite animals.

~HOMER SIMPSON

Kate was relieved that her fartleking was finished. She put her arms on top of her head to cool down and let the post-run endorphins kick in.

The front door opened at the Kennedy residence, as Mark and his oldest sons made their way to the car.

"Hiya, Kate," the boys mumbled.

"Good morning, gentlemen. Hey, I was wondering if I could hire the two of you to help with some jobs around the guesthouse over the next couple of weeks. Would you like to earn some extra cash?"

"We would. Sure," Benjamin said, speaking for both of them.

She watched them climb into the back seat, scrunch down and close their eyes.

The smell of bacon wafted Kate's way. Mark rolled down his window. "Go on in, Kate. Deirdre has something she wants to ask you. There's a little bit of breakfast left over, but you'd better be quick about it if you want a bite."

She waved as they drove away. She imagined that a father of seven had to work extra hard just to make ends meet. His bosses at Seagate must be very impressed with him. She was happy for the way things turned out for this college buddy of hers.

Before she could knock, Deirdre opened the door. On their way to the kitchen, they scaled a mountain of shoes and passed through a doorway bearing tic marks sketched in permanent pen—a home-made "Watch Me Grow" chart. "The smell of your Irish bacon was too hard for me to resist, and Mark told me that there might be some left over for a starving neighbor."

A little voice at the table responded with, "Auntie Kate, you plonker! It's not good form to beg, and it's not called *bacon*, it's called *rashers*!" It was six-year-old Mary Cecelia, putting a forkful of broiled tomato into her yolk-stained mouth.

"Mary Cecelia, don't be bold! You don't call adults *plonkers*." After reprimanding her youngest daughter, the mother turned toward Kate. "Sit yourself down now, Kate." Deirdre pulled out a chair, wiping the toast crumbs off with a towel. "I've the leftovers in the cooker. Let me get a plate for you, and I'll take a cup of tea while you eat."

Kate sat at the table and whispered to the frowning Mary Cecelia, "You're right. I'm sorry for my bad form." She wanted to add, "What's a plonker?" but didn't want to get the child in more trouble.

As Deirdre busied herself in the cupboards and set the tea to boil, Kate could hear the older girls fighting upstairs.

"Won't you plait my hair?"

"Bugger off, Mary Margaret! I'm busy. And I had that sock first!"

"Fine, but you look like a cheap doxie, Mary Kathryn! Wipe that make-up off!"

From the foot of the stairs their mother chided, "Girls, girls… stop all that givin' out! You're bound to wake up the twins. Now mind your time… it's nearly half-seven. Hush and rush!"

She turned toward the table. "Sorry, Kate. Girls are prone to chick fights. The lads now, they're a quiet lot. Hardly open their gobs in the mornin', or at night for that matter. I t'ink, so far, that the boyos are easier to raise." She slid a fried egg onto a floral Aynsley plate.

"Ah now, the chisellers must be havin' me on. Did they really eat the whole two packages of rashers? I don't believe it!" Deirdre looked in various places around her kitchen, as if she might find them under the toaster, on top of the refrigerator or under the faded tea towel bearing a likeness of Dublin Castle.

"That's okay, Mammy. I have some on my plate that Auntie Kate can eat," said Mary Cecelia, now with red tomato juice on her school uniform.

"Well, thank you so much. What a good sharing-girl you are!" said Kate.

"Ah, that's grand, luv." Deirdre smiled at her fifth child. She turned to Kate, "Just t'ink...most couples would have stopped at number four—if not before. What a sorry place the world would be without our Mary Cecelia!" She kissed the top of the girl's head.

Kate took a bite of the meat. "I believe I've heard you say that about each of your kids."

Deirdre whipped the tea towel over her shoulder like a seasoned chef. "So I do."

At that moment the other two girls rushed into the kitchen, gave some good-bye hugs, grabbed Mary Cecelia, and hurried out the door. In their wake, they left a trail of debris: a brush, a barrette (or 'slide' as the Irish say), a notebook and a single stretched-out sock. Kate thought this lady really needed a vacation—big time!

"Deirdre, now that I'm living right next door, please, *please* let me watch the kids for you sometimes. It's good for my soul, you know. Why don't you talk to Mark and make some plans for a getaway?"

"You're a grand friend, altogether, for the offerin', but actually, I wanted to talk to you about a girls' holiday."

"For you and me?"

Deirdre flung *The Irish Times* toward her friend. "Did you read in the paper that George Clooney will be down the country in Tullahought? Mark and I saw this bit o' news on the telly last night. The townsfolk are turning his visit into a festival. The O'Garas just so happen to own a caravan in that area of Kilkenny—which is near the bit o' turf that I hail from, and I'm always lookin' for an excuse to get back there. Morgan O'Gara and I had a chat last night, and we want to take you there. We'll stay at the caravan."

"But my first guests are due to arrive shortly."

"Didn't you say the place was nearly ready? Surely Catriona can manage on her own for a few days."

"Yeah, well, she's definitely protective of the place and I know she's experienced, but I'm concerned about her stability."

"Ah now, I'm guessin' Myrna informed you about the delicate situation. Poor Catriona … her head's in a muddle about Declan's demise. But she's a grand manager and … soon enough she will show you her generous heart. You can trust her to take over. She won't even miss you."

"I'm sure she won't, but I think she'll disapprove of my taking a … a holiday … so soon."

"Right. But you won't be able to go on holiday once the guesthouse opens. Besides, I'd be daft to say I didn't need to get away myself—as you rightly noticed this fine mornin'." Deirdre ran a hand through her hair. "there's great craic at Power's Pub in Tullahought, and I'm guessin' there'll be some brilliant people-watching and maybe a bit of a sing-song. And who knows, perhaps we'll even catch a glimpse of the man himself. We'd leave tomorrow and stay just t'ree nights. Whatya t'ink?"

Kate put her fork down. "Mark doesn't mind that you're going there … to chase a movie star?"

"Not at all! He knows it's really just an excuse to welcome you to Ireland proper-like. Plus, he knows I'm too smitten with him to be throwin' myself at some gombeen, like some scrubber would."

Kate's mind took a second to translate Deirdre's last sentence. "Okay, but will he be up for watching all the kids?"

"Aye, he'll be grand. The older kids will help." Deirdre grabbed the ceramic teapot. "Let me top off your cuppa while you make up your mind."

"Well … I guess I can handle Catriona's disapproval … so, I'm in! But promise me that Pierce Brosnan won't show up there!" They clicked teacups with a whoop and a holler.

CHAPTER 16

I believe in fairies, the myths, dragons.
It all exists, even if it's in your mind.

~JOHN LENNON

The next morning, Catriona Ryan chuckled to herself as she shut her front door. A deep blush began to rouge her plump cheeks. That man of hers—the great *amadán* that he was—had just attacked her in the kitchen again. She could still feel Declan's arms wrapped around her in a bear hug. She had been washing the banger grease from the fry pan when she heard his passionate "Catriona, Catriona, Catriona!" Of course he said this while grabbing the large expanse of her buttocks and playfully squeezing it, mussing up the skirt she had just ironed. And ohh...the kissing and nibbling of her neck made her wiggle and waggle. But then she had to leave for work.

As she continued on her way, she glanced down at her skirt and her smile faded. There were no wrinkles. She inhaled and reset her shoulders.

Up ahead, a child was putting a letter into the green cylinder Post box on the corner. The sight reminded Catriona of how badly she and Declan had wished for little ones. But, it wasn't in God's plan, and this was the cross they had to bear with grace. Nevertheless, they had decided to fill their lives with children. So they doted on nieces and nephews and minded the neighborhood children. They sponsored an Ethiopian boy named Bereket—which means 'Blessing,' and they supported Nuestros Pequeños Hermanos orphanage in Honduras. They also volunteered at St. Columba's primary school.

The Ryans loved "their" kids. At the moment, they were in the throes of planning surprises for a couple of them; just the thought of it made her heart race. And wasn't it grand of her Declan to go along with the whole rigmarole and to never mind the cost?

Tonight I'll make that man a gorgeous meal: Lamb chops, colcannon potatoes and parsnips and we'll listen to Frank Sinatra. And maybe, just maybe, I'll let him attack me in the kitchen again.

As she reflected on her big plans, she looked about. It was such a lovely morning that she hadn't even bothered to wear a cardigan on her five-minute walk to work. It was the type of fair morning that reminded her of waking up at the farm when she was a young wan. She longed for the glow of the sun on the gentle green drumlins and thick hedgerows; the smell of the newly cut hay in the fields and smoke escaping from the hearth; and oh, how she missed the taste of fresh milk and beef.

She passed a garden ornament of a horse that always reminded her of the chestnut colt of her childhood named Kid Shelleen. There was nothing like taking him out for a run in the fields, gliding over the land. But before Catriona rode a horse like the wind again she knew she'd have to lose a stone or two, on account she'd break the poor creature's back. Nonetheless, the next time she visited her parents' farm she planned to take a strong horse out for an easy trot over to Cormac O'Shea's to conduct that little bit of business she and Declan were up to.

She wondered if this nice weather would hold for Kate's get-away with Deirdre and Morgan when they go out the country. She was more than a little annoyed yesterday when Kate hit her with the news that she was going to be gone for three days. But then Declan said it was a sure sign that Kate had confidence in her, as well she should. And then Myrna mentioned that perhaps on this holiday Deirdre and Morgan would introduce Kate to a proper suitor, such as a capable construction worker, an honest shopkeeper or a substantial

68

farmer. However, Catriona would prefer that they direct their efforts to setting Kate's thinkin' to right.

As Catriona strolled down Iona Road, she could see a bit of commotion in front of O'Gara's. It appeared that Dan O'Gara's lorry was being loaded with boxes and bags. She asked, "Whatya up to, Dano?"

"Mornin' Catriona. Surely you've heard that Morgan, Deirdre and Kate are going to stay at our place in South Kilkenny for a couple of days? Well, they're taking this vehicle." He hoisted another sturdy box from the sidewalk and added it to the load. Catriona heard rattling within the container.

"Is it bottles of booze you're loading into that truck of yours?"

"It is. Five bottles of nothin' but the finest in spirits, plus some wine and brandy."

Catriona snuck a peek as she lifted the lid, and her eyebrows rose. She recognized the green bottle to be Jameson, and spotted some Bushmills and Blue Sapphire as well. Another box held Grey Goose and Courvoisier. "It looks as if the ladies will be having a bit of ri-ra."

"Indeed," Dano laughed. "But this stock is not just for *their* enjoyment, it's also meant to be replenishing the shelves in our caravan. Each spring we host some nuns from Archbishop Brady's Shelter for the Destitute and Downtrodden for a bit of a retreat. And of course they like to put a shot of brandy in their coffee while they're on holiday." Dano tugged off his cap.

"Well, aren't you a grand man altogether, letting the sisters use your place."

Dano wiped the sweat from his forehead. "Isn't it imperative for those of us who have made a good go of things to share our luck? And don't you know this fine and well yerself, Catriona?"

Catriona chewed on that cud for a while, agreeing with the barman 100 percent. She thought how she'd like to be included on this jaunt toTullahought, but then everyone knew she was indispensable.

A moment later, she jumped from fright as Kate ran up behind her. "Jaysus, Mary and Joseph! I didn't hear you comin'." Her hand went to her palpitating heart.

"So sorry, Catriona. I didn't mean to scare you." Kate wiped her face with the neck of her running shirt.

"Hiya Kate," the publican called out as he stacked a bag of scones, a platter of cheese and a cooler of sandwiches into the back of the lorry.

"Wow! Aren't those divine? It looks like we're going to have quite the feast on this little trip."

"Yeh don't know the half of it," Catriona said.

Across the street, she could see Terry and Myrna Riley walking toward them. They liked to start their day taking Pooka for a morning stroll. It helped ease the aches and pains of Myrna's arthritis and gave them both the benefit of fresh air. Catriona reached out to pet the dog as everyone bid each other a good morning. Pooka pulled away from her to lick Kate's legs.

"So sorry, Kate," Terry said. "I suppose she likes the salt from the sweat on your ankles." He tried to contain his pride-and-joy with the leash. "Did yeh run on your own today?"

"Yes, and it's so beautiful out now that the rain stopped."

"I'd rather you went running with someone—for safety purposes. But if you're to be bold, and insist upon goin' on your own, would you kindly remember the lesson I taught you when you were staying under my roof?"

"To alter my course each day?"

"Yes."

"I have been, Terry. Thanks for your concern. You taught me well."

"Good girl," he said, pressing a bill into her hand. Then he lowered his voice. "Here's a little gift from us for yer shoppin' in Tullahought. Buy yerself somet'ing you wouldn't get otherwise."

Myrna was nodding and patting Kate on the forearm.

Catriona saw Kate's eyes moisten and heard her say softly, "I'm the luckiest woman on earth. Not many of us get two sets of loving parents."

"What was all that about?" Catriona heard Dano ask Kate as the Rileys went on their way. "Oh, Terry's got a bit of the protective father in him," Kate answered. "You know … gypsies and dirty-minded men."

"I tell Morgan the same thing when she goes off runnin'." Dano shut the back of the lorry with a loud *thwack*. "On this lil' trip of yours, why don't you ladies stick together on your runs, just to please Terry and me?"

Catriona added, "Do, Kate. You need practice heeding advice."

"Okay. Whatever," Kate said. She turned to Dano. "Tell Morgan to bring her running stuff. When I come back with my luggage, should I bring some wine and snacks?"

Catriona snorted, "No need. He's seen to the lot of you, plus a gaggle of nuns."

An hour later, Catriona stood at the front door of The Cobblestones saying her goodbyes and assuming her temporary role as innkeeper. "Enjoy yourself now, Kate … but not too much. I don't want you coming back home and circling over Shannon again."

Kate seemed to bristle as she said, "I've learned that lesson already." She headed out the door whipping a green tote over her shoulder. She stopped short on the steps and turned about. Inhaling deeply, she added, "I really do appreciate your taking over while I'm gone. So thanks for your help, Catriona."

Help indeed! Wouldn't you be a sorry sight without my guidance? She watched the lorry pull away.

All morning long, Catriona baked while she listened to Gay Byrne's radio programme. When she was done, she conserved all her masterpieces in the freezer and made herself a cuppa tea and a chicken sandwich. She spent the afternoon hoovering under the guest beds as she watched over the "hired hands." The Kennedy boys were moving heavy furniture and painting.

71

When at last she was satisfied that all was in good order, she had the boys clean their paint brushes, gave them some fresh-baked shortbread, and sent them on their way.

As she went around the place turning off lights and fluffing pillows, she decided that after she was done here, she would stop by her favorite shop on Grafton Street, which she still called "Switzers" even though it was bought years ago by Brown Thomas. They had a fine full-figured women's department. *I'll buy a new dress for the special night I've got planned for me Declan. And then I'll stop by Superquinn to purchase the food and candles.*

Since the computer was banjaxed, she used a log book to list the jobs the Kennedy boys had completed. At precisely four o'clock, Catriona collected her pocketbook, locked the front door and strolled to the bus stop on Prospect. *Should I make a quick stop at the Liffey Waters Spa near the Gresham Hotel? I could get some of that Tahitian body oil I overheard the newlyweds in the pub talking about.*

Yes, tonight Mr. Declan Ryan was going to get the royal treatment.

CHλPτER 17

I've always been a bit of a loner. I've always felt like an outsider,
and because I didn't have a mother or father figure,
I brought myself up.

~PIERCE BROSNAN

Ultan Ferrian turned off the evening news and threw the clicker across the room of his dank and dingy flat. "Nothin' good on the telly. Only that wanker from *Ocean's Eleven* on holiday in Ireland. The media think we give a flyin' fook!"

He took the laptop out of his Manchester United duffel bag and checked out the free porn sites bookmarked as "Favorites." He found a new photo of a fresh porn star named Ridhim Wilde, so he took out his box of art supplies and did a quick charcoal sketch of the vixen in her little teddy-like number. The lace was a bugger to draw, but an hour later Ferrian felt like he got it right. He tacked the finished artwork onto the wall above the mattress lying on the floor. It hung next to the photo he took of that blond gee-bag in her red Minnesota Twins hoodie. He had Googled the Twins and discovered they were a professional baseball team. Ferrian took a moment to study the goddess's face and body for what seemed like the millionth time. Maybe he'd have a woman like that if he looked more like that gobshite Clooney and was loaded. He'd live in a glitzy mansion and have babes hangin' on him.

His studio apartment in Ballymun, in the northern part of Dublin City, was a rough auld kip. Even though the rent wasn't too dear, he

73

was having trouble piecing together enough money for the month's payment again. The XXX DVDs he made for his entrepreneurial venture weren't selling.

His fascination with porn was costing him too fookin' much. At 35 euros a pop, his pockets were feeling empty these days, and he sure as hell didn't want to give up that pleasure. He should try quitting the smokes and hallucinogens to save on cash, but he knew there was no bloody way he could do that, either. *A bloke's got to have a little fun in his life; that's why God created vices.* He ceremoniously lit a fag and took a deep pull off it.

Ferrian sat in his chair and brooded as he puffed away. In the past when he was desperate, he had stolen a small amount here and there from Doyle's stash at work, but he didn't want to go that route again. He needed that regular paycheck. From time to time, he had lifted cash from unsuspecting people: druggies on the corner, blokes queued up at the chipper stand, or from the pocketbooks of boozed-up bimbos outside of nightclubs. He'd been lucky nobody noticed and he was too smart to ever get nabbed.

He needed more money than those little hits rendered. Ferrian knew what he had to do—something he had done once before when he was in dire straits. He got up, went to the wardrobe, and rummaged around in the back until he found what he needed. Next, he yanked on dark clothing.

"Time to kick some arse."

Ferrian lit another cigarette on the way to his car. He drove a few kilometers to the sleazy tenement called Dolphin's Barn. These quarters were even sketchier than his own. He drove around for a while, scoping out the place.

"Bloody knackers are crawling all over this kip," he said to his reflection in the rear-view mirror. He passed a few dealers, hoping to find one with no reinforcements. But most of them were loitering in twos, or in some cases, a whole gang. He eventually found one loner, but because the gobshite had on a leather jacket, he wouldn't do at all.

And then he found his target.

On a corner where some boarded-up businesses sat, a dodgy bloke was leaning into the window of an Astra Opel—probably filled with people heading to the nightclubs. He was making a transaction and wearing a track suit; both of these points made Ferrian happy. It was a quiet location without the usual pedestrian or vehicular traffic. Very few street lights penetrated the midnight sky.

Brilliant!

Ferrian knew he had to act quickly as soon as the Opel moved on its bloody way. There was no telling when other vehicles might surface, or when scum-of-the-earth might start milling about. He parked his Ka behind a nearby building, confident that, since it was in bad form, the hoodlums would leave it alone until he returned. He got out of his car and pulled the hood over his ginger hair. Walking east, he put his hands in the pocket of his charcoal hoodie.

Creeping stealthily was a skill that Ferrian acquired during all those years he had to make himself invisible. Whenever his scrubber of a mother was busy with her boyfriends, which was often, little Ultan had to move around the flat as if he were non-existent. He figured if he would've become a sniper or a spy for the IRA back in its heyday, he could've pegged off a fair share of fookin' Brits—all because he could move unnoticed.

He shielded his body behind the building, and glanced down the road a few times to monitor the scene. When the Opel pulled away, he was able to creep over to a covered doorway. Now he was just a mere 12 meters from the stupid chav and could see the Celtic cross tattoo on the back of his shaved head, underneath a tilted ball cap. Four-and-a-half meters was the optimum distance for this to go down properly. Taking another look-see, Ferrian determined that it was now or never. Pulling the Taser M18L out of his pocket, he walked forward and aimed the laser right between the shoulder blades of the dealer. When he was four meters away he fired.

Thwack, crackle, zzzzzzzap!

The man in the track suit didn't know what hit him as the two metal probes, trailing their wires, penetrated the fabric of his jacket

and t-shirt. He immediately fell to the ground, completely incapacitated as 50,000 volts of pulsing electrical current caused uncontrol-
lable contractions of his muscle tissue. The sad freak was under the
influence of something illegal, but Ferrian knew that didn't matter.
The volts and 18-watt power output were still capable of completely
overriding his central nervous system. Ferrian felt so powerful—
being able to take down whomever he wanted, regardless of the
person's mind-power and body-strength, by simply pulling the marvelous trigger. But he didn't have much time to bask in this glory. In
a couple of minutes the target's brain would be able to control his
extremities once again.

Ferrian ejected the Taser cartridge, and it fell to the ground. He
left the dart-like probes and their attached wires in the target's back.
The man's skeletal muscles were still doing the herky-jerky, making
him look like a right eejit. Ferrian stood over him and quickly rummaged through the scumbag's pockets.

"Brilliant!" He mumbled as he pulled a wad of euro notes from
one. "And fookin' brilliant!" as he removed a bag full of pills from
the other.

He shot out of there like a bullet from a gun, making sure nobody had noticed him. He concealed the Taser in his hoodie as he
sprinted. The weapon was priceless to him because it was the only
damn thing he got from his mam. He stole it when he was 16 from
the overcoat of her boyfriend Mick. "Mick the Prick" used to beat
little Ultan worse than all the others put together. Ferrian took the
Taser on the night he thought the thug was going to kill him with a
rolling pin. He was left with a broken nose, a missing tooth, a frac-
tured cheek and two cracked ribs. This "Inheritance," as he fondly
called the Taser, helped him survive after he ran from home that
night and began living on the streets.

Twenty minutes later, Ferrian sat in his white Ka. He had pulled into a parking lot so he could go through his loot, counted a whopping €1,435 and gave the stash a big ol' kiss. This would definitely tie him over for a while. Next, he fished the bag of drugs from his pocket. Ecstasy—the street form. His artist's eye took in the vibrant hues and simple markings. Each was branded with a different symbol: a smiley face, a butterfly, a peace sign, and other such child-like designs.

Ferrian always found it amusing that the manufacturers of this drug made the stuff look like candy in order to attract the young. But it was popular with users of all ages. He could sell this supply for about €400 to a bloke he knew in his building.

"Jayzuz ... I'll be livin' the life of fookin' Riley!" He popped a yellow pill into his mouth after a petrol lorry passed and its headlights had stopped illuminating him. Since the night was young, he decided to buy a few pints of the black stuff at a sleazy pub in his neck of the woods, and then maybe hit the underground adult pleasure store. But first he had to stow his newly acquired property in a safe place at his flat. Tonight would be bleedin' deadly! He'd have a massive amount of cash to aid in the mix of a whole cocktail of vices.

"A bloke's got to celebrate his good fortune!"

CHAPTER 18

A good snapshot keeps a moment from running away.

~EUDORA WELTY

L uke and Buck were lucky to find a B&B. It was the last vacancy in Tullahought, and they had to share a double bed. Mrs.Mc-Donough, who owned the white pebble dash residence, was kind enough to make them ham sandwiches on this beautiful afternoon. They ate as they walked down the country road toward town. Luke watched as Buck was in wildlife heaven, taking photos with his Canon 50D of things that caught his fancy: a red deer in a marsh standing next to a stalk of bogbean, a cluster of primroses along a stone wall, a child skipping in front of the forest, and two lambs frolicking in the meadow. He switched to a zoom lens to capture a close-up of waxwings perched in a berry tree, on migration from Scandinavia.

The photography slowed their pace, and Luke was relieved when Buck tucked the camera away, saying, "I figure I can use some of these shots for the Tullahought piece, and I'll stockpile the rest." He hoisted his black backpack onto his shoulders. "I'm telling you, someday my work will be worth millions!"

Luke smiled at the pseudo-confidence his rugged friend was displaying. Buck reminded him of himself ten years ago. People even said that they looked like brothers, with their bright blue eyes, dark hair—although Luke's was beginning to grey—and athletic physiques. But when it came to height, Luke at 6'2" had his little buddy beat by four inches. And he never let him forget it.

"Come on, Buck," he said, "try to stretch those little legs a bit more."

"Give me a break. I've gotta carry this heavy bag of equipment around like a pack mule. All you need is a stinkin' notepad...Oh yeah, and a pen. Humph!" Buck trekked on, muttering, "I know you just dragged me here so you could get away from Nora, but I'd like to see you try to..." Luke stopped short, and Buck plowed right into his back.

"What the hell'd you stop for? That's just what I need...to drop this bag of expensive shit!"

"I must be seeing things," Luke said, giving his head a clarifying shake.

"What was it...another deer? A leprechaun? Clooney on his Harley?" Buck started to unzip his bag.

"Better."

"Whattya mean?"

Luke rushed forward. "You're gonna think I'm crazy, but I think I just saw The Lady in Red, as you call her."

"Yeah...you're right. I *do* think you're crazy. What are the chances she'd be out here?"

"No, I'm serious. It's gotta be her. I'd recognize that stride and ponytail anywhere. Come on!" Luke started to jog down a road following a sign that pointed toward a Stone Age burial ground. Buck lagged behind, juggling the camera in his hand and the heavy pack on his shoulders.

Luke heard a *click, click, click* coming from behind and he yelled over his shoulder, "Did you get it?"

"I dunno, but at least I had my telephoto lens handy. Where'd she go?"

"I don't see her any more. God...do you think she went up *there*?" He asked, pointing to the peak of Booley Hills rising above the village.

Buck looked through his lens for a while and finally gave up with a shrug. "Who knows? But man ... you weren't kidding. If that really was The Lady in Red, well then, she really *is* fast!"

Luke continued to look about the area, but like a fairy, she had disappeared into thin air once again. Buck called to him, "Come here and look at the shots I got. I think there are *two* people running together."

Luke looked into the frame of the camera. "See what I mean?" Buck enlarged the subject of their interest. "Right here on the right ... that's another person wearing a natural colored-top. That's why it was hard to see him or her with the naked eye."

"Yeah, you're right. Dang, what if it's a guy? Maybe she's married."

"Or maybe she's not. I've never seen you so bewitched." Buck looked at Luke with one eyebrow cocked over his eyeglasses. "Maybe—if she's lucky—we'll see her in town today."

CHAPTER 19

Every day brings a chance for you to draw in a breath,
kick off your shoes, and dance.

~OPRAH WINFREY

After her run through Tullahought, Kate phoned the guesthouse to make sure everything was running smoothly. Catriona seemed sound and didn't mention Declan.

Kate grabbed a scone from the kitchen and stepped outside. All was quiet on the caravan front. She filled her lungs with clean country air and thought about how perfect their girls' trip had been so far. Yesterday, after getting settled in, they had walked around a crowded Tullahought, bopping into little shops and listening to street musicians who were in town all because of George Clooney. For lunch they had greasy fish and chips from a chipper stand. In the evening, they ate food Dano had prepared and drove to a packed Power's Pub for traditional music during an Irish *seisiún*.

Eventually, they had returned to the caravan for a nightcap and watched *The Help* on the DVD player, using rolls of toilet paper to wipe their tears. The day ended with laughter as they gorged themselves on chocolate tart, relieved that someone named Minnie hadn't baked it.

As she nibbled her currant scone she replayed an interesting conversation from last night. Deirdre had announced that Mark's twin brother, Joe, would be visiting Ireland around Easter.

"I didn't know Mark had a twin," Morgan said. "Did you know that, Kate?"

Kate recalled that she had responded with a nervous laugh as Deirdre offered a quick explanation. "Indeed, she knows full well that Mark has a twin. The two were head-over-heels in college until she broke his heart."

Morgan leaned forward and put down her fork. "Why? How?"

Kate explained, "Mark and I were in college together at St. Thomas in Minnesota, and he set me up with his twin. But Joe was going to a university that was two hours away ... and neither of us had a car." She took a gulp of wine, eyeing her friends over the rim of the glass, hoping they would not demand more of an explanation.

"I thought she said you broke his heart," Morgan pried.

Deirdre was using her napkin to clear a few crumbs from the table. "She did indeed! Joe told us the break-up was her idea."

Kate remembered she had squirmed in her chair, trying to play it down. "It was about distance ... and timing. I was leaving to study in Ireland. I really thought Joe and I would get back together after that semester apart—but then I met Bryan."

Then Deirdre made a memorable comment: "I'm thinkin' that maybe you'd have been better off if you'd stayed with Joe. Wouldn't we have been grand sisters-in-law?"

"Yes, we *would* have," Kate had replied, with what she hoped was an air of finality.

"Right." Morgan was not about to put the matter to rest. "Is it too late now for the two of you?"

"I never thought about it," Kate lied.

"He's still single?" Morgan asked.

Deirdre nodded. "He's still nursin' his broken heart. But I should tell you straightaway that he's not the same as he was back then. I'm thinkin' he's been a bachelor too long."

"Oh, I'm sure he got over me long ago. Besides, I need a romance like I need a big hole in my head! I need to devote all my energy to the guesthouse right now."

Kate stepped out of her daydreaming, and down the steps of the caravan, trying to get the thought of Joe's upcoming visit out of her head. She took a determined bite from the scone and looked around.

She was alone on the property this afternoon because she had decided to stay back while Deirdre and Morgan were out buying Easter candy for their kids.

The O'Gara's property stretched for acres—or hectares—or whatever the heck they called it in Ireland. Morgan and Dano were planning to build a cottage on this spot someday. The charming town of Tullahought was visible in the valley, and the hills could be seen making a statement out on the horizon. Morgan had explained that Tullahought—or *Tuluch Dhocht* in Gaelic—meant "eight hills."

It was obvious to Kate why this village had been designated a "Tidy Town" and honored in the competition many times over. It was not only squeaky clean, but so gosh darn cute as well. It boasted colorful storefronts with hanging flower baskets, old manor homes, tall Celtic crosses, and stately old St. Nicholas Church.

Kate finished her scone and busied herself out in the shed. She rummaged around for some tools. *Why not help out with the gardening for about 20 minutes? I could do some stretching while I tidy up the area a bit and then wash up before the other two return.* She took a moment to switch on her iPod. Bruce Springsteen was singing *Born in the USA*, and she blasted it through her earbuds. She began by touching her toes and pulling some weeds to the rhythm of The Boss's magic.

She giggled as she turned on the hose. The water was freezing, but it felt good when it splashed on her; she was still sweaty from her run. Morgan was an avid marathoner, and had amazing endurance, but Kate had the edge on speed, due to all the fartleking she'd been doing lately.

While they ran, Deirdre had stayed back to read the latest American book that Mark had given her: *John Adams* by David McCullough. "You gals go ahead and do yer runnin'. I'll get my own exercise just holdin' this t'ing up to my eyes." Kate knew her friend well. She had no doubt that Deirdre would read a few pages of the best-seller, put it aside, and then sneak in some chapters from a romance novel. Kate had spied *Tango with Me* in Deirdre's suitcase.

She wet her hands and splashed the coolness over her face, arms and legs, soaking her little red running shorts. She gave the plants a good dousing, grabbed the basket of gardening tools, and set about pulling weeds. The soil felt good on her hands, and she didn't mind getting it under her fingernails. Some of the greenery she couldn't identify. Were they weeds? She wished she had Michael Farley's talents.

Reaching for a dead blossom that was hanging low on a bush, Kate bent over and stretched her hamstrings in a pose similar to yoga's Downward-facing Dog. She used the pruning shears and lopped off the wilted bloom. *Ohh, that stretch feels awesome!* Holding the pose for a while, she snipped away. She bent into a squat, and then straightened up again, thrusting her keister skyward repeatedly to the beat of the music as if someone had pushed her "play" button.

She wiped the sweat off her face, careful not to pull out her earbuds, and began singing at the top of her lungs, her derriere still pumping to the drumbeat.

Using a muddy trowel as a makeshift microphone, she sang a few more songs with gusto. Singing was not her forte. No amount of alcohol was enough to embolden her at a karaoke bar, but it felt so good to belt it out like she did in the shower.

Her hammies were loosened and that natural high was kicking in. "Life is beautiful!" she yelled up to the clouds as she moved about aerobically.

Eventually, her yoga stretches morphed into something akin to the Chicken Dance. When she went to nightclubs, she was too self-conscious to dance because someone once told her she jerked like Elaine in *Seinfeld.* She recalled the old adage, *Dance as if no one is watching,* and this hidden natural stage set her free.

She continued with this self-expression for several minutes, whooping out *All the single ladies, all the single ladies* ... until she felt a tap on her shoulder.

CHAPTER 20

And those who were seen dancing were thought to be insane
by those who could not hear the music.

~FRIEDRICH NIETZSCHE

When the ladies pulled up to the caravan, Deirdre knew at once that something was wrong with Kate. As Morgan came to a stop, an antique oak dresser in the bed of the truck gave a *thud*—which seemed to jolt Kate out of her trance.

Deirdre jumped out of the lorry, tossed her shopping bag to the ground, and dashed to the front step where Kate was slouched. "My God, Kate, are yeh okay? Yeh look stunned."

Morgan rushed to help. She touched Kate's cheek. "And why is your face all muddy?"

"What?" Kate asked, confusion clouding her eyes.

"Your face … it's smeared with mud." Taking her camera out of her pocket, Deirdre took a quick picture. Pushing a few buttons she said, "Here, wait 'til I show you." She held up the photo so Kate could see for herself.

"Oh my God! A muddy face on top of everything … I don't believe it!" She wailed.

Deirdre noticed the garden tools strewn around and the hose still running. "I see you were out workin' in the garden. Did you hit your head or sometin'?"

"No, but I wish I had. I wish it was all just a dream."

"Come now, Kate my girl, you're not makin' much sense," Deirdre said, as they coaxed Kate in the door. "Why don't you tell us the whole lot?"

"Two men stopped by and they…"

"Oh, Jaysus, God, no! You didn't get raped, did you?" Morgan shrieked. Deirdre was thinking the same thing.

"Raped? No!"

"Then what happened here while we were gone?" Morgan eased up on Kate's biceps and Deirdre led her to the sink.

Kate cleared her throat. "George Clooney and some other guy stopped by to ask for directions."

"What? Go on! You must be jokin'!" Deirdre cried, jerking her head up.

Morgan stood there "catching flies" with her mouth wide open, too gobsmacked to speak.

"Nope. It's no joke." Kate shook her head. "I was … multi-tasking … and I made a fool out of myself in front of an A-list actor … again."

"What was it you were doin'?" Morgan asked.

Kate splashed water on her face and wiped it on the tea towel. "Well, I was pulling weeds and singing and dancing at the same time … and you know how badly I sing and dance."

"Don't tell me they saw you!" Deirdre gasped.

"Yep. I don't know how long they were watching, but they were laughing when they tapped me on the shoulder and scared me to death."

"Janey Mack!" Deirdre said. "What if they took a video of your performance? They could post it on YouTube!"

Deirdre felt relieved when a chuckle escaped Kate's mouth. "Well, they asked me if I was starting a Twitter flash mob … I guess they were afraid more crazies would jump out of the hedgerows and join me."

"Tell us straightaway … Is he as mighty as he is in the films?" Morgan asked.

"Mighty? You mean handsome? ... Oh, yes! Even better."

"Jaysus! And the two of us out shopping while you're hobnobbing with the famous!" said Deirdre.

"Tell me, did you invite them in for a drink? Did you take a photo?" Morgan asked. "He's truly a grand figure of a man."

Kate tossed her head back and laughed. "Are you kidding? I just wanted them to go away."

"What else did yer man say? Finish the story," Deirdre said.

"Um ... they said not to quit my day job." Kate blushed and added, "And I remember at one point Clooney said I was kinda cute; I think he meant pathetic."

"Ah now," Morgan cooed, "aren't you the envy of everyone who made the pilgrimage?"

Deirdre patted Kate's arm. "She is indeed. And aren't I still kickin' meself for being in the candy store and missin' the eye candy."

Kate wrapped an arm around each of them. "Ladies, let's open a bottle of the nuns' brandy—cuz we could all use a drink right now."

CHAPTER 21

I was in a bar and I said to a friend,
"You know, we've become those 40-year-old guys
we used to look at and say,
'Isn't it sad?'"

~GEORGE CLOONEY

"All right, let's talk about what we've got for this article so far," Luke suggested to Buck as they sat in the family room of Mrs.Mc-Donough's B&B. Buck had just interviewed the McDonough family for a blog post on guesthouses in Ireland. Now, with that finished, they could concentrate on the Clooney project.

Luke began: "It's been over 160 years since his great-great-grandfather, Nicholas Clooney, aged 18, left Tullahought for Kentucky in 1847—which was the height of the Irish potato famine, or The Great Hunger. The auld sod beckoned, and so this week George rides in on his Harley—setting all the female pulses racing like mad."

"Lucky son-of-a-bitch," Buck exclaimed quietly, apparently not wanting to offend the owners of the house. "Well, I read Clooney chose Ireland because when he was in Toronto a while back, Bono told him about all the great places Ireland has for bike enthusiasts, like the two of them."

"Good background. I'll need that reference." Luke took a sip of tea and added, "There was a relative named Sarah Clooney who worked on the carpets that graced the Titanic. Not sure if this woman made 'em or laid 'em; still working on that bit of info." Looking up from his notes, he asked Buck, "What did you shoot after we separated this afternoon?"

"I chased down Clooney's cousins at that reunion they held at the Community Hall. Their names are Peter and Paul Purcell; father and son. They drove me to the townland of Knockeen and guided me to the old Clooney cottage. Dilapidated thing nestled in the foothills; someone will probably pay a fortune for it someday. I got a great shot of these cousins in front of the vine-covered ancestral pile, with its rusted, green iron gate off to the side." Buck bit into some homemade brown bread and freshly churned butter. He then yelled into the kitchen, "Mrs. McDonough, this is the best blasted stuff in all of Ireland!"

She waddled out through her swinging doors, her face beaming. "Aren't you two gents kind! T'anks a million for complimentin' my bakin'. Here, let me top off yer tay." After she had poured a little into their cups she said, "Put in your story that the Clooney name in Irish, *O Cluanaig*, means 'rogue' or 'flatterer.' Fitting for someone in Hollywood, don't you t'ink?"

"Perfect," both men answered with a smile. She opened her *Irish Surnames Dictionary* in order to prove it.

"Well, I say we head into town and hang out at Power's Pub to interview some of the locals and fans," Luke said, looking at his watch. He felt like their Clooney piece needed a little punch, or an interesting twist to pull in the readers.

"You betcha! I get to question and photograph all the gorgeous females, and you can talk to all the others," Buck said.

"What else is new?"

By ten o'clock Luke had interviewed Mr. Jackie Foley the schoolmaster, Father Malone from St. Nicholas Church, Captain John Tuohy with the Gardaí, Kenny McMahon the musician, and toothless horse breeder Damien Rock, the town drunk—all old men.

Now he was wrapping up his interview with the publican of this fine establishment, Daniel McQuillan, another old man. He verified some interesting details. The pub was over 200 years old, so most likely the Clooney ancestors would have enjoyed a few pints under its roof. And the place frequently hosted The Clancy Brothers and other famous Irish musicians.

After thanking Mr. McQuillan for his time he decided to call it quits and ordered a pint of Guinness. He looked about the place and spotted Buck sitting in a snug—a small room within the pub where match-making used to occur. He was with a crowd of women, snapping their pictures and having a grand old time.

He scanned the patrons, but didn't see the Lady in Red. As he waited for his brew to be pulled, Kenny McMahon began singing *Danny Boy*. That had been Christy's favorite Irish tune, and it always choked him up a little. Needing a distraction, he quickly placed enough euros on the bar and headed toward Buck and his entourage of females.

"Buck, remember me? Your buddy, Luke?" He took a seat next to the two gals, a redhead and a blond. He noticed that Buck was clicking notes into his phone with more urgency than usual.

"You're going to love this story," Buck shouted over Kenny's singing. "It's pretty dang funny."

"What?"

"Well, let me introduce you first. Ladies, this is my co-worker, Luke O'Brien with the *Associated Press*. Luke, this is Deirdre Kennedy and Morgan O'Gara—both from Dublin."

Luke looked at the women for a moment. They appeared to be in their late thirties or so, and he thought he had seen them before. "Where in Dublin are you from? You both look familiar."

"Glasnevin," Morgan answered. "My husband and I are keepers of O'Gara's Pub."

"Oh yes, you're Dano's wife."

"I am." Then looking at her friend, Morgan said, "Deirdre here lives just 'round the corner from us with her husband and seven children."

"Oh, you must be the ones who take up a whole pew at St. Columba's?"

"If the family you're thinkin' of is coppertops all 'round, then'tis us, indeed."

"Yes, all redheads; a beautiful family. Well, it's nice meeting some of the neighbors. I live at the condos that sit on the nuns' property." Luke shook their hands.

"Ah yes," Deirdre said. "You just live a stone's t'row from the two of us." She peered at him. "So now... an *Associated Press* reporter are yeh? And this little country festival is makin' international news?"

Before Luke could respond, Buck jumped in, "Yeah, well... last month he got shot at while covering that Interpol drug bust in Galway, so they decided he was ready for the big time."

Luke shook his head explaining, "Well, I thought I'd paid my dues, but I guess... you know... Millennials feast on celebrity gossip, and now that's what passes for hard news."

Morgan bounced in her seat. "Can we tag along when you interview himself?"

Luke smiled at her enthusiasm. "He declined an interview. Just gave me a quote. The focus of this piece is the reaction of the locals, and the tourists... looking for an excuse to carouse."

He turned toward Buck, "Well, what's the story they told you?"

"What I've got so far is that Morgan and her husband own a place out here in the country. She and Deirdre went shopping today and left their other friend named..." Buck peeked at his notes. "... Kate McMahon, at the caravan. Kate stayed back to do some gardening."

Morgan interrupted, "Actually, Mr. Hubbell, Kate didn't stay back to garden initially. She wanted a bit of relaxation after she and I did a long run this mornin'. Tendin' the garden was an afterthought, like."

Luke's sip of Guinness turned into a gulp. He saw Buck's eyes widen. Buck regained his composure first and quickly grabbed a camera from his backpack. He scrolled through a few pictures. Holding the Canon up to Morgan's face he asked, "By any chance is this a photo of you two running?"

Morgan took a look. "Well now, indeed. That'd be me in the beige…Why did you take this photo of us?"

"Well…I was aiming at Booley Hills…and you were in the foreground." Buck pointed to his screen. "And the Lady in Red is…?"

"That's our friend, Kate. We were running to the prehistoric landmarks on the peak above Tullahought. I wanted Kate to see 'em."

Buck arched an eyebrow. Luke's heart was jumping. He cleared his throat, but he couldn't spit out any words.

Buck continued, "You say her name is Kate McMahon?"

"'Tis."

"Is there a *Mr.* McMahon?" Buck pushed.

Deirdre narrowed her eyes and folded her arms as she sat back on her stool. "Ah now, that's an odd question, but I'll answer it nonetheless. There *was* a Mr. McMahon, but he passed on t'ree years ago. Kate just moved here from America recently, and she bought the McFadden Guesthouse."

"We nailed it!" yelled Buck, looking at Luke and slapping his fist on the table as the facts gelled. Luke felt the blood drain from his face and rush to his limbs.

"Nailed it?" the gals asked. "Wha'?"

"Ahh….nothing. Sorry. I just mean we were lucky to run into you and hear that Clooney story." Buck kicked Luke under the table.

It jarred him. "Clooney story? What're you talking about?"

Buck held up his palm to delay answering, and instead asked Deirdre, "Where is Kate at the moment?"

"She's just stepped out to make a few phone calls to family in Minnesota. She couldn't wait to tell them George Clooney spied on her doin' the Moon Dance."

"What about Clooney?" Luke asked, but Buck silenced him with his palm again.

"Wait…did you say she's from Minnesota?" Buck asked.

"So she is," Deirdre answered, cocking an inquisitive eyebrow. "My man's from there, also. I was guessin' you were from that state as well, because of your horrid accent."

Buck laughed. "Well, there ya go. I'm actually from right next door in Wisconsin. You know there's nothing better than a midwesterner, even though we talk funny. Now this guy here," Buck slapped Luke on the back, "He's from California, so he's more superficial than everyone else ... and he's widowed, too, like your friend Kate."

Luke thought he caught an exchange between the match-making eyes of Buck and Morgan. Morgan held her pint up above the sticky, wooden table and said, "Kate claims she's not in the market, but, let's have a toast to shopping around. Sláinte!"

"Sláinte!" was echoed by everyone at the table, except Luke. A question was floating around his ruffled brain. *What in the hell will I say to Kate when she joins us at this table?*

CHΛPCER 22

When I wear high heels
I have a great vocabulary and I speak in paragraphs.
I'm more eloquent.
I plan to wear them more often.

~MEG RYAN

Kate was ready to have fun. She had just finished a lengthy conversation on the phone with her friend Rose, the one friend she had left in Stillwater. Rose thought the Clooney story was a hoot and a half.

Kate felt the wind pick up with the promise of rain. The stars were usually bright in the countryside, but tonight none were visible. There was a cloud cover as thick as Bailey's Irish Cream. She put her cellphone into the back pocket of her jean skirt and stepped into Power's Pub. It was warm in there because of all the bodies, but it looked to Kate like everyone was into the sing-song and enjoying the craic despite the heat. The entertainer's name was Kenny McMahon and he was singing *Go Lassie, Go*. She was tempted to buy the guy a drink and find out if he was an Irish cousin.

Kate wove her way through the crowd. She was wearing the new red stilettos she had purchased with the money from Terry and Myrna—something she wouldn't have bought otherwise. They were fun to wear but they were killing her feet, and she needed to sit down. She ignored the admiring glances from the men at the bar, as her heels continued to *click, click* on the wooden floor. She made her way through a group of drooling old-timers and spotted her gal-pals in the corner snug, talking to a couple of men who had their backs to her.

Kate blotted away the sweat that was starting to run down her temple. Then she smoothed the front of her cobalt blouse as she worked her way to the table. Morgan spotted her first and said, "Well look who blew in with the tempest. Hiya, Kate."

The two men seated with her friends turned their heads to look at her. The taller one shot to his feet and overturned his stool. Kate thought he looked familiar and couldn't pull her eyes away from him. The other three were snickering as if they were in cahoots.

"Have I met you before?" she asked. His face was pale but his features were handsome, and his eyes were an unbelievable blue.

"We haven't met, but I watched you jogging in Glasnevin ... I mean I wasn't 'watching' you ... but we had a drink together ... I mean at the drinking fountain." He took a gulp of his Guinness. "You're really fast ... I mean, you passed me up the other day."

Spandex Man! She could hide her surprise, but not her delight. Seeing him for the first time without sweaty hair, she noticed his attractive silver strands. Her smile widened as he raked a hand through his waves, and there was no band on his left ring finger.

She hadn't had a drink yet, but her mind was reeling, and she steadied herself by grasping the back of a chair. *What was he trying to say? He's obviously no smooth-talker. Oh yes, something about me being fast.*

"Oh, I'm not that fast really, but sometimes I fartlek."

"*What?*" He asked. Their friends at the table almost choked on their drinks.

She giggled. "I fartlek—it's a Swedish word for a type of tempo running. My high school coach used it for training, and we hated him for it." She tilted her head and crinkled her nose. "Hey, you sound American, although you have a touch of an Irish lilt."

"Yeah, I guess I do. I should introduce myself ... I'm Luke O'Brien and I'm from San Francisco, but I've been working in Ireland for eight years. I'm a journalist for the *Associated Press* ... and I ... write ... better

95

than I talk." He wiped his hand on his jeans before shaking hers. "The reason I'm in Tullahought is that I'm covering the hoopla over George Clooney's visit. Your friends were just telling me and my partner... I mean co-worker... Anyway, your friends told me Clooney caught you doing the Moon Dance."

Kate glanced past Luke's tall shoulders to her girlfriends, and laughed. Her gal pals started giggling, too. She rubbed the tears away from the corners of her eyes with a cocktail napkin, hoping she didn't smudge her mascara. "Oh, geez! I wish it had been something as normal as the Moon Dance. What the poor guy witnessed was horribly embarrassing, and I wouldn't call it dancing at all."

CHAPTER 23

Fall in love with a guy who ruins your lipstick …
and not your mascara!

~UNKNOWN

When she laughed, Luke was smitten.
Noting her positive attributes gave him a head rush. She had a natural smile and seemed so full of life. This gal didn't take herself too seriously or appear to be high-maintenance like … a lot of beautiful women he knew. She had the bonus of a killer body; a nice athletic build. And he was drawn to those seductive red stilettos, not only because they emphasized her femininity, but also because she couldn't sprint away from him again.

All of these details tumbled through Luke's mind like cream in a butter churn. He picked up the milking stool that had toppled to the floor, and then motioned for her to take the spot next to him at the table. "You look hot … I mean warm … let me get you a drink."

Buck, Deirdre, and Morgan gave each other a look tinged with conspiracy. Buck said, "Why don't we let these two have a little quiet conversation so Luke can get the rest of the Clooney story." The three Cupids made a hasty exit and huddled near the snug's entrance, so nobody could enter.

"What would you like to drink? Beer? Whiskey?" He asked.

"Ah, I'm taking it easy on the little green man these days," Kate said, using the slang term for Jameson's. "It was whiskey that made me so … thirsty … that morning in the Botanic Gardens. But a nice cold cider would be great."

Luke balled up a wad of moist napkins and threw them at Buck's back. When Buck turned around Luke said, "Hey buddy, since I can't squeeze past you, make yourself useful and get the lady a Bulmer's, please."

"I am being useful. I'm playing Swiss Guard, so you two aren't disturbed." Buck took the euros from him and headed to the bar.

For the next half hour or so, Luke scrawled in his notepad while he sipped his Guinness and Kate nursed her cider. Once he was into his reporter mode, he found her easy to talk to, and his words no longer got caught in his throat. When she crossed her legs he could see all that running paid off. Her toned calf muscles teased him. He coughed to pull himself from the sensual stimulation, but it was hopeless.

Her stool kept inching closer to his as she strained to hear over the crowd, and her citrus perfume massaged his memory, reminding him of the orange groves of his California childhood.

Her eyes shone like diamonds, and her hair hung over her shoulders, tied up with a black velvet band—fitting perfectly with the words to the song Kenny was now belting out. This was by far the best damn interview he'd ever conducted. How could he be feeling this way about someone he just met? His favorite blogger, Mark Perry, once wrote that if there is chemistry between two people, it takes only a nanosecond to recognize it. One more nanosecond like this, however, and surely there would be spontaneous combustion.

He took his time getting her whole story. The two of them laughed easily. The journalist in Luke appreciated Kate's honesty and the fact that she included important details, even the embarrassing ones, like the part about discovering her dirty face afterwards. When she talked about her keister jiggling in the air as she rocked to *Single Ladies,* it was a technical knockout.

That song served as a segue to a subject he'd hoped to broach. "Speaking of that song, your friends told me you're single … that your husband passed away a few years ago. I just wanted to say I'm sorry for your pain. I lost my wife ten years ago, and it still hurts."

Kate pushed a strand of hair over her shoulder, releasing another waft of tantalizing citrus. "Yeah, it's hard. Thanks for your kind words, Luke." She placed her ringless hand on his forearm. "I'm sorry for your loss, too."

Luke knew that her compassionate touch was meant to soothe him, but it caught him off-guard, and his arm involuntarily jerked away. His restrained hormones were jolted as if by jumper cables. It took every ounce of self-control to just sit there, when his impulse was to crush his mouth onto hers and devour the lady.

CHAPTER 24

A boy's best friend is his mother.
And there's no spancel stronger than her apron string.

~IRISH PROVERB

Kate was surprised when he pulled his arm away. She saw him open his mouth, then shut it without uttering a word. *Did I overstep his boundaries by touching him?* She took a sip of cider and looked away. The hopeful sweetness of the beverage rolled over her tongue.

Luke made a hasty retreat saying, "I'm going to grab us another drink. It's really getting hot in here. I'll be right back."

She swallowed the cider. The drink imploded into tart flavors.

Why the heck did I touch his arm? She stood and opened the nearest window. Rain splattered down hard on the window sill. The humidity seeping into the room worsened the sticky heat. She glanced through the transom and took comfort in the lights of the village, shining through the wet droplets. The church's stained glass was glowing, beckoning visitors. Lanterns lit the sign on the store across the way: *L. Hurley Provisions.* Beyond Tullahought a few miles, she could make out the twinkling lights of the next town, Carrick-on-Suir. The beauty couldn't be captured in a travel brouchure, and Spandex Man just added to the interest of the place. She reminded herself that she didn't need a romance right now and would never be able to trust a man again. *Oh well, I probably scared him off anyway.*

She looked up as she blew a lock of hair out of her eyes and spotted an ancient ceiling fan. She located an electrical switch behind a floor plant, flicked it on and delighted in the blessed breeze.

Luke's notepad flew open and a piece of stationery fluttered out. Kate reached under the table to retrieve it and saw that it was a letter to his mother. *Should I? Do I dare?* They say you can learn a lot about a guy from the way he treats his mom, but she didn't buy into that theory. Bryan-the-con-artist had always treated his mother just fine. Why would she want to learn more about that journalist anyway? *Remember, you need a romance like you need* ... but before she could finish that thought, bad manners and curiosity got the best of her. She squinted as she held out the paper at arms length and let her eyes adjust to the dim lighting.

Dear Mom,

Happy birthday! I sure miss you and wish I could be there as you celebrate your 60th. Thanks for being the sweetest Nazi-of-a-mom a son could have. I can't begin to thank you enough for everything you've sacrificed and all you do for our family. I can't help noticing you've done a great job raising some incredible kids.

Love you more than Mexican food.

From your oldest and favorite son,
Luke

P.S. Enclosed is a skirt I bought for you in Donegal. I know how you love Magee tweed. I thought the color would be great on you, and it's short enough to showcase the "best legs in the Presidio."

Kate smiled. Apparently Luke O'Brien was a light-hearted lover of Mexican food. Her favorite, too. And he seemed like a darn good son. Against her better judgment, Kate had to admit she liked the whole enchilada ... so far.

Oh, gag. She liked the whole enchilada? Where was her hole-riddled head?

And obviously, he was a "leg man." She shifted in the stool so the ceiling light could fall on her legs. She crossed her ankles, glancing at her high heels. Would he notice?

"Careful, Kate," she muttered with a sigh. Buck turned around. One of his eyebrows arched up. She had forgotten he was standing guard by the door.

"You okay?" he asked. "You're talking to yourself."

"Um, yeah," she answered, hiding the letter under her purse.

"Good. It looks to me like Luke's doing a great job getting your story. I've never seen him gab so much before." Buck stepped closer to Kate. "I wanted to tell you something before that ding-dong gets back with the drinks."

"Okay ... what is it?"

"Just between you and me, Luke's a really great guy, even though he doesn't know how to talk to women very well ... "

Kate held up a hand to stop him. "Whoa ... I've been burned before, and I'm not really in the market."

Buck looked around the pub and then continued, "Well just in case, I think you should know that he gets really bad ingrown hairs on his back and has oozing warts all over his body."

"Whaaat?"

At that moment, Luke entered the snug, squeezing past Buck. He set the drinks on the table. She felt his eyes roam over her legs. When those piercing blues rose to her face, he asked, "Who died?"

"What? Who died?" she asked, now slipping her legs out of the spotlight and under the table.

"I said, 'Who died?' because your face looks morbid. No! I mean you have a morbid look on your face."

Kate peered at the two men in the snug. They were acting strangely. But wasn't she, too? She reached for her drink. "Oh, um … Buck and I were just talking."

When Luke turned toward his friend, Kate slid the letter back into his notebook and said, "He was telling me that … um … that you …"

"Don't believe a word this gobshite says."

Buck shrugged. "Hey, I was just stating that you're a really nice guy … and you're basically unattached." He laughed as he made a quick exit.

Luke looked like he didn't know what to say next. He glanced around the snug. Kate hoped he'd try to sneak a peek at her legs again, but instead his eyes fell on his notepad, with the letter peeking out.

"Forgive my friend's kindergarten humor. I'll bet he told you that I have really bad foot odor and that I have lice or something."

"More along the lines of ingrown hairs and oozing warts."

Luke shook his head. "And he's my best friend. You can believe the nice-guy part, though." Luke's biceps bulged under his t-shirt as he took a swig from his pint. He set the beer on a Guinness coaster printed with: "Are you enjoying perfection?"

Kate's mind was buzzing. *Oh my God, he's yummier than that guy on the cover of Deirdre's romance novel.* She shook her head. *Remember, Kate, all you really need is to make a success of the business.*

Luke interrupted Kate's internal battle. "Wow, it feels much better in here. I see you're smarter than everyone else in this pub, and thought to turn on the fan."

"Maybe I just have better eyes than most of the patrons in this place and found the on-off switch."

"Yeah, your eyes are great, and my vision is pretty good, too."

She threw him a quizzical look. Was he going to pay her legs a compliment?

"When I was ordering our drinks, I saw you reading the letter I wrote to my mom."

Her cheeks flooded with heat.

He added, "I happened to see you through the snug's glass panels."

She entertained thoughts of sprinting out the door, but she was wearing the damn stilettos. She covered her face with her hand and mumbled, "Oh, oh ... busted!"

"Don't worry, I won't bite your head off," Luke said with a grin. "I'm a nice guy, remember? Warts and all."

CHAPTER 25

It is easier for a father to have children
than for children to have a real father.

~POPE JOHN XXIII

Around midnight Mark Kennedy's head hit the pillow like a bag of mince. As he pulled the covers over his chest, he decided his wife was his number one hero. How in the hell did she keep up with all seven of their offspring, day in and day out? Mark felt like he'd been kidnapped by the townsfolk of Munchkin Land since Deirdre left on her girls' holiday. But even though they were a ton of work, and they robbed him of privacy and cost him a shitload of money, he knew he wouldn't trade having all these kids for anything.

His thoughts turned to his twin brother, Joe, who had never settled down and was childless. They'd tried to talk on the phone earlier today, amid all the chaos of Mark's household. Joe lived on Hayden Lake near their northern Minnesota hometown, Staples. He pictured Joe sitting alone on his dock, fishing, a Bud Light sitting near his Rapala tackle box. "We're excited for your visit," Mark had said, motioning to Jack and Benjamin to put their pizza dishes away. He then stepped into a puddle of milk.

"Well, I'm excited to see all of you guys soon and the inside of a pub or two as well."

"Oh, we'll be doing our fair share of pub crawling, I'm sure." Mark bent down to wipe up the puddle and then used that same rag to wipe Gavin and Murphy, who were covered in pizza sauce. The young twins started to fuss at the cold wet rag.

"Great! We'll have to encourage Kate to join us."

"She'd love to, I'm sure. So, are you still sweet on her, or what?" Mark asked with the phone pinched between his ear and shoulder. This freed one hand so he could use that same rag to wipe the table while holding a crying twin. His wife would be proud of his multi-tasking.

"I guess you could say I think of Kate from time to time. She's the 'fish that got away'... and she swam right into that asshole Burke's net when I was about to reel her in."

Mark had to place the phone to his chest so he could yell to Mary Margaret, "Stop banging on that piano, would you please? I'm talking to Uncle Joe.

"Sorry about that, Joe, it's a little crazy around here. Deirdre went to Tullahought with Morgan O'Gara from O'Gara's Pub. They took Kate with them for a sort of welcome-to-Ireland getaway."

"Ah... and you're stuck home babysitting?"

"It's called 'parenting,' dude, but anyway..." Mark didn't get a chance to finish his sentence because Mary Cecelia was pulling at his shirt and pointing to some math homework. He nodded, indicating she should ask her big brothers for help. He heard the Hoover come to life and turned to see Mary Kathryn vacuuming the next room, without being asked.

"Mark... Mark... are ya there?"

He put the sniffling twin down, grabbed a pile of dirty clothes from the back hall and headed to a quieter corner in the kitchen where the laundry facilities stood. "Yeah, I'm here. Sorry. What were we talking about? Oh yeah... you and Kate." Mark threw the clothes into the washing machine and added detergent. He dropped the phone with a loud *clank* and retrieved it quickly. Then he hoisted himself onto the swishing machine.

"Mark, are you there? Did the kids tie you up or something? Mark?"

"I'm here, Bro. Sorry, but I had to get some laundry started. We're up to our necks in dirty clothes."

"No problem. I was just wondering if Kate is seeing anyone?"

"Not that I know of. She's stressed out about making a go of it here. Why? Are you gonna ask her out or something?" Over the roar of the washing machine, Mark could hear a chick fight brewing. He chose to ignore it and ducked into the bathroom.

"I'm not dating anyone right now, so I might just ask her out. I'll have to see how things go on my visit."

In the distance, Mark heard a big crash and a collective "Uh, oh!"

"Shit! I gotta go, Joe. Talk to you later."

Lying in bed, Mark could hear the rain splattering the window. He put a pillow over his head, thinking about the broken teapot. An antique Royal Doulton from Deirdre's granny. He had Superglued it back together, but it was ruined nonetheless. At least Mary Kathryn had knocked it over accidentally and hadn't hurled it at someone's head. That's all he would have needed—a trip to the emergency room. Mark groaned under the pillow when he thought about how upset his wife was going to be over the damaged heirloom. He could tell her he'd been using the loo when it happened. Perhaps he'd play up the multi-tasking thing and say he was doing a load of clothes and bathing the twins at the same time.

Rolling over, Mark's arm met the empty left side of the bed. He never slept well without his feisty, sexy wife next to him. He thought about her pale, soft skin and how it was always warm, no matter the temperature. She always smelled so tempting. Even her curly red hair gave off an erotic scent. Some nights she carried a floral aroma to their bed, at other times a soapy sandalwood fragrance.

He smiled to himself, thinking about how often people remarked that, because they have a lot of kids, they must have a lot of sex. The cruel truth is that nobody has *less* sex than parents of a big family.

He dialed up the heating blanket and closed his eyes. Their bedroom door squeaked open, even though he could swear he had locked it.

"Da?" Opening his left eye, Mark saw Mary Kathryn at his bedside. "I can't sleep. You forgot my blessing."

"Sorry, Pumpkin. Let's take care of that." He scooped her into his arms, and carried her back to bed. She smelled like garlic. *Shit! I forgot to remind them to brush their teeth!*

"Comfy?" He asked as he tucked her in, kicking himself for not spending more time with this middle daughter.

"Aye."

Mark glanced at the clock and read that it was 12:08 a.m. "I want to thank you for being such a big help. I didn't even have to ask you to hoover, and you read the twins a bedtime story."

Mary Kathryn rolled over to face her daddy and placed a hand on his stubbly cheek. "Do you think Mammy is going to be mad at me when she gets home 'cuz I broke Great Granny's special teapot?"

With a yawn Mark answered, "She'll be sad that it broke, and she might Hulk-out a bit, but I'm sure she'll eventually forgive us." He planted a kiss on top of her hair and traced a cross with his thumb on her forehead.

"I was just trying to make chamomile tea for Mary Cecelia 'cuz she had a sore tummy and that's what Mammy does when we're sick like..."

God, girls talk a lot—even when they're tired. "Don't you worry about it, Pumpkin. I'll explain everything to Mommy."

A commotion erupted down the hall.

"Da!" One of the big boys yelled. "Mary Cecelia just spewed all over the carpet."

CHAPTER 26

I only take a drink on two occasions:
when I'm thirsty and when I'm not.

~BRENDAN BEHAN

Luke took a drink from his Guinness and glanced outside the snug. He caught sight of Pat Power—the former Mount Sion and Windgap hurler—posing for pictures with Kate's two girlfriends. Luke strained to hear Kate's apology over the merriment of fiddle and accordion. Patrons were singing along with Kenny McMahon:

What's a fella to do? ... And then I lost my heart to a Galway Girl.

"I am so sorry," Kate said, "I had no right to go through your things. The letter just sort of blew onto the floor when I turned on the fan. When I picked it up, I couldn't resist reading it. I'm a compulsive reader."

Luke was losing his heart to a Minnesota girl. Kate crinkled her eyes when she laughed, like Christy did. And it was as if his late wife was telling him to just relax and ask the nice lady out. He had never perceived such a mystical message from her before; one more thing that was missing with Nora.

When Kate had touched his arm a moment ago, something exploded. Crud! He didn't even know what to call it—wonder? Chemistry? *And I'm supposed to be a wordsmith!* Well, he knew one thing for sure: he was enchanted by The Lady in Red—even if she did nose a bit into his private stuff. But he couldn't fault her. In fact, she was probably smart to read it, from a safety standpoint. After all, he was practically a stranger. He just hoped that letter didn't make him look like a momma's boy.

He reached for the letter. He noticed it was a little moist. "They say you can learn a lot about a guy by the way he treats his mother."

"I've heard that," she said. "Maybe that's why I snuck a peek." Kate threw him an innocent grin.

Damned if she didn't just admit she wants to know me better! "Well, what did you learn?"

"That we have something in common."

"We do? You mean other than running, losing a spouse, and oozing warts?" He was actually thankful to Buck for adding a dimension of comic relief to the evening.

"Yes, well … By the closing I could tell that you like Mexican food, and I'm crazy about Mexican food, too."

"Margaritas and all?" Luke asked, looking out the window at the rain.

"Sí, señor. On the rocks with salt."

"Ditto. What else did you learn?"

"I could also tell that you're good to your 'mammy'—as the Irish say."

"'Indeed'—as the Irish also say." Out of the corner of his eye Luke could see Buck putting his camera away and mouthing, "Ask her out!"

"And you admire your mother's … legs?" She seemed genuinely curious. He watched, nearly panting, as her hand smoothed over her own legs.

"Oh … Um … that's a family joke. It was a favorite quote from my Dad. Honest."

"And you call her a Nazi-of-a-mom?"

"She raised five boys, basically on her own. My dad died when we were young. Mom was a loving, one-woman Gestapo."

For the next twenty minutes, the two Americans chatted about their childhoods. Kate discussed her father's recent death, but said nothing about her husband's.

Luke was finding it easier to talk to her, but every time he tried to ask her out, he fumbled. He needed to tie up loose ends with Nora first.

At one in the morning the barman yelled "Last call" and Kenny began singing *Men at the Bar, Unite.*

Morgan poked her head into the snug. "We best be goin', Kate."

Luke held out his hand for a shake. "Thanks so much for sharing your story. It certainly will add humor to my piece, which my editor will appreciate." Looking into her eyes he added, "I sure enjoyed meeting you, and I..." The words were stuck in his throat like a chicken bone.

And then Buck appeared. "Luke, are you ready to go?"

"Yeah, I'm coming," he forced himself to say.

Kate stood up. "Well, thanks for the Bulmer's. It was nice meeting you, too, Luke."

And then just like that, The Lady in Red walked quickly away in those sexy stilettos. A sigh of frustration pushed its way out of his mouth.

"Did you ever end up asking her out?" Buck asked.

"No, I'm not exactly free, yet. But I was about to set up another interview when you interrupted me, pal."

"Do I have to ask Kate out for you? And will I need to break up with Nora for ya first?" Buck snatched the notepad out of Luke's hand and nodded toward the door. "She's in high heels, so she can't run too fast. Quick! Catch up to her, Old Man!"

As Luke started to dash, he heard Buck add, "Geez! Will I have to seduce her for ya, too?"

CHAPTER 27

I feel excellent—I can tell you honestly, I just overslept.
~BORIS YELTSIN
(explaining "Circling Over Shannon," as reported by BBC News)

They were used to the wet spring, but for the past two days it had rained a titanic amount. 'Twas as if the angels were overturning their heavenly mop buckets onto the whole of Ireland. Catriona thought about this on her walk to work in the drizzle, which was predicted to dissipate by the 'morrow when the sun would surely show its face.

She heard on the morning radio that "out the country" the potato crop could be threatened once again. The bogs of the Shannon region in the west were saturated sponges of rolling landscape, and there was a threat of a "bog burst"—when great slabs of peat go careening down a slope like a mudslide. Even the stable, rocky expanse of County Clare's Burren had been deluged, which could possibly cause a blight on its famous wildflowers. Levels of the glassy lakes in the midlands were higher than usual, putting some towns, homes and castles at risk. Rivers and estuaries were becoming very bloated.

What's the good Lord thinkin'? A severe flood would really and truly hurt tourism, which in turn would hurt the guesthouse. Kate would find herself on her mam's doorstep like a wet kitten and Catriona's job would be erased like the ring around Declan's collar that she rubbed out yesterday. Just thinking about it gave her the collywobbles.

Taking a slight detour, she saw that the Royal Canal had swollen into a deep, angry swoosh. She watched it a moment as it rushed underneath the footbridge. Catriona was mesmerized by the natural lace-pattern of the swirling foam. It lay atop the torrents of water and changed its composition like a kaleidoscope of sepia tones, rotating again and again.

Catriona stepped off the bridge and headed to the warm guesthouse, happy to get indoors and begin her mopping. After she completed that duty, she would make the light fixtures sparkle so that even if the weather remained dark and gray when the guests arrived, their rooms would be warm and bright.

She was on her second crystal sconce when Kate walked into the parlor. Thankfully, she didn't seem to be hung over. "How was your holiday?" She asked, not knowing it was a loaded question. Over a pot of Earl Grey, Kate told the tale of the Clooney incident. Catriona laughed so hard she had to wipe her eyes until her starched linen handkerchief was as damp as the tulip bed. What she liked even better than the story, though, was her boss's ability to laugh at herself.

They worked side by side spiffing up the place, and when Kate started to unpack her new acquisitions, Catriona held back her comments about the swift changes. Fluffy eiderdowns, ordered on eBay, were placed on the beds. New stylish antiques, bought in Tullahought, replaced worn pieces. The lamps that Kate purchased on Francis Street were put in their proper spots. And a new area rug in jewel tones was laid in the office.

" 'Tis gobsmacked I am," Catriona said, shaking her head.

"Why? Because I'm not behaving like Boris Yeltsin this morning, and I can actually get some work done?"

"Indeed, that is a relief. But actually, I was after thinkin' that the premises are gettin' mighty posh. Those touches you're adding were the same changes Mrs. McFadden always wanted to make, but she said they'd need to charge more for the guest rooms if they did."

"That's what I'm planning to do. I just have to get the website updated first," Kate admitted, as she brought an armful of new towels and washcloths upstairs. She was happily humming that piano tune from *Casablanca*.

Catriona seized the moment and followed Kate into the bathroom. As the ladies aligned the linens in the loos, she said, "Since you're in lovely form this mornin' because of your run-in with that film star, and since you're goin' about makin' new changes to the guesthouse, I'd like to discuss somet'ing you might well go for. It's a surprise, and it will require your full support."

Kate seemed interested, but then the door chimed. Catriona lumbered downstairs to answer it, admitting Deirdre Kennedy.

"Hiya, Catriona, I wanted to call so that I could check out the painting you hired our boys to do." Deirdre flitted into the foyer, pranced into the parlor, but then turned around and marched right back, sniffing the air. "My, oh my, Catriona! Don't you smell lovely! Like a piña colada in a tropical paradise. What is that? Perfume? Or are you naughty girls over here having fruity cocktails without me?"

Catriona blushed. "Ah, that would be my Tahitian body oil. I bought it at a fancy new spa in City Centre. A girl will do anyt'ing a'tall to keep her husband mad after her. But with seven chisellers, Deirdre, I'm thinkin' you already know all the magical tricks to bewitchin' one's husband."

Laughing, Deirdre answered, "Indeed I know some secrets. Learned them from my romance novels. But if that lovely oil really works magic, 'tis Kate who might be borrowin' some soon enough."

"What are you talkin' about?" Catriona asked, flummoxed. "Do you mean she'll need a bit o' luck, what with your husband's twin coming to town? I've heard he once was sweet on Kate."

Kate hustled down the stairs. "Oh, for goodness sake! It was ages ago that Joe Kennedy and I dated. He's way over me by now."

"Truth be told," Deirdre said, "I do t'ink Joe is still smitten with Kate, but I'm not so sure they're well matched. Time will tell. But who I really was referrin' to is the writer of this story." Pulling *The Irish Times* out of her bag, Deirdre opened it to section B and pointed to an article by Luke O'Brien. It had a photo of the gorgeous George Clooney beside it. "Catriona, did Kate tell you that she was asked out by this journalist? That he just so happens to live at the condos down the road? A man she has spied runnin' around Glasnevin—we call him Spandex Man."

Catriona was gobsmacked for the second time that morning. She felt her jaw drop and surely her eyes bugged out like a mongoose. "She told me she embarrassed herself silly in front of that film star, and showed me that article, but she didn't mention an enchanted interlude with a real-life journalist." She threw her hands into the air. "And didn't he describe her as a Grace Kelly lookalike with courtly legs? No wonder she's in good form today and full of tremendous energy. Please, Deirdre, tell me all about it before she hushes you up."

Kate reached for the newspaper. "Now ladies, let's get one thing clear. Spandex Man...er—Luke, did not exactly ask me out. He asked if he could interview me about running a B&B."

Deirdre countered, "Surely you have brains enough, dear friend o' mine, to know when a man is hitting on you." Deirdre yanked the paper out of Kate's hand, rolled it up and thumped her over the head with it. "You didn't see him askin' Morgan—who was also sitting in the lorry—if he could interview *her*, now did you? She's something of an innkeeper, too. O'Gara's rent out those rooms over the pub, as everyone knows."

Kate held her hands up in surrender on her way to the door. "Oh, go ahead, Deirdre. You might as well tell Catriona the rest of the story." With hot pink cheeks, Kate stepped out into the garden, mumbling something about wanting to talk with Michael Farley.

As soon as Kate closed the door behind her, Deirdre's words leapt from her mouth like a horse out of the starting gate. Catriona learned the details of how Kate met Luke at Power's Pub and how they chatted until last call.

When Deirdre was done, Catriona said, "I'm tryin' to picture the scene. Did this Luke O'Brien run through the pourin' rain after her?"

"Indeed. Wait 'til I tell you! He peered into many cars until he found her in Morgan's lorry. He pounded on the window of the back seat to get her attention and wiped the rain from his face. When Kate rolled down the window, he yelled through the curtain of raindrops like a nervous actor delivering his memorized lines: 'Kate, could I call on you next week sometime? I'd like to interview you about your business.' He said it was to help out his friend Buck, who has a side hustle writing a blog."

"And how did she answer him?" Catriona asked, as she dusted the books on the shelves and glanced out the front bay window. She spotted Kate standing by the submissive blossoms of the columbine—a symbol of the sensuous Aphrodite.

"She said she'd be delighted to meet with him any time. And oh, Catriona...you should have seen the hopeful look on her face. She was gazing out that window at him as if he were Romeo in a sexy pair of tights, serenading her beneath a balcony."

"You make a lovely *seanchaí*, Deirdre, you really and truly do." Catriona placed a rag-toting hand on her hip.

"Many t'anks," Deirdre responded to the compliment about her storytelling talent. "Aye, 'tis a grand story, but that's not the end of it. What happened next is very romantic...Wait 'til I tell yeh."

"Oh, do tell! What did he say?" Catriona stepped closer.

"Em, after Kate told Luke he could call on her, he grabbed her hand and kissed it—right there in front of Morgan and me. And then he looked into her eyes and said..." Deirdre reached for Catriona's hand, re-enacting the courtly scene.

"What did he say? What did he say? Tell me now, Deirdre Kennedy...Go on, don't dawdle!"

"He said, 'Hot dog.'"

"Hot dog?" Catriona was confused and disappointed.

"Yes," Deirdre said all starry-eyed. "Truth be told, with his dreadful American accent it sounded more like *hot daug*. Isn't that just the most romantic t'ing you ever heard?"

"Hot dog?" Catriona pulled her hand away and stammered, "Romantic? Are yeh off yer nut? The bloke's a big-time writer—and all he can say is 'hot dog'? That's blasphemous and not romantic a'tall! What manner of man says such a childish t'ing?"

Laughing, Deirdre countered, "Well, Mark says that hot dogs are a beloved icon over there in the States, right up there with baseball and apple pie. And actually, Catriona, what with the kissing of the hand and all—it *was* romantic and a bit chivalrous, as well. I guess you had to be there."

"Indeed I wasn't there. Somebody had to tend to business. And I'm thinkin' this Spandex Man could take a few lessons on romance from me Declan." With that said, Catriona shot Deirdre a sixpenny look. Deirdre met her stare and narrowed her eyes.

"You need to go easier on Kate, Catriona. A romance is always good for a widow ... at any age. It can help her embrace the present." Deirdre picked up a book, glanced at its pages, and then set it down. Catriona could tell she wasn't finished givin' out advice. "As far as Spandex Man goes, don't be too hard on the bloke, either. The poor, sufferin' soul lost his wife ten years ago. And the best t'ing about him is that he's a church-goin' man. I know, because he recognized me from the pews of St. Columba's."

That statement went right to Catriona's massive heart as if it were defibrillated. She turned away from the dusty volumes and re-set her shoulders. "Ah, go away!"

"No. 'Tis true. He really is a regular to the pews. I'm not jokin'."

"Isn't that grand now!" Catriona replied in a softened cadence. "Well, since he's a church-goin' widower, I guess I could be on my best behavior when he knocks on that door."

"But there's a complication. You see, I t'ink perhaps Kate hasn't given up on Mark's twin."

Catriona pointed a finger at Deirdre. "The two Yanks will be most welcome when they come callin'. But don't be expectin' me to serve them any hot dogs! I'll not be stoopin' so low as to prepare that strange American sausage in this kitchen. Just how in God's name do they eat those t'ings anyway?"

"With ketchup, mustard, pickles, onions, cheese and chili."

"Oh, dear ... that's disgustin'!"

CHAPTER 28

Love is like a beautiful flower which I may not touch,
but whose fragrance makes the garden
a place of delight just the same.

~HELEN KELLER

I wanted to thank you for helping with the gardening," Michael heard Miss Kate say. He watched her as she gingerly placed her feet in the spots of gravel that weren't too muddy.

"I like your g-garden," he replied, pulling some wild thistle from the crushed rock path. It was easy to yank because the soil was so mucky. Pooka meandered over for a visit, and he rubbed her belly with a dirty glove.

"I know you're usually picking flowers for the church when you're over here, but I noticed that you also pull weeds, dead-head the blooms and prune the bushes, plus much, much more." As she jabbered, he moved from Pooka's warm tummy to the border area to clip some spent daffodils.

"Michael, I want to ask you to be my official gardener. You do such a nice job and I was thinking that we could have a ... business agreement." Miss Kate pulled her damp hair into a ponytail. "I could really use your help when you're not at school or busy swimming or working at the church. I'd pay you the first week of every month, starting today. What do you think? I hope you'll do it, otherwise I'll have to hire somebody else, someone who probably wouldn't love my garden as much as you do."

Michael hopped up and down clapping his gloved hands. Pooka was excited, too, because she ran in circles around them. "Janey M-Mack, M-Miss Kate, that'd be brilliant! I get a little m-money from Father Criagáin, but if I get more I'll be filthy rich like John Wayne." They shook hands on the deal and then he spun her around hoedown-style. Sometimes cowboys and cowgirls danced like that. She giggled when he ended the twirling with a bow. He smiled, feeling the points of his crooked eye teeth.

"Thanks for the dance, Michael. I love to dance even though I'm not that good at it."

"We dance after swimming sometimes. Dancing is a m-massive good time. Especially if Elvis is playin'."

She hummed *Love Me Tender* as she bent down to touch the columbine. Michael noticed that Miss Kate's eyes looked happier than usual today. Maybe her holiday was brilliant. He had heard the women inside the guesthouse talking about a man. Was this new man why Kate was so merry like?

Moving from the columbine to the immature larkspur, Kate asked, "Tell me, Michael, how'd you do at the swim meet?"

"I was a m-mighty torpedo, faster than a speeding bullet!" He got up from the ground and ran down the puddled path in his cowboy boots, rotating his arms as if he were doing the freestyle. Pooka ran beside him barking. They returned to Kate a little wetter and mud-splattered. "I got second place in the 50 m-metre race. And I got a medal as big as a biscuit. And M-mammy and Da gave me carnations."

"Wow! Congratulations! When do you race again?"

"I don't know. Coach Keanne says pretty soon. And S-Special Olympics World Games are comin' up. M-maybe I'll m-make all the other blokes eat my bubbles."

Miss Kate giggled. "Well, I'm really proud of you, Michael. I can't wait to cheer you on. I think I read in the paper that your Olympics are in May. If I recall, Mrs. Ryan has taken reservations for the event. People will be coming to Dublin from all over the world."

He went to his Adidas sack, pushed his eyeglasses up the bridge of his nose, and removed a can of Pepsi. He took a swig and plopped a gummy worm into his mouth. While chewing, he slipped his pruning shears from the sack and went to work on the rose bushes near the front of the house.

After Miss Kate went with Pooka to the back garden, Michael saw a white Ka park in front of the Kennedy's home. *Oh, no! Not the white car!* A tall man got out of the car, slipped a light jacket over his uniform shirt, grabbed a bag, and walked to the front door of The Cobblestones. When he rang the bell, he looked at Michael mean like, as if he were taking a gander at a monkey in the Dublin Zoo.

Michael rocked back and forth for a bit, hitting his head until he saw nice Mrs. Ryan answer the door. The housekeeper said, "Oh, howya? Would you be Spandex Man?"

"What?" The man asked. It was obvious to Michael that he was annoyed. "What is Spandex Man?"

"Are you Himself? The widower Kate met at Tullahought?"

"I am not!" The lout answered as if Mrs. Ryan were off her nut. "I'm Ultan Ferrian," he said, and handed her a business card, as if he were the most important person on earth.

"Oh right! You're the computer repairman. Sorry. Come in, why don't yeh? I'll show you to the office."

When the door shut, Michael made his way to the Ka. Peering inside the windows, he spotted a black stocking cap that looked like the one The Edge from U2 wears, but this one had a picture of a computer stitched on the brim. He also spied a pack of Pall Mall cigarettes, food wrappers, and a messy pile of papers that said "Invoice" on the top. Michael sounded that big word out. The name "Ultan Ferrian" was written on the top as well. He didn't have any trouble sounding that out because he just heard the bloke say it.

When Kate and Pooka returned from the back of the house, Michael said, "I don't l-like Ultan F-F-Ferrian." He rocked back and forth a few times.

"What?"

"I don't like the m-man in your house."

"Oh, is the computer man here? Did Mrs. Ryan show him in? Don't worry. We needed him to come."

Michael began hitting his head. He wanted to tell her why he didn't like Ultan Ferrian, but he wasn't sure how to put it in words.

"It's okay, Michael," Kate said. She patted his forearm and it soothed him. They worked together in silence for a time while Pooka took a nap under the lilac bush.

Mrs. Kennedy must have spotted them from her window and she trotted over to join them in the garden. Miss Kate showed her where Benjamin and Jack could add crushed rock to the paths.

Suddenly, Mary Cecelia rushed toward them, calling, "Mammy! Maaaammy!"

"What is it, luv?"

"The twins made a horrible mess and Da said to fetch you."

"Ah, sugar! What did they get into now?"

"They found that great, big box from Granny and Granda—the one you hid in the press."

"Are you tellin' me they found all those bottles of maple syrup from Minnesota?"

"Aye. And it's all over kingdom come." Mary Cecelia rolled her eyes. "There's a trail goin' from the press, into the parlor, where they filled one of Great Granny's teacups."

"Jaysus! Not my granny's t'ings again!"

"Yep, but they didn't break it. Then there's a trail of syrup goin' into the lounge. Oh, and there's a path goin' up the stairs and into the bedroom you got ready for Uncle Joe. They made a syrupy lake on his pillowslips."

"Japers!" Mrs. Kennedy said.

The lass continued, "And they both got syrup on their socks, so there's sticky footprints all over."

"You must be jokin'!" poor Mrs. Kennedy said, looking pale.

"No. Come quick, before Da explodes."

Rushing out of the garden with Mary Cecelia trailing behind, Mrs. Kennedy yelled over her shoulder, "Take me back to Tullahought, I need another holiday!"

"H-Here, take Pooka with you," Michael called. "She can lick the m-mess off the floors."

Mrs. Ryan emerged and said, "I heard through the window about the syrupy mess. That's a fine kettle of fish, then. Kate, why don't I punch out over here, and give Deirdre a hand?"

Michael heard Miss Kate's response as she headed into the guest-house: "I'd say she could use all hands on deck. I'll zip over right after the computer guy leaves."

Michael wanted to get away from Ultan Ferrian. He hustled to "Duke," but didn't throw his leg over the saddle. He didn't want Miss Kate to be alone with that bad bloke. *What would John Wayne do, if his deputy was busy licking floors?* He sat on the ground to think, rapping his head as he rocked back and forth.

CHAPTER 29

The problem with some people
is that when they aren't drunk, they're sober.

~W.B. YEATS

U ltan Ferrian was sitting at the antique desk when that fat lady walked into the room again. *She's as dense as bottled shite, that one. What in Hades was all her blather about a Spandex Man?*

"I'm heading next door to help our neighbor. I just wanted to let you know that Mrs. McMahon, who owns this guesthouse, will be with you in a moment. Cheerio!" And just like that she waggled out of the place, blubber and all. *That one's such a whack job not even the tide would take her out.* He laughed at his own cleverness and continued to work undisturbed for a while.

And then a vision entered the room.

"Hello. I'm Kate McMahon, the owner. You don't know how happy I am to see you!" she said with a thick American accent.

You've got me pretty excited, too, lady! Ferrian was sure it was the blond goddess he'd seen out and about—the runner. He thrust his hands into his pockets and tossed her an irresistible smile. "Grand meetin' you, as well. I'm nearly done."

"Great! Just yell if you need me. I'll be in the kitchen."

Like a creative master studying his subject, he drank in her facial features. She stared at him for a moment with inquisitive eyes, then left the office. He clicked on his phone and tapped away until he found the photo he had taken of her—the one where she was out walking and wearing a red hoodie. Yep, it was her all right.

For fooks sake! I run into her by chance after I've been searching the area for days. If I play my cards right... He looked at his reflection in the computer screen and smoothed his frizzy orange hair. The hooker he picked up the other night—after he scored money and drugs off that dealer—said that his wavy hair was a turn-on. He'd been told by others, too, that he wasn't bad looking.

Well, well, well... this is turning out to be my lucky day! Straining his neck a bit, he tried to sneak a peek. But, she wasn't visible.

"Damn!" he whispered, and then turned back to the job at hand. His boss, Doyle, wasn't expecting him back at the shop for another hour. Since he was almost done here, maybe he'd have a spot of time to case the joint a bit. And who knows? Maybe he could take a run at that fine piece of arse. He tested the keyboard by typing: *Shazaam!*

Everything with the desktop was in fine order again, thanks to the brainiac in the room. As he collected his junk, he spent a few moments thinking of some lines he could use on that vixen. He whispered one of the only things he remembered from Irish classes before he dropped out of school—a bullshite line he used in the pubs on gullible tourists: "Tá tú iontach álainn." Which translated as: "You are amazingly beautiful."

And then he stealthily headed out of Kate's office.

By snooping around a house a bit, a man could learn a lot about a female. He figured that by pretending he was searching for the proprietor, he could take a look-see. With his bag over his shoulder and a clipboard in hand, he walked into the parlor. He noticed earlier how homey it was—a lot nicer, indeed, than his auld kip. Now he took a closer look because he was searching for clues into her life. On a bookshelf in the corner he found a silver-framed photo of Kate in a fitted evening gown. He removed his phone from his pants pocket and quickly took a picture of that photo. In it she had her arms draped over some lucky gobshite in a tuxedo. Who was he?

Didn't that bugger housekeeper say that the runner-lady was a missus? Could this be the fookin' husband? Or maybe her da?

Down the hallway he found the door to the toilet. Ferrian was no eejit, he went right to the medicine press. *What is her drug of choice? Anything interesting?* There was nothing but bandages and antacids.

He could hear rattling at the opposite end of the house. By the sound of a kettle's whistle, he knew she was making tea. He figured he had a few seconds to nose around in the back of the place. Treading quietly—using that skill he had acquired as a kid when his mother had her fellas over—he opened the far door to her private apartment.

The first thing he noticed was the girly décor: a floral eiderdown on the bed; lights dripping with rhinestones; and a romantic print hanging on the wall. Peering at the bottom corner of the print he saw the name "Rembrandt."

Classy bitch.

There were books on the shelf: *Gone with the Wind, Pride and Prejudice, The French Lieutenant's Woman* and paperback novels. He never read much, but he knew that uptight females chose these books because of the cover art. He bet Kate was as horny as any slut on the docks.

Interestingly, this bedroom didn't contain anything masculine at all. No belts haphazardly hung over the chair, no sports magazines on the nightstand, and no boxer shorts crumpled on the floor. When Ferrian opened the wardrobe, only dresses and other frilly stuff were hanging there. *Maybe she's a rarin'-to-go divorcée with no man around to get in the way. That'd be brilliant!*

He stuck his head into the master bath. It was all nice and tidy, and again, lacking anything manly. Everything was white: the tub, tiles, towels, candle, bath mat and walls. But there was one glorious splash of color next to the shower. Keeping one ear tuned to the kitchen noise, he stole up to the shower door and plucked the silky, sapphire-blue item off the hook.

"Oh la, la," he whispered. In his hands was a lovely little number that was more feminine than sexy. The sun was streaming through the small window, playing upon the folds of the smooth cloth. *She could really fill this thing out!* His creative mind was already conjuring up images.

He was startled by a ring tone. His shoulders relaxed when he realized that it was just her cellphone sounding from the kitchen. Through the open doors, he could hear fragments of the conversation. "Hi, Mom ... yeah sure ... I'm really excited for Lee to get here." He wondered who Lee was. Knowing that Kate would be occupied while she gabbed, he took out his cellphone once again and snapped a photo of the nightie. When he got home he would do a colored sketch of her wearing it. Stroking the silky material across his cheek, he sniffed a lavender scent. *Mmmmm, nice.* Reluctantly, he hung the nightie back up and then retreated from her private area.

Once in the hallway, Ferrian caught sight of something familiar on a hook by the back garden door. He recognized at once the red Minnesota Twins hoodie Kate was wearing the first time he spotted her taking a walk. He touched it while eavesdropping on the phone conversation just beyond the other side of the wall.

"... Tell Lefko and Basil and everbody in Sun City I said hello. It sounds like you're settling nicely into the Sands of Time. When are you gonna come to Dublin for a visit?"

Ferrian looked at the time on his phone. He'd best be going soon. But he continued to listen to Kate's chit-chat, mesmerized by her voice.

"Yeah, Mom. It's going fine. Please don't worry about me. I know, I know ... your futon. Thanks, but I hope I don't have to take you up on your offer. Spread the word that I open for business on Easter Monday. My computer should be working sometime today. I'll send you a link to the updated website—you could pass it on to your contacts for me." Ferrian was glad to learn that crucial bit of information about her not opening yet. Things would be very quiet around here for a while until the guests started to arrive. He pictured her spread out on a futon.

The air nearly crackled with lecherous excitement. Because his palms were sweaty, the clipboard slipped out of his hands with a clatter to the floor. When he turned around after picking the damn thing up, the innkeeper was standing right there in the hall. She was looking at him with the phone to her ear and appeared confused.

"Ahh … Mom, hold on." She gave him the stink-eye and asked, "What are you doing back here?"

"Oh, there you are, Miss. I was just lookin' for you." He came closer to her. She looked so sultry in those jeans and white T-shirt. He pictured her in that sapphire lingerie, and had an urge to overtake her right there, right now, and show her what a man he was. From past experience, he knew he could be quick if necessary. In fact, he could be over and done with the deed before that fat housekeeper could waddle her pathetic arse over here and spoil the opportunity.

"Tá tú iontach álainn," Ferrian said, watching her face.

"Pardon me?"

"Emm … it was just a bit of the Irish I was speakin' to you." She didn't seem impressed. He was hoping that she'd turn to putty in his hand, and that he could take advantage of her hesitation. Even though women wanted action and not words, they definitely liked to be spoken to in foreign languages by good lookin' blokes. But Ferrian could tell that this Yank would be a hard sell.

"I was just asking you in Irish if yer husband was around to sign these papers."

"He's … I'm the …" She seemed uncomfortable, and he could see her looking in the direction of the back door. When he turned around to see what she was looking at, there in the windowpane, was the face of that gacky looking mentaller. *Damn! There went my chance.*

The face popped down, but Ferrian figured the eejit was still lurking.

A voice crackled through the cellphone: *"Kate? Are you there? Are you okay?"*

He'd better stop feeding her lines and act the impressive businessman now. "I fixed the computer for you, Ms. McMahon. I reinstalled your software and swabbed the circuits with rubbing alcohol. Here's my card. If you want me back, just phone. Now I have some paperwork that you or himself need to sign." She took the pen and he noticed she didn't wear a wedding ring. He took another step closer when she finished signing. Was that fear or excitement in her sexy blue eyes? Whatever the hell it was, he found it a turn-on. He gave her a copy of the invoice.

"I can go over a few t'ings on the keyboard with you now."

"Ah, no thanks. I'm sure you repaired it just fine. My neighbors are expecting me and if I don't get over there right now, they'll send someone over here."

A desperate knock on the window of the back door pulled Ferrian back to reality. He wanted to scream out in frustration, but he was a good actor, and pretended like he wasn't narky and pissed as hell.

"Ahh, my gardener's still at the door. He must need me." She hurried toward the back, looking over her shoulder.

He wanted to say, "Well so do I, lady!" but instead he muttered, "I'll show myself out," and headed for the front door.

From his car he caught a view of Kate standing near a puddle by the side of the guesthouse. Even though it had started to drizzle, she stood there watching him pull away. In his rear-view mirror her white t-shirt seemed to lay moist against her skin. At her side was a Dalmatian, barking at his car. Next to them was that window-licker, and Ferrian sure as hell wanted to bite the head off that bollocks.

Damn! She was just startin' to get hot for me. That gacky kid sure knows how to spoil a spot of fun. Craving euphoria, he steadied the wheel with his knees, fished a bag out of his pocket, and spilled its contents into the palm of his hand. The Ecstasy pills resembled a colorful collection of gemstones. He chose one that was garnet-colored and branded with a heart.

"Fookin' perfect!" He popped it into his mouth and then turned on his windscreen wipers.

At least he knew where she lived now.

CHAPTER 30

I don't see myself as the Hunk of the Month.
~PIERCE BROSNAN

One week later

The sun finally shone bright and gentle when Ireland welcomed this fine April morn, after days of monster rain slamming its fists into the terrain of the island. Now the rays caressed the bruised land like a mother nurturing an injured child. As Kate jogged, she could see a rainbow and it seemed to envelop Glasnevin in a decorative patina. But, despite the glorious change in weather and the display of prismatic color, her heart was gloomy. She had not seen Luke while out for her runs, and what put even more of a damper on her spirits was the fact that he had not even called or stopped by the guesthouse.

You don't really care, Kate, do you? You need a romance right now like you need a hole in your head.

While she took a shower, she tried to sort out her emotions. She felt thrilled and yet anxious about the opening of the guesthouse. She was feeling better about Catriona's reliability, but the woman acted like she owned the place...and her insistence on that damn wrench hanging off the stove was infuriating!

Grabbing the loofa sponge, she gave it a double dose of lavender gel. Forcing herself to turn to other subjects, her mind shifted to Joe Kennedy. She was determined to rein in her excitement about his upcoming visit. And then there was Spandex Man. Why had she allowed herself to get caught up in the oldest game in the world? It had been over a week since their encounter in Tullahought. In that time, whenever her phone rang or the doorbell chimed a lightning bolt shot through her body. Why, oh why, did she give a flyin' flip anyway?

In merely six days guests would be arriving at The Cobblestones. She had enough on her plate right now, including a crash course in the new bookkeeping software. She had no time to be stewing about romance—or the lack of it.

As she dried off and slowly rubbed lavender lotion onto her legs, she closed her eyes. Darned if uninvited images didn't keep popping up. The brush of Joe's lips on her neck as they sat fishing on the dock, back when they were in college. The chivalrous kiss Luke bestowed on her hand as he stood in the rain.

But dang it, why hadn't he called or stopped by? He didn't seem to be ticked about her snooping around and reading the letter to his mother. Maybe he just wanted to get the Clooney story out of her. Didn't he admit that her story added just the right punch he needed to jazz up his article? His sweet clumsy lines—were they just to manipulate her?

When she went to the kitchen, she found Catriona scouring the sink. "Good mornin' Kate. Isn't it a lovely sun-filled day? Rain is all well and good for a while, if you're a frog. Did you see that beautiful rainbow when you were out runnin'? They're harbingers of good luck."

"Yes, I saw it. And I could use a little bit of luck right now."

Catriona looked Kate square in the eye. "So tell me, is it Joe Kennedy you're pining after? Or perhaps that Spandex-wearin' hot-dog-eatin' bloke?"

Is she prying or trying to be friendly? "I can't waste my time worrying about men—when we have more pressing things at hand, like our food supplies. Now that our computer is fixed, we could order some of those O'Flynn sausages on the internet. I'm still dreaming about how tasty they were when I had them at a B&B near Bunratty."

Kate saw Myrna's slim figure through the lace curtains. Catriona led her into the kitchen. "Hiya," Myrna said with a wave of her gnarled hand. "I just wanted to run over and give Kate a couple of house-warming gifts. Here, open this one first," she instructed, padding toward the cooker.

"Watch out for that … wrench … er, spanner," Kate warned as she accepted the gift. She started to laugh when she opened it. "Oh Myrna, you're a hoot and a half!" She handed it to Catriona who was wearing a confused look. "Hoot and a half means … you're very funny. And Myrna is reminding me of how I once made a fool of myself in front of Pierce Brosnan."

Catriona rolled her eyes. "I can't wait to hear that story." She studied the gift, a framed 8x10 photo of Pierce Brosnan flashing a seductive smile. Using the sleeve of her sweater, she rubbed the glass and said, "Indeed, he makes me break out into a hot flash."

"Yes, Catriona! He's even more of a looker when you see him in person, as Kate well knows." Myrna presented the other gift, a photo of George Clooney in a matching gilded frame.

Over the peal of laughter Myrna explained, "After I heard about your Tullahought escapades, I thought you could start a collection."

Catriona took the corner of her apron and began fanning herself. "Oh, my Lord … the two are steamy as boiled parsnips—like me Declan!"

It was Kate's turn to roll her eyes. Myrna placed a restraining hand on her shoulder.

Catriona prattled on, "We should hang these up in the dining room so all the female guests will start their mornin' happy."

Kate shook her head and took a yoga breath. "No, Catriona. They don't quite go with the antique décor in there."

Myrna quickly jumped in, "Besides, the men folk might not feel appreciated, with their ladies moonin' over the film stars."

"I know what I'll do," Kate said. "These will hang proudly in my private quarters so I can drool over them in my spare time."

"By your bed?" Catriona asked. "Weren't you just tellin' me before Myrna arrived that you've been dreamin' of sausages lately? And perhaps hot dogs, too?"

Myrna cut in, "Three years is a long time to forego male companionship."

"Well," Kate said, "I did have a few dates, but it's awkward, you know..." She faced Catriona, "...when you're a widow..."

Myrna clutched Kate's biceps, shook her head, and offered, "Well, I have a feelin' somet'ing good is brewin' for yeh. Did you see that rainbow this mornin'? I t'ink love is in the air."

Catriona squeezed past the wrench. "Wasn't I just after tellin' her the same t'ing? Joe Kennedy arrives soon, and that hot dog bloke will phone when he's good and ready. And when he comes a-courtin' maybe I'll be lucky enough to see him in his Spandex!"

Myrna laughed as she let herself out.

Kate and Catriona moved into the office to finish updating their website. A few cancellations had occurred because of the iffy weather. In fact, The Cobblestones was only 50 percent booked for the first month, and 40 percent booked for the second month. Kate was determined to remain positive and told herself that with last minute travelers and a lot of hard work on the website, there was a chance they could get those numbers up by the summer months.

"I have another pressing situation. Remember when I was tryin' to tell you something the other day?" Catriona said. Tapping her pointer finger on the desk, she added, "And I'll need your full cooperation with this matter."

"Okaaay." Kate's core muscles pulled taut.

"Remember when I told you to leave the hirin' of the part-time maid up to me? Well now," Catriona began unloading the dishwasher, "I've discussed the situation with Declan and we'd like to surprise Terry and Myrna by bringin' Helen home from Australia at Easter. Didn't I used to mind that sweet girl when she was a young wan? Declan and I grew to love that lass." A plate didn't pass inspection, so she brought it back to the sink. "I've spoken to Helen. She feels that she's proven her independence now, and would be delighted to move back home—if she had a guaranteed position here. So we were t'inkin' that you could take her on when Molly Flood leaves."

At the thought of an act of kindness for the Rileys, Kate's resentment evaporated. "That's a great idea! I'm surprised I didn't think of it myself. But it's only a part-time position. I can't afford more." Kate grabbed the plate, squirted it with soap, and felt a wave of inner warmth toward Catriona as she dipped it into the tepid water.

Catriona responded, "Didn't she inform me that she's currently jugglin' three jobs Down Under? No wonder she wants to return to Ireland. And if she could find a lifeguardin' job in Dublin, and have no rent to pay, she could well hold it together with just a part-time job with us." Catriona clinked a bowl into the press. "Helen was bound and determined not to take a half-penny from her parents, and it would take donkey years for the lass to save enough quid for the flight home."

"You mean you're paying for her ticket home?"

"Well, 'twas Declan's idea, and since God has been generous to Declan and me, why not spread it around? We can well pay for her flight and she'll accept it from us."

Kate was surprised that she didn't bristle this time when Catriona talked about Declan in the present tense. *So, this is the Catriona the neighbors know and love.*

"Of course we can put Helen on the payroll. How very nice of you, Catriona, to find a way to bless the Rileys." Kate extended the dripping plate like an olive branch toward her housekeeper.

Catriona smiled and blushed as their hands met.

135

CHAPTER 31

I am so lucky I get to do so many things.
I just want you to know,
even though I have Down syndrome, it is O.K.

~SARAH ITOH, SPECIAL OLYMPIAN (TRACK)

Michael Farley plopped down beside a puddle in front of his home and glugged the last bits of his Club Orange soft drink. Using a stick, he pounded the aluminum can into the shape of a raft-like boat, being careful as can be not to cut his fingers on the sharp pointies.

"B-Brilliant!" he said when it was seaworthy. Reaching over, he set it sailing into the puddle, and then shifted position, removing pocketsful of change, and flinging the copper pieces into a pile by his bum. With a *plink*, he placed the coins onto the boat, one at a time.

He reached under his jacket once again to remove more money and his hand brushed a folded-up pamphlet. He pulled it from his trousers and glanced at the cover. *Tíg An Oiléan* was printed on the front.

An impish chuckle escaped his lips. "I get to g-go to camp!" he said to his reflection in the puddle. Opening the pamphlet, he saw photos of the camp's buildings on Valencia Island off the west coast of Kerry. Horses in a stable posed for the camera as they chomped carrots. On the next page, kids who looked a bit like him were pictured holding their crafts.

Going to camp would give him a chance to be with other people like him, which is why he liked the Special Olympics. Maybe he'd make new friends who loved swimming, flowers and horses. Maybe his new chums would watch John Wayne films with him on the camp's big-screen telly while eating gummy worms.

He turned the pamphlet over to study the map on the back and pushed his glasses in place. He saw that Valencia Island was near Skellig Michael, an island named after his patron saint—Michael the Archangel—who helps folks beat the bad blokes. Skellig Michael looked like a mountaintop jutting out of the Atlantic. He heard that the tourists like to climb the slippery steps and visit the monastery ruins way up top there somewhere. Along the way, they see loads of lovely puffins nesting on the cliffs. And didn't Da say that Hollywood bigwigs might film the next *Star Wars* there? Maybe he could go to this place, as well.

Michael's ears picked up the sound of yelling. His eyes darted to the right where two boys were running toward him. One had on a blue bomber jacket, and the other was wearing a gray rain slicker.

"Hiya! I'm g-going to camp!" He waved to them, but they didn't look at all nice. Michael leaned away, frightened, but not fast enough. The lads stomped in his puddle, splashing water onto his special pamphlet.

"Oops! Sorry, yeh retard!" the one in the bomber jacket said.

As the lads legged it down the street, laughing, Michael used his sleeve to wipe the droplets away from his super special pamphlet.

"I d-d-don't like the R-word," he mumbled. Sadness sat on his slumped shoulders.

Some people called him slow and he didn't mind that too much. He knew that everyone's mind worked at different speeds. Granny's was slow; sometimes she'd forget she put bread in the toaster and it'd get all black and smoky. But some folks' minds worked quick-like. Coach Keanne was good with numbers; he always knew how many laps his swimmers had done and their times. John Wayne's mind worked fast as lightning when he drew his gun and fired at villians.

Sometimes people said Michael was not the full shilling, and he didn't like this too much, either. It meant he was missing something, but he wasn't. All his body parts were there the last time he checked. Dr. Callaghan said he had all of his brain, too, even though it was a bit slow.

Michael knew he was different from most folks, and Mammy drilled into him that "no two people are the same; that's what makes the world an interesting place."

Taking a calming deep breath, he looked at the kids on his pamphlet who had Down syndrome like himself. He kerplonked another coin onto his boat and looked around. Down the road, he spotted Miss Kate trotting toward him. A folded-up yellow umbrella swung from a strap at her wrist. The lads who toppled his boat ran past her. She threw Michael a wave and hustled to his side. He felt fine and good now.

"Hi Michael! Did those boys who just ran by yell something mean to you?"

"Y-yes." He tossed another coin onto his boat. It had an Irish harp stamped on it.

She squatted next to him. "Michael, people who say nasty things to others are bullies."

"M-m-most people are nice to m-me, but sometimes people say rough t'ings. Da says even John Wayne had people s-say mean t'ings to him."

"Yes, I'm sure he did. In *The Quiet Man*, his girlfriend's brother was real mean to him. They even got into a fistfight. Did you see that movie?"

"Indeed. Don't they sh-show it all the time on the telly for the tourists? I like his westerns better. They have cowboys. I like c-c-candy, too, but didn't I give it up for Lent? Including gummy worms?" He pointed to Miss Kate. "Did you give up c-candy for Lent?"

"No, I gave up muffins … and whiskey, for a while, I guess you could say." A smile tugged at her mouth.

"Da gives up the drink for f-forty days, and he doesn't cheat. But I cheated a few times, but only because I f-forgot. Honest."

Miss Kate giggled as she glanced at the front door. "Are your parents home, Michael? I wanted to talk to them about our business agreement. You know, about becoming my official gardener."

"Da is out, but Mammy is home. She's c-cooking a plaice fish I caught with m-my da. I like plaice, they have bugged-out eyes like a flounder." A fishy smell swam out their kitchen window and under his nose. Fish was all good and dandy to eat, but he liked meat best because that's what cowboys cooked at their campfires.

"Shall we go inside so I can visit with your mom before dinnertime?"

"Right."

Michael handed Miss Kate his pamphlet as he scooped up his orange boat and coins from the cold puddle. They headed to the door.

"What's this?" she asked, unfolding the glossy pages.

He jumped up and down. "I g-get to go to Mick O'Connell's camp!"

"Who's Mick O'Connell?"

"Wha?" He stopped and looked at her. "Everyone knows he's the f-famous Kerry footballer. Da says Micko could p-pull down the ball from the skies. And didn't he start a c-camp on Valencia Island where he's from? And doesn't he have a son like m-me?"

Miss Kate handed him the pamphlet after he fisted the coins into his pocket and placed his boat on the step. "That sounds like a heck of a deal, Michael."

"Wha'? Heck of a deal? Bejappers! You Yanks talk f-funny indeed!"

CHAPTER 32

No man is poor who has a Godly mother.
~ABRAHAM LINCOLN

Kate followed Michael though the red Georgian door of the Farley home. In gentlemanly fashion, he took her umbrella and coat, and put them in the foyer closet. She heard him yell, "Mammy, we have a g-guest! Hurry then!"

A petite woman rounded the corner, wiping her hands on a dish towel. Kate extended her own hand. "Hello, Mrs. Farley, I'm Kate McMahon, the new innkeeper."

"I was guessin' 'twas you. Call me Peggy. How lovely to meet yeh. T'anks a million for hirin' Michael. The lad said you even offered to pay him."

Michael interjected, "We have a 'business agreement'!"

Peggy smiled at her son and continued, "I was goin' to stop by the guesthouse and t'ank you, Kate, but you've beat me to the visit."

"Do you have a moment to talk about it?" Kate asked.

"Of course. Don't you have perfect timing? Our fish won't be done baking for a while yet, after Peter returns from work." Peggy saw that her son was tip-toeing into the kitchen. "Michael me lad, no sneakin' any more Club Oranges or other fizzy drinks while Mammy is busy." He turned and gave his mother a sheepish grin. "Why don't yeh straighten yer room since the rain is bucketing down and yeh can't play outside at the moment?"

140

Kate watched Michael remove the pamphlet from his pocket and place it atop the heater. Maybe to dry it? He waved to them as he went upstairs.

"Boy, he sure is excited about that camp," Kate said as she sat on the settee.

"He is, indeed. It's a place for people with mental disabilities. 'Twould be a spot of fun for Michael. But … Just so you know … he'd be missin' a few days of work when he goes."

"Oh, don't worry about that. It sounds like a fantastic opportunity for him."

Peggy went into the kitchen and returned with a tea tray. "Your manager, Catriona, is familiar with the camp on account she has a sister who lives on the island. She has graciously arranged for us to stay in her sister's spare cottage from time to time when Michael's there."

"Oh, isn't that thoughtful of Catriona to arrange that for you?"

" 'Tis indeed. She's a lovely woman … although she's away with the fairies from time to time."

Kate looked over her teacup and nodded. She was finding it easier now to overlook that aspect of Catriona's mental make-up.

"It's goin' to be hard for Peter and myself to be away from the lad. We haven't been parted much from him, you see."

"I've enjoyed getting to know him." Kate sipped her tea. "That son of yours toils so hard on the property—in all sorts of weather. In fact, I told him that I would rather hire him than someone who wouldn't do as fine a job."

"Aren't you a lovely lady for the offerin'? People with Down's value work, and it's imperative that they dwell in the possibilities. As you've probably noticed, Michael completes tasks reliably when they are part of his routine. However, because he's so careful, he's not very fast. Yet, the job will be done well."

Kate was impressed with the way this mother summarized what had to be the biggest challenge of her life.

Mrs. Farley straightened the sofa pillow at her side. "How often would you like him to help? I don't want the lad to be pesterin' you."

"He's not a pest, honestly. I told him he could work when he has a few minutes here and there, and isn't busy with his responsibilities at St. Columba's. How does that sound?"

Peggy's hazel eyes misted over. "Lovely. It's grand of you. T'anks a million."

"I should be the one doing the thanking. He makes time stand still and brings a youthful energy to the place."

Michael appeared, holding a collage of swimming pictures that smelled of glue and markers. He presented his gift to Kate by thrusting it toward her with short fingers in broad hands. "I m-made this for you with t'ings from my paper collection! I'm goin' to S-Special Olympics World Games … and c-camp!" His face was beaming. Turning to his mother he nudged up his glasses and said, "Pooka is outside. Can I go ride m-m-my bike, M-Mammy? Rain stopped."

"You may. Yes."

He bent over so his protruding lower lip brushed against his mam's cheek. Then he galloped out of the room. Kate noticed his Ben Franklin glasses were crooked, but he didn't care. He was living in the current of now.

"That lad! He gets so excited about t'ings. He became eligible to go to the World Games on account he won a gold medal in the finals last year. Ahh … That was so excitin'! There was an application process and then interviews. You see, the Committee doesn't just choose the best athletes; it fills the slots with candidates who are well rounded individuals and leaders in their communities. Me Michael … a leader! Fancy that!"

A wave of warmth spread through Kate's chest. She was surprised to find herself sharing the mother's pride.

"What a blessing he has been to us. He's a God-kissed child." The mother picked up a photo of their family, taken when Michael was a newborn. "Sure, didn't the very first blessing he brought me occur before he was even born? And that was to deepen my love for my wonderful husband.

"I can never tell you how afraid I was when we were first told that our baby would have Down syndrome. I doubted my ability to understand it and to cope. 'Twas overwhelming and I had too much of my own idea of what 'normal' and 'perfect' meant. And I was afraid Peter would want no part of it.

"But then my husband took me in his arms and said the most endearing words I've ever heard. He said: 'He is goin' to be exactly the person God wants him to be.'

"Didn't his sayin' those t'ings make me want to follow him to the ends of the earth?" Peggy traced a finger around the photo.

"But wait 'till I tell yeh the strange part—we had never discussed such a possibility before we were married. I've learned you never really know the full measure of the one you marry until you've weathered some storms." She replaced the picture on the table and smiled at Kate. "How did I get so lucky?"

Kate felt something shift inside her. "Hearing you say that makes me think perhaps luck *does* play a big part in our selection. Thank you for sharing that insight."

Maybe choosing Bryan was a stroke of bad luck, not just a result of her bad judgment. She felt like she'd just taken a baby step—deciding to stop beating herself up.

Kate fingered a swimming medal displayed on the end table. "And Michael's lucky to have you and Peter for his parents."

"Ah, no. Aren't Peter and I the lucky ones? He gives us so little strife and so much pleasure. But when he was a youngfella, he was forever breakin' out to explore the world. And 'twas fearless he was! Walkin' with our child was like trying to corral a kitten—we'd nearly have to hold him by the scruff of the neck, lest we lose the lad." The mother opened a window and looked about until she spotted her boy riding Duke safely on the street. Her coral-painted lips curved upward. "It's a grand t'ing altogether that he has a bit of independence now."

Kate could hear him hollering outside in his make-believe play: "Well, shine my spurs!" The women smiled in unison.

"I should warn you," the mother continued, "he's fiercely stubborn and has his share of temper tantrums—which I'm sure you've witnessed."

Kate set her cup down. "I've seen him hit his head and rock back and forth when he's upset about something."

"Right. We call that 'rockin' and rappin'." It's a sensory processing t'ing. It relieves stress, so they say."

"Well, so far we've managed just fine." The kitchen timer buzzed. "I'm sorry for disrupting your dinner preparations," Kate said as she took her coat and umbrella.

"Not at all! It was grand having a visit with you." Poking her head out the door, the mother called, "Michael me lad, I'd like you to see Miss Kate home and then come back straightaway." Turning back toward Kate, she said, "Cheerio, Kate. Welcome to Glasnevin! You're a lovely addition to the neighborhood."

Michael was straddling his bike, waiting to see her home. He smiled when he saw the swimming collage clutched in her hand. A soft rain started to fall again. She opened her umbrella and fiddled with it while a white Ford Ka drove by and turned down the road up ahead.

"I don't like Ultan F-F-Ferrian!" Michael said as he rapped his head.

"What's the matter, Michael?" she asked, but he didn't answer. He started droning a steady guttural wail.

"Hummmm..."

His mammy poked her head out the door. "Michael? Michael, what is it? What's got you now?"

"Don't go home, M-M-M-Miss Kate. Don't go home! Hum-mmm..."

Peggy rushed to him, took his hands in hers and pressed her forehead against his, saying, "That's my lad... that's my lad."

To Kate it looked like Peggy was transfusing her love into his brain. He relaxed his shoulders.

Peggy tuned toward her. "I'm sorry, Kate. I guess he doesn't want our visit to be over."

"No! No! I d-don't like...Ultan F-F-F..." He broke from his mammy's grip and grasped Kate's arm. "Don't g-go home!"

His mam said goodbye and led Michael, humming again, into the house.

Kate stood in the rain marveling at motherhood until she saw an upstairs light go on, illuminating cowboy curtains.

CHAPTER 33

Good Friday is the one day in the year
when you cannot buy a drink in Ireland.
But it doesn't stop people from trying.
~NIALL O'DOWD (*IRISH CENTRAL*)

It had been three years since Mark Kennedy had seen his brother; much too long for twins to be apart. But when an American boy falls in love with an Irish colleen, no ocean can keep them apart. And even though Mark missed his family back home, he had his own large clan in Glasnevin now, and he wouldn't change a thing.

He would love nothing more than to see his twin happily married, too, with a brood of his own. But he wasn't sure if that was what Joe wanted. And would he ever find the right woman? Maybe Joe's visit to Ireland would spark things up again between him and Kate. They would see soon enough.

At the Dublin Airport, near the baggage claim doors, he spied his "lesser half"—as they referred to each other. Joe was waving a ball cap in the air.

Mark pulled his wife's Ford Transit minibus to the curb. He hated navigating the big, honkin' 14-seater. After opening the driver's door, he jumped out and embraced his brother.

"Christ, you're gooood looking!" Mark said to his double.

Joe answered with: "Wow! Look at that svelte body. You must be working out!" He patted his own waist.

Mark took note of the extra poundage and said, "Better keep your sweater on when the women are around."

"You think that'll help?" Joe asked, as he hoisted his luggage into the back of the vehicle. "Maybe I'll get a little lucky while I'm over here."

As they left the airport, Joe said, "Hell, look at this rain. I was picturing good weather."

"I warned you! But the rain might just work in your favor, Romeo."

"Why? Because it's an excuse to keep my sweater on?"

"Yeah, but also wet weather means more chicks flocking to the pubs and sitting around the fire. They get all romantic. In fact, it was raining on the night I met Deirdre in O'Gara's Pub."

"I'm sure the whiskey and Guinness help in the romance department, too."

"It did that night, surely."

"You're starting to sound like an Irishman."

"Yeh don't fookin' say!"

For the rest of the drive home they talked about each of Mark's seven kids and Joe's job. Joe was excited that his company, Polaris, was doubling its research-and-development space, bringing hundreds of engineers and other professionals to Minnesota.

"Any chance you'd come home, Mark?"

"I am home. Although a part of me will always be back in Minnesota, you know that." Mark passed the condos in their neighborhood that were on the convent land. "I know the folks miss me like hell, but this is where I hang my heart now. I don't dare go back there for a visit without the kids, and it costs a flippin' fortune to take them along. At least we can send Mom and Dad plane tickets each year, and they love coming to Ireland."

"Yeah, but . . . I still don't get to see your handsome face often enough."

"I know. Well, here we are. And right there is Kate's new business."

Joe jerked his head around.

As soon as the red minibus was parked, several bodies descended on Joe like a swarm of honeybees. Deirdre threw her arms around his neck and kissed his cheek. Benjamin and Jack hugged him self-consciously, and took his luggage. The girls needled him with kisses and then led him into the house. As they headed toward the kitchen, Mark noticed a path of crushed cookie on the floor. His brother looked like Hansel being led by a passel of Gretels as they followed a trail of crumbs.

"Mmm ... something smells fantastic," the uncle stated when the heap found its way to their destination.

"Mammy's makin' fish stew since it's Good Friday and we can't have meat," Mary Margaret informed him.

"And the stew has cockles and mussels in it, just like the Molly Malone song. I thought that would be a nice Irish welcome for you." Deirdre thrust a twin toward her brother-in-law.

"Ah, yes ... I remember the Molly Malone statue downtown. Nice curves." The bachelor uncle sat at the table with the boy on his lap. "Now which twin are you?" Mark noticed that Joe grimaced at the Nutella on Gavin's fingers.

"Oo-mada-yanna-dada," the toddler answered.

"I think he's trying to say that you look like Da. They do that 'twin talk' t'ing. Granny said you and my da did that as well," Mary Kathryn explained, as she lifted the handle on the milk dispenser and filled her cup, dripping it on the floor. Mark saw Joe grimace again.

Little Murphy toddled into the kitchen from the bathroom, pulling up his pants. "Eew-potty-no-no-no-wanna-seeee?" Apparently Deirdre interpreted this as meaning something was amiss in the bathroom she had just cleaned. She went to investigate.

Mark grabbed two beers from the fridge. "I've got you a Guinness, Joe. Might as well start your Irish vacation right. *Sláinte!*"

"Cilantro! ... or whatever!" Joe took a sip. "Man, it's like magic on the tongue."

Gavin, still sitting on Joe's lap, seemed confused; he kept looking at his dad and then his matching uncle. "Dada? Dada?"

"Whaaaaaa. Whaaaaa!" Now Murphy started to cry, realizing there were two dadas in the room.

Deirdre came back into the kitchen. "What's all the fuss? And why are you two gentlemen having some of the black stuff when we're supposed to be fastin' on Good Friday? Aren't even the pubs closed today? Save your drinkin' for tomorrow, you big *amadáns!*"

Both men looked at Deirdre like bad little boys. Mark answered, "Well, we just wanted to celebrate our reunion. It's just one beer. I don't think God will strike us down." Deirdre answered him with The Look. He grabbed his bottle and that of his brother and dumped them in the sink.

"A pity to waste something so heavenly," Mark said to the sink as he watched the liquid swirl down the drain. The sink gurgled loudly as if belching a "thank you" in reply.

"But Mammy," Mary Margaret said, "your fish stew has a whole bottle of wine in it!" She punctuated this comment by staggering around the kitchen and then falling down. This got the twins to switch from crying to giggling.

"Quit actin' like an alco, Mary Margaret, you eejit!" said Mary Kathryn.

"A whole bottle of wine is in our food?" Mark asked as he turned to his wife and gave her a male version of The Look right back.

"That's a different matter altogether." Deirdre turned her back to him and began to sweep up biscuit crumbs for the second time that day.

He pinched her butt, thinking he was doing it on the sly.

"Eew! That's disgusting, Da!" Mary Margaret said, her eyes wide. "And parents aren't supposed to have sex on Good Friday! Sister Agnes said so."

"I might as well become a monk and move to Glendalough!" said Mark.

"Not me!" declared Joe.

"What's sex?" asked six-year-old Mary Cecelia.

"Ah, Mark Kennedy, aren't you bold? Look what you've started, man! Upsetting the chisellers! All because you wanted a Guinness," Deirdre said.

"That's not all I wanted."

Joe hid a smirk behind a twin's head.

Now Deirdre gave both of them The Look. She instructed the children: "Benjamin and Jack, go finish coloring the Easter eggs with the twins. Girls, come help me iron the Easter clothes and polish your shoes." Then looking at her husband and his twin she said, "Mark, why don't you show Joe to his room before Frick and Frack take maple syrup to it again. Dinner will be ready soon enough. And no sneaking Guinness up there, boyos."

When she was out of earshot Joe said, "Hell hath no fury like a woman who thinks she's the Lent police."

"No kidding!" replied Mark. "Talk about Irish temper! Deirdre is a boiling tea kettle constantly letting out steam." Then he added, "It's the only way she can keep the lid on her passion for me!"

"In your dreams, Stud!"

After the fish stew dinner (made with that whole bottle of wine!) Deirdre and the girls were occupied with baking a porter cake for Easter (made with a whole bottle of stout!), while the older boys cleaned the dishes.

The big twins took the little twins into the parlor and watched a soccer game on the telly. Within minutes Murphy and Gavin were in the throes of a wrestling match. Or was it a cuddle session? Their Easter-dyed fingers were wrapped around each other's bodies as they rolled around the carpet, making humming sounds.

"Do ya think we did that?" Joe asked.

"Mom was watching them when she was here and she said that we acted just like they do. That's probably why we freaked out so much when they separated us for kindergarten."

"Yeah. Weird. But we turned out okay."

Deirdre appeared at that moment and said, "I beg to differ." She smiled at Joe and wiped the dusting of flour off her shirt. "I just saw Morgan O'Gara drop Kate off. They went to the Passion Play at Christchurch. If you want to call on Kate you should go over now. Her quarters are in the back of the guesthouse. She'll hear you if you knock on the back door."

"I'd love to see her. I think I *will* stop by for just a minute."

"Before you go, I just wanted to say t'anks a million for all the gifts you brought the chisellers. Now you've done it. They won't be leavin' you alone." She got on her tiptoes and gave him a peck on his cheek.

Joe blushed and admitted, "Actually, Mom went shopping for me." He glanced at the twins who were covered with their blankies on the sofa now, tiny thumbs plugging their mouths. "Would you look at those two? This is the first peaceful moment in this house since we walked in the door."

CHAPTER 34

Beer is proof that God loves us and wants us to be happy.
~BENJAMIN FRANKLIN

Joe glanced out the side window as he zipped up his fleece jacket. He could see Kate's blond head as it bobbed around her illuminated apartment. Did her hair still smell like honeysuckle? And how would she greet him after all these years?

And then he thought he spied a dark figure crouched in the bushes along the brick of her home.

"What the hell?" he said out loud, rushing out the door.

By the time he had reached Kate's yard, he no longer saw anything suspicious. But he did hear something—gravel crushing, a dog barking and footsteps running. He followed the noise across the street and became disorientated in the dimness. *Where'd he go?*

Just when Joe thought he'd lost the trail, he spotted a male shape on the front lawn of the guesthouse. He ran toward the figure, grabbed hold of the offender's jacket and pulled him to the wet ground. The guy let out a surprised scream and the two bodies rolled around on the grass.

The Cobblestones' front light went on. Joe had the upper hand and was straddling the peeper at the moment the door opened.

"What's going on out here?"

He recognized Kate's voice, and then another, brighter, light flared on.

"Mark, is that you?" Her voice grew louder as she rushed toward them.

"Kate, it's me…Joe Kennedy. And I just saw this guy peeping into your windows." He heard her gasp.

The figure below Joe's body began to struggle and whimper. As he looked down at the Peeping Tom's face, he saw that the guy had Down syndrome. Joe quickly loosened his grip and rolled off him. "Oh, shit!"

Joe heard a car somewhere nearby—peeling away. He reached out toward the person he had just pinned to the ground and said, "Hey, sorry. I must have made a mistake." The younger man sat up and began to hit his head and make a droning noise.

"Michael, Michael…are you okay? It's me…Miss Kate." She bent over them. Joe felt her closeness before he saw her face. She quickly turned her back to Joe and began fussing over the victim, straightening the guy's glasses, which had gotten off-kilter in the scuffle. Then she took hold of the young man's arms and massaged his biceps so he'd stop assaulting himself. She put her forehead up to his ear and said, "It's okay Michael. You're not hurt, you're just frightened. This is my friend from America. He's Mr. Kennedy's look-alike twin. He didn't mean to frighten you. Let's get you home. I'll bet your parents don't know you're here so late at night."

"What was he doing here?" Joe asked. His heart was still racing.

A Dalmatian came up to them, panting.

Kate explained, "That's Pooka—the neighbor's dog—and Michael's my gardener." Pooka scampered to Michael and licked his tears. Joe noticed that the dog seemed to calm down the young man.

"This guy works here? In the dark?"

"Well, no…usually in the daylight."

"We have a b-business agreement," Michael stammered. "And I-I-I'm a sh-sheriff. The b-bad m-man had a g-gun."

Joe turned his palms up and shrugged. "A gun? What? I don't have a gun!" He looked at Kate. "What the hell is going on?"

153

Now Kate shrugged. "He was probably taking care of the flowers and pretending he's John Wayne. Would you mind walking him home with me? He lives just down the road."

She stood up and Joe got a good look at her in the lamplight. The years had been kind to her figure. Her lips were covered with a sparkly gloss. He sucked in his gut and yanked down his jacket. A vision of long-ago kisses flashed in his head.

"Of course I'll go with you. It's the least I could do. Christ! I feel like such an ass!"

"Don't s-say 'arse.' M-Mammy doesn't like that word. I don't like Ultan F-F-Ferrian."

They turned toward O'Gara's and the church. The moonlight guided them. Joe glanced at Kate as she handed him a white bike. Their hands brushed as he took the handlebars from her.

"What is he saying?" Joe asked.

"That he doesn't want you to swear."

"I got that. I meant the other thing."

"I don't know. Sometimes it's hard to understand him when he's upset." Then Kate looked at Michael and ruffled his hair. "Michael, thanks for being the neighborhood sheriff. But you should only do your cowboy business when it's daytime."

"Sheriffs help p-people."

"Yes, Michael. But only help them when it's light out. Safety comes first." She gave him a stern smile.

They delivered Michael to his home and explained everything to his parents, who said that Michael had been upset the whole evening and they thought he had finally fallen asleep. Apparently he sneaked out for some strange reason.

"I'm awfully sorry," Joe said to the parents repeatedly.

Peter Farley slapped him on the shoulder as they were leaving. "Indeed, aren't we thankful havin' him safe at home? I'll add another lock to the doors tomorrow."

Peggy promised Michael a warm bath as they bid goodnight.

Pooka escorted them on their short walk back to the guesthouse. When they arrived safely, the dog gave a contented bark and then scuttled toward the home across the street. A soft rain was beginning to fall again.

"It's good to see you, Kate. You haven't changed—I didn't get to tell you this earlier because of all the commotion."

"It's good to see you, too. Can you come in? I'd love to give you a tour of my new place."

"I'd appreciate a tour. And I promise I won't attack you like I did that poor guy. God...I can't believe I assaulted a kid with Down's. I feel like such a thug." Joe kicked off his mud-caked Nikes and left them on the doorstep.

"Don't be so hard on yourself, Joe. It was an honest mistake. You were just trying to be like John Wayne." She ushered him in, took his coat, and laid it on a chair.

"Yeah, but still...I can't shake the notion that I saw someone looking into your windows; someone taller, leaner and faster than your gardener."

Kate shuddered. "Really?"

The last thing he wanted to do was upset her. He felt like kicking himself for the second time that evening. "Well, it was dark. I might have imagined it. You know...jet lag." Joe went up to the fireplace and leaned on the mantel, trying to corral his thoughts. He decided that he'd talk to his brother about it later. "How about if I check things out around the place and then make us a fire?"

"That sounds great. It would help me relax. I'm feeling a little shaky." She turned toward the hearth and he put a protective arm around her shoulders. She settled in to his chest and slipped an arm around his waist. Tilting her face upward, she flashed that smile that had won his heart when they were just 19. Then she made him an offer he couldn't refuse.

"Would you like a Guinness? I think our nerves could use one."

"Oh man! I'd love one! But don't tell Deirdre. It's midnight some-where, right?"

CHAPTER 35

The Pooka...
Is very mischievous and combines play with work.
Shakespeare, it is said, used him as the model for Puck.
~JOAN LARSON KELLY (*IRISH WIT AND WISDOM*)

Ultan Ferrian drove slowly by The Cobblestones one more time after he had been chased off, and didn't like what he saw. It was raining, and his wipers left streaks on the windscreen, but he could still see well enough—and the scene made him cheesed off. Standing by the front door was Kate with a tall man. It was obvious she was flirting with the wanker. When he saw the ball-bag take off his shoes, and go into her home at this late hour, he decided he might as well go back to his kip, since she was probably going to entertain the lout all night. All women were scrubbers like his mother.

Who was he anyway? The man looked familiar. He knew it would come to him sooner or later. He lit a Pall Mall and turned on SPIN 103.8. He loved the smoky voice of DJ, Nikki Hayes. But, he hated the song she was playing right now: *Your Body* by Christina Aguilera. It made him frustrated.

"The neighbor!" Ferrian said out loud after he took a pull off his cigarette. *That's who that little vixen was flashing her bedroom eyes at... her bloody neighbor! The one whose house is full of snot-nosed kids? Aren't they a fair pair of cheaters!* His moral outrage put him in a black humor altogether.

Ferrian headed north to Ballymun. He smoked the cigarette down to a stabber and then tossed it out the window. What a shite day it had turned out to be.

When he got to the lift in his apartment building, he whacked the "up" button a dozen times. He couldn't have his spot of fun because she had invited that pain-in-the-hole into her place.

Ferrian entered his flat, took off his mucky runners and went to his wardrobe. He dug around and eventually uprooted the box from the clutter in the back. Reaching into the pocket of his charcoal hoodie he removed his Taser M18L gun, but he had only one cartridge in his pocket. He must have lost the other one tonight, but that didn't matter. Before putting these things back into their hiding place he kissed his piece and said, "Better luck next time, Baby!"

He settled on the sofa, fished his phone from his pocket and looked at one of the frames. "*Tá tú iontach álainn,*" he said with a raspy voice. It was a photo of Kate; one he had snapped tonight, while peeking in her bedroom window. It was an action shot. She was removing her jacket and her breasts were pushed against her t-shirt as she pulled her arms through the sleeves.

Yes, amazingly beautiful.

He decided to sketch the photo with his charcoals and add it to his collection. If he couldn't have Kate in the flesh tonight, he'd have her in his creative mind. To help with the details of her face, he grabbed the packet of group-shots that he acquired from her front step. A few days ago he was on his hunkers behind a bush at The Cobblestones. When he looked around, he noticed an envelope sticking out from under the door mat. It had "Kate" written across it, and when he tore it open, he found some photos and a note which read: *Luke wanted me to tell you that he was called back home to California for a family emergency. He will phone you when he gets back to Dublin. Here are some pictures I took of you and your friends at Power's Pub. Enjoy, Buck.*

Ever since he'd nicked that envelope, Ferrian kept saying to himself, "Fuck Buck!" and wondering who in the hell this Luke was. And he still hadn't figured out where *Mister* McMahon had gotten to. Christ, he'd have to hire Sherlock Fookin' Holmes to solve these bloody mysteries.

For two hours he worked away at the table, lost in his art and lost in time. He was amazed when he glanced at the clock on his phone and saw that it was almost midnight. But there was one more sketch he wanted to produce: an image of that annoyin' Dalmatian. He wondered who owned the dog. He knew her name was *Pooka* because he had heard that gacky-looking fella call her that.

Jaysus, I'd like to eat the head off that dog! He recalled from one of his classes that the pooka was a curse to travelers because it would swoop them up onto its back and throw them into a muddy ditch or boghole. And tonight, after he got run off of Kate's property, didn't that bloody Dalmatian nip at his heels all the way to the car? The damn thing pursued him right into the murky furrow along the Royal Canal.

He held up the image he had created. It was very different from the typical portrayals of Dalmatians. It featured an ominous being that was more black than white, and its fur had a jagged texture that would cut the hand that braved petting it. It had razor-sharp claws and long fangs. Drool was dripping from its mouth. Ferrian had one more detail he wanted to add to the beast. He reached into his bag and grabbed yellow and red pencils—for the evil eyes. When he was satisfied with the illustration, he tacked it up onto his wall alongside the ones of Kate. He chose one from the display and slipped it into a red folder. Someday he'd show that doxie his *many* talents.

He grabbed a bag of crisps and pulled the computer out of his duffle bag. He had an insatiable appetite for porn and it took more and more of it to fill his empty places. The free stuff wasn't doing it for him anymore. Thanks to the money he got off that dealer, he now had more access to harder-core stimulation.

The material was potent and addictive as crack cocaine. As he sat in the darkened room he could feel his pulse race, and his sweaty hands slipped off the computer keys.

CHAPTER 36

Keep the faith!

~VINCE FLYNN

Kate tossed and turned in bed all night. She felt sorry for poor Michael and for Joe, too. They were both trying to play the gallant hero. And she couldn't shake a feeling of impending doom—a premonition or something. Was Joe just covering up for his embarrassing mistake or did he really think there had been a Peeping Tom? His attempts at reassuring her weren't very convincing. He made her promise to keep her cellphone by her bed, and when they kissed goodnight neither one closed their eyes. Sleep evaded her even when she tried to recapture the safety of his arms around her. And oddly enough, in the heaviness of her mind, thoughts of Luke kept creeping in.

At 4:18 a.m. she gave up and pulled on her robe. Perhaps chamomile tea would offer one more chance to fall asleep. While the kettle was boiling, she forced herself to dwell on positive thoughts. *Won't Terry and Myrna be excited when our surprise is revealed at the pub tonight?*

She stepped outside to see if *The Irish Times* had arrived. Bending down, she caught sight of a black and yellow object under the bushes. She quickly stepped onto the dewy ground and grabbed the piece of litter. While she waited for her tea to steep, she looked at the plastic thing in her hand. It looked like an ink cartridge with a lightning bolt logo stamped on it.

"Weird," she said, placing it in the junk drawer. Maybe it had fallen out of Michael's cinchsack. One of his collectibles.

When the water in her cup turned honey-colored, she carried her tea and newspaper back to bed. She put her things on the nightstand and slid under the floral sheets. *Will I ever get used to sleeping alone?* She tried to read, but her whacked-out mind wouldn't let her concentrate. Was she experiencing pre-opening jitters? She didn't think so; in fact, she was feeling over-prepared for Monday.

But she needed to keep her focus on her business. She found herself wishing Joe Kennedy's resurgence wouldn't muddle the picture.

Their reunion brought something else to the surface. Some long ago submerged guilt. In her youthful self-centeredness she had stepped on his feelings when her heart skipped over to Bryan. And she felt even worse when he told her last night that he had slipped into a back pew at Bryan's funeral. Today will be interesting. They had made a date to go fishing. Maybe, just maybe, some part of her *was* ready for a romance. But how could she ever trust a man again? Perhaps she could flirt with the thought of taking a baby step in that direction.

Kate took a sip of her tea and then clanked the cup on its saucer. She snuggled further into the bed and pulled the sheets over her head, mumbling, "Argh … What's a girl with trust issues to do?"

She could hear her mother's voice: *Just keep your options open … and not your legs!* And her friend Rose, back in Minnesota, reminding her to be alert and watch for red flags. And then there was Peggy Farley's suggestion that luck plays a big part in the selection process.

She popped her head out from under the eiderdown, and her eyes fell on the framed photo of George Clooney. Looking at the handsome devil made her think about the whole Tullahought incident. She took another sip of tea, threw down the newspaper and reached for her Vince Flynn novel. Opening the cover, she removed the article about Clooney's visit to Tullahought that Luke O'Brien had written. She had put it there for safekeeping. She must have read the thing a dozen times. As she reread the story this time it made her heart race. Not because of the hunky actor who was showcased in the article, but because of the hunky journalist who had written it, and the mystery of why he hadn't called.

A few times she had thought about calling him, but her pride and those trust issues got in the way. Part of her hoped that someday she'd have the opportunity to see him in person—but just to read him the riot act.

After three dry years, she now had two men dancing in her head. Kate listened to the drizzle hitting the windowpane.

Dang! ... now the thought of a romance got her all "hot and bothered." Or could this be a hot flash? Geez! Could she be going through perimenopause at 36? If so, she'd better hurry up and get on with life.

CHAPTER 37

There are finer fish in the sea than have ever been caught.

~IRISH PROVERB

Kate glanced over at Joe as they stood a few feet apart in the surf. She wondered if he, too, was reminded of all those lazy days they had spent on the Minnesota lakes, hauling in their fair share of walleye, northern pike, perch—and even a muskie once. His family had the muskie mounted for his birthday present that year.

A wave of guilt washed over her reverie. It was on one of those fishing dates that he had hinted at a proposal. And shortly after that, Kate had tossed a wet blanket on his plans when she broke the news that she had fallen in love with Bryan.

As if Joe were reading her thoughts, he said, "You know, Kate, you broke my heart when you left me for that asshole."

"Yep, you're right. He was 'nothing but an arsehole with legs'. And I can assure you I'm still paying for that decision." Kate set her shoulders and prepared to take another baby step. "Can you forgive me, Joe?"

"It took me a while to get over it. Maybe that's why I never settled down, but don't think I stopped noticing the other fish in the sea."

"I got a bite!" she exclaimed as she set the hook and started to reel in. She saw Joe wedge the handle of his rod between some granite boulders and then grab the net.

"That a girl. Nice 'n easy does it," she heard him say.

Kate clenched her teeth as she watched the tip of her pole curve toward the water's surface. Her heart was banging in her chest.

"You got it! You got it!" he said, moving closer. But at that moment the fish decided it didn't like this tug-of-war and took her line out farther.

"Oh, no!" she exclaimed over the *zzzzzz* sound of her stubborn fishing line. She kept turning the handle on the reel and pulling the rod up with all her might. She ran down the strand a few yards and then back.

"You're doing great with that monster. He'll get tired and then you can land him."

"Him? I think this is a female. I'm calling her Nessie," she said between grunts and more sprints.

Joe laughed. "I'd say you're both fighters. Man, you're in great shape."

After what seemed like hours, the creature must have tuckered out. Kate could feel the surrender on the other end of the line. She slid her eyes in Joe's direction and shouted, "You never answered my question ... Can you forgive me?"

"Oh, sure ... no problem."

After all the psychological energy it took for her to ask, she was taken back by his easy answer. *That's a man for you. He just wants to rush through the emotional steps.* Even so, she felt welcome relief and a sense of possibility for their future. Strength returned to her arms. "Ready or not, here she comes."

Joe positioned the net and she tugged it in, feeling empathy for her worthy opponent.

"Oh, my God!" she said, looking at Nessie.

"I think I'm gonna need gloves for this one."

An oldtimer combing the beach approached them. "That's a lovely Tope shark you've gotten yerself. A female, I'd guess, because they tend to be loners." After he helped them get it off the rig, they snapped a few pictures and Kate felt better when they released it back into the sea. Then he told them, "Must be 50 pounds or so.

Good t'ing your spool was loaded with heavy line because those sharks, they clamp down like pit bulls."

An hour later the anglers were enjoying a hurried picnic on the beach before they had to be back in Glasnevin for the gathering at O'Gara's. They were thankful the weather had held. A light sea breeze charged the air with a taste of salt. Crabs scampered sideways into crevices in the nearby boulders. A couple of kayaks skimmed along the shore. She scooted closer to Joe and pointed out the five islands of Skerries. "That one is St. Patrick's Island, where he landed to begin his mission." Joe moved closer to look over her shoulder. She could feel his breath on her neck and it made her tingle with expectation. Her hair blew across her face and he brushed it behind an ear, letting his fingertips linger on her cheek.

"The look on your face when you reeled in that thing was priceless," He said as he pulled her in for a kiss. His lips tasted like chocolate and an old familiar warmth rolled over her like the surf on the sand. *Is this what I want?*

He was kissing her more urgently now and she tried to just live in the moment. Time was running against her. They didn't have much time here on the beach and his time here in Ireland would soon be over. But at her age she needed to sprint toward her long term goal.

She offered no resistance when he guided her downward onto the blanket. Was she just lonely or were hormones hijacking her determination to concentrate on business? She enjoyed spending time with him, but did she know this new Joe well enough to get involved again? She wanted to kick herself for being too willing to trust, but she was having too much fun rolling around on the blanket. However, the spell was broken somewhat when her hand came to rest on his beer gut. He was wearing a sweater last night so she hadn't noticed it then. *Maybe I can overlook this in order to have what Deirdre has.*

When they were both out of breath, she raised up on an elbow and searched his eyes. "You know, it wasn't the right time for us back then, but as they say ... 'For everything there is a season.'"

He smiled. "We can give it another try ... if you'll come home, Kate."

"Whoa ... I just got here. And we need time to get reacquainted."

Joe scrambled to his feet. "I'm not asking for a commitment, ya know, but I'm only here a few more days."

Kate began collecting their things. "Well, let's make good use of the time."

As they loaded the van, she struggled to change the subject. "Um ... I can't wait to share our fish tale with Michael Farley and his dad. It was so nice of them to loan us their equipment and tell us how to find their good-luck spot." She reapplied her lip gloss. "I hope Michael will be out in my garden when we get back so I can show him the pictures right away."

Joe took a long, slow swig of Pepsi, his eyes focused on hers. "I can't believe you hire that kid to do your gardening."

She stiffened. "Why's that?"

"Well, you know ... he's ... slow." He took another sip. "He's mentally slow and he's physically slow. I'm a business guy, and in the business world, hiring a disabled person doesn't always make sense."

She crossed her arms to reel in her patience. "Well, I've been in business for about ten years myself, and I've learned to hire people I can count on. You'd change your mind if you got to know him."

Joe shrugged with a smile.

Heading south on Strand Street, Kate was impressed with how well Joe did driving on the left side of the road. Eventually she would have to learn, but since she lived near a bus line, there was no rush.

They were quiet until they passed the iconic Ardgillan Castle, a hidden gem where tea parties, weddings and rock concerts are held. Joe gave a long whistle.

"See ... you're being enticed by the charms of Ireland, too."

"Ya, well, I could never live here, though."

His words hung in the air between them.

When Malahide Castle loomed ahead of them, he whistled again. "It's almost as big as this flippin' van." He tapped the steering wheel.

"I don't know how Deirdre can stand driving this monstrosity on these narrow roads."

"I suppose it's the only thing nine people fit into. If they have any more children, they'll have to get a bus," she laughed.

"Geez, they should learn to control themselves better. For Pete's sake, haven't they heard about birth control?"

"I rather imagine they have," Kate bristled. "Anyway, it's nice of you to supervise their bedroom activities. Maybe you should write it all down for them before you leave."

"When did you get so sarcastic?"

"Seriously, they have such a great bunch of kids. Do you know how lucky Mark and Deirdre are to be parents? How lucky you are to be an uncle? I'll never have nieces and nephews."

"Yeah, they're great kids, but they shouldn't have pumped out such a big litter."

"Oh really? Which ones do you think they should send back?"

"Um…Well, I'm just sayin'…" They drove in a heavy silence for a stretch, and then he added, "I'm thinking of the financial aspect of it all; kids cost a shitload of money."

"Well, Mark is going to be shocked when he discovers that!" She laughed at her own joke. *Maybe Deirdre was right. Maybe he's been a bachelor too long.* "I believe Mark is investing in things that matter."

As the tension stretched between them, Kate glanced out the van window and saw children playing in the Dublin suburb they were now passing. She thought about something Deirdre once said: that raising a big family was more than just multiplying the hard work and the cost and the stress—It's also multiplying the rewards—the sources of love in your life.

It was Joe who broke the silence again. "You know, Kate, you've changed. You seem a lot more assertive and you never used to be so touchy." His tone softened as he added, "I guess it's not surprising, with all the shit you've been through."

Have I really been too touchy? After all, he did forgive me.

They pulled into the Kennedy's drive and began unloading the huge vehicle.

"Well, I guess I'll be seeing you at the gathering tonight at O'Gara's, and maybe after that … we could sit by your fire again."

She smiled when his lips brushed her forehead. "And maybe we could go for a run while you're here? I remember you used to jog a little back in college."

"Oh God, I gave that up years ago. You should, too. It's bad for the knees, ya know." He removed the fishing equipment from the two carseats. "I get my exercise these days from lugging around a tackle box and rod. At night, I move my muscles by filling out spreadsheets and answering emails." He slammed the car door and grinned. "I think you runners are crazy."

Kate slammed her door, too.

CHAPTER 38

*Sex appeal is fifty percent what you've got
and fifty percent what people think you've got.*

~SOPHIA LOREN

O'Gara's Pub was warm and welcoming that night, especially after a brisk walk in the rain. A fire crackled in the fireplace and to add to the ambiance some candles were lit here and there. As Kate waited at a table, she smelled roasted chicken with rosemary, shepherd's pie and salmon. Laughter and the clinking of glasses provided happy background noise.

"Catriona, over here!" Kate called, as she spotted her manager standing next to the antique shillelagh hanging by the entrance. She had heard the wooden club was made by Dano's Great-grandpa Culligan. He kept the weapon near the door in case a hooligan needed a whack.

As Catriona plopped onto a low stool and wriggled out of her rain slicker, Kate said, "Thanks again for making tonight possible."

"I can't be takin' all the credit. 'Tis goin' to be a grand evening altogether." Catriona leaned over and, to Kate's surprise, gave her a pat on the shoulder.

Kate sniffed the air around them. "My, you smell nice, like that Tahitian body oil again."

Catriona blushed. " 'Tis Declan's fav ..." She put a hand up to her cheek and let the sentence hang.

Kate smiled inwardly. Myrna had mentioned that Dr. Roddy had given Catriona a bit of homework at her last appointment. She wasn't to speak of Declan at all on Saturdays. And this was Holy Saturday. *Good for her.*

"Well now …" Kate said, "I think everything is set for the Rileys' surprise. I've been talking to their son John and he said that Terry and Myrna don't suspect a thing."

Catriona bounced on her stool. "I get so excited thinkin' about it! I'm shakin' like a chicken. Oh, shhhh … here come Terry and Myrna."

"We're over here!" Kate yelled with a wave of her hand. The Kennedys blew into the pub and headed to their table too. Kate scooted over to make room for Joe, but he took a seat at the other end of the table.

Catriona peered at Kate and then at Joe with raised eyebrows. "How was the fishin' this afternoon?" she asked.

Kate reached for her phone. "Um … good. I caught the Loch Ness Monster. Here, look … We took a few photos before we let her go."

Dano's sister, Kelly O'Gara, appeared at their side to ready the table with serviettes—or "napkins," as the Yanks called them. She sported a green Jameson apron, which couldn't hide her Sophia Loren-type figure.

Kate said, "Kelly, I saw you in the Passion Play yesterday. You're a talented actress—a convincing Mary Magdalene." She noticed that Joe's eyes snapped up from the photos of the shark.

"T'anks a million," Kelly said, flinging her curly black hair behind a shoulder. Kate caught Joe casting a covert glance at Kelly's curves and cleavage. She felt a heaviness well up in her own chest.

When the barmaid bent down to set a coaster beside Joe, he sat up straight, pushed the phone back at Kate, and said, "So you're an actress, Kelly?"

"I am. A starvin' actress, so you could say. I mostly work in theater promotion these days. Are the lot of you ready for a drink?"

"Some more than others," Deirdre said smiling at Mark and Joe.

"Thank God Lent's over! Now we can drink in front of the Beer Police!" Mark elbowed his brother, startling him out of his visual groping.

Kate couldn't blame Joe for being enchanted by the lovely actress-barmaid who had baited him by just being on the premises, but she was beginning to identify with that shark. Caught and released. *Did that romp on the beach mean nothing? We'll have to address it when he comes over later.*

Deirdre leaned into the group. "We'll be up 'til the crack of dawn, fillin' and hidin' the Easter baskets. Hopefully this year we won't forget where we put 'em, like last year."

"We never did find Benjamin's basket until mid-summer—in the fuel shed," Mark admitted. "The chocolate bunny was a melted mess."

"And it smelled of petrol," added Deirdre.

Myrna looked off into the distance. "It will be a quiet holiday for us again this year; mostly just Terry, Pooka and myself. Stephen and his kids will be at his in-laws. John will be spending half the day with his friends and then joining us later. And well, of course, we won't see Helen. It's been t'ree years now since she moved to Australia, so it has. If it weren't for the computer we'd have forgotten what she looked like."

Kate's eyes met Catriona's. Kate reached into her bag and removed her phone again, sent a quick text, and gave Catriona a thumb's up. The surprise was ready.

Terry noticed the exchange. "What shenanigans are you ladies up to?"

"Ah, nothin'," Catriona lied.

The door to the pub opened and ol' man Poppy Flynn shuffled in.

"Hiya, Poppy! Won't you be joinin' us?" Terry said.

"Ah, now ... That would be lovely." He trudged over in a pair of shoes that had to be older than the shillelagh on the wall. The heavy, wooden heels made a loud scraping sound on the oak floor.

"He can have my chair," Joe said. "I'm going up to the bar." Kate watched as Joe picked a stool near the beer pulls. It just so happened that Kelly was standing there building pints of Guinness.

She heard Kelly explain to Joe, "Me da used to say, 'Remember, the profit is in the foam.'"

Kate swallowed her irritation with a gulp of chardonnay and shifted her attention. "Don't you look handsome, Poppy, in your blue jumper?"

Poppy looked into the Harp Irish Lager mirror hanging near their table. He smoothed his thick grey hair with a hand flecked with liver spots. "I do, yes. I get better lookin' each day. I'm hopin' to be around to see meself tomorrow."

Kate's phone was vibrating. She quickly read the text, looked at Catriona, and held up one finger.

A minute later the rear door was opened by John Riley. He was holding his car keys and a cellphone. The young lady at his side walked stealthily to the back bar and spoke to Kelly. The barmaid removed her apron and tied it around the other woman while they both smothered giggles. Then Kelly handed her a tray full of pints.

Kate's heart pounded as the young lady in the borrowed apron approached their table. A smile as bright as a turf fire lit the lass's face as she stood behind Terry and placed a Guinness in front of him. "A pint of the black stuff fer you, mate!" she said with an exaggerated accent from Down Under.

"I didn't order a..." Terry's words evaporated as he looked up, gobsmacked. His eyes bugged out.

Myrna jumped with a yelp. "Jaysus, Mary and Holy St. Joseph! My baby!... Is it really yourself?" She rushed to her daughter.

"I don't believe it!" Terry exclaimed, as he shot to his feet and enveloped both wife and daughter in his arms. "Where in the world did you come from, pet?"

"From Australia, of course! I only just got here." Helen brushed the chestnut fringe off her forehead, as other patrons encircled them.

"What's goin' on? Is the pub on fire?" A befuddled Poppy Flynn asked over the buzz of excitement.

Catriona turned to Kate. "We did good, Kate. You're the kipper's knickers."

Poppy yelled, "If the bloody pub's on fire don't you bowsies forget to grab the whiskey!"

"Whisht, ol' man! Don't be daft! 'Tis a surprise! Helen Riley is home from Australia," Catriona explained.

Terry stepped back to the table. "Catriona! We can't t'ank you enough. We hear Helen's visit is your doin'."

"And it'll be a happy Easter after all, so it will," Myrna added. She turned to her husband and said, "Terry, we'd best rush to Superquinn for a ham unless you want toast and marmalade for Easter dinner tomorrow."

"Wait 'til I tell yeh..." Catriona said, looking at the Riley clan. "You'll be eatin' dinner at my home. Haven't I gotten everyt'ing ready?"

A hush settled around the table. Deirdre whispered to Kate, "Having guests into her home is it? Sure, she hasn't done that since Declan's demise."

Kate's gaze fell on Catriona. *Maybe she's taken a baby step.*

Myrna looked confused. "You're inviting us for Easter dinner? But you've done so much already. Helen's round-trip ticket was too dear."

Helen jumped onto a chair, rising above their heads. "Listen up now..." She paused, looking at the corner where Joe and Kelly were giggling. Kelly muffled her noise with a hand while Joe threw Kate an embarassed glance. "Ma and Da, there's more to your surprise. 'Twas a *one-way* ticket Catriona bought for me. I'm not just here on holiday. Kate has offered me a job at The Cobblestones."

"Home to stay is it?" Terry asked, putting an arm around his speechless wife. Helen nodded, wiping away a tear.

Poppy Flynn took a big gulp of his Jameson and then held up his tumbler. "This is cause for a grand celebration! How about a singsong?"

172

"Oh please don't ask Kate to sing. Everyone will make a mad dash out of the pub … no offense, dear," Deirdre said.

"None taken. Singing is not one of my talents. Just ask George Clooney."

To get the chortling crowd's attention, Helen said, "I'd like to sing one of my favorites from Down Under, if you don't mind." The pub erupted in whoops and hollers. "And I dedicate this to Catriona and Kate for getting me back to Dublin." In an engaging alto, she sang *Waltzing Matilda* with gusto.

Helen had a voice as melodious as the harp that Brian Boru plucked at Killaloe. At a nearby table, several Aussies were going mad. One approached Kelly and ordered a drink "for the sweet colleen who sings like a sheila."

Dano hastened to Helen from behind the bar. "You still have that gift, lass."

"T'anks, Mr. O'Gara. In Australia I lifeguarded at the beach during the day, I coached a secondary swim team and I moonlighted by singing for my beer money."

Poppy's ears perked up. "Ah, to be a young fella at one of those beaches. Wouldn't it be lovely to see this nice set of vocal cords in swim togs?"

"Bugger off, Poppy! That's my baby girl you're speakin' of," Terry admonished. "If you can't shut yer gob, how about if you sing a song for my princess?" Terry held up his pint.

"Aye. I'll give it a go." Poppy paused to collect his thoughts. "As ye know, most Irish songs have one of the following themes: fightin', feckin', seafarin', or homesickness. I t'ink I have just the one up here in me noggin." He tapped his head and cleared his coarse throat. "How about one from this area of Dublin, *The Auld Triangle*?" Catriona and the other patrons in the bar nodded their heads or said, "Ah, yes."

Poppy took another gulp of whiskey. "Let me tell the tourists about this piece." He pointed to Joe and the Aussies. "*The Auld Triangle* was written to introduce Brendan Behan's play called *The Quare*

Fellow. It's about an inmate at Mountjoy Prison on the day he is set to be executed. And did yeh know, Behan himself was incarcerated there because of his IRA activities. The prison lies near here on the Royal Canal." He pointed south. "And on the path along the waters is a statue of yer man Behan." Poppy wet his whistle and began to sing.

A hungry feeling came o'er me stealing . . .

When the song was finished, Helen went up to him and said, "Mr. Flynn, t'anks for singin' that lovely song for my homecomin.'"

"Not at all. But now that you're a grown lass, you can be callin' me Poppy." With a wink to the young lady he instructed, "Now put your lips up to my cheek and say 'Poppy' five times!"

CHλpᴄᴇʀ 39

My husband's a handsome hunk, but wait 'til I tell you—
He's SMOKING HOT when he's scrubbing pans
or changing diapers… shirtless!

~KATHRYN MACDONALD SCHNEEMAN

It was times like this glorious Easter morning that made all the hard work and sacrifice worth it. Deirdre glanced at the chisellers who were strewn across the room like dice on a game board. They were still in their jammies, and baskets and candy wrappers littered the floor. From where she lounged, she could read contentment on their wee mugs. There hadn't been one row so far. "'Tis a proud mam I am," she said to her husband. Mark smiled at her over his newspaper.

Life was grand. Sure, the house was rarely tidy, but the children were healthy and happy. Those were the important things. And didn't she have the best husband in the whole world? Aye, at times he could be the right eejit, but they still had a fierce love.

Deirdre reached over for Mark's hand, accidentally grazing his thigh. She chided herself because now he'd think she was in a frisky mood.

Mark put *The Irish Times* down and sure enough, he whispered in her ear, "Hey, Mrs. Easter Bunny, I have a fire in my loins. Wanna hop upstairs for a quickie?"

"You *amadán*! Do you t'ink I have the time for that? Is the Easter dinner goin' to cook itself?"

He gave her a playful look. "I see you're wearing Old Ironsides."

Mark liked to name her sleepwear. The set she was wearing had an obstacle course of buttons and snaps. It was very modest. That's why she was sporting it on a morning when family was about. Mark much preferred a navy blue slip he had dubbed Monica Lewinsky. And then there was her favorite plaid flannel gown which started out nobly as Mary Queen of Scots, but morphed into Mary Queen of Spots when it was splattered with a few drops of paint. It was so comfy that she couldn't give up on it, so she gave it a royal bleaching. That didn't go too well. Now the plaid had big white clouds dominating it. Mark christened it anew: Very Clean of Spots.

"Mammy, can I finish my Cadbury bunny for breakfast?" It was ten-year-old Mary Margaret asking.

Oh blessed interruption. "Sure, luv. Eat one of your dyed eggs first."

Deirdre poured another cup of Bewley's from her granny's repaired teapot. She looked at the cracks on the lid and spout that had been glued. Mark had been nervous, thinking she'd get her Irish up, because the teapot broke during his watch. But truth be told, she cherished it even more with these imperfections because more history had been added. Like the history recorded in her nightgowns.

Joe entered the room and eased into a chair. Indeed, he looked like he was polluted last night. At 2:21 a.m., Mary Cecelia had come to their bedside and poked her on the arm like a woodpecker with ADHD, saying, "Mammy, Mammy, I saw the Easter Bunny. I did, I did, I did!" After questioning the child, Deirdre realized that she had seen her Uncle Joe's shadow tip-toeing down the hall, sneaking in late like a delinquent teenager.

"Mary Cecelia, tell Uncle Joe about how you saw the Easter Bunny last night."

By the look on his face, Joe was only half-listening as she blathered. "... and then he left you a basket full of cigars and Guinness, Uncle Joe. I saw it by your door when I was followin' him. When he went into your room, I ran to Mammy and Da's bed to tell them."

She threw her uncle a broad smile devoid of its two front teeth, but Joe didn't respond.

Mark patted his daughter on the shoulder. "You're a very lucky girl to have seen the bunny."

Deirdre handed her brother-in-law some of Mark's coffee. "Here, you look like you could use a spot of something strong before you break into that Guinness. Is it a sore head you have?"

He took a big gulp and said, "Yes, but it was worth it." Choosing a purple hard-boiled egg from one of the twins' baskets, he rapped it on the end table and then rolled it underneath his palm. Deirdre watched as he ate it and then started opening the foil from a chocolate Cadbury egg. *The last thing his wide girth needs is that yolk filling made of glucose.* As if he could read her mind, he padded into the kitchen and rummaged through the fruit basket, in search of a pear that was free of bite marks. Finding one, he rubbed the fruit on the robe he borrowed from Mark. With his other hand, he scratched his buttocks.

"Jeepers, Joe," Deirdre said looking from her brother-in-law to her husband. "You two have the same mannerisms. You're bloody clones alright, except for that tire you've sprouted. And of course your different lifestyles." The brothers both winked at her as if on cue.

"Freaky." Turning to her children, she ordered, "The lot of you get ready for Mass! Benjamin and Jack, I'd like you to dress your little brothers for me. Their clothes are pressed and folded on their dresser."

Deirdre sighed and turned back to Mark and Joe. "While I get some work done in the kitchen, would you mind straightening up this room a bit? It looks like Candy Land exploded in here."

"Sure. No problem," they both said in unison.

Freaky, Deirdre thought once again. She yawned and then admonished herself for staying up so late last night. But the craic was brilliant at O'Gara's and she was glad that she didn't miss the Rileys' surprise or the sing-song that followed.

She tied an apron over Old Ironsides and washed her hands. Spotting movement out the window, she pulled the curtains aside and peered closely. A man was poking around Kate's garden. He was tall, but not as muscular as her Mark, and it definitely wasn't Michael Farley. Deirdre thought it odd that the bloke had on dark gang-banger clothes with the hood tied tight around his head. It was the type of outfit she'd never allow her boys to wear, especially on Easter Sunday. Could it be a workman? A curious neighbor or potential guest? She thought not, especially since he was squatting behind bushes like a creeper.

When she looked out the window again, he was gone. Perhaps it was her wild imagination or a will-o'-the-wisp. Could she be seeing things because she didn't get enough sleep last night? But still, this just didn't sit right with her.

"Mark, come here," Deirdre said. She explained her concern and told him to go out there and check it out; which he did, even though he was still in pajamas. When he returned a few minutes later, he looked at her like she was off her rocker and said there was nothing unusual about the place. Deirdre decided to let it rest. Nevertheless, she kept glancing out the window as she toiled in the kitchen.

The cured Limerick ham had been soaking overnight. It was smoked in juniper branches and the scent of evergreen still clung to the liquid. She hefted the ham—and the bin of water it sat in—from the fridge to the sink, cursing as it sloshed on the floor. She knew she'd need help draining it, so she called, "Hey Mark, I need help in here!"

As she busied herself at the boiling pot of praties, she heard him march into the kitchen. She barked orders over her shoulder, as sweat dripped into her eyes, "Drain this stewpot, refill it ... and then carry the bloody t'ing back to the stove."

She had already assembled the ham's seasoning to add to the caldron—brown sugar, pepper and a dash of mace. She imagined it a love potion as she carried it across the steamy kitchen and planted herself behind her man. Peeking over his broad shoulders, Deirdre couldn't help but notice his manly scent, like musk mixed with stale whiskey. Some women might find this a bit of a turnoff, but Deirdre found it beyond sexy. Sliding her free hand down the back of the plush robe, she cupped his bum.

"Do you still want to go upstairs for a quickie?" she purred.

From the doorway a voice boomed, "Wife, that's my brother's ass you're pinching!"

CHAPTER 40

Do not abandon yourselves to despair,
We are the Easter people and Hallelujah is our song.

~POPE JOHN PAUL II

Ultan Ferrian had been holed up at The Cobblestones since earlier that morning, watching from outside as Kate left for Easter Mass with the pack of red-headed neighbors, including the bloke she was hanging on that night when the bloody dog attacked him. After she left with them, and the street was deserted, he broke into the back of her home by using a lockpick he'd ordered through the internet.

Once inside, he nosed around the place, helping himself to some cheese and biscuits. He explored the drawers and shelves in the loos to see if there was anything worth nicking. There wasn't. The strongest drug the lady had was still fookin' ibuprofen.

When he heard the key turn in the lock, he ducked into the back closet. He held his breath until he heard her humming within her private quarters. Now he could creep quietly into the hall. Crouching, he gawked through the sitting room door—which she'd left ajar, unsuspecting.

Jaysus! He finally got a glimpse of her … and the wait was well worth it. She was in a lacy camisole set, bending down to stretch her long, lean legs. The sight was bloody unbelievable! He was wishing she still had on the red spike heels that he had spied her in earlier as she tromped off to church.

When Kate's humming stopped, Ferrian was caught off guard by her outburst of song:*"Christ the Lord is Risen Today-ay,"* with a voice that would make a dog howl.

He repositioned himself, being careful not to disturb the door in case it had a squeaky hinge. What he saw was holy hilarious. The blonde was cha-chaing near her bed while she grabbed some clothes from a drawer and then shimmied out of her half-slip, screeching *"A-a-a-a-a-lay-ay-loo-oo-yaa!"* The next thing he knew she was hopping into her trousers like a clumsy friggin' ballerina who'd had too many pints. His hand flew to his mouth to smother a snort as he watched the free show. Her moves, even though unsexy, made him want to tango with the teasing doxie.

His insides turned warm and pulsed with excitement. Sweat emerged on his upper lip and forehead. *This is your chance. Don't blow it, yeh gobdaw.*

Just as he reached into the pocket of his hoodie to take out his "inheritance," the front doorbell chimed above his head. A strong knock followed, with a: "Kate, it's Terry and Helen. Are yeh in?" Kate fell to the bed, half in her jeans.

"Yeah, I am. I'll be there in a minute," she shouted.

Ferrian was more than a little cheesed off. While Kate hustled into her clothes, he fled out the back door. He sped past a hawthorn tree, retreated behind the garden shed and got on his hunkers. The brick wall behind him was a fortress; no one could spot him from behind. The apple trees and thick ornamental grass provided the protection from a full frontal view.

Damn! I did it all arseways. Better lie low.

Near his shoulder on the wall of the shed, two crickets were stuck together, mocking him. He squashed the copulating insects with his index finger, terminating their ecstasy. *If I can't get laid, then nobody rides 'round the house.*

At a sound coming from next door, Ferrian shifted his body. He could see that the noise had come from a lass of about 12 years. A bit young for his palate, but perhaps the same age as some of the illegal images he had seen offered on the internet recently.

It appeared the colleen was hiding Easter eggs. Her long copper hair flowed in waves over her blooming chest. *Just enough for a tease.*

Ferrian removed his phone from his trouser pocket and snapped a few pictures. Then he concealed himself in the shadows.

CHAPTER 41

The story of Jesus from Cana to Calvary
is one long war with demons.
He knew the beauty of the flowers of the battlefield,
but He came out to do battle.

~G.K. CHESTERTON

When the Easter egg hunt was finished, Michael Farley clutched his prize and stepped out of the Kennedy's back door. "T'anks a m-million," he yelled one last time.

The twins were outside giggling as they stuffed leftover cellophane grass down each other's knickers. Michael looked around for their big brother Jack who'd been sent to supervise them. He spotted him sitting in the van, texting.

Michael joined the twins. "Didn't we have f-fun at the Easter egg hunt? And didn't I f-find that big golden one? Want to see what was in it?" Michael slid from his pocket a heavy, plastic figure of a horse. It had a Schleich logo on it. Mrs. Kennedy told him that it was made in Germany and that she had hoped he'd get that toy.

Pooka raced up to them and licked Murphy's chocolate-smeared fingers and then wandered into Kate's garden, sniffing a trail. Gavin followed the dog.

"No, no, no Gabin!" Murphy reprimanded. He hesitated for a tiny bit and then waddled into Kate's garden, too.

"Come b-back, boyos," Michael called.

They didn't mind, and then he heard a noise and peeked through the hedgerow. Two bare baby bums were on display. The twins were having a piddle by the shed. Michael grimaced and covered his eyes.

Should I fetch Jack?

When he peeked again, he saw Pooka squatting near the twins at the base of the apple tree, and heard her growling. *She doesn't growl very often. Is she annoyed?* When the little fellas pulled up their trousers, the dog started scraping, digging her hind legs into the ground and kicking pee-dirt behind herself. It was flinging everywhere—and didn't that make the twins laugh like SpongeBob?

And then a stranger's voice bellowed: "Jaysus!" It roared from the area of the apple tree. The twins jumped and shrieked.

Michael rushed over there and caught sight of a man behind the garden shed. The fella was on his hunkers, snarling, and his hand was wiping dirt out of his red hair. It was the mean man who fixed Miss Kate's computer—that Ultan Ferrian. *What is he doing here?*

Their eyes met. Michael froze.

"Shite! Not you again—Yeh fookin' mentaller!" The man said. The twins started to cry. Pooka growled, baring her fangs.

"The lot of youse ... shut the fook up!"

Murphy and Gavin ran up to Michael and hid behind him. Pooka went up to the man and barked. Ultan Ferrian reached into the pocket of his hoodie and pulled something out. Michael knew what it was. He'd seen them in the cowboy films, and he had seen this man holding it before—the night Mr. Kennedy's look-alike brother jumped him.

It was a gun!

"Call the bloody dog off me, yeh retard!"

When Michael heard that R-word, he grabbed the heavy plastic horse from his pocket and threw it at the hooligan, bopping him hard on the head. The gun tumbled to the ground.

"Ouch! Bugger!" Ultan Ferrian yelped as he picked up his gun and fumbled with it.

Michael felt the twins tighten their clasp on his legs. Now Pooka was nipping at Ultan Ferrian's hand. The wicked man kicked Pooka—hard—in her ribs. Pooka yelped.

Michael's tummy lurched, and while he was bending over, Ultan Ferrian made his escape to the front of the guesthouse. Pooka recovered and chased him down the street, barking like a banshee.

A chill shot down Michael's spine as the twins let go of his legs. He fell to the ground and began to hit his head and moan. He heard Jack call to them from Kennedy's garden: "Twins! What's all the fuss? Wasn't I lookin' all over for yeh? Michael ... you're still here? Are yeh okay?"

Michael couldn't speak. He just kept rockin' and rappin', but he heard Gavin yell, "Ba' guy! Ba' guy!"

And Murphy hollered, "Shite!"

185

CHAPTER 42

Work is the curse of the drinking classes.

~OSCAR WILDE

While winding through Glasnevin, Luke O'Brien glanced out the cab window. He was fighting an urge to jump out of the taxi.

"Make a right turn up here," he instructed the cabbie. There was an air freshener hanging from the rearview mirror, but the pine scent couldn't hide the stench of the driver. Besides his sweaty body odor, he smelled like a long-neglected ashtray. And when he spoke, his rancid breath filled the car.

On St. Alphonsus Road the cab came to a screeching halt. They had almost hit a dog. Luke saw the Dalmatian race away in hot pursuit of some poor lout. The cabbie honked his horn and within seconds the dog and man were out of sight.

"Ah, you can just drop me off here. I'm right there, at the convent," Luke said. He couldn't wait to inhale fresh air.

"And don't you make a fine Mother Superior?" the cabbie said, pushing devices on the meter.

Luke removed a wad of euros from his pocket and counted out the fee, plus a tip, which he fancied being spent on a huge bar of lye soap. "Here ya go. Happy Easter."

The walk to his condo helped to wake him up. When he got to #230, he stopped at Pat Callahan's place and collected his mail. "Welcome back, Yank," his neighbor said.

After a hot shower Luke felt almost human again. He dialed Buck's number.

"How's your mom doing?" Buck asked.

"A heck of a lot better than she was, thanks."

"Was it a heart attack?"

"Acute heart failure, actually. We're just lucky she didn't need a transplant." Luke unzipped his suitcase and then added, "Say, listen, I'm calling because I wanted to know if you were able to get hold of Kate McMahon for me."

"And here I thought you were phoning just to wish me a happy Easter and to hear how my quick little jaunt to Cabo was. I should have known you're just using me to get to some lady."

"Happy Easter. How was your vacation?"

"My vacation? Why, thanks for asking. It was a blast. We all burnt our lily white skin to the shade of a strawberry margarita. You should see me now; I'm peeling like a hunk of birch bark."

"If you're talking about yourself, I'd leave the 'hunk' bit out," Luke joked, unpacking his dirty laundry. "Did you meet any gorgeous *señoritas* while you were down there?"

"My sister tried to set me up with a gal named Vida from the pro shop when we were golfing one day, but I don't want to do the long distance thing."

"I don't blame you. Which reminds me … just down the street is an intriguing innkeeper … "

"I know. I know. Yes, I did get in contact with Kate. Nobody answered the door, so I put the photos into a big envelope and wrote: *Luke is hot for you. For a good time call 304-43 …* "

"… Yeah, Yeah. Real funny," Luke said, as he rolled his suitcase to the closet. "No, seriously."

"Okay, Don Juan. I really did put an envelope containing pictures under her doormat. But instead of telling her how frantically you're rutting, I wrote something like: *Luke got called away on family business. He will contact you when he returns to Ireland. Yadda, yadda,*

yadda. Now tell me goodbye, and call that Lady in Red before some burly Irishman scarfs her up."

"I will, as soon as I get through a few emails," Luke said, turning down the covers on his bed. "Thanks, buddy. Between my mom's emergency, the different time zones, and the deadline for my Easter Rising article, I just knew I wouldn't be able to get in touch with her, and I didn't want her to think I'd forgotten her." Luke grabbed his computer and sat on the bed.

"So, I gather you also didn't have time to break up with Nora?"

"Ah, nope. But it's on the top of my list. Right after those emails."

"*Adios, Muchacho.* Keep me posted."

By the time Luke answered seven emails, he was asleep with his face on the keyboard. His subconscious mind conjured up a scene of The Lady in Red. There was a sense of mystery, urgency and danger. When he awoke briefly at 2 a.m., he cursed that it was too late to call Kate, or even Nora. But he was thankful that, unsettling as his dream had been—and so realistic—it hadn't included images of his mom's catheter, his cabbie's stench or, worse yet, Buck's peeling body.

CHAPTER 43

Men are like bagpipes:
No sound comes from them unless they're full.

~IRISH PROVERB

Serving the Kennedy clan Easter dinner was no easy matter. The only time Kate had seen so much food was when she was booked solid for an event at her B&B in Stillwater. Today she felt like she was on kitchen duty at an army base. With all the commotion, there was no chance for a private conversation she needed to have with Joe.

"Everyone line up at the buffet," Deirdre, the platoon commander, hollered. Even the matching menfolk, Mark and Joe, joined the rank and file.

"Here you go, luv," Deirdre said as she sliced the ham and put it onto each person's china plate. Kate followed by plopping a scoop of her carrot soufflé onto the plates, and then a slice of quiche. Both were recipes from Rose's cooking shop back home. Everyone was free to help themselves to the other fare: roasted potatoes, colcannon potatoes, champ potatoes, boxty potatoes and potato salad. When it was Joe's turn, he busied himself with the chutney, avoiding her stare.

Extra tables were unfolded in the dining room. The twins sat on footstools pulled up to the piano bench, which their sisters had set with a tea towel and a tiny vase of forget-me-nots.

"Fold your hands and get ready for prayer," Mark instructed his brood when everyone was seated.

Some kids were still poking at each other, but grace was said nonetheless. Looking around the room at his children, Mark added, "And we thank God for our many blessings, especially for our food today and our good health…" He stopped at this point, tears pooling in his eyes. He looked up at the chandelier to keep them from escaping. He bit his bottom lip.

Deirdre leaned over to Kate and whispered, "He always blubbers during grace at the holidays."

"May God keep us all…" Mark blew his nose.

Mark's hungry brother interjected, "… safe, now and forever. Amen."

Deirdre leaned over a second time and whispered to Kate, "Twins! Mark and Joe always finish each other's sentences. Telepathy, or some such. 'Tis intriguing, I say." Then, glancing to her left, she bleated, "Mary Margaret, mind the salt. When you're older it'll go right to your cellulite."

The dining room was Grand Central Station. A bevy of bodies seemed to be constantly getting up for more food, pouring more sparkling juice and passing soda bread.

The most memorable mishap, however, was when Mary Cecelia, while chewing her food and giggling at the same time, ejected a piece of grated potato from her nose, to the delight of her siblings.

Kate watched as Deirdre forked another slice of Limerick ham onto Mary Kathryn's plate, and then planted a big kiss on the child's head. As a guest at their table, Kate thought she knew how Ebenezer Scrooge must have felt when he stood amongst the shadows with the ghost. To a childless, single person, life in a big family seems like mysterious, happy chaos; being in its midst is a trip down the rabbit hole. Kate found it a thrilling adventure, but Joe looked like the Mad Hatter waiting for time to pass.

When all were nearly stuffed, Kate noticed that there was hardly a morsel left of that hearty banquet. The vultures had devoured nearly everything. Only a bit of ham remained—barely enough to make bean soup another day. When Benjamin and Jack served dessert, a little twin climbed onto Kate's lap, feeding her maternal hunger. He wanted her to spoon gooseberry crumble into his mouth. "Keem! Keem!" He said as he pointed to the dollop of clotted cream sitting on the plate next to his dessert.

"Sorry, Gavin. How could Auntie Kate forget the 'keem'?" She scooped some onto her fork and sang, "Here comes the airplane. Yum. Yum." It was obvious he didn't mind that she croaked like a frog. With his mouth full, he gave her a smile. Kate kissed his puffed out cheeks and noticed that some dirt was still caked in his right ear. Obviously, she missed that spot earlier in the day when the toddlers needed to be cleaned up after playing outside. She recalled how they had been sporting grass and mud stains. And they seemed upset.

She wondered what that was all about. The adults had tried asking Michael what had happened in the garden, but he had just rushed home. Benjamin and Jack didn't know what caused the disturbance, either.

Mark clanked his wine glass with a knife. *Ding, ding, ding.* "It's time for the session. Everyone get ready to perform your party piece." The kids scrambled in all directions as they grabbed sheet music, instruments, Irish dance shoes and poetry books. As the fire crackled in the parlor's hearth, the adults were treated to free entertainment. To begin the show, Mary Kathryn danced a reel to the beat of Benjamin's bodhran. Then Mary Margaret sang the lovely *Fields of Athenry,* followed by Mary Cecelia singing *What Shall We Do With a Drunken Sailor?* Next on the playbill was Jack and his guitar. He broke from Irish tradition and belted out a song he had composed himself called *Tequila Eyes.* Kate wondered how an 11-year-old knew about margaritas, cantina fights and lovely *señoritas.*

Before the twins could take stage and steal the show, Mary Kathryn stood up again and recited, by rote, her mother's favorite poem called *O Do Not Love Too Long* by W. B. Yeats.

Kate felt Joe's eyes on her as they listened. *Yesterday I thought we could resurrect our romance, but then last night, before I could sort out my feelings . . .* She couldn't ruminate on this at length, however. The curtain was about to rise for the twins' grand finale.

For his solo performance, Gavin did a couple of somersaults, nearly hitting his head on the hearth. When everyone exclaimed, "Ooh!...Ahh!" and "Yikes!" he was energized and decided to kick his circus routine up a notch. So, next he added some ballerina twirls and cartwheel attempts. Fueled by more applause, he broke into some breakdancing, Michael Jackson style. He kept looking over his shoulder for his partner, but Murphy was a no-show. After he took his final bow, people started looking backstage for the missing performer. Deirdre rang the ship's bell, but he still didn't show up.

Kate searched upstairs and discovered him—sound asleep on the floor next to the crib. Gently she lifted him onto her shoulder. His face nestled into the crook of her neck, where she felt the warmth of his peaceful, rhythmic breaths.

She recalled, with a pang of guilt, that she had been ugly with envy when Deirdre had emailed the happy news that they were expecting twins. It was soon after Bryan drowned, at a time when grief and betrayal were all-consuming and the underlying pain of infertility was haunting her.

She carefully slipped Murphy into his bed, forcing herself to let go of that shadow of guilt as she did so. The envy was gone and she now felt true happiness for her friend. She would not, however, let go of the dream of having her own child someday. She covered him with his favorite blanket.

"Oh, you found him." Joe's voice crept in from the nursery doorway.

She felt her pulse quicken as he approached and said, "About last night..."

"Shh...We can talk about that later," she whispered. "Look how peaceful Murphy is."

"Boy, you're really into kids these days."

"Yeah, well, I'm running out of time..."

He took a step back. "Don't look at me. I'd rather be an uncle."

She looked at him, but all she could see today was his beer belly. It might as well have been studded with three red flags.

They went downstairs and called off the search party for Murphy. Mary Cecelia was clearing the table. "Auntie Kate, did you hear that I saw the Easter Bunny last night?"

"You did?"

"Indeed. It was at 2:21 a.m. The bunny was goin' into Uncle Joe's room when I saw his shadow." Kate gave the other adults a quizzical look as Mary Cecelia left the room.

Joe raised his palms. "Okay, I confess. It was me coming home late from O'Gara's. I helped Kelly close up after last call."

Ahh, so that's why he didn't show up at my place. He was closing in on Kelly.

"Right," Deirdre said, crossing her arms and peering at Joe through a copper tendril that had sprung loose from its clip.

Joe shifted from one foot to the other. "Kelly seems like a great gal—and she'll be moving to the U.S.—to Chicago—soon. She got a job at Steppenwolf Theatre."

"Well then, what about Kate?" Deirdre looked at Joe and then at Kate. "What about the two of yeh? Are yeh done and dusted?"

"What? Done and dusted?" Joe ran a hand across his stubble.

Kate hoped the hurt didn't show on her face.

Joe shrugged her off like a moth-eaten coat. "You don't mind, do you, Kate?"

"I have no claim on you, Joe. Besides, we want different things—different lifestyles."

Deirdre grabbed a newspaper from the sofa and made a feeble attempt to resuscitate Kate's pride. "I believe Kate's keen on someone else, anyway—the smashing journalist who wrote an article in today's paper."

Joe's eyebrows rose. "You never mentioned this guy to me."

Kate glanced at *The Irish Times* clasped in Deirdre's hand. She knew an article by Luke O'Brien titled "The Easter Rising and its Effects on America" was on the center page. She had read it earlier, before Mass. *How was it that he had time to write this piece, but didn't have time to call me?* "Oh, umm, I never mentioned him because...we might be done and dusted...before we even got started," she admitted.

"Well, he'd be a fool not to pursue you," Joe said.

Kate managed a smile. "Apparently, I've got a whole stable full of fools."

Joe's hands went to his heart. "Ouch!"

Mark cleared his throat, grabbed a dirty bowl and headed toward the kitchen. "Man, I'm staying out of this one."

Deirdre unfolded the newspaper and looked pointedly at Kate. "'Tis a complicated story Luke wrote, with a lot of research involved. Perhaps now that he's done with it, he'll finally pick up the bleepin' phone."

Kate was encouraged that Deirdre hadn't given up hope. She considered her a master at romance. "Well, I have enough on my plate right now." Kate reached for her bag. "I should go. Since tomorrow is opening day, I need to hit the hay early. Check-in time is four o'clock."

"Hold your horses. There'll be no hay until we talk about somethin'," Deirdre insisted in her mommy-knows-best voice. "I've been t'inkin'...tomorrow you'll have guests, including your brother Lee, and I won't have to worry about you after that. However, my intuition is actin' up again, so tonight I want Mark and Benjamin to stay with you." Kate started to protest but Deirdre continued, "I know the lot of you t'ink I'm off my nut, but there's been too many strange goings-on around here lately and I don't want my friend over there alone."

Kate wanted to assure them that she would be okay. She just wanted to get home and sort everything out.

Deirdre folded her arms. "And there'll be no discussion about it. What with the fact that Joe thought he saw a creeper at your window the other night and I may have seen a prowler earlier today. And let's not forget somet'ing obviously upset Michael and the twins..."

"But..." Kate stammered, but was shot down by The Look.

"I mean it! Mark and Benjamin will walk you over to the guest-house and enjoy a bit of a sleep-over." Turning to her husband, she said, "Bring your sleepin' bags and pillows so Kate's guest rooms stay tidy. You can crash on the sofas near her private apartment."

"Yes, ma'am."

"Now Deirdre..." Kate began again, hoping that her friend was just overreacting because of all those suspenseful romance novels that filled her head.

"Not at all. I insist. Besides, I'm doin' this for selfish reasons, as well." After a yawn she continued, "I'm hopin' to get some good sleep without this *amadán* around to ask me for love. He's been in a frisky mood today, all right."

Joe interrupted, "If I recall, someone else was a little frisky in the kitchen this morning, too, and I happened to get caught in the middle of it."

Kate looked at her friends for an explanation.

"Long story," Mark said. "Give me a minute to grab my stuff."

Kate turned to Deirdre. "Thanks for everything. You worked so hard."

"Not as hard as you'll be workin' tomorrow, with your grand openin'." Deirdre pulled her into a hug and continued, "I'm so excited for you. You'll see ... everything will work out for the best. Now get some sleep."

As Kate and her bodyguards walked to The Cobblestones, they noticed a white car peeling away. In the dark, Mark removed a pen from Benjamin's case and wrote the license plate number on his hand. All they could remember, however, was 00-D-734. Nobody got the last few digits. But at least they had something ... Just in case.

"I'll lock your doors ..." started Mark.

"... and windows ... Just in case." Joe finished his twin's thought before he crossed the street to O'Gara's.

Mark called after him, "Let's not have a repeat performance of the Easter Bunny tonight, okay bro?"

CHAPTER 44

Artistic talent is a gift from God and whoever discovers it
in himself has a certain obligation:
To know that he cannot waste this talent, but must develop it.

~POPE JOHN PAUL II

It was just his luck that those urchins decided to pick that specific tree to piss on. What the hell? Didn't they have the whole garden to choose from? And that blasted dog nearly bit his leg off. Jaysus, he'd love to sink his own fangs into that bollocks!

When he made the service call, Ferrian had overheard the lovely Kate say that the guesthouse would open Easter Monday. Tomorrow. This was going to complicate things. There'd be more people crawling all over the place now, and he didn't exactly want an audience—or did he? Besides the guests, that numpty manager would be around, too, putting her nose where it didn't belong. Jaysus, that woman was annoyin'!

His Easter breakfast had consisted of two beers. Now he was hungry. He went to the press and removed a can of tuna. From the pocket of his hoodie he recovered a yellow dyed egg. *Wasn't I clever to reach out and help myself after watching that lass hide them?*

As he peeled away the broken shell he was ten years old again. He had a real Easter basket that year. His teacher, the plucky Miss McGraw, the only person who ever seemed to give a shite about him, had made up a basket. Just for him. He had followed her home from school one Wednesday because he couldn't go home. She invited him in for biscuits, milk, chit-chat and an art lesson. He returned every week after that for "Wonderful Wednesdays." However, before the end of the school year, his mother uprooted him again, and Miss McGraw was erased from his life. But he often recalled her words: "I'm glad you reached out to me, Ultan. Never be afraid to reach out for what you need."

As he chewed the egg he massaged the bump on his noggin. *For fook's sake ... I didn't need this. What the hell did that mentaller throw at me? A toy horse was it?*

When he was finished eating, he popped a purple pill, downed another bottle of beer and removed some art materials from the Bushmills crate at his feet. Then he flipped to a fresh page in his tablet. Turning on his mobile, he went to the photos he had taken earlier that day. Among them were shots of that uppity skirt taking off her clothes, and doing those dance moves. Surely she wasn't brazen enough to get hired in the strip clubs, but her clumsy innocence was a turn-on. *If she only knew ...* he thought as he began drawing.

Well, actually, she would know that she was being watched. Soon Doesn't every woman hope to have an admirer?

When he finished this masterpiece, he'd put it in the red folder he nicked from Computer Serve. Then he'd add some of his other portraits of Kate, too. On his way to work tomorrow, he'd park near The Cobblestones until he found a kid he could bribe with a cigarette to put the folder by her front door. He wanted her to know she had a fan—a mystery man. It would force her to think of him, obsess about him, and shudder with fear—even in her dreams. Sharing his intimate pieces of art should do the trick.

God, I'm brilliant!

Later that night, he planned to do a sketch for Kate of his favorite example of Renaissance art, *The Nightmare*, an oil painting done by Johann Henry Fuseli. It depicted a voluptuous woman appearing lifeless as she slept. Her snow-white limbs were draped over a bed. A crouching demon hovered over her, and the blond maiden was helpless to resist the tormenting spirit. In the background, a black pooka horse was watching from the shadows. Its eyes were glowing, and it appeared to foreshadow impending evil.

"Some artists are sick bastards, all right," he concluded.

CHAPTER 45

Love is never defeated,
and I could add,
the history of Ireland proves it.
~POPE JOHN PAUL II

On Monday morning, Michael's mother set a glass of orange juice in front of him. "I'm happy to see yer in better form this mornin', lad. 'Tis a grand, sunny day for The Cobblestones to be openin'." She patted his slicked hair. "Do an extra nice job for Miss Kate today, handsome. A beautiful garden is a sure way to impress the guests."

Michael glanced under the table. He was glad to see that his da had on the slippers he had bought him for Easter, and Mammy was wearing the daisy pin his teacher helped pick out for her. He had used his own money, and his parents almost cried when they found them in their baskets.

Michael ate his poached eggs and then grabbed another piece of toast from the rack. He was anxious about going to the guesthouse. He was glad his folks were going to walk with him to the church first. His mammy was the pastoral assistant at St. Columba's and his da was the business administrator there. Today was payday, and Father Criagáin was going to give Michael his regular pay, plus a tip. Da said he could spend the cash at camp. Maybe he'd buy some Turkish Delight. Coach Keanne would want him to eat kiwi and apples, though, on account the World Games were coming up.

At church, Michael changed the water in the flower vases, said howya to Father Hurley, the helper-priest, and then went to the office.

"I don't like Ultan F-Ferrian," Michael said to Father Criagáin when he received his paycheck and a tip of fifteen euros.

"Sorry, Michael?"

"That b-bad bloke. I s-smacked him with a horse on Easter."

"Are yeh wantin' me to hear yer confession, lad?"

Father Criagáin's phone rang and he had to talk in private. Maybe it was a man who couldn't stop the drink. Michael went outside by the front of the church. As he stood by his bike, he put the check and euros into his old bank bag and then zipped it shut. He needed to get to the guesthouse to work and find that toy horse he threw at Ultan Ferrian.

That's when he saw a familiar car driving by at a turtle's pace. The driver looked right at him with super mean eyes. Michael started hitting his head with closed fists. "Ahhhh! Ahhhhhh!"

Mrs. Hickey, from around the corner, was on her way to church to light a candle. She must have noticed that he was upset, because she rubbed his back. By enticing him with a cough drop from her pocket, she was able to calm him down. He didn't mind that the cough drop was old and had bits of tissue stuck to it.

As Michael sat on the cobblestones sucking the cherry lozenge, he noticed that the car had stopped near the guesthouse. Then he saw Ultan Ferrian handing something red to two boys.

Michael's horse and the gardening would have to wait. He didn't want to go to Miss Kate's now. He was not being a good sheriff, because he was scared. His parents taught him to pray when he was scared. So he got up. He'd go light a candle. He could sit by that nice Mrs. Hickey. Didn't Miss Kate need prayers today?

As he walked to the church doors, he looked around, making sure his mother wasn't about. Satisfied that she wasn't, Michael muttered, "Ultan Ferrian's an arse!" He removed the beads from his pocket and kissed the cross.

CHΛPϾƐR 46

It's paradise in a bottle.
It creates a very strong,
positive emotional response in people, like Tahiti itself.
~ERIC VAXELAIRE
discussing monoï oil's appeal (Elle article by April Long)

Catriona had donned her favorite dress for the opening. She chose some practical Bøcs shoes, because she knew comfort was paramount today. She got up extra early to prepare a warm breakfast of eggs and black pudding. She set a pot of tea in front of Declan's empty chair and placed this morning's *Irish Times* beside it. Perhaps tonight she'd build a fire and pour a tumbler of whiskey for him. And since he was often achy during the rainy season, maybe she could give him a backrub with the Tahitian body oil.

Maybe.

As she ambled up the sidewalk to the guesthouse, the piña colada scent of her musings melted away.

"What is this?" she asked Mark and Benjamin Kennedy, who were leaving by way of the front door. Sleeping sacks and pillows were clutched in their arms, and it looked like their hair had been styled with the Cuisinart. After they told her about the mysterious goings-on, Catriona was thankful they had safeguarded Kate overnight.

"Bejaysus! The last t'ing we need is a pervert peekin' in the windows," she said to the lads, her forehead lined with gullied creases.

As soon as they headed home, Catriona decided to do a thorough walk-through herself. Could there really be some evil eejit out there? Her inspection, however, suggested everything was safe. The Kennedy gents had made sure to lock all the windows, and she would leave them so—a pity, on such a fine day.

The sun was out and casting those magical prisms on the walls, which would delight the guests. People expected rainbows in Ireland. And if it started raining? Well, the tourists would come to expect that, too.

By 8:00 a.m. Kate appeared in the kitchen, looking fresh and alert. She had decided not to go for a run that morning and Catriona was relieved to see the lass using her head. Kate explained that she really thought Deirdre was just making a big fuss about nothing at all, but they agreed to err on the side of caution.

"I think we'll be in good hands," Kate said as they dusted the crystal sconces once again. "My brother was a wrestler in high school, and our cousin Nick grew up on a farm in Pennsylvania. He's pretty tough, too." Kate got off her step ladder. "Let's keep this quiet, though. I don't want to worry the other guests needlessly."

"Right. However, won't it be helpful having yer relations under this roof, in case there is indeed a hooligan prowlin' about?"

Myrna entered the guesthouse, carrying a tray. "Pooka and I wanted to bring you a gift for getting our Helen back home to us." She removed the tea towel. "I was up baking scones early this mornin', so I was. I wanted them to be fresh when yer guests arrive."

Catriona smelled cardamom and apricots. "Aren't you the bees' knees? And didn't yeh just save me two hours of work?" She brought the delectables into the dining room, placing them next to the tea server and Belleek vase of tulips.

"No, *you two* are the bee's knees, so you are. It's like I won the Lotto havin' you as friends." Myrna blew her nose on a lace handkerchief. "'Tis lovely havin' Helen back in her little pink bed. And she's satisfied that she has proven she can make it on her own."

"Well, we're excited she's home. We both love that girl. It will be nice having her work with us here at the guesthouse," Kate said. "I just wish I could pay her more. Perhaps someday."

Catriona caught a fleeting grimace cross Kate's face after she spoke. *The poor lamb. She has good reason to worry… about meeting payroll… and perhaps a pervert, too.*

"Helen told me you should ring if you need help later today. She phoned Coach Keanne this mornin' and offered to work on flip turns with the Special Olympians. She used to organize swim drills at Manly Beach in Australia."

"Did you say Manly Beach?" Catriona asked. "Perhaps we should pack Kate off to that place to find a man with a nice hairy chest and a big…"

"Catriona! Give over with that rubbish!" Myrna's eyes widened to the size of a 20-pence piece.

"What? I was goin' to say 'a big bank account.' Get yer mind out of the gutter, Myrna."

"Ladies," Kate interrupted, "the way things are going, it just might come to that. I might have to search a third continent… If I ever feel the need to date again."

Catriona knitted her thinly penciled brows. "Em, but the last I heard you had two lads on your doorstep."

Kate shrugged. "Well, Joe dropped me like a hot potato… I guess I had it coming." She ran a finger along the bookshelf. "And Spandex Man never materialized."

"He'll come around soon enough, so he will." Myrna patted Kate's shoulder as Kate grabbed her handbag.

"Well," Kate said, "I'm off to O'Gara's to get some whiskey."

Catriona was befuddled and Myrna asked, "You're not *that* desperate, are yeh now? Morning drinking is it? 'Tis only half eight."

"I thought you swore off the whiskey," Catriona added.

"It's not for me, you sillies. Dano and Morgan texted me their well-wishes and said to stop by. They have a bottle of Jameson for us, and I thought some of our guests might enjoy an Irish coffee with those yummy scones."

"What a grand way to celebrate the openin'," Myrna said. "You go on, now. I told Catriona I'd help with the final round of dustin'. I might as well put my hands to good use when the arthritis isn't actin' up."

CHAPTER 47

It is not a secret if it is known to three people.

~IRISH SAYING

W hat are you smilin' about?" Myrna asked Catriona after Kate had left the guesthouse. "It looks like you're up to somet'ing." Catriona was underneath a table, polishing its legs with lemon oil. Myrna knew they wouldn't both fit under that same table—due to the size of the dear woman—so she opted to polish the tabletops instead.

"Hmm? Oh, wasn't I just t'inkin' of another surprise Declan and meself... I mean... another surprise *I* have planned?"

Myrna smiled. *Is Dr. Roddy making progress?* "Another surprise? What manner of surprise is it?" she asked, wiping wisps of hair away from her eyes, and smearing her cheeks with the rag while doing so.

"Ah, now. I'd have to kill yeh if I told yeh." Catriona winked, and peered at her friend. "Myrna, you've an oily mess on your face. Why don't yeh go and freshen up while I place a phone call?"

Myrna purposely left the powder room door ajar as she cleaned her face and puzzled. *What is Catriona up to now?* Cupping an ear, she earwigged.

"...Ah huh. He phoned, did he?" she heard Catriona say.

After a bit of silence, Catriona spoke again, "Sorry? You must be jokin'!"

Myrna registered shock in her friend's voice.

"Oh, 'tis grand all right."

Myrna wondered what could be grand.

"Boy or girl?" Catriona asked.

Holy God in Heaven Almighty! What is this all about? Droplets of water dripped from Myrna's washcloth and dribbled down her cleavage.

"Is the wee one healthy? How about immunizations?" Catriona questioned, and then added, "Is the mother in good form?"

Myrna couldn't take the suspense any longer. She rushed into the dining room and mouthed to her friend: "What? Who?" but Catriona just hushed her. *Who does she know that's in a family way? Is she adopting? Is she hallucinating about adoption? Jesus, Mary and Holy St. Joseph! ... And wasn't I just thinkin' she was takin' a turn for the better?*

Myrna's heart sank as she heard her friend continue, "Is the babe nursin' all fine and dandy then?" The mother of three almost felt the letdown in her own breasts.

"'Tis lovely indeed!" Catriona said as she clicked off the phone. She grabbed Myrna's hands, twirled her around, and hollered into the air, "Hip, hip, hooray and a monkey's uncle!"

When the two finally collapsed onto the sofa, Myrna asked, "What's all the fuss? What are we celebratin'? Tell me. I'm sufferin' an anxiety attack."

Catriona's mascara was beginning to drip—now she'd be the one who'd have to clean up in the toilet. She used an apron corner to brush off her face.

Then at last she shared the good news. As Catriona prattled on, she grabbed a broom and went outside to sweep the front step; her bum jiggling with each swoosh.

Myrna saw her friend bend down to pick up a red folder lying beside the door. Catriona continued to reveal her plans as she stepped back inside and opened up the folder just briefly. "This is a bit odd," she said in an absent-minded way. Myrna watched as Catriona placed the folder on a pile in the office. It must have been of no importance.

"... and wait 'til I tell yeh, Myrna ..." Catriona chattered on about the glorious news of her surprise, dispelling Myrna's earlier suspicions.

CHAPTER 48

A man on a horse is spiritually
as well as physically bigger than a man on foot.

~JOHN STEINBECK

The horse he got from the Easter egg hunt had a bit of mud on its hoof. Michael wiped it off using his sleeve. He was glad he finally found it under the perennials by the shed. He and Mrs. Ryan were out working in the gardens when he spotted it.

"Into the stable you g-go," he said, stowing the horse in the basket on his bike. Before Mrs. Ryan went inside to clean up, she said, "Every cowboy needs a horse."

From his cinchsack, Michael grabbed the second half of the chicken sandwich Mammy made for him. He took a few bites and then saw a wet Pooka coming his way from the direction of the Royal Canal. *If she went swimming, she must be mended after that mean man kicked her.*

"Here you g-go, g-girl." Michael tossed the rest of the sandwich to the dog. "T-t'ank you for helping m-me and the twins yesterday." He took a steadying breath. Thinking about Ultan Ferrian made his hands go wibbly-wobbly. He gently scratched Pooka's ear. "I w-wish I was brave, like you, Pooka. At least I s-smacked the bloke when I threw my horsey at him."

As if the dog could tell Michael was blue, she licked his face and then rolled onto her back beside him. He smiled as he began to rub her tummy. "You s-smell like the Royal Canal. Mind yourself in that canal. It's flowin' fierce n-now with all the rain we've had. Da said so."

He hugged the stinky dog. "I get to swim pretty soon, too, but at the pool." He saw a rental van arrive. "It must be four o'clock." Mrs. Ryan said that people would come to sleep at the guesthouse when it was four o'clock. He stood at attention when he saw Miss Kate come outside to welcome them.

"Michael, would you mind helping us carry these bags inside?"

"Aye, M-Miss Kate." He picked up the biggest bag, because that's what a gentleman would do and he had real, real strong arms from pulling his body through the pool.

He filed in line behind the tourists as they went inside. The group huddled around the reception stand. He was proud of Miss Kate because she sounded so innkeeper-like. Listening, he could tell she was good at her job. He was noticing the little things: how she smiled a lot, looked them in the eye, which Da said is good manners, gave them keys with pretty beaded ribbons dangling from the end, and handed out packets with maps of Dublin. Then she said in her American accent, "Please make The Cobblestones your home away from home. To begin your stay with us, we have some homemade scones over here on the sideboard." Michael watched as she led them to the dining room. "We also have tea and the makings for Irish Coffee."

Mrs. Ryan pranced out from the kitchen with a steel mixing bowl in her hands. "I have fresh cream for the lot of yeh. It's whipped just right so it floats on top of the mug." The people lined up to the sideboard while Kate and Mrs. Ryan showed the visitors how to assemble the perfect Irish Coffee: a spoonful of raw sugar stirred into a mug filled three-quarters full of coffee, with a shot of Irish whiskey added next, and then the lightly whipped cream poured on top.

"*Slainté!*" They were taught to say "Slon-cha!" but their accents sounded horrid.

Miss Kate announced, "Notice the lovely tulips beside the scones? I'd like you to meet our gardener, Michael Farley." She then turned his way. "Michael, these are some graduate students from UCLA in

California. They're in Dublin for an Irish Studies course." Michael shook hands with a Beth, Ann, Molly, Vince, Rick and Kim.

"California? By Hollywood? Do you like John Wayne?" Before he knew it, the students were high-fiving him and talking about their favorite films.

The door opened and some more guests arrived; a bunch of blathering ladies from America who were all Magee relations. They were on a shopping trip, and Mrs. Ryan told them about the shops at Grafton Street, Powerscourt, Cow's Lane and Henry and Jervis Streets. She also answered questions they had about the famous Magee store in Donegal. His favorite fancy lady in the group was named Angie. She was super tall and super pretty. He told her he was going to Special Olympics World Games and she clapped and took a picture of him. Then she used her phone to tweet the news. Didn't she make him feel like a big movie star?

When the Magee flock flew into the dining room, they reminded Michael of buntings and catbirds at his feeder. They fluttered about as they nibbled scones and sipped tea.

A man's voice rang out behind him, "You must be Michael the gardener. I recognize you from your picture."

"My-my picture?"

"Yes the framed pictures of all the staff on the check-in stand," the man said. "I've heard a lot about you. I'm Kate's brother, Father Lee McMahon." He shook Michael's hand.

Another man was with him. "And I'm Nick Miller, their cousin. Nice to meet you."

"My sister asked us to bring you something from the Wild, Wild West." The priest reached into a shopping bag and pulled out a brown cowboy hat.

Michael jumped up and down. "T'anks a m-million, pardners," he said in his best western drawl, plopping the hat on his head.

Miss Kate lifted the brim, smiling. "You're welcome, my friend. The gardens wouldn't have been ready for the guests if it weren't for you."

"Indeed. W-we have a b-business agreement."

"Why, he looks just like a sheriff," chirped one of the buntings to a magpie as they migrated past him pecking at some scones. When the one called Angie said how handsome he looked, it made him blush. She took another picture.

"Why don't we show everyone to their rooms?" Miss Kate said to Mrs. Ryan.

Alone, Michael moseyed toward the check-in stand on exaggerated bowlegs. He wanted to look at that framed picture of all the staff members. There it was, right where everyone could see it when they come to the guesthouse. Michael puffed out his chest and grinned at his image in the mirror. He felt like a Hollywood big shot as he ran his hand along the brim. He wished he'd had on this new cowboy hat for the picture.

The phone on the stand rang. Michael looked around but he didn't see anyone about. It rang again, but still nobody hustled toward it. He picked the cordless thing up and held it to his ear below his snazzy hat.

"Howdy."

"Umm, is Kate McMahon there?" said a man's voice.

"No sirree, but I'm the sh-sheriff."

"Is this The Cobblestones—the guesthouse?"

"Please make The Cobblestones your home away from home, y'all." Michael used his best southern accent as he emulated what Miss Kate had said to the guests earlier.

"Pardon me?"

"I got a new c-cowboy hat today, pardner, and we have a business agreement."

"Sorry, I must have the wrong number." Michael heard a *click* and then hung up the phone. A few moments later it rang again.

"Howdy."

"Is this The Cobblestones?" The same male voice asked.

"This is the Wild, Wild West."

Click.

CHAPTER 49

A tune is more lasting than the song of birds.
And a word is more lasting than the wealth of the world.

~OLD IRISH PROVERB

Shit," Luke said aloud, looking at his cell. Now if that wasn't the weirdest damn phone conversation he'd ever had. Was that guy drunk or something? The number listed on The Cobblestones' website must be wrong. He'd have to alert Kate to that fact—if he ever got in touch with her.

He couldn't get Kate off his mind ever since he first saw her out running. That must have been about a month ago. Even though they seemed to hit it off so well in Tullahought, they still hadn't reconnected. He felt like the opportunity to have The Lady in Red in his life was slipping through his fingers. The need to act quickly was stressing him out, but, damn, he had been called out of Dublin again, and it was as if evil forces were at play trying to keep them apart. *I'm supposed to be a pro at researching people; it's in my job description, for Chrissake.* Kate McMahon wasn't on Facebook, Linkedin or Twitter, and her email link on the guesthouse's website was an auto-reply reservation form. He'd have to knock on her door when he got back to Glasnevin.

He was walking near Eyre Square in Galway's City Centre, after interviewing some of the locals in this Irish speaking area, where brogues are thick as sheep's wool. His editor, Dan Kelly, had asked him to do yet another lightweight feature story—this one on the

Irish language. It was recently reported that the male Irish accent was rated #1 for sexiness in a poll of 5,000 women worldwide. It had knocked the French down a few notches from the spot they had held for a few decades. Italian came in second, followed by Scottish. If he had been born with an Irish accent, and if he could speak as fluidly as he wrote, perhaps he'd have better luck with the ladies. So what's a fella to do?

A display in a flower shop window caught his eye. An arrangement bursting with color. The place had a storefront like a pub and the lettering above the yellow door said *O'Neill Floral.* He went inside.

Some older American women were at the counter. They said they were planning a dinner party at the cottage they were renting, and needed to fill a few of their newly purchased Waterford vases. An older gentleman was helping them. His nametag said *Patrick O'Neill.*

"All right then ladies, that's all fine and good, but may I suggest yeh add white roses to those Bells of Ireland? They can represent the snows of Michigan that yeh miss so much." When Patrick said this in his thick Galway accent, the women turned to putty in his green thumbs.

"Aaah. Mmmm," they breathed with heaving breasts.

When Mr. O'Neill went to the back of the shop to wrap up the women's purchases, the heaviest lady said, "Golly, that man's a hunk. He sounds like Sean Connery."

"I thought Sean Connery was Scottish," said a woman wearing purple and red.

"Who cares what nationality he is? He's yummy!" said a granny with a gray bun bopping on the top of her head. She looked around the shop and then whispered, "And so is that florist."

"The Irish brogue and the gift of blarney are the secret weapons of the Irish," a walrus of a woman said. Luke noticed that her chin kept jiggling for a few beats after she spoke her mind. She had a few whiskers and long eye teeth.

Patrick returned through a curtain of plastic ivy garland. He accepted payment from the bopping bun lady and then bestowed on them a bit of an Irish blessing: "May yer thoughts be as glad as the shamrocks, and may yer hearts be as light as a song."

"Aaah. Mmmm," the matrons breathed again.

Luke held the door open for the assemblage of perfumed biddies. The lady swathed in purple and red looked Luke up and down, and said, "This gentleman's a piece of eye candy, too."

"Yeah, but is he a sweet talker like Mr. O'Neill?" the one with the bun asked.

"If I were forty years younger I'd be chasing you around this shop," the walrus grunted to Luke before exiting. Her wattle jiggled like gelatin all the way out the door.

Good thing I'm a runner! Luke thought, chuckling about the whole scene. He took a small notebook from his pocket and jotted down the gold nuggets that had rolled from the florist's mouth. It was perfect fodder for his writing assignment. He believed Patrick could get women to eat out of his hand every time he opened his gob.

"Geez, how do you do it?" Luke asked Patrick when he returned to the counter.

"Do wha'?"

"That." Luke pointed to the group across the street.

Patrick gave an impish chuckle. "Weren't they bold, though? When there's a pack of them turned loose, their husbands never know what they're playin' at."

"It's not just that, it's your silver tongue. I almost had to take out some fainting salts for them. They likened you to Sean Connery."

"Did they, now? Isn't he Scottish?"

"Yeah, well ..."

"It's the accent. All the tourists love it. Sure 'tisn't the looks on me; I've a face like a busted cabbage." The florist snipped some Baby's Breath. "Women like men to be tender, chivalrous and courtly. Even the bold ladies could use a bit of attention. Mind you, none of them want us grabbin' at 'em and pokin' at 'em. Don't they all deserve to be treated like queens? 'Tis true, they are the most worthy ones." He placed the tiny blossoms in a bucket of water. "It just so happens that we Irishmen have a natural gift of gab—and it's not from kissin' the Blarney stone. Who'd do that, anyway, when the locals use the t'ing as a public toilet?"

Luke turned to a new page in his notepad. He told the man he was a journalist and asked if he could quote him for a story.

"Course. Wouldn't I feel flattered, though? Now, have yeh the need fer anyt'ing else?"

"Yeah, some flowers for a woman ... I mean, for a grand opening of a guesthouse."

"Right," he said with a wink. "Has this particular innkeeper captured your heart? I do know this: She'd love to be serenaded with flowers and poetry. Don't they all?"

"Looks like I came to the right place. Do you deliver to Dublin?"

"Indeed. Now you just let Patrick O'Neill work his magic." Patrick looked around his shop. "What's yer pleasure?"

Luke pointed to the display in the window's cooler. "I like that eye-popping one."

"'Tis lovely, indeed. I can have a fresh bouquet delivered to her tomorrow." The man went to his computer. "Now then, what would you be wantin' on the card?"

Luke froze. It had been so long since he'd worked at being beguiling. According to Nora, he was about as romantic as a tin of beans. He drank his coffee black, liked to watch football in the man cave, and scratched his butt whenever he damn well pleased. But given the right incentive, he thought he had potential. He knew he needed help, though. At least he wasn't ashamed to ask for it. "I've got some Irish blood, but I don't have an Irish tongue. What would you suggest I write, Mr. Irish 007?"

"Is it help you're askin' for? And yourself a wordsmith?"

"Yeah, but I don't do poetry. In fact, I nearly failed that class in college. And lately I've been failing—spinning my wheels—in the romantic arena."

"Well then, let me be so bold as to say that you Yanks t'ink too hard." The shopkeeper raked a hand through his thick gray curls and then faced his customer. "Just let yer words flow like a well-poured Guinness, and remember to speak from yer heart, lad."

"My words flow when I'm the objective reporter, but when I need to say what's in my heart ... well ... sometimes the words get stuck in my throat ... like a hairball that I can't cough up. You Irish are double-blessed. You can write from the heart, and you can speak from the heart—as if both come naturally."

"Indeed. The written words are intertwined with the spoken word, like the ivy and the holly behind me." Patrick pointed to the fake greenery dangling from his office doorway. "Different forms of storytellin' have been part of our culture for generations: music, poetry, playwritin' and poppycockin'. Are ye writin' this down then?"

"Oh, yes!"

"Of course, it helps if yeh have a bit of wit." He said this with a twinkle in his hyacinth blue eyes. They selected one of the shop's floral cards and the two men put their heads together, composing a message for Kate.

Patrick read their final draft aloud. "What do yeh t'ink?"

Luke was gobsmacked. It sounded so good when recited in a Galway accent. "Hot dog!"

Patrick inhaled with a gasp and gave his pupil a stern look. "Hot dog? I tell yeh to speak from the heart and you say *hot dog*?"

"My dad said that a lot when I was growing up. He died when I was a kid. Old memories, I guess."

"Nevertheless, that's some hairball, lad."

Luke said that he would also like to have a bouquet sent to his ailing mother in America. He chose a dozen white roses with Queen Anne's Lace and Bells of Ireland. It was similar to those the American biddies had chosen.

"What message would yeh like on *her* card?" The florist asked. Luke knew this was a test; a trick question.

"Roses are white, violets are blue ..."

"I hope yer only messin'."

"Yep. I'm not *that* pathetic." Luke closed his eyes and rubbed his forehead for a moment. "Umm ... Dear Mom, I miss you already. So happy you turned the corner. May these flowers brighten your day."

"Not bad, lad. Why don't yeh add somet'ing to spice it up a wee bit?"

Luke started to sweat. *Something spicy?* "Umm ... Umm ... I love you more than Mexican food?"

Patrick hesitated over the keyboard. "Since this is yer mum, I'll let it pass. But that'd be rubbish if she were a lady-friend who needed romancin'."

Luke paid the florist and shook his hand. Mr. O'Neill looked him in the eye and said, "Practice speaking from the heart, and letting yer words flow like Guinness, lad. Or yeh haven't got a chance in hell."

As he left the shop, he glanced at his phone and noticed that Nora had texted five messages. If he'd had more time, he would have asked the florist to give him the right words for a break-up.

CHAPTER 50

It's a good thing that when God created the rainbow
He didn't consult a decorator
Or he would still be picking colors.

~SAM LEVENSON

Kate was delighted with how well yesterday's opening went. As she folded towels alongside Molly Flood, she thought about how smoothly this morning went, too. Breakfast sailed by like a curragh skimming in the breeze. So did the kitchen and guestroom cleaning. There was a lull in the activity at the moment because their guests were out enjoying the sights. The California graduate students were whiskey-tasting at the Jameson distillery. They told her a pub crawl was to follow, meaning that a liquid dinner was on their itinerary. Lee and Nick drove to Lahinch at the crack of dawn for a 12:10 tee time. After playing a round at the old course, they planned on visiting a rectory nearby. Kate hoped the greens weren't too wet to play. She loaded a pile of whites into the washing machine and chuckled.

"What's so funny?" Molly asked.

"I was thinking the retail industry in Dublin must be thrilled to see the Magee women. I'm sure they're scarfing up inventory right and left. Sweaters, Waterford and Belleek will be flying off the shelves." The two joined Catriona in the kitchen.

"Well now, everyt'ing's been runnin' grand, I'd say. Everyone seemed well pleased with their accommodations and food so far."

Catriona rattled around the press and removed some walnuts to add to her tarts.

"I'm glad to see that you're baking. The Magee women might need to replenish the calories they're burning during their power shopping, and the grad students might need to add something solid to the whiskey that will be churning in their guts."

Catriona leaned over the damn dangling wrench and pointed her wooden spoon at Kate. "You know what that devil whiskey can do. When those eejit students return in a buckled condition, they'd best not tango with my freshly cleaned toilets."

Kate cocked a brow. *Just when I thought we were making progress, she backslides.* She exhaled slowly, "Remember, they are paying guests and our mission here is hospitality. And re-cleaning the loo is sometimes a part of it."

"Indeed. Don't I well know it?" Catriona grasped the wrench and jerked it to the right to pre-heat the cooker.

"Well now," Molly said with a grin, "I'll make sure to teach Helen the philosophy behind toilet cleaning."

Both Kate and Catriona chuckled at Molly's comment as the tension was flushed away.

Kate looked out the window. Next door, Benjamin and Jack were scrubbing some chalk designs off their house. "I need to ask the Kennedy boys when they will have time to move some furniture for me."

Opening the door, she nearly tripped over a wrapped bouquet of flowers sitting on her step. She brought it inside.

"What have you got there?" Catriona asked while putting a tart into the oven.

Kate opened the wrapping, exposing an array of brilliant color. She noticed it looked as though someone had already separated the tissue paper. She plucked the tag hanging from a stem. "It says to add water immediately, but there's no card. And the florist's name is not on the box."

"That's odd," said Molly, discarding the clear wrapping and fuchsia paper as she lifted the vase from the box. "Who could they be from?"

"I don't know," Kate said, "Perhaps my mom. Maybe my friend Rose in Stillwater or some neighbors here in Glasnevin."

"Maybe your Spandex Man sent 'em," Catriona said as she added water to the vase.

"No, I don't think so. I'm convinced I scared him off." Kate picked up a spatula. "In fact, I'm a little ticked off at Mr. Spandex Man for not contacting me like he said he would." She whacked the spatula into her palm. "What's with men, anyway?"

Catriona lifted an eyebrow. "Let's t'ink of happy thoughts now, shall we?" She held the flowers up to the window and exclaimed, "Ah look, it's a lovely rainbow."

Kate set her shoulders, determined to lift her mood. She remembered Deirdre saying that rainbows are harbingers of good luck. She closed her eyes and smelled the flowers, recalling her brother's words. *Ahh ... these gifts of nature ... a reward for my own hard work ...*

When she lifted her lids, she spotted the returning Magee ladies flocking to the front door, toting a gazillion shopping bags. The women were fluttering about, flying on a shopper's high. Michael, having just arrived on his white bike, in his western boots and hat, was running to give Angie a hand. Then he grabbed the matriarch's bag. They chirped their thanks.

His joy was contagious and Kate caught it through the window.

As he mounted his bike seat a bit later, he returned Kate's wave with a tip of his cowboy hat. Angie must have kissed him, she thought; there was lipstick smeared on his cheek.

Yep. And the goodness of other people.

Kate looked at her bouquet again. *I'd better try to find out who sent this rainbow.* She retrieved her phone and called her mom.

CHAPCER 51

I hate flowers—
I paint them because they're cheaper than models
and they don't move.

~GEORGIA O'KEEFFE

Ultan Ferrian pulled into a pay-and-display parking space near The Cobblestones guesthouse. In his hand he held a card from *O'Neill Floral*. It read:

May everything go well for you, Kate McMahon,
as you run The Cobblestones.
May this bouquet remind you
of a writer who's been trying to phone.
May you have all the happiness and luck that life can hold.
And at the end of all your rainbows,
May you find a pot of gold.

"What a crock of shite." Ferrian lit a cigarette and took a deep pull as he coiled up on the driver's seat. "What is all this blather? It makes me want to puke." He filled his lungs with smoke again and blew it out his nostrils.

He turned the card over and noticed that someone had scribbled a note. *I've been having trouble getting hold of you. Please call me on my cell.* The bloke had written his phone number on the card and signed it *Luke*.

Who was this Luke?

Ferrian seethed. The name Luke was also written on that manila envelope he lifted from the guesthouse's doorstep a few days ago; the one with the photos of Kate and her friends in a pub. It was obvious this wanker was actin' the Romeo and tryin' to put the moves on Kate. Didn't the eejit know that women preferred action over words? Jaysus, they didn't want to be serenaded with ABCs. But of course yer man Luke wouldn't know this fact; he was a fookin' writer who gets paid to write rubbish.

Ferrian punched the phone number into his contact list and then tossed the card out the window. If this poem was any indication of Luke's artistic skill, then the gobshite was one pathetic writer, especially when it came to the flame of passion.

Memories swirled in his mind like a host of dust devils. He recalled a Christmas Eve of his childhood when he overheard his mother getting it on with one of her regulars. She belted out what women really wanted: "I'm so sick of words! If you're on fire...show me!"

I need another bloody plan. By the time he had smoked another cigarette down to a stabber, he knew what he would do. There was no way Kate weighed more than nine or ten stone. Surely he'd be able to drag her to the car. And once he got her into his hideout—while she was still groggy—he'd slip her a Mickey Finn. He wasn't sure how long he'd enjoy her company. He'd just play it by ear. But he needed to act fast before that maggot Luke got his way with her.

Ferrian threw the stabber out the window; it scorched a hole in the florist's card lying on the concrete. He wondered how Kate enjoyed the sketches in the red folder he'd left for her. Did they frighten her a little? Did she feel a yearning, knowing that she had a mystery man out there somewhere? He enjoyed imagining what her reaction must have been when she came to the erotic sketches in the middle of the pack. He'd bet his life she'd been aroused to the fookin' point of rapture.

It was a pisser that the high he got from porn was short-lived. Lately, after sliding into the lust, he'd experience a vast black hole, again and again. The feeling made him rage; he hated the cold cave of emptiness.

He opened a package of crisps and remembered another line that his doxie-of-a-mother shouted to one of her new patrons: "God Almightly, man! Aren't yeh hung like a showdog!" He knew what women wanted all right, and wasn't he a showdog himself?

Slouching in the front seat, Ferrian made himself as small as the hairs on a gnat's bollocks. He didn't want anyone to spot him while he fed another craving. He reached into a plastic bag and removed a green Ecstasy pill. His stash was shrinking. Stamped on one side of the tablet was a four-leaf-clover.

"Indeed, it looks like this showdog is goin' to get lucky soon."

CHAPTER 52

*Only Irish coffee provides in a single glass
all four essential food groups:
Alcohol, caffeine, sugar and fat.*

~ALEX LEVINE

The next morning, Catriona visited with Myrna Riley in the kitchen of The Cobblestones. She cleaned the slippery residue adhering to the oatmeal pot while Myrna made them each a cup of tea.

"So, 'tis goin' well then?" Myrna asked.

"Better. The summer looks slow, except for the days surroundin' the Special Olympics. But we've been takin' a few reservations for next fall, for some massive American football game."

"Right," said Myrna. "Terry mentioned it. Notre Dame will be playin' the Navy this year in the Emerald Isle Classic. A throng of Yanks will be touchin' down in Dublin."

Catriona poured the soapy water out of the pot. "Indeed. And I ordered more O'Flynn sausages this morning. The guests are sayin' they're the best they've ever had. Word will spread about our gorgeous breakfasts."

"That's fine and good, but what I was really after was … Is it goin' well with … yeh know … the surprise?"

" 'Tis grand altogether, Myrna, but keep it under yer cap."

"So I will. Where is Kate?"

"She skipped her run and is makin' some phone calls. She'll be done soon enough. Since all the guests are out, I can manage fine."

The women heard some giggling coming from upstairs. Molly Flood was instructing Helen Riley on how to take over her responsibilities. They heard Helen ask, "What do you do with the disgustin' t'ings you find in the waste bins?"

"You put them in the rubbish bag. And wear latex gloves—a practical tip comin' from a nursin' student."

"And what if I find something disgustin' on the sheets or towels?"

"Roll all the linens up into a ball and whisk them into the washin'. And wear the gloves." There was more giggling, and then Molly asked her pupil, "Do you know the proper way to clean a toilet?"

"Didn't my mam teach me? I spray on a heavy layer of disinfectant and scrub like mad."

"And wear gloves. Oh, and remember … our mission is hospitality, so think fond thoughts of the people who made the mess."

Downstairs, Catriona said to Myrna, "Helen's goin' to do a grand job altogether."

"Good t'ing I taught her how to properly scrub a toilet and make a bed."

When Myrna left, Catriona walked to Michael Farley's home to meet with his mam. Along the way, she passed a white car, parked at the curb. A man sat at the wheel with a hat pulled far down on his head. It looked like he was waiting for someone. By the looks of the pile of cigarette butts on the street outside the driver's door, he'd been there a long time.

Her curiosity was smothered by thoughts of the next big surprise she was planning—if the Farleys gave their blessing. *Won't it be grand?*

As she continued on her way, she wrapped her long cardigan around her big middle. It had started to sprinkle again, but that didn't diminish the spring in her step. She spied an old copper penny on the ground and bent over to pick it up, humming a tune:

If you have no daughters
If you have no sons

Give them to your neighbors
Hot cross buns!

When she returned from the Farley's, she and Michael replaced the wilted tulips with a small bouquet of daffodils in the dining room. Each time she looked at him, a smile crept over her face. They had said their goodbyes to the Magee ladies who were headed to Waterford to hit the crystal retail store, and the graduate students who were on their way north to the Bushmills distillery. They had welcomed a few new guests and had a few walk-ins, but weren't there still beds beggin' for bodies?

While Catriona swept the front stoop, she looked at the "Vacancy" sign hanging in the front garden. She let out a long, slow breath.

Kate came around the side of the guesthouse, glanced at the sign and let out a similar sigh.

"Don't be discouraged. It takes time to build a business. Even the McFaddens had a slow start," Catriona said.

"That's not the only thing that's got me down."

"Ah, now... that Spandex Man will be showin' his face soon enough."

"Oh, don't remind me of Luke."

"There's nothin' wrong with dreamin', lass. I'm a bit of a dreamer myself." She noticed Kate winced.

They went inside and made Irish coffees to go with the chocolate Guinness cake Catriona had baked.

Cousin Nick smacked his lips. "Wow, Catriona! This cake is divine. You could open up a thriving business in Pennsylvania." His smile revealed teeth as white as what was left of his hair.

Catriona could feel her face turn as red as a well-smacked backside.

"Aren't you going to join us, Kate?" Father Lee asked.

"Um, well, I'll have some cake, but I'm taking a break from whiskey. I'm afraid I had too much my first night here, and I made a fool of myself in front of Catriona the next morning."

"You don't say," Father Lee said.

"Father," Catriona said, placing a glass cover over the cake stand. "I'm a bit of an expert on the topic of inebriation. I grew up with a few tipplers in the family." She patted her hair and glanced sideways at Nick. "Do you gents have time for a funny story?"

Wiping chocolate crumbs from his mouth, Father Lee said, "Of course. Maybe it'll be fodder for a homily some day." When the others in the room echoed his enthusiasm, Nick stood up and politely pulled out the chair beside his.

As she plopped herself down, she looked up at Nick and quickly lowered her glance. His attention had her bumfuzzled. "Oh my! Don't I feel like a duchess, though?"

When she looked about her, she witnessed a mischievous grin passing between Kate and Father Lee. Ignoring it, she plunged into her story. "When I was a young girl out the country, my friends and I belonged to a farming club. We'd have a bit of a social while working on crafts, cooking projects and the lot. We also learned about livestock, crops and to be sure—growing potatoes."

"Sounds like the 4-H club I was in as a farm kid," Cousin Nick said, wiping away his whipped cream mustache.

"Right," Catriona said. "Having grown up on a farm yerself, then you know the beauty of these types of gatherin's for the young folk."

Nick nodded. "So this is a true story? Not an Irish tale?"

"'Tis true. I'm not one to tell tales." Catriona continued, "Usually we took the bus to our club, but this particular day I begged me da to let us girls use his lorry."

"That's a truck," Kate explained to the visitors.

Catriona continued, "After a few jars he finally gave in. So off we went."

"What's a jar, Ma'am?" A guest from Virginia named Gaertner asked. He was sitting at a nearby table.

"A pint, or a glass of beer, mostly." Catriona pointed to one on the stand. "Right, then. On the way to our meetin' we purchased some cigarettes. We were smokin' as we drove and thought we were gettin' away with it. But durin' the meetin' we heard sirens. Somebody yelled that a lorry was on fire in the street. And sure enough it was me da's."

"Oh, no!" The Virginian exclaimed.

"Indeed," said Catriona. "After the fire brigade had put the flames out, a fireman came up to our meetin' room. He could tell 'twas my lorry, for wasn't I cryin' like a wee babe? He told me that the back seat was destroyed but that I could drive it home. So, all five of us girls crammed into the front seat and drove toward my house, and I parked the darn t'ing down the way a bit."

"What did your dad say?" Father Lee asked, after taking a sip of his Irish coffee.

"My friends all came inside with me to help with the explainin'. Weren't we all relieved when we discovered that he wasn't home? He was out with mates at the pub. So, I planned to tell him the next day. But wait 'til I tell yeh ... When mornin' came, me da looked out the window and scratched his head and said, 'Bejappers! Why would I be parkin' the lorry down the street?'"

"You must be jokin'," Molly Flood said. She had taken a break from the dishes to listen to the story.

"No, indeed." Catriona giggled and continued, "Da went out to move the vehicle and that's when he discovered the burned-out back seat."

"What did he do?" Kate asked as she collected the mugs.

"Didn't he promise his wife and children that he was goin' off the drinkin' and smokin' altogether, because of what he'd done. He thought he was havin' blackouts."

Father Lee asked with a chuckle, "Did you ever confess the truth, Catriona?"

"I did indeed. In the confessional the next day. My penance was to be open and honest." She paused as Dr. Roddy's face flashed before her. "But mind you, I didn't tell me da until the day he received his Five-Year Pin for sobriety."

227

"That poor priest must have been fighting to hold back his chuckles," Father Lee said, as everyone laughed and the party dispersed. Only Nick stayed behind.

Catriona stealthily pinched her cheeks for a rosy glow. "Well now, Nick, I'm glad you enjoyed my story. Now I best be gettin' home." She reached into her apron pocket and held out two leaves. "But first I have somet'ing for you." She turned to the fine-figure-of-a-man and said, "I noticed you were smellin' the inside of your golf shoes when you got home from the west. If you put a bay leaf inside them, by evening the odor will be removed. And your shoes will... smell like corned beef instead."

"My, oh my! If you find that aroma attractive... then into my shoes they go. Thanks Catriona," he said.

She peered over her shoulder at him as she slowly bent down to fetch her handbag. She felt his eyes follow her out the door. *Am I imagining this?*

As she fluttered down the road, her feet came upon the mountain of cigarette butts which must have been left by the bloke she spotted in the white car earlier. Among the pile she noticed a card with *O'Neill* legible between the scorch marks. She grabbed it and blew off the ashes. There were burn holes seared into it, too, but Catriona could still make out a bit of the writing:

--you have all-------------------------------.
---------the----------------------,
--------------pot-----------.

Pot? What is this rubbish? On the back there was a part of a phone number and what looked like a signature. Did it say Mike, or perhaps Jake? Would they be dealin' drugs on this corner of Glasnevin? She put the card into her bag. She'd toss it away in the bin when she got home. *So now I'm after pickin' up litter from potheads!* She kicked the butts down the sewage drain with a harumph. *Only eejits smoke in vehicles!*

CHλPCER 53

I am a drinker with a writing problem.
~BRENDAN BEHAN

Acold chicken dinner lay neglected at Luke's side. He was finally writing that article about the two Bloody Sundays. Today he had been concentrating on the 1972 incident in Northern Ireland when 26 unarmed Irish protesters and bystanders were killed by the British Army during a civil rights march. He had obtained a copy of the investigation report. It stated that the killings were both "unjustified and unjustifiable." He also had a copy of the formal apology made by the prime minister on behalf of the UK.

Luke reached for his notebook. Earlier in the day, he had interviewed Mrs. Middleton, the 90-year-old he met on the street a while back, when that idiot in the white car almost hit him. The little old lady was delightful. They met at her home in Glasnevin and shared a pot of tea, and darned if the granny didn't insist on waiting on him. She was so excited to have someone from the press interview her, and thankfully her memory was clear as vodka.

"It was the most significant event of the Troubles of Northern Ireland, lad," she told him as she passed a piece of barm brack. "Because those who died—may the good Lord bless 'em—were shot by the British Army rather than paramilitaries. And did I tell yeh that it was in full view of the public and press? Indeed it fueled the IRA."

And then, when Luke was nibbling on a currant from the cake, she dropped the bomb. "Did I tell yeh, Mr. O'Brien, that I know an eye witness to the horrid event? Me son Liam's coworker was one of the injured … a Barry Harrington. Sure 'tis fortunate he wasn't one of the 26 killed."

Luke coughed. The currant shot across the room and landed near the television stand on her fancy rug. "Would you happen to have his contact information?" he asked, and then crawled on his knees to retrieve the vittle.

"Didn't I t'ink you might be wantin' the information? So I asked me Liam to write it down when last he visited." The woman tapped her mouth with a finger. "Now let me t'ink … Where did I put it?" She rose with the help of her cane, hobbled over to a shelf and rummaged around.

"Here 'tis."

"Hot dog!" he said, and then he got up from his knees and kissed Mrs. Middleton right in the middle of her parlor. "If Mr. Harrington agrees to an interview, I'll have one hell of a story."

Her eyebrow shot up.

He said, "Oh, I'm sorry … one *heck* of a story." He pulled his phone from his pocket. "And if the piece wins the Harold Kurvers Journalism Award, then I'm taking you out for dinner, Mrs. Middleton."

"Ah now, aren't you a sweet little pumpkin? That would be lovely … as long as it's not for hot dogs."

Barry Harrington did indeed agree to an interview. In fact, he was so enthusiastic that they talked for nearly two hours. He offered to make copies of the original articles, correspondence and photos pertaining to the horrific event. He had kept all this in a file and promised to mail it "straightaway."

Luke was sure this article was going to be one of his best. Tomorrow he'd begin researching the first Bloody Sunday, which took place in Croke Park in 1920. He wrapped up his writing for the day, poured a cup of coffee and stepped out onto his balcony. The Cobblestones guesthouse was aglow in the lamplight—welcoming guests home.

Why hadn't Kate McMahon phoned? He wondered. She should have gotten the flowers yesterday, and he had written his phone number on the card that was stuck into the bouquet. Wouldn't most women call to thank a guy for flowers on the day they arrived? He was no expert, but that was his guess.

As if on cue, his cell sounded. Could it be her? It was coming from an unknown number. "Hello?" he said.

"Is this Luke the writer?" It was a deep male voice.

"Yes. Who's this?"

"None of yer fookin' business." The man had a coarse Dublin accent. "All you need to know is that Kate McMahon belongs to me. Yer to have nothin' to do with her. Do you understand, yeh gobshite? No more flowers, nothin' at all."

"Hey listen, buddy..."

"Just don't mess with her." *Click*, and the phone was dead.

Luke tried calling back the number, but there was no answer. Was Kate seeing someone? Certainly not a low-life like this guy. He'd been having some interesting phone conversations lately. What in hell was going on?

He glanced at the guesthouse once more. *Since I don't have her number should I suck it up and walk over there?* Grabbing his jacket he headed out of his condo, but when he reached O'Gara's he saw her embracing two men as they stood on her front steps. *Well, it looks like she's okay. She's either too busy or she's blowing me off. Maybe she really is seeing someone.*

Luke turned an about-face and walked into the pub—and into the comforting arms of a warm, frothy Guinness. He looked into his pint. *If I end up having that dinner with Mrs. Middleton it might be the best damn date I'll have this year.*

CHAPTER 54

It's better to light a candle than to curse the darkness.

~ATTRIBUTED TO

ELEANOR ROOSEVELT, GENGHIS KHAN AND CONFUCIUS

Michael Farley wiped the remnants of potato leek soup from his protruding lower lip. Then he took the serviette and wrapped a piece of brown bread in it for Pooka and galloped out the door. When he got to Duke, he plunked the treat into his basket and pedaled to church, where he lit a penny candle—one of the green ones by St. Joseph. He needed all the help he could get because Special Olympics World Games were coming up.

When he got back on Duke, Pooka was sniffing around his basket. "Hiya, Pooka. I have s-somet'ing for you." He unwrapped the bread and tossed it in the air. The dog jumped up, grabbed it with strong jaws, and devoured it as she trotted behind the bike, following Michael to the guesthouse. Before it got much darker, he wanted to put more mulch around the annuals he had planted.

Father Lee and Cousin Nick were smoking cigars on a bench in the back, under the hawthorn tree. "Hello, Michael," Miss Kate's brother said. "Since the rain let up, we thought we'd come out and smoke the stogies we bought near Lahinch." Michael liked the way cigars smelled but his mammy thought they were horrid. Pooka sauntered to the men and licked their hands. *She must agree with me*, thought Michael.

He liked the two men because they were nice to everyone—including Pooka. He went over to a pile of mulch, happy to collect it with the wheelbarrow, because pushing that thing around was massive fun.

"Can I help you with the gardening?" Cousin Nick asked, putting out his cigar. "I do a lot of this stuff on the farm. The smell of mulch reminds me of home and the cattle; maybe that's because it has manure in it."

"Surely," Michael said, handing Nick some gloves. He hoped this kind of mulch didn't have a lot of dung in it. That'd be disgustin'! He noticed that the man didn't even care that his fancy trousers got a bit of mud and mulch on the knees.

Pooka came up to Michael and licked his face, causing him to giggle. Nick said, "I can see you like animals, Michael. I have a pet cow named Cindy. Boy, she's a pretty Brown Swiss. And before my wife went to heaven, she used to have a cat named Joyce that would ride on my shoulder and cling to my bibbed overalls for a free ride."

"Do you have a horse?" Michael asked. He spread some mulch around the pansies, and noticed that a few of the lights in the guest rooms were flicking on.

"No, but our neighbors do."

"I have a horse named Duke." Michael pointed to his white bike. "John Wayne n-named one of his horses Duke. Do you like John Wayne?"

"It's a sin to not like John Wayne."

"'Tis?" Michael crinkled up his nose.

"I'm just kidding," Nick said with a chuckle. He scooped mulch around some marigold seedlings.

Miss Kate came out, carrying a tray of beverages, whiskey for the men, and a Fanta for Michael. He'd already had his limit of fizzy drinks that day, but he rarely turned one down. Michael wondered why Miss Kate wasn't having a whiskey. She handed Michael a card. "Congratulations for doing so well in swimming." She turned to the men and explained, "Michael was chosen a while ago to compete in the Special Olympics. Tell them what your nickname is, Michael."

"T-Torpedo. 'Cuz I swim s-super speedy like this ..." Rotating his arms, Michael ran around the grass. The others clapped and cheered.

With a thirst, he chugged his minerals and then looked at Miss Kate. The garden light was shining on her pony-tail and it looked golden. She was wearing a red hoodie that said *Twins* on it. *Isn't that funny? She must really like the Kennedy twins.* He set the can down and then studied her face. To be sure, there was something about her eyes that looked sad, which made him sad.

"The flowers look beautiful, Michael," she said as she bent down to rub Pooka's belly.

Michael gestured toward her and exclaimed, "*You're* beautiful!" because she was—on the inside and the out. That's what his mam said.

"Ah, Michael, you always seem to know what a person needs to hear. I was just inside thinking about how old and ugly I feel."

It hurt Michael to see her eyes get glittery with tears. He reached out and patted her head with a dirty glove. "W-well, you *are* old. But you're not ugly." He felt compelled to tell the truth, and that was a good thing, because now the three big people were all laughing.

Father Lee brushed bits of manure muck out of Kate's hair, and asked, "What's got you down, Katie?"

"Well, A few days ago, I thought Joe Kennedy and I might become an item again. But it wasn't workable. And I'm okay with that, except it kinda hurt when he jumped right over to a younger, hotter woman—that Kelly O'Gara from the pub."

Father Lee cut in, "Oh, Katie, she's not ..."

"Yes she is, and we all know it." Miss Kate smiled and plopped on the bench next to her brother. "And then this new guy I was interested in said he'd call, and he didn't. I think he was just using me to get that funny George Clooney story. Compared to the pain and loss I've already been through, this is nothing. This is minor league stuff, and I have more important things on my plate right now. But it still hurts."

Cousin Nick set aside his gloves and stood in front of Miss Kate. "I'm sorry you're going through this."

She sniffed. "I guess I kinda put myself in this situation. Why was I so open to trusting again?"

"Now, Kate, remember—for everything there is a season," her brother said. Michael saw Father Lee squeeze Miss Kate's hand. "Dad would be so proud of you. By taking this big risk—moving to Ireland and starting this business—you've proven that you have the courage to change the things you can. But remember it's also important to accept the things you *can't* change—and that includes the behavior of others."

Father Lee's words reminded Michael of the tipplers' prayer that he had seen on a plaque in the chapel.

"You can't make somebody love you, even though you deserve to be loved," Nick said.

Michael saw that Miss Kate's nose was running. She wiped it and said, "If Catriona were here she'd say that you can, however, render them helpless—with her Tahitian body oil."

The men gave each other a gacky look and then laughed. Michael joined in on the laughing, wondering what was so funny.

Nick put his gloves back on and said, "Kate, I have a feeling that when you least expect it, Mr. Right will fall at your feet."

Michael checked his pockets and pulled out a euro. "I'm g-goin' back to church to light a g-green candle for you M-Miss Kate, and pray that a n-nice cowboy falls at your feet … and doesn't get a gash." He could hear the threesome chuckle again as he jumped on Duke, the Dalmatian deputy at his side.

CHAPTER 55

Let the wife make the husband glad to come home,
and let him make her sorry to see him leave.

~MARTIN LUTHER

In fluffy slippers, Deirdre drifted to the electric tea kettle and hit the "on" button. She glanced out her window and saw Kate starting on her morning jog. *Oh bugger! Don't I feel like a lazy bones? Indeed, that woman is not the full shillin' if she's runnin' in this rain!*

But Deirdre knew she wasn't lazy at all—just a bit slow-like in the exercise department. Hadn't she already washed a stack of dishes, put in a load of laundry, overseen the lunch making, and driven the boys to school? All in her bathrobe—and it not yet half-seven.

The boyos were mortified that she wasn't dressed proper-like as she chauffered them about. "Jaysus, Mam, what if a garda pulls you over, fluffy, pink slippers and all?" But she figured the Dublin Gardaí had seen worse. Didn't she read that they had just pulled a naked fat man out of the sewers? There was no mention as to why the bloke was down there in his birthday suit. Maybe he liked the feel of slime on his skin. Indeed the world had its fair share of gobshites.

Deirdre caught another glimpse of Kate trotting down the road and sighed. She could tell her friend was a bit disappointed lately because of Joe. And that journalist hadn't phoned. What was his name? Ah yes, Luke O'Brien. Perhaps she should phone the man herself to investigate. When she glanced out the window again Kate was a speck on the horizon, a white car trailing behind her in the dark rain.

The button popped up on the kettle and she poured the boiling water into a mug that said, "I child-proofed the house but they still get in!" While the tea was steeping, she grabbed her romance novel from its hiding place under the divan cushions. On the cover was a picture of a big-bosomed woman removing a mini gun from her bodice; a don't-mess-with-me look was on her face. The title, *Reckless with the Rogue,* was written in metallic curlicues across the top.

To the sound of the rain, she curled up on the cushions and pulled her robe tight. She loved the days her mam took the twins for a few hours. Sometimes, just for the heck of it, she'd strip off her clothes and streak through the house in her pelt because she could. Sure, it was juvenile, but it made her feel so free. She gave a mischievous smile and looked about the house. Her husband was at work, all the chisellers were gone, and Joe said he'd be out 'til noon.

Should I? Maybe she'd just run the dirty socks that were left on the floor to the laundry right quick and then back again. She stood in the middle of the parlor and removed her plush robe and navy blue nightie. A breeze blew in through the lace curtains and kissed her nakedness. Just when she bent over to grab the socks, she heard a noise coming from the garden.

"Jaysus, Mary and Joseph!" Deirdre squealed as she dove for cover behind the divan. The door made a squeak as it opened, and she heard heavy footsteps. She peeked out. It was a man all right; but was it Mark or Joe? She couldn't tell from her vantage point.

Bugger it! Her sleepwear nestled a few metres away, beyond her reach. Footsteps clonked on the kitchen floor again, getting nearer the parlor. Deirdre curled up like a hedgehog and didn't let her lungs stir. The footsteps were muffled. He was on the carpet now! She heard a sharp intake of breath.

"Deirdre?"

She still couldn't tell if it was her husband or brother-in-law. *I swear to God I'll never streak again! Not even when the twins are grown and out of the house. Never, ever!*

"Deirdre? Where are you? And why is 'Monica Lewinsky' lying on the floor?"

She popped up like Jack-in-the-Box. Sure, only her husband knew the names of her jammies. "You big *amadán*! What are you doin' scarin' the bejaysus out of me? Didn't I t'ink you might be Joe?" Her copper tendrils weren't quite long enough to hide her charms in a Lady Godiva fashion.

Mark looked her over with sweet delight. He had her romance novel in his hand. "My meeting got cancelled. Why don't I take you upstairs and you can show me how ruthless you can be with this rogue?" He danced the book in front of her eyes and threw it down. Then he knelt on the divan so that his head was right at breast-level. And *ohhhh*, the kissin' was makin' her body tingle and shudder like in that scene where Felicity shamelessly succumbs to her rapacious rogue.

"What if Joe gets back early from his coffee date at Bewley's?" Deirdre panted. She really didn't want him to stop, however. He was orchestrating her body like a maestro, and soon enough she'd be singin'. Now he was nibbling her neck right beside the Sheela na gig necklace he had given her. The fertility charm dangled from its chain and stroked her sternum.

Mark teased in a husky voice, "I've a fire in my loins, Hot Mamacita, and only you can put it out."

"I don't want to put it out. I plan to stoke it until we get interrupted." Deirdre ran her nails down his back. "There's a good chance baby number eight might start bakin' in me oven, though."

He licked her ear. "Eight's..." He sucked her neck. "a..." He bit her shoulder. "nice..." He kissed her clavicle. "number."

"You reckless rogue!" was all she could gasp.

CHAPTER 56

Drink is the curse of the land.
It makes you fight with your neighbor.
It makes you shoot at your landlord—And miss him.

~IRISH PROVERB

Kate had always loved running in the rain. There was something about it that was exhilarating and cleansing. She wiped away the raindrops dripping from her forehead. Like a mirage, an image of her possible future flashed before her: running—thirsty and fatigued—in the scorching heat of the Arizona desert. Kate squeezed the wildflower she had plucked near the playground with renewed determination. After crossing the Tolka River, she came to a "V" in the path and decided to go left toward the treeline, like usual. Behind her, she sensed movement along the other branch of the path, which snaked along the bottom of the hill. She thought nothing of it, and wiped droplets from her face.

Since the rain was starting to pick up, she wanted to get home as quickly as possible. Nobody was in front of her on the path, so she decided to fartlek. For some unknown reason, she was suddenly gripped by a cold fear. An urgent need to run like the wind, as if some force were pushing her, saying, "Faster, faster!"

Within the cluster of weeping willows, her legs started their rapid drive. Because of the trees' umbrella-like coverage, the ground was dry there, making her flight easier. The flower tumbled from her hand.

As she neared the end of the grove, she heard someone from behind shouting her name. But before she could turn around and look, she heard a *Zzzzzaaaap!*

CHAPTER 57

There is something terribly morbid
in the modern sympathy with pain.
One should sympathise with the colour, the beauty, the joy of life.
The less said about life's sores the better.

~OSCAR WILDE

It hurt like hell. All he could do was lie there, face-down, on the ground for a few minutes, moaning like a wimp. He felt like he was on fire and his extremities were jerking around. He panicked, *Oh my God, am I dying?* His body tingled as though swarms of angry hornets were using him for target practice.

For a moment Luke thought he was in the ring again, boxing for Notre Dame's Bengal Bouts. *Who is my opponent? Did I get sucker-punched?* Damn, his head was pounding. He must have whacked it when he kissed the canvas.

Just when he decided he was down for the count, he was aware of someone beside him. Was it his corner man? He tried to turn his head, but it was plastered to the ground and wouldn't obey his command.

"Are you all right, sir?" an angel's voice asked. She shuffled a little and then put something soft and red under his head on the blacktop. The color pulled him out of his brain fog a little. *Okay, so I'm not in a boxing match. But… what kind of a hit did I take?* He recalled that he'd been running a distance behind Kate McMahon, and that she was wearing a red shirt. Was this Kate? The woman removed his ballcap.

"Ooouch!" he groaned.

"Luke, it's you! Crud! What the heck happened?"

Now he knew it was Kate for sure. He wanted to talk, but he couldn't get anything out except baby noises. *Shit, what a pathetic loser!*

His mind was getting clearer, but he was having trouble piecing things together. Why did his ass feel like a sword was puncturing it? And why did his back feel like he had taken a kidney punch?

"Luke, it's me, Kate McMahon." She squatted on the path near the brambles and turned his head to the side, so he could see her. Water dripped off the brim of her cap. She crouched closer still, and he saw the goosebumps on her legs. With a wet hand, she wiped the rain from his face.

"Geez, you have some kind of a wire coming out of your back. It looks like it's stuck in there with some sort of a … a dart thingy." She looked around the park and then into his eyes. He couldn't stop blinking. At least his damn eyelids worked. "And you've got another one of those wire things coming out of your … your butt."

That sobered him up. He tried to recall what happened. He had seen a red laser dot darting among the willow trees. He'd called out to Kate, sped up, and then heard a clicking noise.

"Damn, I was Tasered," he said. His jaw clenched. "And, um … will you … pull the prongs out? They … hurt like hell."

He could see her make a face under her brim. "Ahhhh, sure. How, exactly?"

"I don't know." He lifted his throbbing head and tried to look at his backside. It wasn't a pretty sight. "I guess … put your fingers … around the darts and … tug."

She hopped up and straddled him with her tennis shoes in puddles. "Okay, here goes." She yanked out the one in his back.

"Oooouch! God that … kills!"

"Sorry," she said. He managed to swivel his head toward her. She was looking at his light blue Spandex shirt and crinkling up her face. "Oh gross, it's bleeding."

"Don't worry about that … just get the other one out."

"Um …" She hesitated. "I'm gonna have to touch your butt."

"I wish it were … under … different … circumstances." He tried to wink at her, but the effort hurt his head.

Now she sounded peeved. "Maybe I should just leave it there."

He didn't understand her anger. Maybe his remark was too forward. Thinking about it made his head hurt more. Maybe he had a concussion from slamming his forehead into the pavement. "What?"

"You told me ages ago—in Tullahought—that you'd call me, and you didn't. Not that I was waiting by the phone or anything, but I didn't hear a thing from you." She plopped on the ground next to him. Mud splattered onto his face. He noticed that besides her shorts, the Lady in Red wore only a black running bra now. The scarlet pillow underneath his head must be her shirt. "Were you just toying with me in order to get that Clooney story? Huh?"

"I don't … know … what you're talking about." God, he wished she'd just get that damn thing out of his ass. "I tried calling, and … Buck left a note … on your doorstep." He took a few deep breaths. "And then I got this … really odd phone call … from some Irishman saying to … leave you alone; that you belonged to him." His gluteus maximus gave a spastic shudder that caused him to jerk. "Can we just … talk about this later? Will you please pull that … second dart out?"

"What? I don't *belong* to anyone. Who would call you like that and lie?"

Kate looked like she didn't believe him. Her eyes bore into him deeper than the blasted prongs.

Through gritted teeth he said, "I don't know … who he was … I tried to find out … but … couldn't. It's been … crazy … My mom was sick … I've been in the States."

She squinted.

"Honest!" Luke lifted his head and glanced at her again. Her pissed-off look dripped from her jawline along with the droplets of rain. A sprinkling of compassion was starting to soften her features, though.

243

"Well … Okay. I guess we can talk about this later. I'm just really confused." She straddled him again.

"You think … *you're* … confused?" Luke mumbled. "When you pull that … sumbitch out, could you please … apply some pressure this time?"

Her left hand cupped his buttocks roughly while her right hand gave a quick yank.

"Owwww!" Luke felt immediate relief in his backside, but his head still throbbed when he lifted it. He grabbed the red shirt and hobbled up. "Thanks, Kate, I owe you big time." But she was pre-occupied, collecting the Taser wires. He could tell she was thinking about something deep when she got to the cartridge.

"I've seen this before," she said, wiping the rain from her face. "I found one of these in my yard, but it was unfired and I didn't know what it was."

Luke's journalistic mode started to kick in. Someone was definitely aiming for Kate instead of him. At first he thought it was some delinquent kids messing around, but now he doubted that. He rubbed his temples and ruminated. *Christ, I remember seeing a red laser spot on Kate's yellow shorts, and I shouted to her.* The next thing he knew, he'd sped up and was thrown to the ground. Had he gotten in the line of fire?

"Do you have a phone on you?" He asked through the bullets of rain.

"No, I didn't want it to get ruined in this weather."

"Same here." Luke touched her arm. "Come on, Kate. Since your place is closer, let's head over there and report this to the gardaí."

"Um … Okay. But let's go to the back door. I don't want to upset my guests."

His eyes searched the surrounding area, as he wrapped the t-shirt around her shoulders and they hobbled toward The Cobblestones.

CHAPTER 58

You gotta love livin', baby, 'cause dyin' is a pain in the ass.

~FRANK SINATRA

After breakfast, Catriona wished all the guests a good day on their sightseeing escapades. The golfers, Father Lee and his charming cousin, had left at the crack of dawn, hoping to play 18 holes at Howth Golf Club, if the rain would let up. She pulled a few sprigs of heather from Kate's mysterious rainbow bouquet, arranged them in a bud vase, and set it on Cousin Nick's nightstand. Then she phoned her former neighbor, Cormac O'Shea, to check on her surprise.

She wondered where her boss had gotten to. Usually Kate would be done with her run and shower by now, but Catriona hadn't even seen her yet. It wasn't like Kate to miss out entirely on the early morning routine. Just when she was going to knock on Kate's apartment door she heard noises in the back hall and beheld two soaked creatures making muddy footprints on her floor. And didn't she just mop it yesterday?

"Catriona, could you please get us a couple of towels?" a goose-fleshed, half-naked Kate asked. "We need to call the police."

"The gardaí?" Catriona wilted like a head of warm lettuce. "Are yeh all right?"

"We had an incident in Griffith Park. I'll explain in a minute."

Jaysus, Mary and Joseph, didn't it sound dire though? She went to the hot press for towels. Kate rushed to her room and returned with a mobile.

"Don't forget to dial 999 here in Ireland. Not 911," the man in wet Spandex said. He bent down to take off his shoes and groaned.

"Holy God in Heaven! Yer bleedin'!" Catriona bellowed.

The man touched the wound on his forehead and shrugged his broad shoulders. She handed him a towel, and noticed how the wet Spandex shirt formed to his body like a sausage casing. This bloke had a lot of muscular meat on him for a fellow his age. Could this be the infamous Hot Dog Man?

As Kate stepped toward the kitchen to make the call, he turned to Catriona as if he could tell she was wondering about him. "Hi, I'm Luke O'Brien." She hoped he wouldn't guess that she was fawning over his muscles. His right hand, streaked with scrapes, was thrust out for a handshake. It, too, appeared powerful.

"Right. I'm Catriona Ryan, the manager of this place." She put her chubby, chafed hand into his and lifted one eyebrow. "I've heard about you indeed, Luke O'Brien. And none too good." Her comment made him uneasy. She could tell by the way he hesitated while rubbing his hair with the towel. "A gentleman doesn't leave a woman hanging. A wee bit of cat-and-mouse is fine and dandy, but ignoring her for eternity is a bold t'ing altogether!"

Yer man looked gobsmacked. He cringed as he wiped off his backside. "Um, gosh ..." he said. Words seemed to be getting caught in his throat for a moment. "I'm confused. Didn't Kate get a bouquet I sent her from O'Neill's Floral in Galway?" His eyes darted around and fell on the wilting arrangement sitting on an end table. "There it is. I'm pretty sure. It used to be fuller and more colorful, though."

Something triggered in Catriona's noggin. *Could this really be the giver of the mysterious bouquet?* She excused herself and fished her pocketbook out of the desk in the office. Digging around the Black Hole—as Declan called her handbag—she found the remains of the burnt card which had been in the street near that pile of cigarettes. She'd forgotten to throw it away. Indeed, the top was inscribed with *O'Neill.* Through the scorch marks and smeared ashes she re-read:

--you have all-------------------------------.
---------the----------------------,
--------------pot-----------.

Perhaps this card blew off the arrangement, and wasn't part of a drug deal after all. And poor Kate, not knowin' that himself had indeed tried to contact her. *What had the greeting originally said? No matter.* She remembered Deirdre saying that Luke was a church-going man. A smile spread across her face as she walked back into the parlor.

Kate had changed into decent clothes, and Spandex Man was sporting Kate's Twins hoodie. It stretched across his chest and biceps, but who was looking? As they waited for the garda, Catriona showed them the floral card and explained the situation as best she could. Relief soothed Kate's features like a cucumber facial.

'Tis a grand t'ing altogether to discover one was not jilted after all, Catriona reflected. And it was obvious that Spandex Man was thrilled about Kate's new attitude toward him. The atmosphere didn't seem as blustery as it appeared earlier. *Now, what on Earth happened in Griffith Park?* The suspense was killing her, but she gave them some space for private conversation.

A few moments later, the doorbell sounded. "Ms. McMahon? Mr. O'Brien? I'm Officer Timothy Flynn. I was told by the dispatch about your misfortune. I grew up in Glasnevin and I don't like to hear about such goings-on."

"You're Poppy Flynn's youngest, aren't you?" Catriona asked.

"I am." He removed a notebook from his pocket.

"I've met Poppy at O'Gara's," Kate said.

"Indeed. He's ancient and a right pain in the neck. Do I need to apologize for his actions?"

The hint of a smile tugged at Kate's worried mouth. "He asked me to put my lips up to his and recite his name five times."

Now a smile creased Luke's face. He shook his bloodied head and put a hand to his temple.

"Ah, it's useless. He's been off his nut for quite a few years now." Officer Flynn twisted his biro and asked them to tell about the incident. As the story unfolded, Catriona gave thanks to the saints above for their safe deliverance. Wasn't it lovely that Spandex Man was there to take the hit? What if Kate had been attacked or abducted? Catriona wiped the sweat from her upper lip. Surely tonight she'd be working the beads off the chain.

"Officer, I need to show you something." Kate walked into the kitchen and returned with a small black object in her hand. "I found this near my front steps a few days ago, and forgot about it until now. As you can see, it matches the Taser cartridge that was shot into Luke's back and ... butt."

Catriona could tell that thoughts were tumbling around the garda's head like clothes in a dryer. While making notations, he asked, "Has anyt'ing else peculiar happened lately?"

And then Catriona remembered ... the red folder. "Janey Mack! I have somet'ing to show you." She fetched the folder and they looked through its contents. She hadn't given it much of a look-see before, and now she was kicking herself. It was full of strange sketches; some were sketches of Kate with Morgan O'Gara and Deirdre Kennedy in a pub. And some were shocking! In fact, they bordered on obscene, like something in one of those filthy American magazines.

Luke removed the pub pictures from Catriona's hands. "These are copied from photos that my associate, Buck Hubbell, took of the ladies when we interviewed them out in Tullahought." He touched the bump on his forehead while he thought a moment. "This psycho must have stolen the pictures from Kate's doorstep. Buck told me he left them there in a packet with a note and my phone number. Kate never received the stuff, did you, Kate?"

"Nope." Understanding dawned on her face. "So you *did* try to get in touch with me after all? The flowers ... the note and the pictures ..."

"Of course. I'd have been crazy not to."

Love was starting to perfume the air, right in the midst of the ugliness. It made Catriona miss her Declan more than ever.

Garda Flynn cleared his throat.

Luke abruptly turned his head away from Kate's gaze. "Hey, I might have the guy's phone number. I got a weird call ... I'll have to show you later ... I left my cell at home."

Myrna and Helen Riley rushed into the guesthouse. They must have seen the Garda car. Officer Flynn asked them if they had seen anything unusual, but nothing came to their minds. Catriona showed them a charcoal sketch of an evil-looking Dalmatian wearing a collar that said *Pooka*.

"Whoever did this artwork is demented, so he is," Myrna said, looking nervously through the open window at her pooch. Pooka was safe next to Michael by the officer's car.

Timothy Flynn replaced his pen. "Indeed. This looks like a stalker case. I want this neighborhood on high alert. Call the headquarters if anyt'ing else unlikely happens. And Ms. McMahon, I don't want you runnin' alone a'tall, and make sure you are extra careful at night. We'll send patrols around your place."

"Oh, no! What about my guests? What will happen to my business?"

The air pulsed like a heartbeat. Catriona knew this was the crux of Kate's fear and jumped in: "Officer, we cannot let this pervert ruin what Kate has built here. If the guesthouse is not a success, she'll have to move back to America and live amongst snakes and scorpions."

The Garda sucked on the end of his biro, glancing outdoors. "Ah, now. Wouldn't you say, however, that she already lives amongst predators?" He flipped his notebook closed. "We'll do everything possible to ensure Ms. McMahon's safety and to guard the premises. Your guests should be okay, because it's the innkeeper he wants, so take extra precautions."

A greasy cold crawled down Catriona's spine.

"Thank you, sir." Kate's voice was barely a whisper.

The Garda handed them his card and snapped photos of Luke's injuries—including his Spandexed bum. He promised to swing by Luke's condo later to check his cell. Then he collected the cartridges, folder and drawings for evidence. A sketch titled *The Nightmare* was on top. Its vileness made Catriona shudder. The demon mounting a woman, with a black pooka horse watching. *What manner of man would draw that?*

Everyone went outside except for the cold joggers. They sat on the divan to warm up by the fire. It had stopped raining, thankfully. A group of curious neighbors had gathered in front of the guest-house. Garda Flynn explained the situation and asked if anyone had seen anything suspicious.

"On Easter weekend, my brother and my wife thought they spotted someone peeking into Kate's windows," Mark Kennedy said. Catriona noticed that Mark's shirt was on backwards, and there appeared to be a hickey on his neck. No wonder Deirdre's curls were extra wild this morning, and her cheeks afire. Mark said something about a white Ford Ka and ran inside to retrieve a piece of paper with its partial plate number. The mention of a white car pulled Catriona from looking at Deirdre's bed-head.

"Em, Timothy, sir ... I t'ink I saw the same vehicle parked a few days ago down the road. A man was inside it, but I didn't get a good look at him." Catriona rubbed her chicken-flesh arms. "He must have been there a while, though, because he left quite a pile of cigarette butts on the street." Her eyes became focused as the incident registered. "There was a florist's card at the bottom of the butts. Perhaps the Taser Man stole it from the bouquet sitting on our steps." She handed the card to Timothy, who carefully put it in a plastic bag and added it to the evidence.

"And just this mornin'," Deirdre said while taming her mane and smoothing her clothes, "I saw Kate leave on her jog. A white car was followin' behind her in the rain. I couldn't tell yeh the make and model. I'm useless with those t'ings."

The nice officer made notations and gathered contact information from the crowd. Once again, he told everyone to be on the lookout. He ruffled Pooka's ears and then let Michael mess with his siren and lights before heading out.

Catriona re-entered the guesthouse and spotted Kate and Luke conversing on the divan. She re-filled their teacups, stoked the fire, and told them what Timothy Flynn and the neighbors had discussed. She busied herself to give the two of them privacy, but she couldn't help tuning one ear to the couple. Soon enough she heard something lovely.

Luke said, "Kate, I owe you for giving me the shirt off your back. So, um … so, I was wondering … would you go out for dinner with me tonight? Maybe we could have a hot whiskey first—I'd say we earned one this morning."

Ah Kate … not whiskey on your first date! Catriona put a hand to her stomach and then snuck a peek at the pair of them. Seeing Kate's smile lifted the burden of fear off her shoulders a wee bit.

"I'd love to go to dinner with you. But it's *I* who should be thanking *you.* Who knows where I'd be right now if you hadn't … been a slower runner than me." She twirled a strand of hair and made demure eyes at him. "But I'd better have a glass of merlot instead of whiskey."

"Hot dog!" Luke said, removing the Twins hoodie and handing it back to Kate.

Really? Catriona thought. Hot dog? And this man makes a living with words?

Catriona noticed that Luke grimaced when he stood up and said, "I'll have to find a place with cushioned seats." He rubbed his bum and then groaned while pulling on his runners. "How's seven o'clock sound? I'll pick you up."

"Perfect. If you don't show up, I'll look for a note from Buck on my doorstep." Kate walked him to the door, and Catriona pumped her fist into the air.

CHAPTER 59

Good cognac is like a woman.
Do not assault it.
Coddle and warm it in your hands before you sip it.

~WINSTON CHURCHILL

When Luke approached The Cobblestones that evening, a young man with Down syndrome was in the garden, holding a bouquet of heartsease. He held the blooms out to Luke and said, "I'm M-Michael Farley. I'm the gardener here. M-Mrs. Ryan said you're takin' M-Miss Kate on a date." He pushed his glasses up the bridge of his nose. "You need to give her flowers, pardner. I know, 'cuz Da gives M-Mammy flowers when he takes her to Dobbins." Michael's protruding lip curved upwards, and he pulled down his cowboy hat a little too far, making his ears stick out.

Luke recognized the voice and smiled. So this was the fellow who answered the phone and said something about the Wild, Wild West when he had called the guesthouse. He couldn't wait to tell Kate over dinner.

"Thanks, buddy. These will definitely give me bonus points. I could use a local florist." Luke patted Michael's shoulder.

"S-sure. We have a b-business agreement?"

"A business agreement?" Luke laughed. "You bet, cowboy."

"You l-like John Wayne?" Michael asked.

"Of course. Have you seen *True Grit*? It's my favorite movie of his. He plays a drunken U.S. marshal in it."

"Indeed, b-but I lost that DVD," Michael said, as he snapped his fingers. It looked to Luke like this was a technique to help with stuttering. "I like cowboys. I'm a sh-sheriff."

Luke spotted Kate in the doorway and struggled to steady his pulse.

"Hi, Luke. I see you've met my gardener Michael."

Luke presented her with the flowers and gave Michael a conspiratorial nod.

He looked Kate up and down, taking in her black slacks and fitted grey top. "You look gorgeous," he said, speaking from the heart and letting his words flow like Guinness.

"Thanks. I only changed my clothes about a billion times."

"Me, too," he said, hoping his khakis and blue sweater would pass muster. When he looked at her again, he had an urge to touch that velvety golden hair. His mom would be proud of his restraint.

"Come inside, I want you to meet my brother and cousin." Luke was surprised to see the brother was wearing a Roman collar. He was comfortable around priests. Over the years, he'd interviewed dozens and had gotten to know some during his years at Notre Dame. He hadn't met one he didn't respect, but darned if the back of his neck wasn't sweating.

Father Lee thanked Luke for helping Kate that morning. "I'm still shocked about her brush with danger." Then he padded Luke's shoulder. "How well does she know *you*? Keep in mind, I was a wrestler in high school."

Her cousin Nick added with a grin, "And I'm pretty handy with golf clubs."

And then the housekeeper, Catriona, joined in. "And treat Kate like a queen ... or I'll cuff you on the ear with a toilet brush!"

"Where are you taking her, and when will she be back?" Father Lee asked as he cracked his knuckles. Luke felt like a teenager picking up his first prom date.

"I'm taking her to a hole in the wall. Only the best for Kate."

Luke chuckled as he guided Kate out the door. Through the window, he could hear Catriona explaining that the Hole in the Wall was indeed a grand place. "In fact, it's a medieval pub in Phoenix Park. The marching soldiers were served beer through a hole in the pub's wall. You can still see it today."

Luke settled Kate into the taxi, and she smiled at him and shrugged her shoulders. "Sorry about all that grilling, but I tend to give the people who love me plenty of cause for concern."

What am I getting myself into?

When Kate smiled at him again, as he climbed into the seat beside her, all his fears melted away. They passed a squad car on patrol as they rounded the corner, and the occupants in both vehicles waved to each other.

"Would you be wantin' somet'ing else?" the bartender at the Hole in the Wall asked.

"The bill, please. We're going to City Centre now," Luke said. They placed their empty glasses on coasters which read: *Uisce Beatha*, with an English translation: "Water of Life." Luke knew that this was the origin of the word "whiskey." And the golden liquid was definitely bringing him to life after their crazy morning and his "prom grilling." After a few swallows his nerves and the wounds in his head, back and ass were throbbing less.

During an hour of great conversation, Luke was grateful for the cushioned stool. They laughed as he told stories about growing up in a family of five boys, and how much their lives changed when his dad died.

Kate talked about how wonderful her brother had been after her husband's sudden death. Luke felt honored that, once half her wine was consumed, she had confided in him about the Triple Whammy. But when she added that she wondered whether she could ever trust a man again, it was a blow to his confidence.

On their way to dinner they walked across the cobblestone grounds of Trinity College. When they saw that the Old Library was open late and the line was short, they hurried into the Treasury, where the Book of Kells was exhibited. They leaned over the display case, marveling at the works of medieval art which were hand-produced by candlelight. Luke's back pain returned as he pictured monks hunched over their desks for hours on end.

They peered closely at the illuminated page on display that day— *The Temptation of Christ.* Its celtic knots and interlacing patterns glimmered in vibrant colors. Everything on the vellum shone with beauty, except for a heinous black form off to the side—the figure of Satan.

Kate shuddered.

Luke placed a protective hand on her back. "How 'bout we get some dinner?"

They dined from the carvery at O'Neill's Bar. In an alcove, they briefly discussed Kate's business for his B&B article. He didn't want to pry too much, especially because he could tell she was worried about her financial security. So, he focused on positive things like her gardens and Michael, Catriona's baked goods, and the big-hearted neighborhood.

"Well, at least your B&B is in a safe location. I promise not to mention that crazy Taser guy in the article." Luke grimaced as he shifted in his seat. "Hopefully the guards will resolve that soon, anyway, and put the jerk away."

"Thanks, again, for taking that hit for me," Kate said.

He wasn't so sure he deserved all that gratitude—he had merely reacted out of instinct when he jumped into the line of that red laser. It didn't matter. The important thing was that Kate was spared from the attack.

She reached over and touched the wound on his forehead. Her fingers electrified him more than that damn Taser gun. "I don't know you very well yet, but you seem like a great guy, Luke O'Brien." She removed her magical fingers to take a bite of lamb stew.

"Things take time," he managed to say, "I hope you'll let me hang around until you get to know me better."

Jigs and reels were blaring from the corner and eventually a voice as mellow as Bing Crosby's sang the old ballad, *I'll Take You Home Again, Kathleen.*

"Is your full name Kathleen?" Luke asked. He noticed that their short stools were a few inches closer now.

She looked up at him coyly from the rim of her glass. Her eyes sparkled in the firelight and she purred, "Yes."

She was sending him mixed signals. *Didn't she just say she wasn't ready for romance?* He decided then that Kate was worth the wait. He would need time, anyway—to get through the hellfire of Nora's fury.

Kate looked at him again with eyes of an enchantress. He felt like Merlin bewitched by The Lady of the Lake. He took a gulp of his cocktail. The drink seemed stronger than poteen, and burned his throat. "Hot dog!" he said, thumping his chest.

"Catriona, says you need to stop saying that. In fact, she nicknamed you The Hot Dog Man." Kate giggled as she broke off a piece of roll. "But I think it's kinda cute."

"My dad used to say that all the time. And he was kinda cute, too."

She laughed again.

"Say, speaking of Catriona, I heard her tell Garda Flynn that you'd move back to The States if your business doesn't do well—and then something about living with scorpions?"

"Oh yeah, well ..." She tilted her head down and peered up at him. "You see, I sold everything to pay back my late husband's investors, and then I invested my dad's life insurance money in the guesthouse. If it isn't fully booked most nights, I'll be a pauper. I'd have to move in with my mom in Arizona and sleep on her futon." Kate massaged her shoulder. "This business is unpredictable, but free publicity like this B&B article you're writing will help. But this rain really hurts tourism ... and now ..."

"And now you're worried about that stalker. I don't blame you." A lump formed in his stomach. He'd just found her and he'd hate to see her move away. "Well," he said, "there's nothing we can do about the weather, but we can make it our mission to see this bastard put behind bars." He exhaled forcefully. "What do you say we get out of here and take a walk?"

They headed toward the Temple Bar area of Dublin. The rain had ended, and the stars were out. The song *Some Enchanted Evening* played in his head. He wanted to express this sentiment to the beautiful woman at his side, but he wasn't free—until he confronted Nora. And he could only move forward with Kate if he handled it honorably.

The cobblestones, glistening from dampness, reminded Luke of a movie set. They strolled along the medieval lanes and passed the Bad Ass Café. Above the door was a sign of a cranky donkey's backside. Luke rubbed his own backside and said, "I know how that bad ass feels." Kate threw her head back and laughed. He noticed how soft her neck looked in the moonlight and her orange blossom fragrance sang to his soul. He reached for her hand and led her to the Ha'penny Bridge, their fingers interlaced in a Celtic knot.

The bridge arched over the Liffey, with lanterns gleaming like magnificent gems. They paused atop the curvature and gazed into the river. Four graceful swans danced a *pas de quatre* in the swollen waters below, reminding Luke of the Irish myth about the Children of Lir.

Beside him, Kate shivered. What a perfect opportunity to put his arm around her, Luke thought. But he shouldn't. Could she hear his heart pounding a staccato rhythm? They stayed there for an infinite amount of time. Then she raised her eyes and held his gaze. Now it felt like his heart was hit by a Taser. *Why is she looking at me like that? She just said she doesn't know me very well.* He broke the gaze and led her toward the taxi stand. *If she looks at me like that again, I don't know what in the hell I'll do.*

When they were saying goodnight outside her private quarters, they nervously scanned the area surrounding the guesthouse, and relaxed when they found nothing lurking in the shadows. And damned if she didn't look at him like that again. He cupped her face with his hands, tilting her head. Before he could weaken, she spoke.

"Thank you, Luke. Tonight was perfect. Much better than this morning."

He chuckled and broke the spell by folding his arms. "Make sure you run with Morgan O'Gara tomorrow. I'd go with you myself, but I have to go up north early. I'm doing some interviews for my Bloody Sunday article. I'll be back by dinner time. If the weather's good, how would you like a picnic at Bray?"

"I'd love that. I'll pack the food." Kate looked up at him. Her lips were polished with a gloss, and they shimmered in the moonlight. Suddenly a frisky Dalmatian came out of nowhere, leaping between them.

"Oh Pooka!" Kate said.

"Your brother sicced the dog on us, didn't he?"

"I wouldn't put it past him."

Next door, two red-headed pre-teen boys came out of their home. It looked to Luke like they were sent out to pick up the toys in their yard. "Hiya Kate!" They yelled over the hedgerow. Their curious eyes took in Luke.

"Hi Benjamin. Hi Jack," Kate answered.

In an upstairs window of the boys' home, a matching pair of little heads peered over the side of a crib. Their waves could be seen in the lamplight. Kate and Luke waved back and laughed. Luke's dilemma was resolved. Then he reached for her hand and gallantly brought it to his lips. His honor was kept intact by this G-rated performance for their juvenile audience.

"I'll pick you up tomorrow at six o'clock. Wear some hiking boots." He touched the tip of her nose. "Now go inside and lock your windows and doors. Give me a thumbs-up if your brother's in." He waited on the steps until she was inside and he heard the bolt turn. Her face came to the window with a thumb pointing up.

He squatted down saying to the Dalmatian, "Next time I'll be free—and you can push me *into* her, not *away* from her. Do we have a 'business agreement'?"

Pooka wagged her tail.

Luke headed in the direction of Nora's flat, determination propelling him forward. His desire for Kate far outweighed his dread of confrontation. Another wound or two would hardly be noticed, and another blow to the head might help him sleep.

CHΛPCER 60

Round up the usual suspects.

~CAPTAIN RENAULT IN *CASABLANCA*

In the last 24 hours, Kate had seen mankind at its best, and its worst. On her morning run she re-hashed that strange incident from her jog yesterday. Who the heck was that guy? Would they ever find out? The thought of what could have happened had it not been for Luke made Kate shudder.

Luke...

She smiled at how perfect their first date had been. So far, she didn't see any red flags. Rose would be thrilled. She thought about his protective hand on her back when they peered at the Book of Kells. His tenderness had been pure and graceful as the swans in the Liffey. And then later how he cupped her face at the back door. She thought about that kiss on the lips that didn't quite happen. No uncomfortable grabbing and groping, either. He just left her pining for more.

Her hamstrings were tight after her run, so she stretched while leaning against the damn "Vacancy" sign. She reminded herself that she needed to believe in her own hard work.

Two of the rooms would be occupied by two European couples named Gott and Draves. They planned to sample the gourmet scene all around the Emerald Isle. They belonged to some sort of gourmet club in Germany and took a trip together each year to "research." Frau Gott photographed the food, and Frau Draves wrote a popular blog about their adventures called, "Feinschmecker Reisen," which translates as: "Gourmet Ride." Kate was hoping to get some free publicity through them.

She waved to Morgan and Dano O'Gara as they walked by for their cool-down. They had been her running partners today. Kate was touched when Dano had insisted on running with them, saying, "I'm not about to let some pervert get you lasses." He intended to bring his antique shillelagh, but left it behind when he heard they were to run a 5K loop. Unlike his wife, Dano wasn't used to jogging.

A kilometer into the run, Dano was a few strides behind. He panted, "Don't worry... I've yer backs, girls." Morgan and Kate slowed their pace, so he wouldn't lose face. And Kate had to hold back her fartleks, but she had to admit that having him along gave her peace of mind. Nonetheless, she kept her guard up, even though they followed a new route per Terry Riley's request. Terry had also offered to accompany them—by driving his car alongside. Kate was touched by the goodness of people.

After the guests had been fed, and the breakfast dishes completed, she took a break outside in the sunshine with Catriona. Within a few minutes they were joined by a brigade of flibbertigibbets, anxious to hear all the details of last night.

"Do you mean to be tellin' me that because of Pooka and my chisellers you missed a burnin' goodnight kiss? I swear I'll shoot them myself!" Deirdre stated emphatically.

"Oh, Deirdre!" Kate said, "Don't you dare say anything to the kids. Actually, it was really cute."

"And now the anticipation will build, making that first kiss even more special, so it will," Myrna said, rubbing her sore joints. "Everyone needs somet'ing to look forward to, so they do."

"Jaysus, that Luke's a hottie, Kate!" Helen said fanning her face. "And aren't I a good judge? Didn't I spend a load of time in the lifeguard chair at Manly Beach?"

The women nodded. They all fanned their faces now, while giggling like a passel of schoolgirls.

"Well, 'tis a grand t'ing altogether that yer man didn't have patty fingers," Catriona said. "And since I approve of the lad at the moment, I'm willin' to loan you my Tahitian body oil for your next date. All you have to do is dab it behind your ears. As I told yeh before, the smell snares men and drives them mad. Indeed there will be no holdin' him back."

"Can I have some of that for Terry?" Myrna chided, to the embarrassment of her daughter. "But wait 'til I tell yeh, it sounds to me like this Luke is marriage material. He has restraint, so he does, and goes to church." She turned to her daughter. "Remember, Helen … There's more to a prospective husband than hot looks. It'd do you good to take notes, pet."

Then it looked like a lightbulb went off in Deirdre's head. "Now Kate, I'm makin' a note to myself to lock up the chisellers tonight, and keep them away from the windows. We'll watch *Downton Abbey* 'til they fall asleep." She grabbed a pen from Catriona's apron and wrote the reminder on her hand.

"And I'll keep Pooka chained in our garden," Myrna said as she, in turn, reached for the pen.

Catriona stood up. "Excuse me ladies, but before I get to the laundry, I need to phone my old neighbor. He should be done with his morning chores on the farm by now." Kate noticed that Catriona and Myrna shared a conspiratorial glance.

"Catriona," Kate said, "what's up?"

"Ah, not a t'ing. I'm just horsin' around." Now she saw Catriona throw a wink toward Myrna.

Before she could make that phone call, however, the Kennedys' front door opened and nine redheads exited with great fanfare. The five oldest Kennedy children were wearing school uniforms. Mark was wearing a business suit, and his twin brother was carrying a suitcase.

Kelly O'Gara sauntered over from the pub. She cozied up to Joe, saying in a come-hither voice, "Cheerio, Yankee." She wrapped her arms around his neck very dramatically and pulled him toward her.

He let his suitcase drop. The audience clapped with delight when he responded, "Here's looking at you, kid," and tipped her back, exaggerating the romantic scene. *Oohs* and *aahs* were heard all around the lovers. Kelly straightened her left leg into the air in a Marilyn-Monroe-eat-your-heart-out fashion.

"I'm takin' notes," Helen said to the ladies around her, reaching once again for Catriona's pen.

"So am I," Kate admitted. At the same time she thought, *Well it sure didn't take Joe long to forget me.* But she was relieved when it dawned on her that she really didn't care. She could let him go as easily as the leaf she plucked on her morning run.

The little twins ran around the amorous couple, disrupting their lip-lock. "Don't be bold," their mother said as she grabbed their hands. "No more interferin' with romance!"

Joe pulled Kelly upright, released his grip on her and walked toward Kate with red lipstick smeared across his grin. "It was great fishing with you again. I know some day soon you'll find the catch of your life. You deserve that, Kate." They hugged goodbye, and then he added, "Stay safe."

Small ginger groupies were waiting for attention. After Uncle Joe gave a round of hugs, he went up to his brother. Mark grabbed him by the shoulders and then placed his forehead up to his twin's. They stood still like that—heads touching, as if lost in time. It looked as if they were communicating subliminally, expressing their sorrow at parting. Kate imagined it was hard for identicals to part, not knowing when they were going to see each other again.

The smaller set of twins looked up at their daddy and uncle and mimicked that embrace. With their arms intertwined and heads touching, they mewed like kitties. Kate turned her attention back to Joe and Kelly as they walked hand in hand to Dano's truck.

Another chapter had closed in her life, and perhaps a better one was just beginning . . . and it was going to be a page-turner, she could tell. With the way her heart felt right now, maybe it was a sign that she was recovering from Bryan's deceit. But how would she know for sure if someone really is trustworthy? Myrna seemed to think that Luke might fill the bill. She guessed time would tell, and luck would have to play its part. And his "smokin' hot looks"—and tight abs— were just an added bonus.

As the truck pulled away, Kate smiled and turned toward the guest-house. *Her* guesthouse. She had so much to be thankful for, and so much to look forward to. She refused to dwell on the stalker, if that's what he was. She felt safe, surrounded by all these good people.

Something to the right caught her eye. Biking toward the crowd was Michael Farley. He kept waiting for his mother who was walking behind him. "Hiya, M-Miss Kate," he said as he pumped his pedals to the fence. A chlorine smell filled the air around him.

"You must have been swimming bright and early this morning, huh Michael?" Kate said. He kicked his stand down and then an-swered her with "Indeed" as he danced up and down and rubbed his hands together in excitement.

"Tell them the good news," Peggy Farley said, looking around at the neighbors. Kate could see the pride in the mother's eyes.

"Wha' is it?" Benjamin asked. "Didn't you swim in the Dublin Dash?"

Michael covered his face with his fingers and squealed. "I g-got third place!" He showed his crooked eye teeth in an expression of delight as the crowd of neighbors clapped and patted him on the back. Even Pooka jumped up onto his chest with her front paws in congratulations.

Peggy Farley wiped her eyes. "Show them your medal, Michael."

He opened his cinchsack and pulled out a bronze disc hanging from an aqua ribbon. Removing his cowboy hat, he placed the medal around his neck. Then he said, "S-Surprise!"

"Congrats, Torpedo!" Jack said. "You must have surely been fast."

"Yes. I said to m-myself, 'Beat 'em, beat 'em, beat 'em' all the way to the wall."

Michael mounted Duke and rode like the wind to St. Columba's to tell the priests his good news. Pooka scampered at his side, wagging her tail. The Kennedy girls in their maroon jumpers accompanied him, too, on their way to school.

"May I talk to you ladies a moment?" Peggy asked.

"Of course," Kate answered, as she led Michael's mother to the garden bench.

Peggy began. "For a while now, Michael has been mumbling what I t'ink is a name of someone. And when he does, he gets upset and does his rockin' and rappin'."

"What's he mutterin'?" Catriona asked.

"'Ultan Ferrian,' or some such. I finally got him to scribble it down, but he has trouble with writing and spelling. Just this mornin' on the way home from swimmin', we saw a white car parked in the schoolyard. Michael was so agitated, and sayin' that nonsense over and over again, that I thought he was goin' to throw himself out of our own car. Then he blathered on about bein' a sheriff and protectin' Miss Kate."

Catriona stood up and paced slowly. "Ultan Ferrian. Ultan Ferrian. The name sounds familiar, but I just can't pull it out of me noggin." She stopped abruptly, hesitated, and then charged into the guesthouse. "Oh my," was all they could hear her sputter.

"What's all the fuss, do you suppose?" Peggy asked.

"I don't know," Kate replied, hoping the woman wasn't flying "away with the fairies." A few moments later Catriona ran back toward them. Her love-handles looked like they were doing jumping-jacks at her sides.

"Wait 'til I tell yeh." Catriona waved a business card in the air. "Michael solved the mystery! He figured out who yer creeper man is. Indeed, isn't he brilliant? Give the lad another medal!" She paused to catch her breath. "'Tis the computer repair bloke. I'm flabbergasted; his card's been on the bulletin board all along, right in front of our mugs." She held the business card down so the other two could read it. "See...'Ultan Ferrian.' That's who was in the white Ford Ka. Surely it all makes sense. Aren't I the right eejit for not puttin' it together meself?"

"Oh my God," Kate said as she pulled out her phone and dialed the number for Officer Flynn.

Timothy Flynn soon arrived in his white car with yellow and blue livery. He was once again taking notes. Michael's mother went to the church to collect her son so the garda could question him. Michael told Flynn in his unique way, using calming techniques, that Ultan Ferrian had once nearly run him over purposely, and had called him *retard* when he came to fix the computer. He explained that Ferrian was peeking in Miss Kate's windows one night, and Mr. Kennedy's twin brother had seen him, too—but he jumped Michael by mistake. Kate helped interpret this account from what she could remember herself about that evening. She was amazed at the story unfolding before them. Myrna wrapped an arm around her.

Michael rocked back and forth on his legs and mumbled some things that Kate couldn't understand. Did she hear the words *gun* and *Pooka*? She watched as Peggy patiently de-coded her son's ramblings.

After a few minutes Peggy straightened Michael's glasses and squeezed his big shoulders. "Right. Michael says that on Easter Sunday yer man, Ultan Ferrian, was hidin' behind Kate's shed. The twins must have discovered him while they were ... umm ... havin' a piddle in the garden." Peggy motioned toward the rear of the guesthouse. "He said that Ferrian kicked Pooka ..."

Myrna gasped.

Peggy shuddered and shook her head. "And I guess he had some sort of gun, which he dropped somehow ..."

Michael tapped his mam on the shoulder. "M-My horsey got him."

"A horsey? You have a horse?" The garda asked. Michael pulled a hard, plastic toy out of his cinchsack to show him.

With his protruding lip curving upward, Michael said, "Indeed. I-I'm an excellent sheriff ... I threw the horsey, and it b-bopped Ultan Ferrian, and then he d-dropped his gun! I don't like Ultan Ferrian!"

Garda Flynn took copious notes and called into his headquarters. Going to the back of his squad car, he opened the boot and dug around. Kate saw him slip something into the pocket of his jacket before he returned to them. He said, "Michael Farley, I hereby name you 'Honorary Detective.'"

Michael looked confused. "No, I'm a sh-sheriff."

Flynn stood corrected. "Okay, I hereby name you 'Honorary Sheriff of Glasnevin.'"

Michael gasped with delight as the officer removed a tin badge from his pocket and pinned it on Michael's shirt—right next to his swimming medal.

The two men shook hands and the officer said, "Thanks, Sheriff Farley... and remember to be safe. Always. Don't take chances."

Before leaving, Officer Flynn talked to some of the neighbors. He even spent some time with Father Lee and the other guests. He assured Kate they would find Ultan Ferrian and pull him in for questioning. "... And phone immediately if you see or hear from the suspect again."

CHAPTER 61

Love is like a picnic;
You can plan it, but you can't predict the weather.

~UNKNOWN

"Come here, pooch, I have something for you," Luke said to Pooka as he stood in front of The Cobblestones that evening. He reached into his Columbia jacket and pulled out a soggy napkin containing a hot dog. The Dalmatian jumped onto his chest and barked until Luke tossed the weiner into the air. Pooka caught it in her jaws and wolfed it down. "Remember, we have a 'business agreement.'"

Kate giggled at the display as she stood in the doorway. She had on jeans and a fitted fleece pullover. Luke noted the pink color highlighted her healthful glow. "Now you've made a friend for life," she said.

In the rock bed nearby, Catriona was planting some herbs with Michael Farley's help. Luke approached her saying, "I heard that you call me 'Hot Dog Man,' so I thought I'd be true to my nickname." Then he winked. "I'm trying not to use that expression so much, but old habits are hard to break."

"Well, if that's the worst vice you have, Luke O'Brien, then that's a good t'ing altogether," Catriona said, sniffing the tiny pot of thyme she was holding.

Michael was staring at Luke. "You look like Sh-sh-shaggy on *Scooby Doo*."

Rubbing the stubble on his chin, Luke responded, "Well, I was kinda going for the Mitch Rapp/George Clooney look."

Father Lee and Cousin Nick squeezed past Kate as they exited the guesthouse. "Why, hello there, Luke," Nick said. "We're on our way to Kavanagh's for some pub grub." He elbowed Luke and added, "I don't suppose you two would like to join us?"

"Thanks, but Kate's packed a picnic. Another time, perhaps."

Nick touched Catriona's elbow. "How about you? Would you care to join us?"

Catriona's apple cheeks reddened. "Me? Oh no! I have to hurry home to fix supper for..." She paused, inhaled, and handed Michael her spade. "Ah, no I don't. I'd be delighted to join you. Let me freshen up first." Yanking up her bra strap, she scurried back inside.

Michael poked Luke on the shoulder, handed him a nosegay and said, "I'm a g-good sheriff. See what Garda F-Flynn gave m-me?" He pointed to a badge on his shirt.

Kate explained that Michael had solved the stalker mystery. The last they heard, Ultan Ferrian had cleared out his flat and was lying low. Somehow, he had figured out that they were on to him. His boss at the computer store said Ferrian hadn't been to work for a couple of days. And a warrant was out for his arrest.

"Way to go, Michael!" Luke said, holding up a hand. "Gimme a high five!" Tomorrow he would make a few calls to his contacts with the Guards. What he wouldn't give to be able to Taser the SOB in the ass.

From around the corner, an old man came shuffling by in heavy shoes. After introductions, Kate mentioned how helpful his son Officer Timothy had been to them lately. Poppy knew all about the "maggot who was spying on Miss Kate." He put his arm around her and said, "What a disgustin' pervert." Then he added, "Although, I can't say I blame the bloke. You're a fine lump of a girl, Kate McMahon, and you have that new-girlfriend smell. Tutti-frutti, I'd guess." He glanced Luke's way. "'Tis a fortunate t'ing altogether for you, Yank, that I don't just take the woman on a date meself!" He elbowed his competition and then bobbled down the sidewalk toward O'Gara's.

"I told you, the lads love it," Catriona whispered to Kate with a nudge as she passed by, joining her escorts and rubbing an oily patch behind her ear. In her wake, Luke got a whiff of that tutti-frutti-new-girlfiend aroma.

Kate smiled and shrugged, "Come on! Let's tackle Bray Head!"

Luke bowed and handed her the nosegay of violets. She smiled, grabbing the picnic backpack, and they headed to the train station. They took the DART south along the coast for about 20 miles. It was a beautiful jaunt, dotted with lovely homes and seaside vistas.

"How long did it take for you to adjust to living here?" Kate asked.

"A year or so, I'd guess. Like you, I moved here for a fresh start. And now it feels like home. I love the people and their lightheartedness."

"And the scenery is spectacular. I'm still getting used to being so near the ocean. But when I'm in the city I feel a little hedged in. You know … all the walls and tight spaces."

"You'll learn to love it. But in the meantime, we'll just have to get you out more often."

"Hot dog!" she said, rewarding him with a smile.

As soon as they arrived at their destination they found a grassy knoll and spread the blanket. Luke could tell Kate had put a lot of thought into their fare. She had ham and three different cheeses, fruit, and leftover potato farls from the Ulster Fry Catriona had served that morning. To accompany the ensemble was a bottle of Pinot Grigio and Bailey's truffles served on antique linens. She told him that while she packed the food, her German guests were snapping photos and writing descriptions. They kept saying, "Wunderbar!"

He sliced a block of farmhouse cheese with Kate's Swiss Army knife on the cutting board. Studying the sharp blade, he said, "I'm relieved Michael was able to identify the creep—your stalker." He reached for an apple and stabbed it.

"Me, too. Now they just have to catch him!" She took the knife from Luke and clicked up the corkscrew. "Michael's better than Nancy

Drew and the Hardy Boys combined." She told him about the Special Olympics as she filled their glasses, and Luke proposed a toast to solving the crime. Mr. Patrick O'Neill would be proud of him. Kate had a way that put him at ease. He liked who he was with her.

They watched people walking by on the beach. Some carried fish and chips from a local chipper and some licked ice cream cones. Luke plopped a truffle into his mouth. He made happy guttural noises and said in a pathetic German accent, "Das ist wunderbar, Fraulein!" Kate made him repeat the compliment so she could videotape it for her German guests.

They finished their picnic and headed toward Cliff Walk. Bray, or *Bré* in Gaelic, means "hill" and this seaside resort had grown up around a natural attraction, Bray Head, which jutted straight up from the sea. People came from all around to climb to the top and enjoy the view.

They hiked hard. Luke wanted the exercise after being in the car for so many hours earlier that day. He told Kate that the Bloody Sunday article was coming along well. "But it's harder than hell interviewing people who experienced such violence. Their stories are heart-wrenching."

There were a lot of people on the path, probably because there was finally a lull in the crappy weather. Kate paused to remove her pullover. Luke took a swig of water, and used the opportunity to study her. She had an athletic physique and gentle curves like the Ha'penny Bridge.

Kate knotted the fleece around her waist and smiled back at him. As they passed a young family, he noticed how she reached her hand out to ruffle the hair of a toddler, sitting in a carrier on the father's back. He'd seen her interactions with the Kennedy kids and Michael Farley. The woman hiking ahead of him had a mother's heart.

At twilight they stopped at a scenic overlook on the trail and were rewarded not only with the grand panorama of land and sea, but a bright orange moon—the waning Easter moon—was suspended over them like a perfect stage prop. They could almost touch it.

"The Irish might call this a 'thin place,' where the boundary between heaven and earth is worn away," she said.

At no time in the ten years since Christy's death had he felt so alive. Would Christy approve if he somehow carved out a future with this lovely lady? At least he was free now to explore the possibility. *What am I thinking? There can't be much of a future for us if I can't even pull off that first kiss!*

The night was clear but the edge of the moon was soft, and that reminded him of something he learned from a story he and Buck had done on Irish folklore. "On a night like this, 'tis said the faeries will be out and about ... for good or for mischief-making," he told her.

"I can't recall ever hearing that one," she said, "but it's easy to believe."

Noticing that no other hikers were in sight, he laughed and reached for her. He put his hands on her shoulders and pulled her to his chest. He thought he saw a flicker of desire in her eyes before she nestled into him.

She wants me, too! Good God, let me get this right!

"Could this be more perfect?" He whispered in her ear.

He put both his hands in her hair and ran his thumbs gently along her cheeks. He reminded himself: *Slow down, her wounds are deep.*

She closed her eyelids and he felt her hands on the back of his neck, pulling his face toward hers. She inched up on her tiptoes as he lowered his head to close the deal.

And he almost did.

"Hey Aidan, a fellow's over here gettin' off with a fine bit of skirt," a teenager hollered as he approached them from over the ridge.

"Go on, mister ... give her a goozer," Aidan bellowed.

"Get a room!" a third kid whooped.

What the hell was this? Luke wondered. Some sort of reformatory field trip? A steady stream of pubescent males trekked their way; each had a backpack bigger than his own scrawny frame. Christ, couldn't a guy kiss a gal without an audience in Ireland these days? His brothers and Buck wouldn't believe this.

Kate *thonked* her forehead onto Luke's chest. Her shoulders were jackhammering as she giggled. Since the magic spell of passion was broken, Luke decided to grab her hand and continue to hike up Bray Head.

Ten minutes later they arrived at the summit. A small crowd was up there enjoying the breathtaking view. Kate asked another teen if he'd take a picture of them with her phone. Luke gladly wrapped his arms around her waist as they both said *cheese*. Standing this near to her was intoxicating, but he wished she didn't smell like her housekeeper.

"What did that old man, Poppy Flynn, say? That you've got that new-girlfriend smell going?"

"Yeah. And you've got that new Eau-de-Oscar-Mayer scent going," she said. "I think it's from that hot dog you had in your jacket."

Without warning, the clouds started to roll in and the wind picked up. White-capped waves began to crash violently onto the shore. Out at sea the water churned angrily as if it were defying evil. Because of all the time he had spent in this cauldron of the Celts, Luke knew to respond immediately to the sure signs of a brewing storm.

A foreshadowing of something sinister was enveloping them like a thick mugginess. Luke feared it threatened to invade their "thin place."

He wrapped an arm around Kate and they hightailed it back to the safety of the DART train. They chose a seat in the rear of a near-empty car, brightly lit, where they collapsed into a long inevitable first kiss, with the backpack poking into his Taser wounds. He was thinking all the while: *This is not exactly a smooth move, I should have shaved, and I smell like a weiner.*

CHAPTER 62

An addiction is a "thorn in the flesh."

~2 CORINTHIANS 12:7

Ultan Ferrian pulled out of the hiding spot he'd found for his car. Yesterday he had changed the plates; you couldn't be too careful when the heat was on. When he crossed Binn's Bridge, he threw his phone into the seething Royal Canal. Brendan Behan's statue sat on the bank near the jail. His shiny bronze nose was being pelted with raindrops. It seemed the fat Irish poet was having a gammy day as well.

"Bloody hell!" Ferrian yelled. He was just as cheesed off as the churning waters underneath him. He didn't like losing.

With his left forearm he wiped the rain from his face. He was hungry as hell and he'd give his right arm for a pack of Pall Malls. He couldn't return to work and he couldn't go on the dole, either, because he was lying low. A while back, through the windows at Computer Serve, he had seen the Gardaí talking to that asshole Doyle. They were on to him. They'd be staking out his kip in Ballymun as well, but he'd given them the slip before—he could do it again. He was old hat at the cops-and-robbers bit. In fact, his former hangouts were still the perfect places to hide. Christ, he almost felt thankful to his skanky mam and Mick the Prick for not giving a tuppenny damn about him. If they hadn't made him split, he wouldn't have developed such brilliant street smarts.

And he wouldn't have his "inheritance" either.

He glanced at the Manchester United duffle bag on the floor of his Ka. In exchange for a dozen Ecstasy pills and a few hot DVDs, he was able to talk his meth-head neighbor into grabbing his stuff before the Gardaí got to his kip. Now it was stashed in the boot of his Ka. Ferrian sighed.

"That brasser innkeeper better be worth all this fookin' trouble," he muttered. "And hopefully that writer will turn tail and run away, like a weasel."

He was gummin' for a pint. *Ah, shite. Where's a body to get enough dosh to tie him over?* He passed a billboard for the Special Olympics World Games. A photo of a kid was on the advertisement. Ferrian studied it with disgust. *Look at that window licker! The wheel's turning but the hamster's dead, all right.* He laughed at his cleverness. Then he looked in his rearview mirror to make sure the Gardaí weren't on his tail.

When the light turned green he surged forward and clicked on SPIN 103.8. The Rolling Stones' *You Can't Always Get What You Want* was playing. He listened to the lyrics. Ferrian knew what he wanted: money, more pills, harder-core porn, and Kate in the flesh. Like the rockers said: if he tried, he'd get what he needed. Well, fookin' A ... he'd just have to try again, now, wouldn't he?

To conserve petrol and to stay out of sight from the Gardaí, he stopped driving. He parked his Ford in a secluded area near the deserted building that had once been a produce warehouse. He had slept in it many a night as a young runaway. This was the place where he would have dragged Kate, to show her his talents—if it hadn't been for that pack of eejits getting in the way.

"Bugger it!" He yelled into the rain as he ran for cover. Jaysus it was lashing! He was sick of running around like a blue-arsed fly, especially in this weather.

Once in the warehouse he picked up an empty vodka bottle and slammed it against the metal shelves, cutting his thumb on the flying shards. He crouched near the shelves and wrapped his hand with an oily rag he found on the floor. Ferrian's stomach growled as he relieved himself in the corner. What he wouldn't give for an Egg McMuffin! But that wasn't going to happen. Instead, he dug into his pocket, popped two potent pills into his mouth, and swallowed them with a glob of spit.

What was his new plan going to be? He dried himself with an old shirt he found on a shelf and slid to the floor. He tore open a bag of salt and vinegar Taytos some vagrant left behind. Mick Jagger's hit was working its way into Ferrian's skull as an ear worm.

The picture on that Special Olympics billboard flashed before his eyes, and then a recollection surfaced from the deep abyss of his anger. *That capper from the guesthouse hangs out at the church—and he carries a money bag in that cinchsack of his. It must contain alms for the poor!*

He grinned as he chomped on a crisp. *For focks' sake! I'm as poor as they come. In fact, Destitute is my second name.*

CHAPTER 63

Courage is being scared to death ... and saddling up anyway.
~JOHN WAYNE

At the back of the guesthouse, lace curtains were blowing in the tempest wind. They looked like angels' wings fluttering in protection. But then again, Michael's teachers did say that he had a vivid imagination.

The smell of bangers and rashers floated out of the open window, making Michael's tummy rumble. He could hear the telly. The newscaster was saying: "There is widespread flooding today across huge parts of Ireland after a period of nearly biblical rain." Inside the guesthouse, Miss Kate was doing the cleaning up after breakfast. All of the guests had left to shop or what-not, except for Miss Kate's cousin and brother, who were planning to take her to the Porterhouse for lunch.

Those nice Germans that talk funny left a few minutes ago. They told Michael they were going to Bewley's on Grafton Street to write about gorgeous things like coffee, tea and cakes. Before their taxi came, Frau Gott took a picture of him by the fireplace. Michael made sure to wear his cowboy hat, sheriff badge and swimming medal. She kept saying something like, "Ja, ja, du bist ein gutes Jungen." Doktor Gott and Kapitän Draves told him that it meant "You are a good boy."

Michael smiled, thinking about it as he touched his hat. The brim kept the drizzle out of his face. No wonder cowboys liked them. Today he was doing tough work, and he didn't want rain in his eyes. He was hoeing in the back to make a fairy garden with minature plants. The ground was as wet as a bog this morning, making the grass easy to yank out by the roots. Indeed he was getting pretty muddy. His mammy would surely make him take his clothes off by the back door and run into the house with just his Y-fronts on. Silly Mammy. He just hoped the neighbors wouldn't be peeking.

Mrs. Ryan had returned from Superquinn a bit ago. As she carried the bag of groceries to the back door she spotted Michael and said, "Aren't you the good fella? Out here toilin' in the wet garden." It made him feel more important than the Lord Mayor herself. Mrs. Ryan was rushing on account of the rain, but he noticed she had that funny look on her mug. Lately, she appeared to be up to something. What could it be? He took off his mucky gloves and removed the cinchsack from his back.

His stomach sounded like booming thunder. Da made eggs this morning, and he cooked them too long, so the yolks were rubbery like a bouncey ball. Michael didn't fancy his eggs done that way; he liked his yolks runny like lava from a volcano. So he had a temper tantrum and didn't eat them. That's why he snuck some sweets in his bag—he was a hungry, hungry caterpillar. Swimming for Coach Keanne and Coach McBarnes did that—made him half-starved. Helen Riley had been at the pool this morning, helping to teach flip turns. She whacked the swimmers on their feet with a kickboard every time their toes would go too high out of the water when they were flipping. Her whacking must have worked. By the end of practice, Coach said Michael had a faster time. So did some of his mates on the Green Machine swim team. They all gave high-fives to everyone on the pool deck. It was brilliant fun.

"Ready or n-not…Here I c-come, Special Olympics Dublin!" He did a hula dance in the soft rain. When he was done, he leaned against the garden wall and dug around in his sack. It was full of paper for his "collection" and other things, but soon he found the packet of gummy worms he had stashed in his bank pouch. Gobbling them up like a baby birdie, he waited in that far corner of the garden for Miss Kate. She sure looked happy the past two days. Maybe her dates with Luke were really, really fun. A few minutes ago she promised to bring Michael a Fanta because she said he deserved one for working in the rain so hard. But wasn't he used to being wet? Wasn't he a swimmer?

There was a sound near the back of the guesthouse. Could it be Miss Kate with his fizzy drink? He turned to look and then froze. It was that hooligan Ultan Ferrian! Michael knew it was him even though he had a black hood tied around his ginger hair. He gulped down the half-chewed gummy worm. *What should I do?*

Without thinking any longer, Michael dove behind the azalea bushes. The noise and action was drowned out by the rain. He wanted to hit his head, rock back and forth, and whine, but then the bad bloke would see him. Trying to calm himself down, he closed his eyes, bit his fist and tried to remember the Saint Michael prayer:

Saint Michael the Archangel, defend us in battle.
Be our protection against the wickedness and snares of the devil ...
Cast into hell Satan and all the evil spirits
Who prowl about the world ...

When he opened his eyes, the coast was clear. Where was Ultan Ferrian? Was he around here somewhere? Was he "cast into hell"? Michael was in a frenzy. *What would John Wayne do?* He decided to stay huddled right where he was, hiding. Eventually he peered out from behind the bush and spied Ultan Ferrian in back of the shed. What was he doing?

A noise came from the door. Miss Kate was coming out of the guesthouse with a soda can in her hand. Michael shook with fright.

He looked over by the apple trees and saw that Ferrian had a gun! It was like the one he had on Easter. It was pointed right at Miss Kate. Michael knew how dangerous they were from all the Westerns he watched. He opened his mouth and screamed like a cavalry sentinel, "R-Run, Miss Kate! Run!"

She hesitated, glancing around for a moment, and then sprinted along the back of the building to the side garden.

"F-faster! Faster!" Michael yelled as he stood up. A red dot was lit up on Miss Kate's back. He guessed that wasn't very good. Then he heard the most horrid crackling noise. It was like a rancher's whip made from a lightning bolt, and it struck her back. Michael watched in horror as Miss Kate fell instantly to the ground, face down, moaning and jerking.

What was that Ultan Ferrian doin'?

Michael stealthily trotted toward Miss Kate and froze behind another bush. He could see two pointy things sticking out of her shirt. They made wee bloody spots by her spine. Wires—or fishing line or something—were coming out of the pointy things and they trailed into a teeny black box lying next to her. Michael saw the man put the gun in his hoodie pocket and then remove some big gray tape. In the blink of an eye, Ultan Ferrian slapped tape across Miss Kate's mouth and around her wrists. Then Ferrian dragged her by her hair like a caveman, to the back of the shed. The wires from those pokey-things—still stuck in her back—trailed behind her. They must hurt something fierce.

"N-ooo! S-S-Stop!" he shouted.

Now the lout turned toward him, and looked at him real mean. A raindrop clung to the tip of his nose as he jeered, "Do you t'ink this retard is going to help you, Miss La-dee-da? Look at the blatherin' eejit, he looks as if he's goin' to piss his pants." The nasty man got on his knees beside Miss Kate. "I don't mind an audience one bit. How about you?"

Miss Kate started squirming on the wet ground. At least she could move a bit now. She kicked at him. Michael could tell she was trying to aim at his willy, but she missed, because her legs didn't work too well. She was getting mulch and mud all over herself and Ultan Ferrian. Her eyes looked scared and mad, and she kept making noises from her throat.

"Stop messin', you stupid ..." Ultan Ferrian never finished his command because Miss Kate's left foot met her target this time. Ultan Ferrian grabbed his bollocks and rolled on the ground. Now he was really getting dirty. He was trying not to make much noise, but Michael could hear him moaning "Ahhhhhhhhh. Shite"

The next thing Michael knew, Ferrian was standing over her again, roaring, "You bloody toe rag!" and he smacked Miss Kate across her face.

Michael plopped on the ground and started hitting his head. He rocked back and forth and uttered sounds to make the bad noises disappear. He wanted to get up and help, but his legs were frozen. He slipped into a daze.

A familiar sound snapped him out of it. *Woof! Woof!* followed by fierce growling. Pooka bolted at the gobshite and received a blow right in the tummy. The kick made pooka hit the corner of the shed with a loud thud. She lay motionless in the mulch, her tongue hanging out of her mouth.

Michael screamed, "N-Noooooo!" Then he covered his face and started to cry as he rocked back and forth at a frenzied pace.

When he peered again, Pooka was still on the ground. It was like she was asleep. He saw that Ultan Ferrian was after messin' with Miss Kate's jeans. Michael looked around but there was nobody else to help. The angel wings lifted in the window, stirring his confidence. He forced himself to stand and ran to his things. He grabbed the handle of the small hoe. Within seconds he was behind Ferrian, holding the gardening tool in the air like Saint Michael's sword. *Should I smack him?*

The button and zip fastener of Miss Kate's jeans were undone. It looked like Ultan Ferrian was trying to tug them down. *What in the world is he doing to Miss Kate? Is he having a look at her knickers?* Michael could see her belly button. Ultan Ferrian ripped off her sparkly necklace and put it into his pocket. She made an angry noise and looked right at Michael. There was mud in her eyes.

Saint Michael must be helping Miss Kate now because Ultan Ferrian shook his head a few times and stepped back.

Michael couldn't take it any longer. He needed to help, too. "You're an arse!" he yelled. Even though his mammy doesn't like the word, it felt brave coming out of his mouth. He brought the hoe down onto the bad guy's shoulder, and then he rushed to the door screaming, "Help! Help!"

"You fookin' mentaller!" Ultan Ferrian howled.

The back door flew open and Father Lee and his cousin charged out. Michael pointed to the area between the shed and garden wall, where the bad thing was happening. Father Lee reached Ultan Ferrian first, pulling him away from Miss Kate, and pinning him to the ground in a wrestling hold. Cousin Nick reached inside the door and grabbed a golf club. He looked real, real mad when he saw Miss Kate. Ultan Ferrian squirmed away from underneath Father Lee and started to run. Nick swung the club at his leg, but whiffed.

Michael stood up. He wanted to take that tape off of Miss Kate and see if Pooka was okay. But when he got closer to them, he saw that somehow Ferrian had jumped onto the bench, and was reloading the gun. Then he pointed it at Miss Kate. "Don't any of you wankers move, or I'll shoot her in the face."

Cousin Nick quickly took another swing, knocking the weapon out of the attacker's hand. It landed a few feet away. But then Nick slipped in the mud, falling backwards onto Miss Kate and Father Lee.

Ultan Ferrian jumped off the bench and reached for his gun.

As Michael started to run toward the front street, Ultan Ferrian was close behind him. When Michael passed the Fanta lying in the grass, he picked it up, and threw the can at the bad man, but missed. *Bejappers! Is he pointing that gun at my tummy now?* He yelped.

Ultan Ferrian caught up to Michael at the side of the guesthouse and grabbed him by the arms. "Give me that bloody bag on your back." The man was hurting his arms and he smelled like a boozer. As Michael struggled to get free, he spotted Father Lee helping Miss Kate in the garden, and he was relieved to see Nick running toward Ultan Ferrian with that club again. Michael was able to pull away and run like a galloping horse all the way back to Duke. Ultan Ferrian must have seen Nick chasing him, too, because he took off running in the same direction.

Now the bad man was coming right at him—with that gun!

Does he want to shoot me? Does he want the bike? Michael wasn't sure, he just pedaled away like the devil himself was on his tail.

He heard from close behind, "Gimme that bag, yeh half-wit!"

Michael kept rotating his feet around and around as fast as he could in cowboy boots. *Why does he want my bag? Does he collect paper things, too? Maybe he's after gettin' my gummy worms?*

CHApTER 64

I am not what happened to me.
I am what I choose to become.

~CARL GUSTAV JUNG

Kate was vaguely aware of being led by her brother to the back door of the guesthouse. She could hear Ferrian yelling, "Gimme that bag, yeh half wit!"

Through blurry eyes, she could see Deirdre standing by the road. The twins were clinging to her skirt. Was she throwing something at Ferrian? She heard a *crash.*

As they stepped through the door, she was aware of Deirdre's shout, "Mark! Mark! Come out here!"

Catriona was standing at the kitchen counter, unpacking a box of sausages. Lee shouted to her, "Call the police!"

Kate hobbled to the stove, grasping the spanner for support. Catriona rushed to her. "Oh, sweet Jaysus! What in the name of heaven was goin' on while I was in the pantry? What wrong has been done to her? She looks like the Swamp Thing."

Lee clasped Catriona's arm. "Ferrian was attacking her...we drove him off...He's chasing Michael now, but a rape did not occur."

Kate's trembling hands slid to her jeans, but she didn't possess the strength to pull up the zipper. *It could have been so much worse for me, but...poor Michael!*

Catriona whipped the sausage links over her shoulder and dialed the Gardaí.

Kate allowed Lee to usher her into the parlor and settle her on the divan. *This can't be happening. I don't believe it.*

Lying on her stomach, she felt Lee place ice packs on the Taser wounds. There was mud and mulch embedded in her shirt and hair. *What keeps scraping my right eye?*

Catriona was standing at the window, narrating the action scene: "Now Ferrian is stealing a bike from the Whaley's house ... Something black fell out of his pocket ... My God! Is that a gun?"

"Where's Michael?" Kate yelled through puffy lips.

"He's just beyond the pervert, pedaling like mad in the rain." Catriona was craning her neck and wringing her hands. "Now Mark Kennedy is dashin' out of his house, waving a hurling stick."

Kate raised her throbbing head. "Go get Luke and Buck," she ordered. "They're at O'Gara's ... Tell them to help Michael!"

Catriona went racing out the front door. The scream of sirens filled Glasnevin.

CHΛPϹƐR 65

Every man is bold until he faces a crowd.

~IRISH SAYING

Myrna was on her way home from Hickey's Pharmacy, hurrying through the rain, when she heard the sirens wail. She clutched her jacket tighter and checked her pocket to make sure the packet of Humira was safely tucked away. Every little movement made her wince in pain when she was due to take her shot. She was nearly home when a gardaí response car sped past, splashing mud on her feet. Sure it was fortunate she had worn wellies.

She crossed the Royal Canal. It was higher than she had seen it in ages. In fact, some areas near Dublin City were flooded. Glasnevin, with its high embankments, had been spared so far. However, a catastrophe was sure to hit if the weather did not improve soon enough.

Up ahead, the response car pulled to a halt—directly in front of The Cobblestones. She froze in her wellies. *That misguided lad? After Kate? Or a guest?* If only her gammy legs could carry her as fast as her heart was pounding! Rounding the corner, she saw a ruckus in front of the pub. Catriona seemed to be in charge. She sent Kate's cousin Nick bounding down the street with a golf club in his hand. Mark Kennedy was at his side with a hurling stick. *What turn of events?* She rushed toward the pub.

"What is it, Catriona?" Myrna blurted. She didn't even ask about the sausage links trailing out of her friend's apron pockets.

"That computer lout attacked Kate and now he's giving chase to Michael!"

Myrna gasped.

The ballyhoo roused the men in O'Gara's and they dashed out into the rain. "Fellas!" Catriona pointed and hollered, "Ferrian's after Michael. Go help the lad!"

"Where's Kate?" Luke started running in the other direction, toward The Cobblestones.

"No, Luke!" Catriona said, "She's fine and good. Just a few scratches. Her brother's minding her. 'Tis Michael needs help now!"

Luke turned around and charged like a rutting bull, ready to trample whatever got in his bloody way. Buck did a grand job staying close behind, his camera bouncing around his neck, ready to shoot.

Catriona turned to Myrna and said, "I wish 'twas a rifle he had instead, God forgive me."

Dano O'Gara bounded out of the pub with his antique shillelagh. "Which direction did they go?" When they pointed south, Himself ran off, wielding the wooden club like an angry chieftain, his bar apron sweeping at his thighs like a kilt without a codpiece.

Next, Catriona steered Myrna to St. Columba's and approached the priests in the nave. They told them of the ensuing battle, and instructed them to find Michael's parents.

Myrna choked up, thinking of dear Michael—the presence of God in all their lives. Indeed he fanned the flame of goodness in the hearts of those around him.

As they stood in the courtyard, Catriona blessed herself and squeezed her palms together. Myrna heard her whisper urgently: "Holy God, you hear me out! Protect our darlin' Michael."

"Come now, Catriona! Let's follow the menfolk," Myrna said, pulling at Catriona's sleeve, determined to ignore the pain in her feet. Catriona ran as fast as her portly legs could go—bingo wings flapping underneath her arms.

At that moment, old man Poppy Flynn bobbled around the corner, shuffling his thick-soled shoes. Surely he was on his way to the pub for a bit of ri-ra. "What's all the bobbery? Wha'? Has Elvis been sighted?" he asked.

They quickly filled him in and dashed off in the direction of the fracas. Myrna knew he was trying to follow them, but the octogenarian moved at a snail's pace. This was no time to fret about being polite.

More sirens blared in the distance. Myrna tugged at Catriona's apron and led her on a shortcut to a schoolyard. "Up there we can watch from the high ground."

The women clutched each other as they paused to catch their breath and view the action. Ferrian was closing in on Michael, who made a sudden turn onto Whitworth Road.

"Myrna, Oh no! They're headed toward the canal!"

The rain had let up and they could see better now. Ferrrian was pedaling right behind Michael on the path along the canal, just below where the women were standing. The other neighbors, still on the chase, had the length of two Gaelic football fields to catch up to the hooligan.

"Oh no, Catriona!" Myrna shrieked, "Michael's fallen off his bicycle!"

The women watched as Ferrian jumped off of his own wheels and ran after the lad. Michael's cowboy boots made it a tough go in the mud, and he soon fell to his knees. Ferrian tugged at the cinch-sack on his back.

"If only we could get down to him!" Catriona cried. But a high fence and thick brambles kept them back. Searching frantically around the schoolyard, Myrna spotted a big plastic tub near a sand pile. Painted on the sides were a yellow sun and the words, "God will provide." She dragged it over to the fence. Catriona stood on it and hoisted Myrna over the fence, pushing her bum.

Myrna landed with a thud on the other side, re-arranged her handbag, and then helped her hefty friend to scale the thing. They scraped their way through the brambles and slipped on the mud, but neither woman groaned or mentioned her pain. How could they when Michael needed them?

Where were the Gardaí? She could still hear the sirens. Were they getting closer? As the two women neared the violence on the linear park, Myrna saw Ferrian grab the bag from Michael's back. The lad was yelling something and kicking his assailant. She could hear the blackguard shouting "Retard!" Glancing to her right, she saw the troop of neighbors a stone's throw away. "Hang on Michael! Help is coming!" She felt drizzle spotting her face and more clouds darkened the sky.

Myrna turned back to the conflict and yelped. The lout was choking Michael! Was he using Michael's own swimming medal?

"My God, Catriona! He's goin' to kill him!" Myrna's legs hobbled faster down the hill, upsetting some mallard ducks that flew out from under a fern, scaring the bejaysus out of her. Catriona stumbled over some roots, but Myrna pressed on.

Only a few meters from the lad now, she saw the neighbors were a bit farther off. *I need a weapon.* She remembered the syringe of Humira in her pocket. She tore away at the package as she ran.

Ferrian pulled the medal tighter and tighter around the lad's neck. Michael made choking sounds as he struggled.

Myrna felt a surge of power as adrenaline rushed through her veins. Clutching her weapon, she charged forward. *Just a few meters now...I can make it!*

Ferrian seemed blinded by his rage and didn't turn as Myrna approached. She snuck up behind him and plunged the long needle into his thigh.

"Ooww! Son-of-a-bitch!" he howled, clutching his leg and letting go of Michael. Myrna's wellies slipped in the mud as she jumped out of Ferrian's reach. She landed hard on her right side and felt her elbow crack. She lay just a few meters from Michael.

Their eyes met.

She tried to roll toward him, but just then the rain-sodden gravel and dirt beneath Michael gave way, collapsing into the Royal Canal. She could hear Catriona and the other neighbors shriek from somewhere close behind her. Ferrian had jumped to safety while Michael struggled to regain his balance. His cowboy boots slipped in the chasm, dropping him onto the ground on his belly, facing the enemy. For a brief moment, Myrna witnessed Ferrian reaching out to his victim. It seemed to Myrna that he stood on the edge of a dark precipice, instinctively but futilely grasping at goodness. Before Ferrian could seize Michael's hand, however, the deep fissure rumbled, and carried the lad down by a mudslide into the waters.

Ferrian fled, limping a bit on one leg.

Time seemed to stand still for one terrifying moment as Myrna rolled up and began to hobble downstream after Michael.

Her heart was in her throat. She called out to him, "Swim lad! Help is coming!" *Ah, sugar! Whatever would Peggy and Peter Farley do if they lost their dear, only child?*

On the cross-street ahead, a garda car pulled up. Myrna called to them and pointed, "Over there! In the canal! Help that boy!" Two officers raced to the bank.

On the path ahead, Myrna saw Ferrian, with Michael's cinchsack clasped in his left hand. He kept glancing back over his shoulder as he sprinted. The neighbors overtook Myrna and were now on his tail like a rabble of angry dogs on a fox hunt.

Myrna saw one of the officers jump off the steep bank into the raging water. He was fighting the current. Two more gardaí threw a lifeline into the waterway.

She looked at the neighbors again. Luke O'Brien led the pack, with his legs working faster than a scenthound's. He reached Ferrian and punched him right in the nose with a quick, straight jab. The photographer trotted alongside the brawl, clicking away. Luke followed his first punch with a powerful uppercut to his opponent's chin. Ferrian crumpled, writhing in pain, a stone's throw from the statue of Brendan Behan.

Another neighbor splashed into the canal to aid Michael.

"Well done, Luke!" Myrna heard Catriona puff as she extracted something long and ropey from her apron. *The sausages?* Ah yes, and she was winding the links around Ferrian's legs while Luke's strong hands secured the ruffian's wrists behind his back.

"Lemme at 'im!" she heard Dano shout.

"Me, too!" Mark growled.

"Someone help the guards get Michael!" the photographer yelled. "I can't swim!"

During the melee, Myrna was relieved to hear more sirens getting closer, blaring in the rain. Three more gardaí pulled up along the stone wall across the canal from her, their blue lights flashing in the gray dampness.

Then her own Helen emerged from one of the vehicles. Myrna gasped, watching her daughter kick off her shoes at the edge of the embankment and dive into the turbulent canal. Using strong strokes, Helen maneuvered through the rapid currents, passing the guards and working her way toward Michael. Two more guards followed her.

Myrna climbed a boulder and scanned the rushing waters. *Where has Michael got to? Where is Helen now?*

"Oh, Holy God in Heaven Almighty!" she cried, holding her flaming elbow and sinking to her knees.

CHAPTER 66

If an evil spirit pursues you at night head for a running stream.
If you can cross it, you're safe.

~IRISH SAYING

The waves were rolling something fierce. No matter how hard he tried, Michael just couldn't get his legs to do a powerful freestyle kick. Then when some debris scraped up his knees, he remembered his cowboy boots. They were making him sink.

His head bobbed down below the surface again. A roaring sound flooded his ears. He tried like mad to get his head above the waves. His body dipped with the current, and then his face rose up. He could feel the air. Michael had time to suck in a giant breath before he somersaulted back under. *Which way is up?* Fear clawed at his throat. The water tasted disgusting.

Am I drowning? He jerked his arms with all his might until he surfaced again. He gulped another big breath. His body rolled itself over onto his back. He heard someone behind him splashing. *Is it Ultan Ferrian?* The current dragged him down again. His mantra echoed in his head: *Beat him! Beat him! Beat him!* And this made him swim better. His head popped out. When he looked back again he could see that the person wasn't that bad bloke. It was Helen.

"H-Help me, Helen!" he sputtered. He knew she used to swim in the rough ocean in Australia. Maybe she could reach him.

The canal rushed south on its way to the River Liffey. He felt its power. The dark, raging waterway kept pushing toward Dublin Bay, showing no mercy. *It's got me! It's got me!*

His shoulder smashed into a boulder, rolling him onto his side.

"Oww!" He spit the filthy water out of his mouth, and squeezed his eyelids.

"'Hoy! Ay-up!" Two gardaí were tossing him a lifeline. He rotated his good arm at a hyper pace, trying to reach it.

"H-help!" He yelled, and then rolled underwater again.

Swim like a torpedo, he urged himself. A picture of St. Michael in his armor flashed through his mind. His stinging eyes found light through the murky water and led him to the surface. Something tugged at his shirt. He thrashed his arm and kicked harder.

"Michael, I've got you!" he heard Helen yell.

He threw his arm toward her, flailing and thrashing, but the current ripped him from her grasp. A wave smacked his face, filled his lungs, and threw him against a moored barge. He grabbed at a ropeline but another wave pushed him back into the whoosh. He coughed, but the filth stayed in his nose.

Thinking about the Special Olympics gave him a boost of adrenaline. He filled his lungs with air and flutter-kicked to keep his head raised. *What if I got hurt? ... I'd miss the race!* Then he thought he caught a glimpse of his parents on the footpath.

"Mammy! Da!" he tried to yell, but only a choking sound escaped.

On the bank of the canal he could see the response cars of the gardaí. Their blue lights reflected off Binn's Bridge, and the flashing made him dizzy.

A log crashed into his chest. "Oww!" Filthy water rushed into his mouth. The pain in his side made it harder to use his good arm now.

If only I could reach the wall of the bridge! His legs were too heavy to kick any longer. And he just felt so tired, tired ... tired ...

More muddy water splashed into his open mouth. He sputtered and twirled until the darkness pulled him under. *Surely I'll be gone to Glasnevin Cemetery.*

CHAPTER 67

I gave up on most of my body parts,
but I'm glad my brothers still have my back.
~CECELIA MCMAHON MACDONALD

Lying on her back, stretched across the divan near the fireplace, Kate could hear her brother pacing and praying, repeating a soothing petition, "Help us to trust in your love and protection … Help us to trust in your love and protection …"

When Lee had pulled the darts out—right after he ripped the duct tape off her mouth—she had thought of Luke—because it made her scream, "Oww! That kills!" just like he did that day when he got Tasered. She understood now the price Luke had paid to save her. Electricity pulsing through his limbs. The jerking and loss of control. *I don't want to think about it anymore.* She imagined his comforting arms around her as she let her mind slip back into a fog.

When she surfaced again, an officer was in the room, asking her questions. *What is he saying?* She tried to focus, but her brain remained stuck in low gear. She felt dirtier than she had ever been and wanted to take a shower. *Is my zipper still open?* Her hand shifted to her pelvis, and discovered a velvety throw pillow had been strategically placed. *Thank God for my brother.*

A garda medic was bending over her, determined to elevate her head. And wouldn't you know, he propped it up with the shielding throw pillow. *Aww … dang! Really?* But just then, Lee played Sir Galahad, tossing his jacket over the unguarded area. The medic gently wiped her face with a warm washcloth, gave her a sedative and treated her eye injury.

"Looks like a corneal abrasion," he said, "probably from being dragged through a bed of mulch." *Oh yeah, he had me by the hair.* She winced when the medic pressed lightly on her scalp, so he avoided that area while bandaging the eye. Then he placed an ice pack over her other eye and swollen lips. *God! My eyes ... I can't see a darn thing ... At least Ferrian didn't break my teeth or bust my nose.*

The detective tried again to ease answers out of her. She mumbled, just the facts, sparing the details and trying not to go wobbly on him. But the ugly facts gave rise to her emotions, and it was all she could do to smack them down again.

The detective was able to reconstruct the attack after discussing her wounds with the medic and inspecting the back garden. "Em, when did the lad ... Michael Farley ... get involved?"

"I think it was when Ferrian hit me across the face ... and called me a bloody toe rag. Whatever that is." She kept to herself the details of that blow: feeling the explosion of a sudden rush of air into her ear canal, seeing red and white orbs flashing inside her eyes, feeling her lip split beneath the duct tape. And being scared ... so terrified.

There was more she couldn't shape into words. The details she wanted to forget: regaining her wits and finding herself lying there by the shed, bound and gagged; the sinister look in Ferrian's eyes as he tugged at her jeans; seeing Pooka's broken body and wanting desperately to cradle it; Michael's face above her—confused by the violence, feeling her pain, summoning courage.

And then there was a realization—that when she found the strength to kick Ferrian's crotch, it wasn't from pure self-defense. It sprang—not so much from that primitive instinct—but from a need to protect poor, dear Michael.

"How *is* Michael?" She spoke into the darkness. With both eyes covered, she wasn't certain who else was in the room.

It was Deirdre's voice that answered, approaching the divan. "He's got an army of defenders."

"And Pooka?"

"My mam's taken care of that matter. I'll take you to the shower, luv," she said, lifting off the ice pack. Kate felt motherly arms wrap around her. "You can lean on me."

Steam filled the bathroom as Deirdre gently slid Kate's jeans to the floor. "I'll pitch all these vile clothes into the dustbin after you're settled in bed," Deirdre said. Through the slit of her left eye, Kate could see that a white towel had been draped over the mirror.

Her legs felt as heavy as her heart when she stepped into the shower stall. The stream of hot water couldn't wash away the filth and shame. *Why was I so careless? Why didn't I take their warnings seriously? Whatever happens to Michael ... is my fault.*

CHAPTER 68

He that raises a large family does, indeed,
while he lives to observe them,
stand a broader mark for sorrow;
but then he stands a broader mark for pleasure too.

~BENJAMIN FRANKLIN

One week later

Deirdre looked out her window as she washed away grease from a skillet, and sighed. The schoolyard flag was half staff, blowing in the wind. She paused in her chore for a moment and closed her eyes. "'Twas a week from hell," she mumbled quietly. She rolled her shoulders as she commenced scrubbing; they ached something fierce from carrying a load of sadness and tension on them.

The lonely gardens of The Cobblestones could be seen from where she stood. They seemed so empty without Michael Farley caring for them. Her big kids missed his hearty goodbyes on their way to school. He always seemed to bring sunshine into their morns. And he even made her moody boys smile with his enthusiasm. She recalled the morning a while back when Benjamin was upset because exams were looming. As the boys put their books in Mark's car, Michael could tell his friend was extra anxious. He had hurried to their vehicle and said, "D-Don't worry, Benji, I'll take the exams for you when it's t-time." His face was full of love. The innocent comment had put things into perspective for everyone that day.

"Ah, Michael..."

She heard little footsteps shuffling about upstairs. A slow smile spread on Deirdre's face. She scraped some fried egg whites from another pan and turned on the faucet to let this one soak in sudsy water.

"Mammy!" one twin yelled as he ran to her, his eyes still heavy with sleep. Because of the angle of his head, she wasn't sure at first if this one was Murphy or Gavin. He looked up at her and smiled with gapped front teeth.

"Mornin', Gavin!" She squeezed him extra tight.

The other twin entered the kitchen wearing footie-pajamas that matched his brother's. "Me good seeper, Mammy?"

Their language was improving. All that speech therapy with Mrs. Crowley was helping. She brought him into the fold. "Yes, luv. You were both good sleepers." She buried her face in their sweet softness and breathed in their innocence.

"Why you ky, Mammy?" Murphy asked.

Deirdre wiped her eyes. "Oh, I'm just so happy to have the lot of yeh." She squeezed them again. "Right. We need to get you dressed for Granny. She's comin' to collect you soon enough." After she had clothed the boys and smoothed out their tangles, they went back into the kitchen to eat. The dishes were never-ending in this house.

"Where goggie go?" Gavin asked, as he spread a heap of Flora on his toast.

"I told you … Pooka got a bad owie, and …" Some things were just too hard for the wee ones to understand.

Deirdre glanced at that article Luke O'Brien had written about the whole tragedy. The lengthy story was pinned to the bulletin board next to their dinner bell. The photos that Buck Hubbell took stared back at her. The shot of Ultan Ferrian caused her to be sick to her stomach. Just the thought of that perverted hooligan made her madder than bloody hell.

A few moments later, when Granny came to pick up the twins, she hugged her mam a little longer than usual. "The thought of what that scumbag did to our friends rips my heart out. And the fact that he was sneakin' photos of our Mary Margaret sends chills up my spine. What if ..."

"No, luv, you mustn't go there. 'Tis best to be thankful for all the blessings we have in our lives, and to embrace every day like the gift that it is."

Deirdre hugged them all goodbye and then rushed upstairs to get dressed. Even though she felt like she had run a marathon already that morning—what with all her jobs around the house—she still hadn't even brushed her teeth or changed out of Very Clean of Spots.

When she got to the master bedroom, Deirdre thought about how her husband had to be restrained from going to the jail and knocking Ferrian's block off. He wanted to lop off the pervert's willy, as well. "Just give me five minutes alone with the bastard!" Mark had yelled to the gardaí when they had called saying they found images of one of their girls on the lout's laptop. No one blamed the father for his outburst one bit.

The gardaí had confiscated Ferrian's computer and flashdrive from the boot of his Ford Ka after a search warrant was issued. Over 14,000 pornographic images were extracted from the files. The authorities told them that the possession of those things, coupled with the attack, should at least get him a sentencing of three years.

Deirdre couldn't allow herself to think about his attacks on Michael and Kate at the moment. She hoped Ferrian would find his new residence at Mountjoy Prison—along the banks of the Royal Canal—for the rest of his maggoty life. Would the demons that led him to do all those things ever go away?

God, the thought of all that vileness in the world made her stomach churn. And yet, thankfully there were sprinklings of goodness all around, too—just like her mam said. All she had to do was think of seven little faces to believe this—and the army of brave volunteers that was mobilized in the crisis.

She put her iPod into its dock near the bed, and turned it to FM 104's morning show. She heard the DJ discussing a topic that caught her attention. He said, "The Special Olympics were started in the 1960s by JFK's sister, Eunice Kennedy Shriver. Now it's a global movement with three million athletes in more than 180 countries involved..."

Ah... Michael so wanted to swim in the World Games. Poor lad! Deirdre wept as she brushed her teeth.

The man continued, "Three-thousand volunteers help run the whole event. In fact, even inmates from Mountjoy Prison were ordered to assist with the Games. I've been told they made podiums, signs, benches, flags and towels."

Deirdre spit into the sink. *How strange would that be if Ferrian had a hand in the Special Olympics, after he'd gone smashin' Michael's dream?*

As she removed her bleached nightgown she kept listening. "About 7,000 athletes from 150 countries have been given a warm Irish welcome."

After she dressed, Deirdre readied the items she had to bring over to O'Gara's pub. In one week's time, the neighbors would be hosting their own event—a fundraiser at O'Gara's for the Special Olympics in honor of Michael Farley. It was the least they could do. A person feels helpless in such circumstances.

She blew a copper curl out of her eyes as she placed a necklace, which she had fashioned out of Swarovski crystals, into a box. Indeed, it was the finest one she had made yet. It should bring a dear price in the silent auction.

Next, she reached up into her wardrobe to a place beyond the twins' reach. When her hands felt the mass of soft yarn, her heart was immediately comforted. She always thought there was something about the weight of a knitting project that soothed the body and soul. Deirdre brought the shawl over to her bed to study it carefully one last time. She tried to remember where she had got the pattern. Was it in the back of Debbie McComber's romance *The Inn at Rose Harbor*? Deirdre wasn't sure. She looked for her favorite spot on the item. There it was... the row that Michael Farley and Mary Cecelia wanted to "help" her with. Indeed, the finished product was a bit irregular. Sure, she could have ripped it out, but she left it there as a reminder that life shouldn't be perfect. She stowed the shawl in a bag, grabbed the boxed necklace and headed down the street. From her garden she could see the big black ribbon tied around the front door of O'Gara's. Bugger! Her shoulders felt like a dead rhino was draped over them.

CHAPTER 69

Life … It's a great and terrific and short and endless thing.
None of us come out of it alive.

~CECELIA AHERN

Luke looked at the photographs displayed in front of him. He and Buck were sitting near the fire inside O'Gara's Pub. The television in the corner was turned to RTÉ—Ireland's news channel, and many of the patrons were glued to it, including old man Poppy Flynn, who seemed to be a fossilized fixture embedded into the barstool. Every once in a while, someone would voice their reaction to what was being discussed on the program.

"Ah bugger it!" Poppy spat through missing teeth. Tears pooled in his rheumy eyes.

"It's tough, all right!" said Joe O'Soucheray, a retired cylinder index specialist for Guinness Storehouse and former mayor of Glasnevin. He scratched his gray hair. Wide shoulder pads captured a drift of dandruff as it fluttered down. He then sipped a potent cocktail called "The Rookie."

"Ah, pity that," Martin Donovan, the former director of finance at Croke Park, spoke from the back corner. Wrinkled skin dangled from his jaw like taffy that was pulled too thin. When he shook his head in dismay the extra folds quivered.

"May he rest in peace," Kevin Brown, retired groundskeeper for Glasnevin Cemetary, uttered. Last night's whiskey and cigarettes clung to his breath and pores.

John Sullivan, a pilot for Aer Lingus, inched his stool away from Kevin's body odor. "Lucky son-of-a-bugger … Died in his sleep, so he did."

"Mr. Tracy … Wasn't he marvelous, though?" said Mrs. Aoife Kiley who was taking breakfast and resting her bunioned feet before heading to work at Dunnes footwear department.

They were referring to the prime minister, Owen Tracy, who had passed away that week. The government had ordered all flags half-staff. To honor the beloved leader, O'Gara's had wrapped their door in a black ribbon.

Deirdre walked into the bar. Right away Luke noticed that she didn't have kids dripping off her like chimpanzees. He also noticed that she looked a little pale. She had been taking all this nasty business real hard.

"Over here, Deirdre," Buck called. "I wanted to show you the photos I'm doing up for the fundraiser. I need the opinion of someone who has an artist's eye—not the eye of a dolt like Luke, here." Buck elbowed him.

"Thanks, buddy," Luke said, biting into his salmon omelet.

The usually spunky woman plunked into a chair like she was tired to the bone. She put her things under the table and glanced at the photos. "Right, then, let me have a look."

Buck poured her some water. "These are the ones I took that day—the ones that the newspaper didn't print. I'd like to have some in this pile of 8x10s framed. What do you think?"

Deirdre looked at the photo of the gardaí standing on the bank. "You've captured the canal's momentum. And Binn's Bridge is lit up nicely in the background. It sets the scene." She put it in the "Yes" pile.

Next, she glanced at a black-and-white of Ferrian handcuffed to Brendan Behan's bench. "He looks stone-cold, just like yer bronze man next to him." She put that in the same pile as the other one.

From behind the beer pulls, Dano changed the television channel and then hushed the patrons. "Hey yehs … Shh! … they're talkin' about the Special Olympics on the telly! Listen up!"

The barman clicked the sound higher. Everyone in O'Gara's craned their necks in order to see better. "BBC World News" was written along the bottom of the screen. A British newscaster was reading from the teleprompter: "following the loss of their prime minister, the Irish are keeping their chins up. They continue to show the cheerful hospitality for which they are famous, as they host the Special Olympics World Games." The chap swiveled his head and looked at the screen on his right. "Victoria Ademite is in the Emerald Isle covering the event…Victoria?"

"Yes, Thomas…" the reporter said in a snooty British accent. Luke noticed that she stood—ironically enough—in front of the monument to Daniel O'Connell, the patriot who liberated the Irish from the Brits.

The stunning blond continued, "I'm standing here in Dublin's fair city where they are celebrating on a grand scale as host to the Special Olympics World Games."

Poppy gave a low whistle. "Don't I wish I could take a run at that fine bit of…"

"Shh, Poppy!" Mr. Taffy Jaw said. "Yeh couldn't take a run at anyt'ing ol' man, even if yeh had a mind to!"

Victoria continued to report: "The opening ceremony was held last night at Croke Park and covered by live radio and television. Since the prime minister passed away this week from a cerebral hemorrhage, the ceremony was officially opened by the president of Ireland, James MacDonald. The band U2 and the Riverdance troupe were headline performers for the opening ceremonies. Nearly 75,000 athletes, spectators and celebrities were in the stands. An amazing event, I say! Back to you in London, Thomas."

From the newsroom, Thomas said, "I hear you're working on a special story, Victoria."

"How right you are, Thomas. You see…while Dublin celebrates its international athletes, the northern suburb of Glasnevin is celebrating something even grander: the miracle of one special life spared—a life that has enriched so many other lives." The telly showed pictures of the Royal Canal next. "Last week, a Special Olympics hopeful, a 17-year-old with Down syndrome named Michael Farley, was attacked by an alleged stalker after he foiled an attempted rape. Michael was pursued in a high-speed bicycle chase, before tumbling into the turbulent waters of this canal, where he very nearly drowned. He was saved, not only by his considerable swimming skills, but also by a band of heroic neighbors, who gave chase to the assailant before the gardaí arrived on the scene. They fought to rescue Michael because over the years, Michael has shown them that love comes in many packages—and that we all have something to contribute to the lives of others."

The camera panned Glasnevin, and then Victoria finished with: "More on this story of Michael's condition and his neighborhood heroes in tonight's news." The channel took a station break and the patrons in O'Gara's clapped.

Over the cheers, Dano yelled, "Terry was tellin' me that the press interviewed Myrna and Helen late last night."

Deirdre turned to Buck and Luke. "That was lovely, now wasn't it? And Myrna and Helen are heroes indeed!"

"Yep, you all are … I have proof in the prints." Buck held up more 8x10 glossy shots. Luke and Deirdre laughed at the portrait Buck had taken, after the chase, of Deirdre holding the smashed remnants of the teapot she had hurled at Ferrian. The twins were at her side, making faces at the camera.

Next they looked at some other portraits that were taken after the event: one of the priests from St. Columba's, posed in front of the church; and another of Father Lee with a protective arm around his bruised and bandaged sister, standing in front of the guesthouse—with their cousin Nick in the background, swinging a club.

"Oh, my God!" Deirdre said, covering her mouth. "I'd forgotten how damaged she looked. Did yeh hear Catriona named her 'The Swamp Thing?'" She put them in the "Yes" pile. "Ah, the posh newslady was right … if it weren't for Michael's bravery, no doubt somet'ing worse *would* have happened to our Kate."

Buck handed her a couple of shots taken at the scene. One was of Dano smacking Ferrian with his shillelagh. Deirdre grinned. "And it shows the sausages wrapped around his legs."

The other photo showed Mark with the hurling stick in his hands, as he *thwacked* Ferrian on the arm. "Would yeh look at his biceps flexin'!" Luke could see pride etched on Deirdre's face. "Didn't yer camera catch how well and truly built he is, Buck?" They went into the "Yes" pile, too.

"What are all these?" Deirdre asked opening a file filled with action shots of Helen Riley. Luke spoke up, "I think our friend here has a little crush." A blush crept over Buck's face.

"I-I was just doing my job, folks," Buck stammered. "Capturing what happens at crime scenes is one of my fortes."

Luke watched Deirdre shuffle through myriad pictures of Helen. The first two were of her diving into the Royal Canal and pounding the current with powerful strokes. There was a series of her reaching Michael and then losing her grip on him. In the next, she was towing the boy to safety with the help of the gardaí. On the bottom of the pile, a photo showed her administering CPR before the ambulance arrived.

Deirdre caught her breath when she pulled out a picture from the next folder. It captured an exhausted Helen hugging Michael, who was crying as he came to. At the bottom of that folder was a photograph of the paramedics ministering to both Helen and Michael. All these went onto the "Yes" pile.

Deirdre reached for another photograph. "Oh my!" she said, "This one is brilliant!" She had found Luke's favorite picture—the one that best showcased Buck's talent. "Aren't you a great storyteller and artist, Buck?"

Luke felt a surge of brotherly pride swelling his chest. He patted Buck on the shoulder and said, "Yep! He's a poor man's Michelangelo!"

This single piece of art had captured the moment perfectly. It was similar to the one *The Irish Times* used, but this shot had more heart and soul—the parents' *Pieta*.

It was of Michael on a stretcher, with his parents beside him. Peter Farley was holding his son's hand to his heart. With his head tilted back, and eyes searching heaven, he looked as if he were giving thanks. It appeared as though his large body was trembling. His left hand grasped the stretcher's safety bar for support.

On the other side of Michael his mother was bending down to kiss her son. One hand was caressing his face and the opposite arm was wrapped around his shoulder. Her eyes were closed, her cheeks wet. Her pale face was scored with intense emotion. And Luke was certain that anyone who viewed this photo would be flooded with a surge of empathy, as well.

"Ah . . . what those poor parents went through!" Deirdre said. "And it could have turned out so much worse!" They all just stared at the image for a while.

Luke tightened his grip on his fork. "I could have killed the bastard!"

"Yeah," Buck sneered, "if Catriona hadn't shoved you aside."

Deirdre laughed and leaned in. "And didn't I hear 'twas Poppy Flynn who restrained you?"

CHAPTER 70

*If you knew how much work went into it,
you wouldn't call it genius.*

~MICHELANGELO

At that moment, Catriona opened the pub's door so that Myrna could push the baby carriage inside. As soon as they entered, the patrons clambered over to them.

"Ah now, let me at her!" Mrs. Kiley pleaded, hobbling on bunioned feet to the carriage.

"Would yeh look at that? Nice and healthy!" Mr. Donovan said.

"Surely she's the best girl in *all* Glasnevin!" Mr. O'Soucheray goo-gooed in baby talk.

Poppy shuffled over toward the action and bent down over the pram. "How about a kiss, girl?" he asked, and then giggled when Pooka obliged by licking his weathered cheek. "Aren't you a great pet, though, makin' a lonely man happy?"

Buck hurried over to get a picture. "Awesome! The dog was the last of the heroes I needed to shoot. The story just wouldn't be complete without highlighting Pooka!"

Catriona stepped aside so he could click away, and then, rubbing her bruised hip, she shuffled over to Deirdre's table near the fire. Kelly O'Gara was pouring a pot of tea.

"Sorry we're late for the fundraising meetin'," Catriona said to Deirdre and Luke, shimmying out of her cardigan.

"No worries. We've been lookin' at pictures. Wait 'til you see the one of you. Buck is going to frame it for the silent auction." Deirdre passed it to her.

"Would yeh look at that!" Catriona giggled, studying the action shot of herself in an apron—muddy bum in the air—wrapping the sausage links around Ferrian's ankles like a rodeo cowgirl roping a calf.

"What manner of woman walks around with a weapon in her apron?" Deirdre smiled.

"You never know when it's goin' to come in handy." Catriona said.

Luke held up a banger sausage from his plate, in a salute to Catriona. "The news said that the people of Glasnevin are heroes—you could become known as 'Hot Dog Woman.'"

Her chuckle started out soft and then rolled into guffaws. Soon enough she was snorting. *I have to admit, I really like this man! Even if he's bold!*

Myrna wheeled Pooka over to the table when she heard the ruckus. "What's so funny?"

"Don't even ask!" Catriona said.

Buck joined them at the table, too, peering at the pictures of Pooka on his camera. "How is Pooka doing? I heard she suffered a minor back injury and some cracked ribs."

"And some cuts on her belly and major dehydration. She had to spend a few days at the vet hooked up to IVs, and as you can see, he had to put a brace around her middle, but she's on the mend, so she is." Myrna beamed.

Buck shuffled through yet another file. "Speaking of needles, Myrna, here's my photo of you. I was able to zoom in on Ferrian's thigh just as you were plunging that sucker into the bastard. Talk about guts!"

Catriona could see Myrna was flattered. Rightly so! She reached over and gave her a hug, being careful not to disturb the bandaged elbow.

Woof! Woof! Pooka sounded a weak bark, demanding attention. Catriona stroked the dog's ears. She watched as Pooka turned toward Buck and placed her head in his lap. The scarlet taffeta bow that was tied around her neck shimmered in the firelight.

Catriona heard Luke whisper, "That dog is the closest you're ever going to get to a Lady in Red, Buck!" He grinned and snatched a photo out of Buck's hand. It was the one of Helen climbing out of the canal in her soaking red t-shirt.

Well now, is yer photographer-man interested in Helen?

Catriona leaned toward Deirdre and said, "Indeed someone should write a novel about the more subtle goings-on in Glasnevin of late! All the romantic suspense could well fill a book."

The front door of the pub opened again and Kate entered the oak paneled room. Her hair was tied up in a ponytail, and her black eyes and scratches were still visible under the makeup she had layered on.

Luke rose to hold out a chair for her. Before she sat down, they looked at each other, sharing a brief Oops-we-just-forgot-that-we-aren't-the-only-people-in-this-room look.

Kate pulled herself away from Luke's eyes and gingerly sat down. She smiled, splitting open the cut on her lip.

Deirdre slid a photo toward Kate. "Wait 'til I show yeh ... Buck got a picture of The Swamp Thing."

"Yikes!" Kate gasped, opening a tube of lip balm.

"Don't worry, we all have our bad days." Luke rubbed his buttocks and then touched the scar on his forehead. His knuckles were still swollen and bore Ultan Ferrian's toothmarks.

Poppy shuffled to the table and looked at Buck. "Can I see those pictures of Helen you were gibberin' about earlier? The wet ones?" Myrna looked at Buck with confusion.

"Ah, go on Poppy! Those pictures are stayin' in a closed file." Deirdre slammed a hand on the folder.

"While you're over here, Poppy," Buck said, looking through his things, "why don't you take a peek at *your* photo?" Buck held up a picture of the old man sporting a determined grin with missing teeth. His tweed suit was a little rumpled and he was wearing only one shoe. In his hand, he was holding the other shoe above his head as he was trying to whack Ultan Ferrian in the nether parts while the gardaí were carting Ferrian away.

"It took me a while to catch up to the lot of yeh, but didn't I give that fecker a fright?"

Dano walked over from the bar, "I might buy that portrait for the pub. It'd make great fodder for conversation. And then I could tell everyone that I was also in line to neuter the gombeen with the shillelagh hangin' right over there."

All the men who heard this comment said, "Ouch," collectively, shielding their own nether parts.

Kate took a sip of tea. "Buck, can we see your shots of Luke putting the boxing moves on Ferrian? I might pay a pretty penny for those at the auction. I could hang them on my bedroom wall next to George Clooney and Pierce Brosnan."

Catriona watched as Kate studied the photos. The whites of her eyes were still yellow and bloodshot and now they were getting all misty. *It's tough all right. Now the poor lass has to ride out a Quadruple Whammy.*

Kate fingered the corners of the photos and looked around at the neighbors. "There was a time back in Minnesota, when I was as low as you can get. My brother taught me to consider three teachings of St. Francis." Catriona watched as Kate held up her index finger. "First, learn from nature that nothing stays the same for very long. Seasons change and we need to let go and learn to . . . trust." Pooka wagged her bandaged tail.

"Second, depend on your own hard work." She glanced out the window at the "No Vacancy" sign hanging for the first time in front of The Cobblestones. "Thank God all this publicity hasn't hurt the business." Relief and pride settled over Kate's swollen features.

"And third," Kate continued, "believe in the goodness of others. This one was a doozy for me . . . I was confronted with the dark side of humanity. But just look at how you neighbors responded to the crisis, and you still have the bruises to remind me. You've restored my faith in the goodness of people." Kate hugged the photos to her heart and couldn't hold back the tears. "Thank you."

Catriona overheard Myrna whisper to Kate, "You just took a baby step toward restoring your trust in men, so you did."

Catriona felt a sudden urge to take charge. She grabbed the fresh tumbler of whiskey out of Poppy's hand and pushed it in front of a gobsmacked Kate.

Poppy took the opportunity to plant a kiss on the top of Kate's head and then shuffled toward the bar, pulling out a hankerchief.

Dano quickly busied himself with building some pints.

Catriona noticed that Luke was blinking a lot.

"Right ..." Deirdre sniffled and reached for a bar napkin. "And isn't the neighborhood better now that Kate McMahon is in it?" She cleared her throat and returned to business. "Here are the items I brought for the silent auction." She pointed out the imperfections that added value to the knitted shawl. Catriona noticed that Kate couldn't keep her hands off Deirdre's second item, a crystal necklace labeled *Prism of Light*. Kate kept holding the strand up to her neck and twirling the beads.

Deirdre was now rattling off the latest contributions for the auction: The O'Gara clan was donating a case of top-shelf liquor; their friends—the nuns from Archbishop Brady's Shelter for the Destitute and Downtrodden—offered to host a dinner at their convent; Helen and Coach Keanne were donating swim lessons; Myrna was offering a baked-good-item-of-the-month club; The German guests at The Cobblestones had promised a Steinbach cowboy nutcracker; and Catriona was putting together a basket of Tahitian body oil products.

"Indeed, 'tis goin' to be a lovely event," Myrna said, looking at her watch, "but we all need to get to the hospital. Michael is expectin' us soon, and he wants to see Pooka, too, so he does." She put an arm around Catriona and added, "And wait 'til you hear what a surprise Catriona has in store for the lad!"

CHΛPTER 71

Our wounds are often the openings
into the best and most beautiful part of us.

~DAVID RICHO

Later that morning, Kate glanced around Michael Farley's room at St. Joseph's Hospital. The space was filled with about thirty eager bodies, including members of the press, An Garda Síochána, and the Dublin City Council. On the walls were homemade signs: "Get back in the saddle, Pardner," "Bite the Bullet, Cowboy," and "Get well soon." The volume was turned down on the television in the corner. The World Games were on, replaying footage of Manchester United football players taking the athlete's oath with Special Olympians.

Kate didn't mind that she and Luke were pressed together at the foot of the hospital bed. Luke had his notebook in hand and Buck milled about, trying to determine the best angle. And there was Michael . . . in the middle of it all, basking in the glory, and quite "full of himself"—as Kate had often heard the Irish say. The cowboy gave a broad smile, even though he had fluid in his lungs, cracked ribs, and a concussion. He had his head, chest, knees and shoulder wrapped in gauze and bandages. On top of it all, the poor guy had a painful bowel obstruction attributed to stress.

She hadn't seen him since the assault and wished she could envelope him in a heartfelt hug. But that was impossible because yards of rubber tubing carried fluids into and out of various parts of his battered body.

Nurse Lampman came in to change the bag of IV antibiotics. Michael told the crowd in his room that he liked her because she looked like Maureen O'Hara. To the joy of the media, he removed a yellow rose from one of his bouquets. With the help of his mother, he handed it to the nurse after she re-taped the IV needle.

"Ah, he's a good boy, all right," Nurse Lampman said to the reporters. "Truth be told, he's after toyin' with my affections." Michael covered his face with a beefy hand and gave a careful giggle until his ribs hurt. The cameras clicked.

He was receiving an award for bravery by Lord Mayor Mary Jeanne Kelly, and that's why the hospital room was filled to the brim. Mrs. Kelly was wearing her gold Chain of Office across her chest. It was a fancy adornment that looked like an athletic medal done up by Tiffany & Company. Kate thought the mayors in America could use a little more regalia.

To the Americans present, the Lord Mayor explained the origin of the mayor's medallion: It was presented by King William of Orange to the City of Dublin in 1698. The decorative chain included Tudor roses, harps, trefoil shaped knots and the letter 'S'—which probably stood for Steward. The Lord Mayor was wearing the original, and she placed a replica around Michael's chest with much fanfare.

"Th-this is better than an Olympic m-medal!" Michael said to the crowd.

A female reporter from *The Irish Times* said, "If you want my tuppence worth, I'd say it suits you fine. Indeed, it spiffs up yer hospital gown!"

"Am I a s-star?" Michael asked, looking at all the heavy gold on his chest. His parents wiped tears away. Everyone else clapped and cheered, and said things like: "Indeed," or "You betcha!"

Pooka—who was also a guest of honor—was wheeled in her pram up to the bed. Michael played with the red ribbon tied about her neck and patted her head.

Everyone was treated to punch and apple strudel—made by the German guests at The Cobblestones, who were so touched by Michael's story. Peggy Farley put a gummy worm on top of her son's piece. After it was all gobbled up, the room cleared out a bit. The O'Garas handed Peter and Peggy Farley a nice bottle of Kitchak Cellars Cabernet. "We thought you could use this," they said with hugs for both.

Cousin Nick produced Michael's cowboy hat from behind his back, saying, "Look what I found on the banks of the Royal Canal." He placed it on the rolling nightstand. "I had to buff it up a little, but it's good as new."

Kate reached for the hat saying, "It's better than a new one, Michael. You have history together."

Father Lee gave him a blessing and then said, "Nick and I will be leaving tomorrow. We'll really miss you." He handed him a holy card of St. Michael the Archangel.

Michael beamed, "I prayed to my p-patron s-saint, and he listened to m-me, Father!"

"I believe he did, Michael."

Michael tucked the card into the brim of the hat and said, "Y'all come back, ya hear?"

With Terry's help, Myrna ignored her arthritic joints and injured elbow and stood on a chair. "Would the lot of yeh be quiet? Catriona Ryan would like to make a presentation." All of the neighbors in the room knew that Catriona had some sort of big surprise up her sleeve, but only Myrna and Michael's parents knew what it was. Kate wondered what the heck it could be.

Catriona placed a wrapped box into Michael's lap and ruffled his hair. With his father's help, he ripped opened the wrapping paper. Inside was a digital frame downloaded with fifteen pictures.

They turned on the device and paused it at a picture of a brown Connemara horse in a green paddock. "Michael," Catriona said, "This horse will be waitin' for you on Valencia Island. It will be boarded there for good, and every time you go to camp, you can ride yer own horse."

Deirdre was the first in the room to gasp. Kate was the second. *What an absolutely perfect gift for Michael.* Kate wished she could see Michael's expression, but her view was blocked by Catriona's expansive dimensions. *But isn't her largesse even more expansive? Well, the woman needs a big body to carry that huge heart.*

Michael asked, "It's m-mine? Wha'? A *real* horse?"

Catriona nodded. "Every cowboy needs a horse."

Kate saw Mark clasp Deirdre's hand. In authentic Minnesotan he said, "Holy Moley!" They let the slide show run through a few more pictures of the horse in different poses.

Michael said, "I'm g-gobsmacked!"

"So am I, son," Peter Farley said. "Mrs. Ryan has been planning this for a very long time. What do you say?"

"T'anks a m-million!"

"Oh," Catriona said with a twinkle, "there's one more t'ing." She let the slide go to the next photo. "That horse became a mammy a while ago. So, Farmer O'Shea said you get the colt, as well. In fact, he's delivering *both* to the island at the weekend."

Michael made happy, squeaky noises in his hospital bed. He accidentally set off the nurse's call button. Nurse Lampman appeared. "What is it, Michael?" she asked, resetting the button.

"I g-get two horses! And the b-baby is white!" Then he turned to Catriona. "What are they called?"

"You get to name them, Michael."

"I-I'm goin' to c-call the brown mammy... 'John Wayne' and the white baby... 'Duke.'"

"I knew it! What a great story," said Luke. "And I've got a gift for you, too, something to keep you busy in the hospital." He reached into a bag and pulled out a *True Grit* DVD. In a lousy western accent he said, "It surely ain't a horse, Pardner, but I reckon there's some cowboys and stallions in it." He walked over to the bed on pretend bowlegs. "Thanks, sheriff, for watchin' out for all of us."

Kate gave Michael a kiss. Later, when it was just the two of them in the garden, she would explain how sorry she was for bringing this on him. For now, she forced a smile. "This cowgirl needs to hop along, too, and get to Superquinn. I'm making Mexican vittles for this cowboy, here." She smiled up at Luke, re-cracking her split lip.

CHΛPͲƐR 72

In a Dublin cell, fresh from detox, Ferrian flung the crust from his chicken sandwich onto the cafeteria tray lying on the floor. It landed on a pile of green beans. "This shite is rubbish!" he huffed.

He got off his cot and removed a letter from a shelf in the corner. The guard told him that some priest delivered it while he was visiting yesterday and said it was from some lady. He must have held the thing in his hand a million times, wondering who'd have written him. When was the last feckin' time he had any mail? He decided it probably contained a death threat.

He flopped onto his mattress, propped a lumpy pillow behind his back and leaned against the old place-stone wall. He put aside the unopened letter and scratched his wab. A magazine lay near the footboard. Some plonker pushing a reading cart left it for him and his cellmate. It was called *It's Garden Time!* Why didn't they have any girlie mags around this joint? Even that fashion rag *Bella* with photos of slappers in tight clothes would beat this crock. No laptop, no cell phone, no sketch pad. *Are they trying to drive me looney?*

Ferrian flipped the magazine open to a picture of some high muckety muck's manor home, surrounded by feckin' flowers. He threw it on the floor and mumbled, "Do they really and truly t'ink we're interested in this shite?"

He saw on the news that the gardening mentaller was on the mend, and they were treating him like a bloody celebrity. Ferrian had to admit, he was relieved. *If that header had become worm food I'd be in the slammer for life.*

He let out a big breath, unaware that he had been holding it in. Shifting on his arse, he picked up the envelope again and held it up to the light. It was useless. He couldn't decipher anything at all except that the handwriting was a little shaky.

Ah, bugger it! I might as well stop pissin' about and just open the bloody t'ing! He tore at the envelope and slid out a sheet of pink stationery.

Dear Ultan,

You don't know me, but I live in Glasnevin. I was there on the day you attacked Kate and Michael. What you did to those two people I love was really and truly awful, indeed. But I wanted to let you know that I saw you reach out to help the lad when he was about to plunge into the canal. I'm writing to you because I think you should know that at least there's one person in the world who knows there is a glimmer of goodness inside you. Isn't that hopeful now?

It was said on the telly that you had a rough childhood, but you're a grown man now and you make your own choices. Perhaps your own mam never told you this, so I'm going to have a go ... Be good. Respect the life God gave you and likewise respect other people's lives as well. And look more kindly on animals. It was my dear dog that you hauled off on. If you ever kick another dog again, I hope the Lord Himself will plunge a gigantic needle into your leg!

Father Criagáin, the priest who will deliver this letter, gave a lovely sermon Sunday last. He said that we, the neighbors, must travel on a journey of forgiveness. I'm assuming yourself needs to contemplate this, as well, seeing as you had it tough when you were a young lad. Perhaps you could meet with Father Criagáin when he's visiting the imprisoned sometime. You'd enjoy him, so you would.

Be strong and mind yourself now. Don't be wasting time during your incarceration. Work at turning away from evil and forgiving your trespassers. Gandhi once said: "The weak can never forgive. Forgiveness is the attribute of the strong."

You can start forgiving by taking baby steps.

Goodbye for now,
Mrs. Myrna Riley

P.S. Please excuse my poor handwriting. I cracked my elbow on the footpath on account of you. But didn't I forgive you already?

Ferrian re-read her words three times. Surely the lady was off her nut. What did she mean when she wrote "Goodbye for now"? *All this because she saw me reach out?* The phrase "reach out" reminded him of his teacher Miss McGraw.

Ferrian slipped the letter back into its envelope and hid it under his pillow for safekeeping. He looked at the door of vertical bars and hung his head. Tears were burning his eyes. *I wonder when this Father Criagáin is visiting this gammy clink again?*

CHΛPTER 73

I don't need more jewelry, clothes or Tahitian body oil.
~SAID NO WOMAN EVER!

One week later

Luke glanced around O'Gara's pub and estimated that hundreds of people had turned out for the fundraiser. He knew this was partially due to a story *The Irish Times* ran about the event. He heard that already over €3,000 had been raised for the Special Olympics through ticket sales, the live auction and matching contributions. Some of the proceeds would go toward swim parkas for Coach Keanne's athletes, and the remainder would be placed in a general fund for the whole organization.

A host of volunteers was recruited to make the event a success. Poppy Flynn sat on a stool by the front door welcoming people with his gravelly voice and toothless grin. On more than one occasion, Luke heard the old man say, "Hello there, pretty lady! Make sure to spend all yer hubby's money tonight!"

Kate was asked to help in the kitchen and told Luke to mingle until her shift was over. Buck was busy taking pictures and chatting up Helen Riley whenever he had a chance. Across the pub, Luke saw Deirdre working the ticket table. A pack of digestive biscuits was next to the money box. The older Kennedy children were in charge of the coatroom, and the twins were chasing Pooka around the pub—while Mark chased after the twins, huffing and puffing. *Man, he sure looks like he could use a beer!* Luke ambled over to the bar to order one for him.

A few minutes later, with a Guinness in his hand, Luke passed the crackling fire and glowing candles to reach Mark on the dance floor. Kenny McMahon of Tullahought was hired to play whatever tunes the crowd paid to hear. At the moment he was singing *The Unicorn Song* and he sounded better than The Irish Rovers. Folks were acting like goofballs, making alligator mouths with their arms, and scratching their armpits like monkeys. Luke laughed, watching Mark and his twins using fingers to create unicorn horns on their foreheads. *That's one lucky guy ... busy, but lucky as hell.* He set down the beer and joined in on the fun.

While dancing, he noticed Kelly and Morgan O'Gara passing around trays of appetizers that Kate had probably prepared back in the kitchen. Dano had the rest of his staff building pints of Guinness.

Along the back wall were the silent auction tables. Hanging above them was a homemade poster with the Special Olympics athlete's oath: "Let me win, but if I cannot win, let me be brave in the attempt." Beneath it was a pack of brave ladies nearly scratching each others' eyes out over the auction items.

Catriona squeezed her big frame through the crowd to join Luke. She nodded toward a woman who was cradling a long, skinny puppy and said, "I thought surely you'd have been biddin' on that pup in the live auction. It's called a *sausage* dog here in Ireland, and Terry and Myrna Riley donated it. Indeed she would make a lovely pet for you, Luke."

"Ah ... no thanks. I prefer the larger breeds. Besides, I've got my eye on that necklace for Kate. I haven't forgotten that you ordered me to get that for her."

"Indeed. Every lass loves jewelry from a man she's well fond of. And didn't Kate have to part with her jewels in order to start a new life?" She motioned toward the kitchen. "Are you serious about our Kate?"

"Absolutely." *Is it getting warmer in here? Why am I sweating all of a sudden?*

Catriona peered into his eyes. "Have yeh told her properly then? She can well turn a man's head, but she's more than just a—'Grace Kelly lookalike with courtly legs'—as you once wrote. She's a woman of substance, as well." She leaned toward him, speaking out of the corner of her mouth. "It took me quite some time to uncover that substance, but 'tis true indeed."

"Yep. She's something special," he said. "I've had my fill of shallow women."

"Right. You best get in touch with yer feelings, and then let yer feelings be known." She smiled with mischief. "And yeh best be quick about it, lest some faster bloke gets to her first. We already know Poppy Flynn has his eye on her."

Luke scratched his head. "Yeh, I know."

"Well, now that *that's* settled . . . off with yeh now! You best be gettin' over to that auction table. Or won't that great lump of a woman, Suzanne Murphy, outbid you? Already she's standin' over that necklace like a bloody sentry guardin' the crown jewels."

Luke waged war against that battleaxe, Suzanne Murphy, until Coach Keanne stepped up to the microphone.

"Michael, would you come to the podium and say a few words?"

Michael took the microphone and said he hoped all this money meant there'd be extra snacks after practices when he was able to return to swimming. He lifted his shirt and tie, exposing his belly, to show the crowd his wrapped ribs. "Dr. Daly says two m-more weeks and these w-will be aaaallll better!"

His mother rushed to his side as the people chuckled. She tugged his shirt back down and whispered into his ear. Michael then said, "Oh . . . Right!" He cleared his throat. "Th-thank you for coming to my p-party. I h-hope you s-spend all yer money!" He waved to the guests.

At 9 p.m. sharp the bidding closed. Luke was able to write his bid number on a line one last time before the bell rang. He pumped his fist into the air and hissed "Yesss!"

"Did you get it, lad?" Catriona asked, hustling to his side.

322

"I sure did!"

"Wait 'til I tell yeh ... Didn't I have to spill a bit of mustard on Suzanne Murphy's dress so she wouldn't beat you to the finish? Jaysus! What a brazen strap of a woman!"

Luke chuckled, wondering which of the two women was more brazen. "You're full of surprises aren't you, Catriona?"

"Indeed. Surely the world would be a desperate place altogether without 'em!"

His confidence fueled by Guinness, he winked and said, "Well, perhaps I'll plan a surprise of my own for Kate in the future ... with a more expensive piece of jewelry, if you get my drift."

"'Get your drift'? I t'ink I know what yer sayin'. And don't I like the sound of it?" She pushed him gently toward the auction table. "Now go claim it before that annoyin' Murphy woman paves the bloody t'ing! The cheek of that one!"

Luke paid for the necklace and stowed it in his shirt pocket—safely away from Mrs. Murphy. He looked around for Kate, thinking she should be done with her shift soon.

In the corner he spotted Mick O'Connell—the former Kerry footballer, with his son who has Down syndrome. Luke had done what he could to bid up the price of Mick's autographed jersey in the live auction. It was Mick who started the camp on Valencia Island. When Luke passed by them he heard Mick tell Michael, "John Wayne and Duke are settling in well, indeed, and eating their fair share of hay and carrots."

From behind, Luke felt warm arms glide around his waist. A feminine body pressed close. He turned around and looked into Kate's eyes, framed by the remnants of two shiners. She looked delighted.

"I'm a winner! I won that basket of Catriona's Tahitian body oil." She bounced up and down.

"Hmmm. I just love it when you smell like your housekeeper. How about we go outside for some fresh air?"

"Mmm ... that sounds great. That kitchen's hot!"

"So are you, my dear!" He grabbed her hand and led her toward the door. As they passed Deirdre's ticket table, she waved them over.

"Wait 'til I tell yeh … I just heard the necklace I made fetched a good sum!"

Kate clasped Deirdre's forearm. "That's wonderful, Deirdre. God! I bet it went to that Suzanne Murphy."

Luke fought the urge to shout "Hot dog!" *I botched the first kiss, but I really pulled off the first gift.*

Next to Deirdre's table, was Poppy Flynn, who was sleeping sitting up, his mouth open like a fish hoping for a leech. His son, Officer Timothy, was standing beside him. He just shrugged his shoulders and shook his head, saying, "The aul' fella can sleep anywhere, so he can!"

A twin ran up to his mom and reached for her can of Coke. "Cive some?"

Deirdre slid the can out of his reach. "No, lad. There'll be no caffeine for the lot of yeh the rest of the night! I want yeh to be sleepin' like yer man, Poppy, here."

Luke leaned toward Kate and whispered, "What a role model to be holding up to your kids."

He guided her outside and they retreated under the lamp in the front garden. He wrapped his arms around her to ward off the cool evening air. The weather had been calm the past week, squelching the chances of a flood. In the distance, The Cobblestones guesthouse was glowing in the night. Kate nodded at the "No Vacancy" sign illuminated in front of it. "I'm so glad I moved here." She hugged him tighter. "And since we're booked solid for the summer, it looks like I'm here to stay—especially since Ferrian's out of the way now."

"Yessss!" Luke said. "… Ah … I'm restraining myself from shouting 'Hot dog!' "

Kate patted him on the chest, clinking the beads in his pocket.

"Oh, I have a surprise for you." He poured the necklace into his open palm.

She gasped and jumped on her tiptoes. "You got it? Oh Luke ... Thank you! You don't know how much I needed a nice piece of jewelry!"

Her joy filled his heart with a deep satisfaction as he clasped the strand around her neck and slid his fingers along the beads resting at her throat. The crystals sparkled in the light. He gave a playful pull at her ponytail.

Kate looked down at her gift. "Gosh, it's so beautiful! Deirdre is one talented lady."

"So are you. I'm proud of you, Kate. Think of all you've overcome—your triple whammy, the trials of setting up a new business ... and especially that bastard Ferrian." He tilted her chin upward. "I'm really happy that things are going so well for you. And that the timing ... for us ... is perfect."

She clasped her hands around his neck. "It does seem perfect. I have everything I need right here in Glasnevin."

He started to bring his lips to hers when the front door opened and Catriona made her exit, wrapped in the fringed shawl Deirdre had made with "help" from Michael and one of her kids.

"Bejappers! So sorry to be interuptin' the romance." She strutted toward them. " 'Twas a lot of hard work, but wasn't it a lovely event? Indeed, my dear departed Declan would have been well pleased."

Luke felt Kate's startled jerk.

"You mean ... Declan ... ?" she stammered.

"Right," Catriona said. "He's gone to Glory, you know. And part of my assignment is to take care of myself and to live in the here-and-now." She tossed an end of the shawl over her shoulder. "Don't I look like that jet-setter Paris Hilton, though?"

"That's just what I was thinking," Luke grinned.

Catriona glanced at the necklace. "Janey Mack! It's smashin' on yeh, Kate. Just look at its sparklin' colors!" She peered at Luke. "And now ... I believe Luke has some words for you, Kate."

Catriona pranced down the sidewalk in a cloud of Tahitian fragrance. Her derriere, swinging proudly, made the fringe sway like a hula skirt. "Cheerio!" she called with a graceful wave.

"What was that all about?" Luke asked.

"I think Dr. Roddy had a breakthrough. And I suppose some attention from my cousin Nick helped, too. I can't tell you how relieved I am... Maybe I can get rid of that damn wrench now that Declan's definitely not coming back." Kate brushed his hair off his forehead. "What did she mean... you 'have some words for me'?"

"Well... um..." He pulled her closer, cupping her face. The cut on her lip was healed now and he traced the scar with his thumb. Her arms held tightly to his waist and her eyes searched his. He wanted to hold her like this forever.

"I think I'm falling in love with you, Kate McMahon."

She smiled up at him, her eyes wide. But suddenly he felt her stiffen and pull away. "You think so? How will you know for sure?" she asked.

"Well, my 'assignment' from Catriona is to get in touch with my feelings. And since I've met you, I've got that lovin' feeling."

She rolled her eyes playfully. "Love isn't just an emotion that washes over you. It's an action verb. It calls for a lot of work, over a long time."

"I know that. And I'm ready to commit to that. But, hey, Babe, it's not *all* work." He drew her back into his arms.

She softened, but continued in analytical mode. "Well, love has so many facets to consider, and we're just getting started."

He released her. "Okay," he said. "I can be patient. Let's consider them together. Can we start with physical attraction? Because I think we've got that part down."

"Yep," she conceded. "It only took a nanosecond to recognize that."

"That's a good start, don't you think?"

"Yes. And we seem to be communicating better lately. No more envelopes on my doorstep and disappearing acts."

"Never again, I promise. I'm finding it easier to talk to you, Kate. I want to share everything with you, face-to-face."

She was quiet for a few seconds, but it seemed like an hour to Luke. He wondered how many bullet points were on this checklist of hers.

"And I really love that you make me laugh, Luke O'Brien. You make me laugh because you're such a dork sometimes."

They both laughed.

She added, "And I like who I am when I'm with you."

Her softening stance made his heart pound.

"But looking ahead is scary. Trust is the piece that's still missing. I trusted blindly when I was young, and that was a big mistake."

What could he say? It seemed so beyond his control. "Remember, I took one in the ass for you … And I punched out your attacker."

It worked. She laughed again. "Oh, I won't forget that! You've proven your … gallantry. And you seem to have other noble qualities, too. But I have to be careful here. I'll need more assurance of your honesty and integrity. That's the arena of my betrayal."

He became thoughtful and then hopeful. Recalling the story of Myrna's advice, he put the next question to her slowly: "So do you think you can … get *ready* … to get ready … to trust?"

She stepped forward into his arms. "Yeah, I'm doing that. I'm taking those baby steps."

Holding her at arms' length, he looked into her eyes and asked, "Well, could you *fartlek* those baby steps?" He pulled her close while she laughed.

Just as their lips met again, the door of O'Gara's opened, causing them both to jump. Luke wondered if a man could ever manage a real kiss without being interrupted in this neighborhood. Michael was letting Pooka out to have a piddle near the front patio.

"Wh-why are you s-snoggin?" Michael asked, straightening his glasses and bringing his hand to his mouth with a giggle.

"Because we're getting in touch with our feelings, that's why we're snoggin'. And you know what, Michael? We might find ourselves in love … someday!"

Pooka, finished with her business, sauntered over—and darned if the dog didn't nudge him even closer to Kate. Luke snogged her one more time.

Michael clapped his hands. "B-Brilliant! Dancin' at weddings is b-brilliant indeed."

"Wedding?" Luke gulped. "Now hold your horses, cowboy!"

Kate added, "Yeah, don't jump the gun!"

Inside the pub, Kenny McMahon began belting out Michael's favorite song, *RV Cowboy*. Michael jiggled his butt and threw his good arm in the air, carefully, so as not to disturb his ribs.

He ain't tall. He ain't dark.
He's the best catch in the motor park …
He's an RV cowboy, his horse is a camper truck.

Michael stood still long enough to hold out his hand to Kate. "M-May I have a go with you on the dance floor, cowgirl? Come on! We have a business agreement."

Pooka barked and wagged her tail. Kate laughed, looking at Luke with a shrug of her shoulders. Prisms danced everywhere as she glided toward Michael.

"I'm right behind you," Luke said, running across the cobblestones. "I want to see you do that George Clooney dance!"

THE END

ACKNOWLEDGMENTS

Cobbling together a first novel requires a village of skilled craftsmen. If it weren't for the significant people God placed in our lives, this story would never have been paved smoothly enough to become a book.

First and foremost, thanks to everyone in our clan. Eric, you are a true gift—a stellar father and a smokin' hot husband. Patiently, you managed the fort, fired up the grill and dished out burgers so that your wife and mother-in-law could rock the keyboard. And to the chisellers: Ben, Jack, Joe, Luke, Katrina, Mary Kate, Cecelia and the twins—Michael and Peter—you rescued us with your technical savvy, identified our false starts, shared swimming knowledge, dreamed up romantic mishaps, and provided fodder for large-family anecdotes. When the story was churning in our heads and Mom and Grandma were "away with the fairies," you understood with nary a harrumph. We love you more than Mexican food.

Papa Charlie, Auntie Angie, Uncle Jimmy and other "relations," thanks for taking the twins fishing, out for ice cream or to "GreenMart," tractor riding at the tree farm or cheering at St. Thomas Academy sporting events so we could have a quiet block of writing time. The maple syrup scene in our book really happened once upon a time when Mom was in the shower. You prevented repeats of those shenanigans.

We'd like to thank "literary critic" Bob McMahon for contributing humor to these pages by just being himself. And Kenny and Joelle for their music and story.

We are gobsmacked by the talent of Erin Rock and her Dublin husband, Damien, who pored over our horrid first draft in order to correct our "Irishisms."

A tip of the hat to our generous "Manuscript Mommas": Angie MacDonald, Tina Draves, Lisa Gott, Lysa Flynn, Morgan Schneeman, Mary Perry and our token "Manuscript Male," Captain David Draves, who were beta readers of our second draft. You fitted us with proper arch supports for taking baby steps. Are you putting to good use that Tahitian Body Oil?

JoAnn McMahon, Tib McMahon, Kaylan Lucius and plucky Megan McGraw—we are truly grateful that you studied our third draft and offered piles of thought. You encouraged us to continue using Irish terms like "manky blob" and your stimulating support strengthened our resolve.

Indeed, we need to thank Megan Lampman for taking time away from her hottie fiance to share her marketing charisma and photography skills. In cyberspace, thanks to Chris Bayer at CJB Editing for fixing our corrupted manuscript—surely we eegits would have thrown in the tea towel otherwise. And Dave Hrbacek—thanks for giving us technical information on photography.

To Senior Commander Tim Flynn for taking time while smoking a cigar to answer Taser gun questions. And of course, to the entire Flynn family for guidance all along this journey. Our pub has an empty stool but our hearts will remember to "Keep the Faith."

Coach Keanne Cameron, thanks for your enthusiasm about the Special Olympics. It's contagious. And to Michael Luecke and the individuals with Down syndrome and their families who showed us how lovable our character Michael could become: Kevin at Kowalski's Market, Brian from the neighborhood, Katie from summer school, Daisy at speech therapy and especially Bridget Brown and her mother Nancy (Butterfly4Change.org). We also found the book *Making a Case for Life* by Stephanie Wincik insightful.

We owe much gratitude to many literary greats: Louise Burke, David Brown and Sloan Harris for their guidance; authors Stephanie Landsem, Mark Levine, Mary Treacy O'Keefe and Erin Hart for their advice and professional critiques; Dr. John Buri and Doug Hennes from the University of St. Thomas (our alma mater) for answering publishing questions; Kaki Stewart and David Tripp for their monumental help; "Queen of Suspense" Mary Higgins Clark for her precious time and kind feedback.

We were blessed to have had as writing mentors: Michael Holbach, Judith Guest, Dan Kelly and Dr. Tom Connery. You taught us that rewriting can make the heart sing. Thank you for helping us believe in the magic of our own hard work.

Thanks, Kevin Brown, for our irresistible cover, and to you, Donna Burch-Brown, for designing the interior of our book. How did we ever find the two of yeh?

A special call out to The Loft Literary Center for all it does to support writers. And to our team at Mill City Press—for fartleking us over the hurdles.

T'anks a million to all the O'Garas from O'Gara's Bar and Grill (St. Paul) for their enthusiasm. What would we have done without your warm booths and strong Baileys Coffees every bleepin' time we celebrated, thinking we had completed our final draft?

Finally, this story would never have been conceived without the Rafferty clan who opened their Glasnevin home to a certain student back in 1986. Thanks to you all— and the lovely Ryan family—for your warm Irish hospitality and continued friendship.

Sláinte! (Cheers!)

ABOUT THE AUTHORS

C.K. MacDonald is the pen name for the mother-daughter writing team of **Cecelia (McMahon) MacDonald** and **Kathryn (MacDonald) Schneeman**, of Mendota Heights, Minnesota. Both authors are graduates of the University of St. Thomas (Class of '88). *Running the Cobblestones* is their first novel.

Kathryn lived in Dublin for one brillant college semester. She is a freelance writer and the mother of nine children, including twins. She stays sane by writing in pubs and running through the streets of St. Paul.

Cecelia, Kathryn's mother, does small things with great love. She is a freelance editor, a retired grant writer and a regular in the pews. The product of a large family of tipplers, she dreams about running away to Ireland.

A second book is incubating—and maybe it'll be twins. Visit their website at: ckmacdonald.com.

CPSIA information can be obtained
at www.ICGtesting.com
Printed in the USA
LVOW12s1341070417
530026LV00003B/103/P